Praise for
THE RETRIEVAL ARTIST SERIES

One of the top ten greatest science fiction detectives of all time.

—io9

The SF thriller is alive and well, and today's leading practitioner is Kristine Kathryn Rusch.

—Analog

[Miles Flint is] one of 14 great sci-fi and fantasy detectives who out-Sherlock'd Holmes. [Flint] is a candidate for the title of greatest fictional detective of all time.

—Blastr

Part *CSI*, part *Blade Runner,* and part hard-boiled gumshoe, the retrieval artist of the series title, one Miles Flint, would be as at home on a foggy San Francisco street in the 1940s as he is in the domed lunar colony of Armstrong City.

—The Edge Boston

What links [Miles Flint] to his most memorable literary ancestors is his hard-won ability to perceive the complex nature of morality and live with the burden of his own inevitable failure.

—Locus

Readers of police procedurals as well as fans of SF should enjoy this mystery series.

—Kliatt

Instant addiction. You hear about it—maybe you even laugh it off—but you never think it could happen to you. Well, you just haven't run into Miles Flint and the other Retrieval Artists looking for The Disappeared. ...I am hopelessly hooked....

—Lisa DuMond
MEviews.com on *The Disappeared*

An inventive plot and complex, conflicted characters increases the appeal of Kristine Kathryn Rusch's *Extremes*. This futuristic tale breaks new ground as a space police procedural and should appeal to science fiction and mystery fans.

—*RT Book Reveiws* on *Extremes*

Part science fiction, part mystery, and pure enjoyment are the words to describe Kristine Kathryn Rusch's latest Retrieval Artist novel.... This is a strong murder mystery in an outer space storyline.

—*The Best Reviews* on *Consequences*

An exciting, intricately plotted, fast-paced novel. You'll find it difficult to put down.

—*SFRevu* on *Buried Deep*

A science fiction murder mystery by one of the genre's best.... A book with complex characters, an interesting and unpredictable plot, and timeless and universal things to say about the human condition.

—*The Panama News* on *Paloma*

Rusch continues her provocative interplanetary detective series with healthy doses of planet-hopping intrigue, heady legal dilemmas and well-drawn characters.

—*Publishers Weekly* on *Recovery Man*

…the mystery is unpredictable and absorbing and the characters are interesting and sympathetic.

—*Blastr* on *Duplicate Effort*

Anniversary Day is an edge-of-the-seat thriller that will keep you turning pages late into the night and it's also really good science fiction. What's not to like?

—*Analog* on *Anniversary Day*

Set in the not too distant future, the latest entry in Rusch's popular sf thriller series (*The Disappeared; Duplicate Effort*) combines fast-paced action, beautifully conflicted protagonists, and a distinctly "sf noir" feel to tell a complex and far-reaching mystery. VERDICT Compulsively readable with canny plot twists, this should appeal to series fans as well as action-suspense readers.

—*Library Journal* on *Anniversary Day*

Rusch offers up a well-told mystery with interesting characters and a complex, riveting storyline that includes a healthy dose of suspense, all building toward an ending that may not be what it appears.

—*RT Book Reviews* on *Blowback*

The latest Retrieval Artist science fiction thriller is an engaging investigative whodunit starring popular Miles Flint on a comeback mission. The suspenseful storyline is fast-paced and filled with twists as the hero comes out of retirement to confront his worst nightmare.

—*Midwest Book Review* on *Blowback*

We always like our intergalactic politics as truly alien, and Rusch delivers the goods. It's one thing to depict members of a Federation whining about treaties, quite another to depict motivations that are truly, well, alien.

—*Astroguyz* on *Blowback*

BLOWBACK

A RETRIEVAL ARTIST NOVEL

KRISTINE KATHRYN RUSCH

wmg **PUBLISHING**

Blowback

Book Two of the Anniversary Day Saga

Published 2014 by WMG Publishing
First published in 2012 by WMG Publishing
www.wmgpublishing.com
Cover and Layout copyright © 2014 by WMG Publishing
Cover design by Allyson Longueira/WMG Publishing
Cover art copyright © Victor Habbick/Dreamstime
ISBN-13: 978-0615688503
ISBN-10: 0615688500

For the readers.
I couldn't do this without you.

Acknowledgements

I owe a debt of gratitude to my husband Dean Wesley Smith, whose creative mind gets me out of more jams than I want to contemplate; and Annie Reed, whose keen eye improved this book. I also need to thank the readers of *Analog SF Magazine* who support my explorations in the Retrieval Artist world and, of course, Stanley Schmidt, who first published the Retrieval Artist short stories.

Author's Note

Dear Readers,

You hold in your hands the second book of the Anniversary Day saga. I didn't know I was writing a saga when I completed Blowback. *At the time, I thought I had one more book left in a trilogy. Silly me.*

If you haven't read Anniversary Day, *the book that starts this saga, you'll need to pick it up before you read this novel. They're tied together, and followed by six more books that will be released one per month in the first six months of 2015.*

Normally, my Retrieval Artist novels stand alone. I suspect those of you who've read some of the previous books expected that when you picked this one up. I didn't plan to write a saga when I started Anniversary Day. *I didn't even expect to write a trilogy.*

I thought I was writing a short novel to explain something to myself that would happen in the standalone book that'll show up in a few years, a book called Talia's Revenge.

I have always planned to write stories about characters other than Miles Flint in the Retrieval Artist Universe. I had started to do that with Talia's Revenge *before I realized I had to explore a catastrophe that happened in her past.*

This entire saga is that catastrophe. Once I've finished exploring that, I will return to the standalone novels you're used to. This book has been reissued with a note on the cover calling it Book Two of the Anniversary Day saga.

We're doing a couple things with these novels. If the books don't feature Miles Flint, they're called Retrieval Artist Universe novels. If Flint has a starring role, then the novels are called Retrieval Artist novels.

Confused yet? If so, here's all you need to remember. Make sure you've read Anniversary Day *before reading this book. And enjoy! You've got quite a journey ahead of you.*

—*Kristine Kathryn Rusch*
Lincoln City, Oregon
August 10, 2014

BLOWBACK

A RETRIEVAL ARTIST NOVEL

THREE YEARS EARLIER

1

Detective Iniko Zagrando hurried through the Port in Valhalla Basin. He had his right hand up to show the bright gold badge on his palm. The badge blared *Police business! Move out of the way!* in that official genderless voice that seemed ubiquitous on Callisto. He dodged chairs outside of restaurants, passengers pausing to read menus, and the occasional alien, looking lost. A clump of passengers huddled near the ever-changing Departures sign—a sight unusual anywhere else, but common here. New non-sanctioned arrivals on Callisto often had their links automatically severed. Not only did it keep them in the dark, it made them feel helpless.

Aleyd Corporation, which ran and owned Valhalla Basin—all of Callisto, really—liked making people feel helpless.

Zagrando ran to the Earth Alliance departure wing, his breath coming harder than he expected. He was out of shape, despite the mandatory exercise requirements of the Valhalla Police Department. Apparently the damn requirements weren't as stringent as the idiots in charge of VPD seemed to think.

He wasn't dressed for this kind of run, either. He was wearing a suit coat, which had the benefit of hiding his laser pistol but was otherwise too hot and constricting, and brand-new shoes whose little nanoparticles had actually attached to his links and warned him to slow down or else the shoes would be ruined by incorrect use.

If he could shut off the shoe cacophony, he would. His links were giving him enough trouble without that.

Instructions had come from all sides: *Emergency at the Port. Requesting street patrol backup and Detective Iniko Zagrando.* In all his years at the VPD—and that was more than he wanted to contemplate—he had never received a call like this, and certainly not at the Port itself.

He was a *detective*. He investigated *after* the crime, not during the crime. And he certainly didn't get his hands dirty with an in-process emergency unless he happened to stumble on the scene.

Two security guards came out of nowhere to flank him and push away other passengers. The passengers emerging from the various departure wings stopped when they saw him, blinking in surprise and a bit of panic.

Welcome to Valhalla Basin, he thought. *It only goes downhill from here.*

But of course he didn't say anything. He couldn't even if he wanted to, he was breathing so damn hard. How had he let himself go like this? Of course, he knew the answer—misery caused a lot of problems. And because he didn't want to think about that, and because things *would* only go downhill from here for him as well, he commanded his VPD bio link to send him a surge of extra energy, something Aleyd happily provided all its public servants—in limited quantities, of course. No sense in having them overuse the energy and collapse in a heap that required massive hospitalization and weeks of recovery.

He had never used his before. Suddenly he felt like he could fly. He left the security guards in the dust.

Oh, man, would he pay for this.

Then he didn't think about it. He hit the Earth Alliance departure wing, and some Port staff members used their arms to point the way as two more security guards found him.

With the staff members there, he realized that someone should have uploaded an illuminated map straight to his links. He should have seen his path outlined in red (for emergency, of course) over his vision, and he should have been able to follow it blindly. And he did mean *blindly*. He should have been able to close his eyes and follow the backup voice instructions telling him how many steps to take and how far he had to go before turning a corner.

He didn't have an automated map and the Port employees knew it. That was why they had shown up. Something was going very wrong.

Although he didn't know what that something could be. Emergency services links were always the last to shut down. Especially on Valhalla Basin, where Aleyd controlled everything and hated relinquishing that control.

Two more security guards joined him, faster guards, who managed to move passengers aside so that he didn't have to weave around them. He didn't have to weave around most of them now anyway.

Either the word had gotten out that he was running through the Earth Alliance wing or that there was some crisis here or maybe, just maybe, someone had actually augmented his emergency beacon so that the obnoxious genderless voice his badge was producing was blaring all over this part of the Port.

Police business! Move out of the way!

Why the hell did the crisis have to happen in the middle of the biggest wing of the Port, farthest from parking and the main entrance? Why the hell wasn't this thing built for easy access *behind* the scenes, where it was important?

He'd been in the back areas of this Port, and it was a twisted maze of passages, tunnels, and viewing rooms that allowed him to spy on arrivals. It just didn't allow him—or anyone in Port security—to get to those arrivals quickly.

Finally, he reached the part of the wing that his private message had directed him to. The Arrivals area for Earth. This part of the Port was festive, with blues, greens, and whites just like the Mother Planet herself. No sense surprising new arrivals from Earth with Callisto's odd coloring, courtesy of Jupiter, which loomed large over this—the second largest of her moons. No matter how much Valhalla Basin it-self tried to look like an Earth city, it didn't even come close. It was too brown, too red, too uniform. No Earth city had a gigantic red ball looming over it.

Plus, the dome itself—with all its regulated light periods and dark periods—was too uniform, too predictable. Earth had winds and storms and blazing hot sunshine. Earth was about beauty and discomfort.

Valhalla Basin was about sameness.

Except today.

Just a few meters to go. Two more turns, if he remembered this section right, and he'd be in the holding area for suspect arrivals. He whipped around the first corner, and someone grabbed him around the waist.

He twisted, but someone else caught his right hand and pulled it down, pinning it to the arm holding him. Then a third someone put a hand over his mouth.

All three of the someones pulled him into a room he hadn't even known existed and slammed the door shut.

Then they let go of him.

"What the hell?!" he said as he turned around.

And stopped.

Three men stood behind him. He recognized only one of them, but that was the important one: Ike Jarvis, Zagrando's handler for the Earth Alliance Intelligence Service. Zagrando had been undercover with the Valhalla Basin Police for more than a decade.

"What's going on?" he asked, more calmly than he had a moment ago.

Jarvis took a step forward. He was smaller than the other two men he had brought with him, but not by much. They were brawny guys, probably enhanced for strength and muscle, but they were naturally tall.

Zagrando had been a good street fighter once upon a time, but he suspected those skills were as dormant as his running skills. No won-der these guys had taken him so easily.

"We have to get you out of here," Jarvis said. His gravelly voice had no hint of urgency, unlike his words.

"Am I blown?" Zagrando had no idea how it could have happened. He'd told very few people about his work with Earth Alliance Intelligence, and none recently.

The last person he had told had been a lawyer from Armstrong, on Earth's Moon. She represented a young girl whose mother had been kidnapped and who died as a result. The girl—Talia Shindo—had impressed Zagrando so much with her smarts and ability to operate under pressure that he had almost blown his cover with VPD to help her.

But he hadn't. Her mother's kidnappers had provided the best lead in his investigation of Aleyd. As he had told the attorney, his work came first.

Still, this moment caught him by surprise.

"No," Jarvis said.

"If I'm not blown, then what's going on?" he asked.

"We need you elsewhere," Jarvis said.

Zagrando shook his head. "I'm finally making progress after a decade in this sterile place, and you want to yank me out?"

"Your progress is why we're yanking you out. We can't do any more here—*you* can't do any more here—without letting Aleyd know that we're onto them." Jarvis had a little half-smile, almost a sneer, that he used when he was trying to smooth over something.

"Listen," Zagrando said, letting the urgency into his voice. "If I leave here for good, Aleyd will know that I was the one investigating them. People don't leave Valhalla Basin permanently without Aleyd's permission."

Jarvis's weird half-smile faded. He nodded his head, just once, in acknowledgement. "Believe it or not, I have always read your reports. I know how Aleyd works."

"Then you know that I can't leave," Zagrando said.

"You'll leave." Jarvis turned toward the back wall. One of the two men who had come with him touched the side wall, and a panel appeared. Zagrando had seen those before. They were tied to the security personnel at the Port.

The man touched the panel and the back wall became grayish, but clear. The Port's version of one-way glass. Whoever was in the next room couldn't see anyone in this room, but Zagrando, Jarvis, and the other two could see what was going on next to them.

And what was going on was a hell of a fight. A vicious fight, with lasers and knives of all things, and nearly a dozen people, many of them Black Fleet from their appearance.

In the middle of it all was Zagrando himself.

Zagrando's breath caught. The clothing was slightly off, and so was the body. It was a younger version of him, without the added weight and the gone-to-seed muscles. The other Zagrando fought like a demon, but he was outnumbered and alone.

Zagrando had no idea who these people were. Jarvis's assistant touched the panel again, and the side wall turned gray. Outside it, several street police officers mixed with security guards from the Port and a couple of panicked administrators. They were all trying to get into that room, but something blocked them.

"They don't know we're here?" he asked Jarvis.

"They don't even know the room is here," Jarvis said. "Earth Alliance Ports have extra rooms just for top secret Earth Alliance business. Without the rooms, the Earth Alliance doesn't sanction the Port."

"Even with Aleyd?" Zagrando asked. He'd been around that corporation too long. Like everyone else on Valhalla Basin, he thought of Aleyd as unconquerable.

"Aleyd started as a small company in the Earth Alliance. They were nothing when they built this Port. The rooms have been here twice as long as anyone has been on Callisto, and there is no record of them outside of the Alliance hierarchy. They don't know about us," Jarvis said. He hadn't taken his gaze off the fight.

"So those people are ours?" Zagrando asked, nodding toward the fight. He wasn't quite looking at it. It felt odd to watch that younger version of him somehow managing to stay on his feet, despite the cuts, slashes, and burns.

"Oh, no." Jarvis crossed his arms. "The only one in there who is ours is that fast-grow clone of yours."

Bile rose in Zagrando's throat. He had forgotten about all the DNA he had donated when he signed on with the Intelligence service. They were allowed to use it to heal him or to fast-grow a clone to get him out of a tight spot.

He swallowed hard, more shaken than he expected to be. "You're going to let him die."

"Yes." Jarvis watched as if he were seeing a flat vid and not an actual fight.

"Good God," Zagrando said, moving toward the window, actually looking at his clone. Strong, still surviving, fighting as hard as he could to live another few minutes. He was outnumbered, and his only weapon—a laser pistol that was a twin to Zagrando's—was on the floor by the door.

Outside the other door, the police and guards still struggled to get in. Zagrando knew they wouldn't, that the men in this room controlled that doorway, controlled that fight.

"We can't let this continue," Zagrando said.

Jarvis gave him a sideways look. "This is what he was designed for. Let him fulfill his mission."

"He has the brain of a three-year-old," Zagrando said. "He doesn't understand *mission*."

"He doesn't understand anything except fighting," Jarvis said. "That's what he was grown for, that's what he does. If you don't die today, then Aleyd will look for you forever."

"Let them look." Zagrando hurried the door, then stopped, and doubled back to the control panel. He peered at it. "How do I get in that room?"

"You don't," Jarvis said.

Zagrando shoved the assistant aside and hit the controls on the panel. Nothing happened. He used both his VPD clearance and his Earth Alliance clearance and still nothing happened.

"You can't do this," Zagrando said. "This is murder."

"I know how hard it is to see a replica of yourself go through this," Jarvis said in a tone that implied he didn't know, "but I have to beg to differ on the murder charge. Fast-grow clones are not human under the law, and if they are designed to die in an experiment or a mission, then their death is sanctioned. We filed all the necessary documents. His death is legal."

"Son of a bitch," Zagrando said, and launched himself at the door. But he couldn't get out. He tugged, pressed his identification against the door, gave the door some instructions through his links, and still he couldn't get out. Then he went to the window and pounded, thinking maybe he could get the attention of the police officers or the guards. But he couldn't. They continued their battle against their own door.

He realized at that moment that his links to the outside world were down. He hadn't heard any emergency notices nor could he send a message to them via his links. Plus the constant noise that Valhalla's government called "necessary maintenance" was gone.

"You can stop now," Jarvis said. "It no longer matters."

Zagrando whirled. His clone was in a fetal position on the floor, blood pooling around him. There was arterial spray on the far wall and on several of the fighters.

"You didn't give him any way to heal himself," Zagrando said.

"On the contrary," Jarvis said. "He has all the links you have except for the Earth Alliance identification and security clearances. He just doesn't know how to use them."

"Didn't know," the assistant said in a conversational tone.

Zagrando slammed the assistant against the control panel. "This is not something you should be discussing so easily."

The assistant didn't fight him. He let Zagrando hold him against the wall. Zagrando put his arms down and backed away. He had wanted that fight; they had known he had wanted that fight, and they hadn't given it to him.

"We have to leave now, Iniko," Jarvis said, his use of Zagrando's first name his only acknowledgement of Zagrando's distress. "We have to get out before they close down this part of the Port."

"Oh, you don't have a secret room for that?" Zagrando snapped.

"Actually, we do have our own way out," Jarvis said. "And you're coming with us."

"And if I don't?" Zagrando asked.

Jarvis turned toward him, his expression flat. "You're already dead, Iniko. Which body those people out there find is your choice."

"I thought we worked together," Zagrando said.

"So did I," Jarvis said with that weird half-smile. "So did I."

SIX MONTHS AFTER ANNIVERSARY DAY

2

NOELLE DERICCI ACTUALLY HAD AN ENTOURAGE. SHE DIDN'T LIKE IT, but she needed them now. Five people went with her everywhere on this trip—two security guards, two assistants to run interference with the local governments, and one person to shadow her everywhere she went. She needed them all, particularly the shadow, because she was prone to making promises just to get people to leave her alone.

And she wanted to be alone right now.

She stood in the rubble that had once been the city center of Tycho Crater. Six months before, Tycho Crater had suffered the worst casualties of the nineteen cities bombed during the Anniversary Day Crisis. The Top of the Dome, a hotel/resort that someone had built against the dome itself, had been a successful target of one of the twenty bombers.

That horrible day, DeRicci had taken her authority as Chief of Security for the United Domes of the Moon to new levels. She had ordered every single dome in every single city on the Moon sectioned just in case—something she still wasn't sure she had the authority for—and that action had saved all nineteen domes from complete collapse. Bombs blew holes through twelve of the domes, but the sectioning prevented the complete loss of those cities.

Including Tycho Crater, one of the oldest cities on the Moon. Tycho Crater had a lot of problems, from its corrupt government to its ancient dome and grandfathered-in projects. The Top of the Dome had been one of those projects, built just high enough so that visitors could see over the rim of the crater that housed the city. And they could also see the city below.

Apparently the Top of the Dome had been a spectacular place to visit until it exploded, then fell—in pieces—onto the city center below. The city center, which couldn't be evacuated without lifting the sections of the dome and threatening the rest of the city.

This part of the dome was still sectioned, but a temporary dome had been built over the holes created when the Top of the Dome exploded and fell. There was atmosphere, not that anyone really wanted to call this atmosphere. The air was light gray, filled with particles and sludge. The free-standing construction filters couldn't replace the dome filters, which still didn't work. Even setting up new filters every twenty-four hours didn't help.

This environment was toxic, and everyone knew it.

DeRicci and her team wore personal space suits that created atmosphere from the neck down. But DeRicci had known she wouldn't have been able to see everything she wanted to see in a traditional helmet. So she wore a thin emergency helmet that emergency personnel carried in case of a dome emergency or an evacuation outside of a dome itself.

The thin helmet felt like light plastic wrapped around her face and neck. When she breathed, the coating (whatever it was) went in and out, then processed the CO_2 into nanofilters that submitted it to the suit below. The air came from small reservoirs built into the helmet itself. She had only two hours of air, which she had hated when she first set up this visit, and which she appreciated now.

She wanted to get the hell out of here.

The rubble remained all around her. Building carcasses jutted out of the dirt and the dust. It was often impossible to tell what was a building that had been on the ground and what was part of the Top of the Dome.

Fifteen thousand people died here. DeRicci knew the numbers— she knew all the death numbers from that horrible day by heart—but she still couldn't quite contemplate what that meant. Fifteen thousand people, all of whom had families and friends and neighbors and co-workers. The amount of personal loss was staggering.

It was even more staggering when she thought of the numbers who had died moonwide. Those numbers hovered around one million right now, but she knew it would continue to climb. People who didn't have family, people who had no one watching their daily moves, would be missing and then someone would guess that they had been in Tycho Crater on Anniversary Day or in Glenn Station or Littrow.

And she was still getting reports from thousands of alien governments, asking for updates on their citizens or on visitors who happened to be on the Moon that day. She had no idea how many aliens died in the bombings: Some alien cultures didn't ever speak of the dead. Others kept their statistics to themselves. Still others were folded into the death rates for citizens of various cities, because so many of these cities were hugely multicultural.

She felt them here. Not all of the dead, but the ones who died in Tycho Crater. The entire Moon—the survivors anyway, the ones who weren't helping with other rescue efforts—watched that horrible day as the people in this section tried to figure out ways to survive without jeopardizing their friends and family.

The very thought of it all made her tear up, and she didn't dare tear up. She was the closest thing the Moon had to a leader right now, and she was of the personal opinion that leaders didn't cry.

Except in the privacy of their own apartment, long after everyone else had gone home.

She was on a tour of all the damaged cities. It was her second such tour. The first had happened about three weeks after the Anniversary Day bombings, when she was certain that the Moon was secure from more attacks. Or, at least, as secure as they could be.

On that tour, she had seen the damage from outside the sectioned areas, but she hadn't gone in. Most of the domes hadn't yet covered the holes blown in them. Besides, the damage was pretty visible. She had concerned herself with the cities that hadn't lost part of their domes, thinking that maybe those bombings might tell her something about the overall plan.

So far, she only had inklings. And she wasn't even certain about those.

"Chief DeRicci." Dominic Hanrahan, the mayor of Tycho Crater, beckoned her from a few meters away. He was a whip-thin man, made even thinner by the tragedy. When she had met him shortly after his election a year or so ago, he had looked like a twenty-something kid. Now he had frown lines all over his face, and the bags under his eyes were so deep they looked like craters.

She supposed she looked just as bad. Her entourage did its best to make her look good every day, but she hadn't had a full night's sleep in six months. And when she did sleep, she woke up terrified that she had forgotten something—or someone—important.

Hanrahan stood alone on a section of sidewalk that someone had cleared of rubble to make walking paths. His pet lawyers hadn't come in here with the group, primarily because the head lawyer for Tycho Crater was Peyti. The Peyti found the Earth-type atmosphere poisonous and had to wear masks against it. Suiting up in an environment like this one proved a challenge most Peyti didn't want to face unless they had to.

DeRicci actually missed the head lawyer. He, at least, was sensible. She wasn't so sure about Hanrahan

He glanced downward, then back at her. He clearly wanted her to do something, but she didn't want to ask him what.

DeRicci suppressed a sigh. She shut off all but her emergency links whenever she went into a disaster site, but all the environmental suits were sound-linked as a double-check for breathing and other problems, something that workers in Moscow Dome had learned was necessary as they started their cleanup. There was a lot of weird toxicity in the air here, and not all suits had been designed to block it.

She toyed with turning her internal links back on just so that she could talk with Hanrahan privately. Of course, he probably didn't want their communications private.

He probably wanted her to see some horrible death site or the site of some great heroism or something. She'd seen a lot of that on this tour, and while she appreciated it, she didn't want to see any more.

The tours were all deeply personal for each and every mayor—the saga of their city was the tale of their Anniversary Day Crisis—but DeRicci carried the saga of the entire Moon on her shoulders, and sometimes the details blurred.

She didn't want them to, but they did.

A psychologist that one of her assistants hired for the entire staff told DeRicci that the blurring was a self-protection mechanism, allowing her and the others still dealing with the crisis to cope. In fact, the psychologist had suggested that DeRicci wait to deal with the worst of her own emotions until she believed the urgency of the crisis was past.

She didn't believe that the urgency of the crisis had passed yet. She wouldn't believe it, not until the masterminds behind this horrible attack were caught. Then she could let down her guard.

One of Hanrahan's assistants held out his hand to help her down the rubble. She smiled at him, but didn't take it. She'd been climbing on this stuff for months. And she tried not to think about how many obliterated bits of people and aliens were still here, how many lives she was walking over so very gingerly.

She tried not to think of it, but she always did, and always with that clutched feeling in her stomach, as if she had somehow failed. Maybe she had. After all, she had been the Chief of Security for the United Domes of the Moon when this happened.

Hanrahan watched her progress over the rubble.

"This is what's left of the restaurant," he said through the sound links, indicating the area below him.

Of course he would show her that. This was his personal story.

She nodded in acknowledgement as she looked at bits of broken tables and glass, flooring materials and shattered crockery. Apparently no one had touched this part of the rubble, either using it as a marker or a shrine.

She supposed it made sense. This bit of rubble held several parts of the story. Assassins had targeted the mayors of nineteen domes, and had killed several of them. One assassin had also killed the Governor-General, leaving the United Domes government on shaky ground. Or shakier ground, since the government was just beginning to truly unite the domes.

The assassin in Tycho Crater hadn't made it to Hanrahan. His security detail had saved him. Instead, the assassin held a bunch of hostages in the circular restaurant. The hostages got rescued. In fact, almost everyone who had been at the Top of the Dome that day had gotten out during the first part of the crisis.

It was only after the evacuation of the hotel/resort that the dome sectioned, leaving the people below to die when the complex fell.

Then DeRicci looked up. Hanrahan was still staring at the mess, looking as haunted as she felt. He hadn't been the most courageous mayor on Anniversary Day. And he hadn't really known how to handle the Top of the Dome crisis. But he was still in office, probably because he had done well afterward.

Or maybe because the citizens of Tycho Crater didn't want to hold another election on top of everything else they had gone through.

DeRicci waited in silence for a few minutes, the appropriate amount of time (she felt) before changing the subject. And the subject change was going to be dicey for both of them.

"So," she said, moving away from the restaurant debris. "How are the rebuilding plans going?"

Several domes had changed plans in the past few months. Many of the plans she had seen in the weeks after the bombing had been discarded. Some cities had decided to abandon the destroyed sections of the dome. Others had made their rebuilding plans even more elaborate.

Hanrahan had been cagey about his plans from the beginning. In fact, DeRicci had never seen them. She was beginning to think no plans existed.

Hanrahan looked away from the mess in front of him. He shook himself a little as if coming back to the moment.

"We're not the richest city on the Moon," he said, "and we've gotten a lot poorer in the last six months. Half our economy was based on tourism."

He didn't have to add that a goodly portion of that tourism came from off-Moon tourists, tourists who had yet to return after the Anniversary Day events.

"We're far away from everything," he said, "and the outside workers are committed to other places that can pay them better."

DeRicci had heard this complaint from other cities. The rebuilding of the Moon would take years and would cost a lot of money. On the one hand, it was an economic boom to the construction industry and several other industries. On the other hand, it destroyed a lot of local industries—tourism included.

Plus, all nineteen cities now competed for limited resources, from personnel to building materials. To get materials from off-Moon cost a lot of money, and many governments didn't want to—or simply couldn't—handle the pricing. Not to mention, some of those cities had only a temporary government to make the difficult choices.

Which was not a problem Hanrahan faced. Unlike many of the other mayors, he was still alive and still in office.

"I just want to see the plans, Dominic," she said. "You know they have to be approved through my office before any rebuilding can start."

He glanced at the remains of the restaurant. "We haven't even cleared the rubble yet."

"Why not?" she asked. "You can't leave this here. It's right in the center of the city."

The damaged sections other domes had abandoned were on the outside edges of the dome, not in the interior. With this mess cutting through the center of Tycho Dome, it was almost impossible to get around the city easily.

"Lawsuits," he said. "Some people claim this is a grave site."

She cursed silently. He hadn't told her that. No wonder he had lawyers trailing him. And if the grave site issue had become important in Tycho Crater, then traipsing around it was a dicey proposition at best.

"Filed lawsuits?" she asked. "With injunctions?"

"Not yet," he said.

"Then I suggest you clear this out before the suits get filed," she said, knowing how harsh that sounded. "The faster you move, the better off you'll be."

He gave her a baleful look. "You don't want me to get re-elected, do you?"

"It's not my concern," she said. "The safety of the Moon is my concern, and having this crap in the middle of a major city could be a safety issue."

"Maybe you should take over the cleanup," he said.

A flush warmed her face. Son of a bitch. He'd maneuvered her into this position. He wanted her to take over the cleanup so he wouldn't be blamed for disturbing the dead, so that he could get reelected.

If he had asked her politely, if he had had a discussion with her in his office, explaining his dilemma and asking for help in finding a resolution, she might have considered taking over the site. But she wasn't going to be maneuvered into anything.

"Maybe you should do your job," she snapped, and turned her back on him, heading carefully back down the path to the makeshift exit.

"Or what?" he said loudly.

It was a good question. The United Domes was a toothless organization. Since colonization began, each dome ruled itself. Only in recent years had anyone decided that the Moon needed a strong central government. The woman who had led the charge to change the Moon's government, Governor-General Celia Alfreda, had been one of those assassinated on Anniversary Day.

DeRicci closed her eyes. She had been doing a lot of extra-legal things since Anniversary Day. What was one more?

"Things have changed, Dominic," DeRicci said as she turned around. "If you don't want to make the hard decisions for your city, we'll find someone who can. And we'll instate him as mayor of this city. I'm sure everyone in Tycho Crater will be relieved."

She wanted to take back the last statement, but she didn't. There were many reasons she hadn't run for Governor-General after the collapse. One of them had just shown itself. Noelle DeRicci was not a diplomat, particularly when someone pushed her. She couldn't be politic if her life depended on it—and she suspected that some day it would.

The difference between the woman she was now and the woman she had been when she accepted this job was this: that woman would have winced or apologized for her harsh statement; this one stood her ground.

Hanrahan's cheeks flushed as well. His eyes glittered with anger. "You don't know how hard it is," he said. "Looking on this every day and realizing what we've lost. We were the hardest hit of all of the cities. We've lost thousands of people, had even more families ruined—"

"I know the statistics, Dominic," she said.

"They're not statistics," Hanrahan said. "That's what you Armstrong people don't understand. Your city is just fine. You haven't lost a damn thing. You have no idea—"

"We were bombed first," she said quietly. "The practice run, four years ahead. We know. And we lost our mayor. Don't you forget that. Arek Soseki was a friend. Governor-General Celia Alfreda was a good friend. I have been to all nineteen cities. I've presided over funeral after funeral, helped with all kinds of plans, and have fought to set up victims funds. So don't you tell me I don't understand. You think this happened to you alone, but it didn't. It happened to all of us. And some part of me naïvely believed it would bring us together. But talk like yours, separating Armstrong's citizens from Tycho Crater's citizens, only divides us. I'll be happy to replace you, Dominic, if that's what you want. But be warned. If I do it, you'll never hold elected office again."

"You don't have that power," he said.

She let out a small laugh. "That shows how little attention you've paid to events outside of Tycho Crater. Who the hell do you think has kept this Moon functioning these past six months? It sure wasn't the council. A lot of the most influential mayors died. And a whole bunch of the most important governmental support staff got obliterated in the bombing of Littrow. I've been running almost everything, and I'm not happy about it. But one thing I've learned is this: If there's a problem, it needs to get solved immediately. And I'm beginning to believe you're a problem, Dominic. Are you?"

He stared at her. His face was even redder than it had been before. His left hand tapped against his left thigh, a movement DeRicci doubted he even knew he was making.

"People died here," he said in a small voice.

"Yes," she said. "And a lot more people survived. We can't help the dead. We can only help the living."

He shook his head slightly. "You're a cold bitch, you know that?"

"Yeah," she said, even as she wished it were true. "You're not the first person to say that to me. I doubt you'll be the last."

3

MILES FLINT ACTUALLY HAD AN OFFICE IN THE SECURITY BUILDING IN downtown Armstrong. He wasn't exactly sure when that happened. Somewhere along the way, someone had steered him to this room. It was on the same floor as DeRicci's office, not far from the room he and his daughter Talia had worked in feverishly on Anniversary Day.

When he had first moved into the room, it had been nearly empty, with a generic desk and an uncomfortable chair. Now it had a desk, a couch, shelves he'd actually filled with personal items, pads, notebooks, and a wallboard that constantly rotated security messages. One wall even showed moonscapes, and he'd been here long enough to have a favorite.

He liked the sunlight on the Moon dust, the Earth bright in the distance.

The moonscapes stood in for windows. Noelle DeRicci's office was the only one with really good windows, something he thought a bit odd. If someone wanted to take out the Chief of Security for the United Domes of the Moon, they could watch her every move from any of the buildings nearby.

Even though DeRicci had reassured him that no one could do such a thing because nanoprotectors coated the windows' exteriors and interiors, he wasn't reassured. He knew better than anyone else that something protected by technology could be breached by technology.

And right now, whether she liked it or not, Noelle DeRicci was the only person standing between normal life and a complete government meltdown.

That was one of the reasons he didn't mind working in this office. He wanted to support DeRicci as best he could.

There were other reasons he worked here as well. One of them was simple protection. Despite his worries about DeRicci's office windows, this was one of the (if not *the*) best protected buildings in all of Armstrong. He was relatively safe here—if anyone was safe, these days.

And he needed to stay safe. Talia depended on him. He had promised her he would retire from his Retrieval Artist work while he raised her, and he had more or less kept that promise until Anniversary Day. Even now, he wasn't really doing Retrieval Artist work. He was doing actual investigative work.

The work was dicey. He was going into areas of the net that made him extremely uncomfortable, following leads brought to him by the detectives working the various aspects of the Anniversary Day crimes, and following leads he and Talia had developed that very first day.

Flint's biggest worry—which he had expressed to no one—was that someone or something absolutely horrible would track him back through some trail he inadvertently left in his digital travels. Most of his job as a Retrieval Artist had been following those trails; he knew they got left all the time.

He also knew that the most cautious person—and he regarded himself as even more cautious than that—left some kind of trail. The key was to minimize those trails and to make sure that no one could follow them easily, if at all.

He had worked a lot of cases, first as a detective for the Armstrong Police Department (where he met DeRicci—they had been partners), and then as a Retrieval Artist. He had learned caution as a Retrieval Artist. One false move and he could cost someone their life.

Retrieval Artists found people who had Disappeared. Those people usually paid a service for a new identity and a new life. Generally, the Disappeared were accused of a crime committed on an alien world or in an alien culture.

When the Earth Alliance was formed, one of the agreements the parties had to sign onto was that in local cases, local jurisdiction held. It sounded good in theory, but in practice it was often nasty. Small things that humans did—such as walking on a bed of flowers and accidentally crushing them—were considered crimes in some alien worlds. And no matter how much a human was warned about the various differences in the other culture, not even the Earth Alliance knew what all the differences were.

The punishments were often severe—loss of life or loss of a first-born child. So corporations usually facilitated the Disappearance of any worker who violated a local law, just so that the corporation could function in a non-human environment.

Finding those Disappeared could subject them to the very punishments they'd been fleeing, so Flint had to be particularly careful when he did his job. He was always aware that his very investigation might cost someone their life.

In this investigation, he was aware that his work might cost him his life or the lives of everyone he held dear. Whoever had caused the terrible Anniversary Day assassinations and bombings clearly didn't care about life at all. They cared about some kind of agenda, and they were willing to kill thousands to achieve it.

Which was why he worked here, instead of in his small office in Old Armstrong. His office had a lot of safeguards, but he had installed and upgraded them himself, leaving trails just in the work he had done.

He had done some similar work on the computer systems here as well as on the digital security systems, but he hadn't done all of the work. Indeed, much of what he had done was tweak what he found, and he worried about the parts he couldn't upgrade.

On some levels, he knew his office in Old Armstrong was much more of a digital fortress. But he figured that whoever or whatever was behind these attacks expected someone from the various police departments on the Moon and from the Security Office for the United Domes of the Moon to investigate. Those people—or creatures—didn't expect Miles Flint, Retrieval Artist. And if they tried to take out any-one who got close, he didn't want to be an easy target.

Nor did he want to bring these agents of chaos to other places in Armstrong, places he usually used to download sensitive information, like the Brownie Bar or Dome University's Armstrong campus.

He had never really worked from a completely protected position before, and he knew it handicapped him. Usually he was a bit more reckless, a little bit more of a believer in his own abilities to escape detection despite the stakes.

But in this case, even after six months, he still couldn't figure out whom or what he was investigating. And he couldn't figure out why they had acted the way they had. He couldn't see what purpose there was behind these attacks. There had been no follow-up, no secondary or tertiary attacks after Anniversary Day itself. He had expected it. So had everyone else.

On Anniversary Day, Talia had noted that the bombing in Arm-strong four years before might have been practice. So if that was prac-tice, she suggested, were the Anniversary Day bombings a dry run for something even bigger?

DeRicci latched onto that theory. She combined it with a secondary theory, derived from the way the attacks had been conducted. First, a group of cloned men assassinated or tried to assassinate leaders all over the Moon. Then, a few hours later, the bombings occurred. The assas-sinations were not the main point of the attack; the bombings were.

DeRicci called this "Distract and Destroy." Flint believed she was onto something with that theory—with all of her theories—but he didn't know what that something was.

What he feared the most was that whoever this was happened to be applying the distract-and-destroy method on a much grander scale. He worried that the Anniversary Day bombings were the distraction, but from what he did not know.

If it was on a grand scale, then he had a hunch that the target wasn't the Moon herself, but the Earth Alliance. DeRicci had already warned the Alliance of this and they said they would follow up, but Flint had no way to know if they had. Six months after the Anniversary Day attacks, he—and the entire investigative team—was still trying to figure out who or what caused the attacks. For every clue someone found, someone else found a clue that contradicted it.

He had never done anything this complex, this frustrating, or this important.

He had six different computer systems opened around his desk, all attached to him. No one else could work them, not even Talia. He didn't want her in this mess.

She did help him when she wasn't in school, but on a separate system attached to the most comfortable chair in the room. His teenage daughter loved to work in the most uncomfortable positions, arms and legs draped, the holoscreen often floating on the chair's back.

He had long since stopped complaining about how she sat and paid more attention to how she worked. Not that he expected her to do bad work; on the contrary, Talia was much more talented on computers, systems, links, and the net than he was—and he had helped designed some of its modern components.

No, he watched because he was worried that she would trigger something that would put her in horrible danger. He had already lost her once; he wasn't about to lose her again.

The door opened, and Rudra Popova walked in with a tray of food and coffee. Popova, a thin woman with long black hair, had been DeRicci's assistant since DeRicci got this job. At first, DeRicci hadn't liked her, but she gradually learned how valuable Popova was.

Flint completely understood how Popova made herself valuable. She was one of those rare people who was both smart and empathetic. Only her empathy didn't come in the form of sympathetic nods or a good ear for problems. Popova figured out what someone needed before they needed it, and then somehow delivered it.

She was the one who found Flint this office, and she was the one who furnished it. And it wasn't until Flint smelled the cinnamon in Popova's special chocolate/coffee blend that he realized how much he needed a break.

Then he saw the roast beef sandwich she had placed in the center of that tray, and he realized how hungry he was.

He could get used to this. He had worked alone for so many years and kept friends at bay, following the instructions of his mentor, Paloma, that he found this assistance both pleasing and uncomfortable. But he didn't mind it either.

He stretched, his eyes bleary from the caverns of information he'd been lost in.

"Thank you, Rudra," he said. "I'm going to take a break. Why don't you join me?"

"I'd like that," she said. "Just let me get a mug."

And then she hastily left the room, her long black hair swinging behind her.

Flint watched with a bemused frown. He'd expected her to say no, like she had every other time he had asked. Popova had suffered a severe loss on Anniversary Day, and she was still skittish. Not that she had ever been friendly before. In fact, early on, she had greatly disapproved of Flint.

Somewhere—and he wasn't sure where—her opinion of him had changed.

She came back in, carrying an empty mug by its handle and a plate with a matching roast beef sandwich. She sat in the straight-backed chair on the other side of his desk.

He had to tap the desk's surface to shut down the holoscreens. She couldn't see them, but he could. In fact, they blocked most of his vision of her.

He grabbed his sandwich, slid the chair to one side so that he wouldn't rest the food on the desk's command surface, and took a bite. The meat was real, the bread made with real flour, the lettuce and tomato fresh-grown. So much of Moon food had imitation ingredients—imitation beef, bread made with Moon flour which, so far as he could tell, was paste—that it was always a joy to get food with flavor.

"Everything okay, Rudra?" he asked.

She poured herself some coffee from the carafe that she had placed on his tray. Then she wrapped her hands around the mug and leaned back in the chair, leaving her sandwich for the moment.

"I hope you don't mind," she said, her black eyes twinkling. "I'm hiding."

He raised his eyebrows. Popova, not only avoiding her work, but smiling about it. Not to mention the smile itself. He wasn't sure he had ever seen it.

"From whom?" he asked.

"More Earth Alliance investigators. I think they're being cloned, honest to God." Then she bit her lower lip, as if she had said something wrong.

But Flint laughed. He appreciated the normal old-fashioned clone jokes. Recent clone jokes were nasty, and the entire city's attitude toward clones had become a lot darker. He worried for Talia, who was a clone of his firstborn, Emmeline. People didn't know she was a clone, but she did. And she was sensitive about it.

"These guys just come in and think they can take over what we're doing," Popova was saying, "and they can't. They don't understand anything about the Moon except that we were attacked."

She sipped some coffee, then set the mug down.

"And," she added in a confidential tone, "I'm beginning to think that Chief DeRicci schedules her trips around these guys. She gets some notification that they're coming and she flees Armstrong."

Flint's bemusement grew. He'd never seen Popova like this. He knew she had a private life but here, with the exception of Anniversary Day itself, she always acted strictly, almost robotically, professional.

"I know, I know," she said, looking at his expression. "She wouldn't do that. She *hates* these trips, but still. I'm not even sure what I'm supposed to tell these guys. I ask them to leave, and they come back later like an incurable disease."

A chatty, *complaining* Popova? That was new. Flint couldn't quite figure this moment out.

"Do you want me to talk to them?" he asked.

"*No!*" She sounded alarmed. "If they find out we have a retrieval artist on the payroll, then they'll really think we're incompetent."

Her eyes widened as she realized what she said. Flint suppressed a smile.

"I mean, I didn't mean that like it sounded. You know. They think we're small fry already. They're going to really think…"

She let her voice trail off. At least Popova was smart enough to realize that she was making things worse.

"It's all right, Rudra," he said. "I understand what you mean. We could tell them that I'm not on the payroll."

After all, that was true. He didn't need money. He already had more than he knew what to do with. Technically, he was volunteering his time here, although he didn't see it that way.

He believed he was doing emergency triage. He was protecting his home, his family, and his community. He knew that most people didn't have his level of skill, and he knew that even if they did, they didn't have the ability to put information together the way that he did.

The fact that it was taking him months to figure this out instead of days worried him. It meant he was up against something he'd never been up against before. It also meant that if someone less capable had been involved, this crime might never get solved.

Like the first bombing, four years ago.

Much as he loved DeRicci, her team hadn't managed to figure that one out, nor had the Armstrong PD. Which made Flint wonder if the Earth Alliance authorities shouldn't be involved. After all, they were theoretically the best investigators across cultures.

Of course, they would have an Earth Alliance agenda, not a Moon-based agenda. But still, that might help.

Popova was watching him. He recognized the look, and it made him slightly uncomfortable. She knew him a lot better than he knew her.

"Do you want to talk to them?" she asked. Her voice had switched. The chatty woman was gone, and the professional was back.

"I don't know," he said. "What exactly could they do if they don't like how we're conducting this investigation? I thought all the crimes—as heinous as they were—fall under local jurisdiction. Noelle's been fighting just to allow her own investigators from the United Domes to observe in some jurisdictions."

Flint knew that because he'd been listening to DeRicci's complaints, and he understood them. He also understood how the local police departments felt. They didn't want a government agency overseeing them, especially one without a lot of teeth but with a lot of ambition.

That was why DeRicci was visiting a lot of sites herself. She was trying to ingratiate herself with the locals in charge. In some cases it worked, and in others it didn't. It would really have helped if Celia Alfreda was still alive. She had the best diplomatic skills Flint had ever seen in a Moon official. That was one of the many reasons she, as Governor-General, had managed to unify as much of the Moon as she had.

"C'mon, Rudra," he said. "Don't tell me you haven't looked this up."

Popova took a bite of the sandwich, her gaze on his.

"The Earth Alliance is all about local jurisdiction," he said. "Believe me, I know. It's one of the things that got me out of the Armstrong Police Department. So what's different here?"

Popova sighed. "Technically, I'm not supposed to tell you."

"You don't take orders from them," Flint said.

"That's right," she said. "Noelle DeRicci is my boss."

Flint's eyes narrowed. DeRicci told her not to say anything? That meant that DeRicci believed that she had done something wrong, something that opened the door to the Earth Alliance, something that—

"Oh, my God," Flint said. "She opened the door when she warned them she thought this might be an attack against the Earth Alliance, didn't she?"

"I didn't tell you that," Popova said.

Flint scanned what he knew of Earth Alliance law and the Alliance itself. He had a lot of knowledge about the Earth Alliance, much of it

33

arcane, but none of it organized. He wasn't an Earth Alliance lawyer or someone who specialized in any kind of Earth Alliance law, except as it pertained to crimes in Armstrong.

Which, technically, this was. And he knew that the Earth Alliance had no jurisdiction unless there was suspicion or proof that the crime wasn't centered here, but it had been directed at, conceived of, or caused by the Earth Alliance itself.

"So when she contacted the Earth Alliance on Anniversary Day, asking for help, and giving them a heads-up that the attacks might occur elsewhere, she gave them an excuse to come here," Flint said, more to himself than to Popova.

But Popova nodded.

"The weird thing is," Flint said, "that they used the excuse. They could have come here and investigated a whole host of things after the Disty crisis or the Frieda Tey incident, but they didn't. They came here after this. They know something."

Popova tilted her head. Clearly she hadn't thought of that. "Why wouldn't they tell us?"

He sighed. "I'm guessing, but I suspect there could be two reasons why. First, the investigators who are visiting us have no idea why they've been sent here."

"You think that's possible?" Popova said. "I mean, everyone knows about the bombings."

"Yes," Flint said, "but these investigators might not know the reason that the Earth Alliance is involved. Investigators often don't know why their superiors send them into the field."

He knew that one from bitter personal experience.

"And the other reason they won't tell us?" Popova asked.

"Well, actually, they might have already hinted at it with you," Flint said. "They think we're just dumb locals without the skills to investigate anything this large. And honestly, when it comes to some of the cities that got attacked, they might be right."

"I can't believe you think they should get involved," Popova said.

"They have the teams, Rudra," Flint said. "They have the money, and they have expertise that we don't have in large numbers. Armstrong does, and so do a handful of the other cities, but what about Littrow? They barely have a police force. And Armstrong doesn't have the personnel to send there. Neither does this office."

"The chief says we have the expertise," Popova said defensively.

"Really?" Flint asked. "Where?"

"Here," Popova said. "We can export people to the smaller towns."

"Not right now, we can't," Flint said. "We still haven't solved the cases here, and we didn't have a bombing. Our bombing teams are in Littrow because of the United Domes Council deaths there, but do we have teams anywhere else?"

Popova frowned at him. "No," she said. She sounded almost sullen.

"What if there are clues in those other towns, things that they have that no one has investigated because they lack the experience to understand what they have?" Flint was getting worked up, and he tried to keep himself calm. Popova wasn't the person he should be having this argument with.

DeRicci was, and she wasn't here.

But she hadn't told him about the Earth Alliance interest. It seemed like she hadn't told him a lot of things.

He understood that and didn't understand it at the same time. He was volunteering his time because he believed this case—these events—were time-sensitive, because he still felt they were one step away from an even larger crisis.

And DeRicci was acting like someone was encroaching on her turf.

That wasn't fair. He knew her, maybe better than anyone. She hated authority and worked best when she was the one in charge, which was why she had done so well in this job.

If she brought in the Earth Alliance, they would be in charge.

But what if there was a way to have them coordinate the entire investigation, bring their large resources to bear on this case, and not relinquish control?

"Let me talk to them," he said again.

Popova shook her head. She clearly thought coming to him had been a mistake. "That's the chief's job."

"Okay," Flint said. "Let me talk to DeRicci first. Where is she?"

"She didn't want to be bothered unless it's an emergency," Popova said.

"Rudra," Flint said softly, "every hour we waste is an hour we lose. We're already six months behind. God knows what we've missed. I'm terrified that we're four years behind, that we could have prevented all of this. We don't have the expertise. I'm not sure the Earth Alliance does either, but they have access to experts from everywhere—"

"We could request them," Popova said. "I've been telling the chief that. We should request experts—"

"But the Alliance can order them here," Flint said. "And we can use them."

Popova stared at him. "We'll lose control of this investigation," she said after a moment.

"That's the point, Rudra," Flint said. "We don't have control of the investigation. We never did."

4

Iniko Zagrando exited the Black Fleet ship onto some kind of pavement. The Black Fleet called the ship a cruiser, but it outclassed half the ships in the Earth Alliance. And the cruiser looked huge on this landing strip, partly because he had nothing to compare it to. Buildings rose in the distance, but there were no trees, no rock outcroppings, no vehicles. Just a lot of flat brown land that suggested that whatever had been here had long since disappeared.

The air was cold and smelled of rain. Earth rain. Zagrando wouldn't even have recognized that smell three years ago, but he'd been through a lot since then. And he wasn't even sure if the smell meant rain would arrive here or if the place always smelled like this.

He'd read a lot about Abbondiado, but he had somehow missed all the information about its climate. He had known only what every school child in the Alliance had learned: that Abbondiado could easily sustain human life—and had, for nearly forty years.

He shuddered, then pulled his sherlskin coat around his shoulders. Illegal as it was, sherlskin was both warm and comfortable. It had a softness he'd never encountered in any other fabric. But, he supposed, you got what you paid for, and this thing cost fifteen times his annual salary in Valhalla Basin.

"Soaking up the ambiance, Zag?" A man he only knew as Whiteley stood just a few meters from him. The names were purposely short.

Whiteley didn't know Zagrando's real name either. Here, everyone thought of him as Zag and never asked for another name.

Of course, most folks in the Black Fleet had only one name. They didn't need any other. They were family, and often their first names or their ship identified which branch of the family they belonged to.

Whiteley was pretty high up in his branch. He was thin and wiry, no enhancements that Zagrando could see. But then, Zagrando had been trained to recognize only sanctioned enhancements.

He doubted that one of the best scouts in the Black Fleet had anything sanctioned on his body or otherwise. The Black Fleet was the largest human criminal organization in the sector. It mostly worked the Frontier, avoiding the heart of the Earth Alliance whenever and wherever possible.

Rumors, however, stated that the Black Fleet had tentacles inside the Alliance, and maybe even had a few of its people placed within the Earth Alliance government.

It had taken Zagrando two-and-a-half years to earn the Black Fleet's trust, although he couldn't really infiltrate it. One detail he had garnered that apparently no one in Earth Alliance Intelligence had known was that there were only two ways into the Black Fleet: You were either born into it or you married into it.

And in both cases, no matter how hard you tried, you never ever left the Black Fleet alive.

Which made it resemble Earth Alliance Intelligence more than either side was probably comfortable with.

The Black Fleet did have what it called *trading partners,* and so far as Zagrando could see, the only difference between the partners and the Black Fleet itself was that the partners hadn't joined the family.

Zagrando had managed to affiliate with a weapons-trading group that had long ties with the Black Fleet, and then rise up in the ranks. He lead the group now, much as he didn't want to.

And once again, the Earth Alliance wanted him to destroy all his years of hard work. This time, the Earth Alliance hadn't "killed" him to get him to do their bidding. They needed him very much alive.

They wanted him to chase a long-dead phantom.

All because a group of idiot clones had bombed a bunch of cities on the Moon.

"I dunno, Whiteley," Zagrando said. "You could probably say I'm soaking up the atmosphere. It's different than I expected."

"Yeah," Whiteley said. "I had that reaction the first time I came here. You see all the vids and hear all that history, and it only shows you what stuff was like fifty-some years ago. I half expect to see a group of thugs, hands raised, chanting at that pale guy like he was the savior of the entire human race."

Whiteley did his best to sound uneducated, but he—like most members of the Black Fleet—was not only extremely educated, he was also frighteningly intelligent. Whiteley knew who had run Abbondiado and how many years it had been since the colony was truly viable.

This place marked the last stand of PierLuigi Frémont, until his own people turned against him and, with the help of the Earth Alliance, managed to overthrow him.

Frémont committed genocide, not just in Abbondiado, but in the two colonies he'd run before that. In fact, he had completely destroyed those colonies before starting this one. Something about this one made it more successful in Frémont's opinion than the others had been, and he let it thrive for decades before he turned against his own people.

When the Earth Alliance finally arrested him, they brought him to a Multicultural Tribunal for justice, and before his trial began, he killed himself. Zagrando always thought it ironic that the man who forced millions to their death couldn't face the consequences of his actions. He killed himself rather than justify what he had done.

But Frémont hadn't been in Abbondiado for fifty-five years. The colony broke apart without him, even though it had seemed like a viable community before he turned against his people. None of the colonists or their families wanted to stay on this land, deeming it "contaminated by its own history," and so they abandoned it.

The buildings remained, or so Zagrando had been told. And other groups had taken over the area, mostly the Fahhl'd who lost their homeland centuries ago, and took over abandoned sites all over the sector.

He wasn't coming for the Fahhl'd, though. He was here to meet with some arms dealers who promised him his own designer assassins.

His handlers in the Alliance hoped these dealers had a connection to whomever had caused the Anniversary Day attacks. No matter how much Zagrando explained that arms dealers never got involved in political events because they liked to provide the weaponry to all sides, the Alliance didn't listen to him. They kept insisting that this attack was different, although they never told him what evidence they had for it.

And, honestly, they didn't have the time to prove it to him, anyway. His contact with his handlers was, of necessity, short and to the point. He wasn't in any position to argue, either. He did what he was told, or he tried to.

His only other choice was to leave the service and, tempted as he was, especially considering how angry he had been at them for the past three years, he had no idea what he would do if he just walked away. He'd spent his entire adult life working in Intelligence, always pretending to be just one thing when in fact he was two or three. The very idea of simplifying scared him to his bones.

Zagrando looked at the vast emptiness around him. A wind blew dust around the huge black ship, coating it, even though it hadn't been here long.

"Why would anyone live here?" he asked.

"Why would anyone live anywhere?" Whiteley asked, which was such a Black Fleet response. The Black Fleet had no base, no planet where everyone gathered. It had several rallying points that only the families knew, and a few others for the special partners, like Zagrando. Mostly those rallying points were preset coordinates in a particularly empty part of space, although he'd heard rumors that one of the points was a Black-Fleet-owned starbase beyond the Frontier.

"Yeah, but here in particular," Zagrando said with a shudder. It felt wrong. It felt off. He had been to a few other places that had provoked a similar reaction in him, but not as strongly.

"I don't know what's bothering you," Whiteley said. "History can't bite you."

He picked up a pack filled with all kinds of material for trade, from prototype weapons to informational devices to various types of currency. The pack weighed almost as much as Whiteley himself. Zagrando had carried it from the cargo hold, but now that they were on the planet itself, Whiteley wouldn't let him near it.

Zagrando understood why. Everyone in the Black Fleet had been betrayed at one time or another. Trust didn't come easily to them.

It no longer came easily to him either.

"It's not the history," Zagrando said. "Something physical bothers me. That wind, maybe."

Or a smell. He'd been unsettled by smells before. When he'd met the Krasna, he'd had to excuse himself from early discussions while he got some kind of air filter. The Krasna themselves smelled of decaying human flesh, and no one had warned him about that. He hadn't been able to stand near them without gagging.

Sometimes smells were subtler. The Black Fleet often flooded an enemy's environmental system with stress pheromones, hoping to anger them or at least put them on heightened alert. By the time the Black Fleet invaded the ship, the crew members were often so tense that they made terrible mistakes.

"It's the history," Whiteley said. "I've brought folks here before and they react the same way. I've yet to meet a human who likes this place. And since humans used to live here, I'm guessing it's nothing more than knowledge creeping them out."

Zagrando didn't look at him as he said that last, although he made a note of it. Whiteley had brought others here. Zagrando hadn't known that. Whiteley hadn't shared it.

Zagrando didn't know what that meant exactly, whether it meant that Whiteley had brokered a lot of deals here or whether it meant that Whiteley used this place to shake down so-called partners. But Zagrando would now be prepared for anything.

"Yeah, you're probably right," Zagrando said. "It's the history."

He knew that the N'gelese could actually sense a stain on land where massive violence and pain occurred. The Disty believed that dead bodies contaminated the environment, not just while the bodies touched the ground, but for all time.

He wasn't sure the alien groups were wrong.

"Let's just get this done," he said, slipping his hands in his pockets. Not only was it windy here, but it was also cold. And that rain smell bothered him as well.

"Get it done?" Whiteley asked. "That's not like you. Usually you take your time, get the lay of the land, meet the regulars, become acquainted with the way things are done."

Yeah, Zagrando thought but didn't say, *that was when my job was to find out as much as possible about all the arms dealers in the sector. I'm on a different mission these days.*

"Yeah," he said, echoing the thought in his head. "That's when I have my own ship and can keep my own schedule. You're the one making me nervous here, Whiteley. An insistence on your ship, not mine. Skeleton crew on board, a limitation on the weapons I can bring. If I didn't know better, I'd think you were out to get me."

Whiteley grinned.

"You know me, Zag," he said. "If I was out to get you, you'd be got already. Besides, I'd torture you a bit. And I'd tell you what I was about. I'm not out to get you. I still think we have years of business ahead of us."

A promise to put him at ease? Or the truth? Or a combination of both? Zagrando wasn't sure. He'd seen Whiteley kill on a whim and he'd seen Whiteley torture his victims just like he said he would.

He'd also seen Whiteley walk away from a supposed friend in trouble with one of the businesses that Whiteley had brought him to.

Zagrando knew better than to completely trust anything White-ley did, no matter how much he wanted to, or how many assurances Whiteley gave him.

Whiteley grinned again and clapped him on the back. "Because I like you, I'll do this the way you ask. Fast. Let's go."

He slung the pack over his shoulder like it weighed nothing, and headed down the trail away from the crumbling pavement. That was the other thing that Zagrando had seen, but which hadn't registered until now.

Everything manmade here was falling apart. The wind, the dust, the ruins, all made him feel like he was somewhere remote, when, the-oretically, a million aliens lived within walking distance from here. A thriving community had risen from the ashes of the human ruins, or so the descriptions of Abbondiado said.

Zagrando took a deep breath, allowed himself one wish for backup that a lone agent never, ever had, and followed Whiteley into the re-mains of Abbondiado.

5

THE LUNCH ROOM AT ARISTOTLE ACADEMY WASN'T REALLY A "ROOM" so much as a wing, with all kinds of cordoned-off areas, special alcoves, and a large open area that rivaled the auditorium in size. Normally Talia Flint-Shindo loved the lunch room. It gave her the sense that she wasn't on the Moon or even on Callisto, where she had grown up. It seemed like a magical place, a place that only existed in someone's imagination.

She particularly liked the floor-to-ceiling windows that overlooked the Academy's spectacular garden. On special days, students could eat outside, under the double-dome. The garden had its own dome underneath the City of Armstrong's dome. The garden's dome had a sunlight pattern all its own, and it was always warm inside. In truth, the garden was a gigantic greenhouse, and it felt like the safest place in all of Armstrong.

Safety was an issue for her, and she had known it before Anniversary Day. But Anniversary Day had destroyed any feeling of safety she would ever have.

The events of that horrible day were even ruining the lunch room. She cringed when she had to go inside.

Aristotle Academy was the most exclusive private school on the Moon. It was extremely expensive, extremely prestigious, and extremely snotty. Kids from all age groups filled the halls. Most were human, although some other kids got in, especially kids of diplomats and the very rich. Those alien kids had to not only understand Standard, they had to be fluent in it.

A few kids came from low income levels. For the most part, the poorest kids were the smartest ones because they all got in under scholarship. Although Talia wasn't poor by any stretch—she had slowly learned that her father was one of the richest men in Armstrong—she was smarter than 99.9% of her schoolmates. She had snooped in the records; she had seen the studies. All the measurements of her intelligence were so far off the charts that in some of them, she blew out of normal, past genius, into something that no one had yet labeled.

Here, though, she worked hard to keep her intelligence under wraps. She kept her grades up, because that pleased her father. It took almost no effort to do so. She could spend an hour each morning on her homework and classes, and ace every single test thrown at her.

But she didn't talk much in class, no matter how hard the teachers made her try, and she rarely helped her friends with their homework, even though she could have. She wanted people to know she was smart. She just didn't want them to know how smart she actually was.

She had another reason not to call attention to herself. She was a clone in a place that had gone from tolerating clones to actively hating them. In the six months since Anniversary Day, it had become okay to vilify clones, both in the media and in person. For the first time in her life, she heard clone jokes, listened to her friends refer to clones as "inhuman creations," and overheard some of the armed security guards outside the school talk about "taking out" any clone they ever saw.

No one knew she was a clone except her father and a lawyer named Celestine Gonzalez, who handled all of Talia's documentation. Celestine had made sure that Talia was designated a human being under the law before Talia ever arrived in Armstrong, and even then—a little over three years ago—her father had encouraged her not to discuss her clone status.

He had said it was because some of the people involved in her mother's death were looking for the clones of her parents' only child, Emmeline, who had died in a tragic accident. But Talia had always wondered if her father worried more about the prejudice against clones.

Talia understood it very well; she had felt it too—still did, if truth be told. Her mother had raised her as a natural child. Talia hadn't known she was a clone until that awful day her mother got kidnapped. Everything changed that day, everything Talia had ever known. From her own identity to her belief in anything her mother told her to the fact that the father she had thought abandoned her hadn't even known she existed.

Whatever she thought about the events that had transpired in the last three years, she had learned one thing: Her dad loved her. He didn't care that she was a clone. She was his daughter, completely and totally, and he did his best to protect her.

She hadn't really appreciated that until Anniversary Day itself. In the weeks that followed that horrible day, she hadn't wanted to leave his side, afraid something would happen to him too. But he made her go back to school and go out on her own. He believed she needed to learn how to survive by herself.

He never hid the fact that something could happen to him too—that it actually might happen to him, since he'd had a dangerous profession when she met him. He kept telling her everything she needed to know if he died, who she could trust to help her through the transition, how to access that fortune of his, and what she should do next.

She didn't agree with some of it, and he knew that. But they both pretended she would do what he asked.

She just hoped it would never come to that.

She walked into the lunch room, avoiding the windows, and headed toward vegetarian wing. She wasn't a vegetarian, although she preferred the vegetarian food here. The vegetables were fresh, the cooking innovative. She hadn't had such fresh food in Valhalla Basin, which was a corporate-owned city. In fact, most of what she ate here wasn't even available there. The corporation that owned everything, Aleyd, only let its own products get sold and served throughout Valhalla Basin.

No one owned the Moon. No one owned Armstrong. Heck, the school itself was some kind of communally owned thing that she didn't entirely understand. She had gone from a place where one company ruled everything to a place where no one ruled anything.

She still had trouble wrapping her mind around that.

Employees stood behind serving tables. When Talia started going to school here, androids handled food service, but after all the bombings, an entire subset of parents got terrified of technology.

Talia wanted to remind them that the worst of the occurrences happened because of human hands, but no one would listen to her. Her dad told her that people would be afraid of whatever they chose to be afraid of, and the truth couldn't change any of that, and that was probably right. But that didn't mean she had to like it.

The vegetarian area smelled of garlic and freshly baked bread. But as she got closer to some of the tables, the smell of fresh apples dominated. Apples of all different kinds covered one of the serving tables. Another had different apple desserts and meals on them. Apparently apple harvest had happened this week, and she hadn't even known it.

She took one of the apple desserts, then went to the freshness bar. There she put in an order for a fresh spinach-and-tomato omelet, and waited while it cooked.

She didn't mind. As busy as she and her father had been since Anniversary Day, neither of them even bothered to cook. They ate when they could. Usually the meal she got here at lunch was the tastiest meal of the day.

Too bad she couldn't eat it in peace.

She was trying to. She had her back to most of the room, and she was trying not to listen. But it was hard. Over the past few days, things had escalated. Her entire class was on edge, all because of some stupid prejudice against clones.

As far as she knew, she was the only clone in the school. But that didn't stop the idiots. They were ganging up on twins, triplets, and even siblings who looked a lot alike. So far, most of the stupidity happened off campus or as sideways comments in class, but she knew escalation was only a matter of time.

And after what happened in Ms. Walters' class this morning, that time was probably now.

"Oh, there they are!" said a male voice behind her. "The Chinar clones. How's life in tandem, clones?"

Talia closed her eyes and made herself breathe, like her dad had taught her. She had to control her temper, he had said. She couldn't be impulsive, he had said. Acting on impulse often led to serious mistakes.

"You'd think they'd dress alike," said another male voice. "Everything else matches. Blow up any cities, clones?"

The Chinar twins were nice. They'd treated Talia well from the moment she arrived at Aristotle Academy, which was more than she could say for some of the other girls. Her father's friend, Noelle De-Ricci, once commented that she'd never want to be a teenage girl again because girls were so mean.

But girls hadn't been mean to Talia (much). Not like these idiot boys.

She turned around. Kaleb Lamber stood closest to the twins. Of course he did. He was a big kid. Talia believe he'd had pricey muscle enhancements to give him an edge in sports, something illegal but still done around Armstrong.

Five of his beefy friends stood around the Chinar twins, who looked like children in comparison. The twins were slight, with wispy red hair and unfortunate hook noses. They weren't pretty, but they were smart and funny, and great to be around.

They didn't deserve this.

"Leave them alone, Kaleb," Talia said. She tried to sound flat and disinterested, a tone she'd heard from her father when he tried to settle someone down, but she couldn't achieve it. She didn't feel disinterested. Beneath what she hoped was a calm surface, she felt furious.

He raised his long-lashed dark eyes to her. One of the many annoying things about Kaleb Lamber was how gorgeous he was. His features were delicate, which made her wonder whether his parents forced him to get the muscle enhancements to look more manly.

Appearances seemed to mean a lot to him, which, she figured, meant they meant a lot to his parents as well.

"Oh, you're their defender now?" Kaleb asked.

"I'm just tired of the stupidity that you and your friends spew all over this school," Talia said. So much for calm surface. A flush of anger warmed her cheeks.

"Stupidity? You're pro-clone now?"

"I'm anti-bigotry," Talia said. This part of the room had gone silent. It seemed like everyone watched, even the staff. "You've gone to this school your entire life. So have Maybelle and Portia. You've known them longer than I have, and you know they're not clones. I don't think you'd recognize a clone if you saw one."

"Really?" Kaleb's fists closed. "What makes you so sure of that?"

"Because you're looking at the wrong thing." Talia felt a little lightheaded, as if she was confessing to something when in reality, she was trying not to. "Contrary to what you saw on the news, clones don't run around in groups. They live their lives just like you do. They look like someone else, but usually that someone is much older than they are or famous or something. They don't hang out together like twins."

She shot a glance at the Chinar twins. They were looking down, as if they didn't want to be there. And they probably didn't. Who liked being the center of this kind of attention?

"So you could be a clone," Kaleb said, those gorgeous eyes of his narrowing.

"I could," she said, her heart pounding. "But so could you. In fact, I vote for you being the clone, with those fake muscles and your obsession with it all. What better way to divert suspicion from yourself than to accuse others?"

49

Like she was doing right now. She was shaking.

Everyone looked at Kaleb. His friends had their heads bowed. They didn't want to be in the middle of this either.

"I'm not a clone," Kaleb said.

"Why should I take your word for it?" Talia asked. "You don't take anyone else's word for who they are."

"Yeah," someone said from the back. "We should look for clone marks."

"Grab him," someone else yelled.

Talia swore. This was not what she wanted at all. "No," she said, but half the lunch room wasn't listening. They were surging forward, determined to grab Kaleb by the head and search for marks.

Talia took a step backward. She hadn't expected this. Kaleb and his friends stood near the table looking stunned as half the school descended on them.

The security buzzer went off. Someone noticed the fight already.

Talia reached for the Chinar twins, pulling them toward her.

"Come on," she said. "We have to get out of here."

She ran behind the food counters, but as she reached the kitchen, one of the security guard stepped in front of her. He was grinning.

"Good show, honey," he said. "But you're part of this. You can't leave. None of you can leave."

Talia cursed. They were going to call her dad again. Sometimes he defended her when she lost her temper. But he was going to be mad about this one.

"Sorry," she said to the twins.

"I'm not," Maybelle said. "Look."

She pointed to the table they had just vacated. A group had caught Kaleb and were twisting his head at an odd angle, looking for the clone mark.

Talia almost reached for hers, but she didn't. Hers was not in the normal place nor was it regulation size. Hidden, because her mother didn't want anyone to find her.

She swallowed back bile. The kids were in a frenzy and the guards were having trouble wading into the mess.

She wanted to believe the frenzy was anti-Kaleb, anti-bullying, but she knew better.

The frenzy was anti-clone. And she had started it all.

6

Sᴜɴʙᴇᴀᴍ Gᴀʟʟᴇɴ ᴘᴜᴛ ᴛʜᴇ ꜱᴏɪʟ ꜱᴀᴍᴘʟᴇ ɪɴ ʜᴇʀ ᴛᴇꜱᴛ-ᴛᴜʙᴇ ʀᴀᴄᴋ. Old-fashioned science in an old-fashioned place. She put her hands on her back and stretched, then peered out the windows of her little habitat.

It had taken her five years to get approval to work in this part of Peyla. Peyla was the home planet of the Peyti. The Peyti had a niche in the Earth Alliance: They fit perfectly into the overall legal system. Their organized minds helped them find the most minute ruling within seconds, often faster than any link could provide the information. Their dispassionate approach to life—by human standards—made the Peyti a lot more ruthless.

Combined, those things made them the best lawyers in the Alliance, and since the Alliance was all about laws and rules and regulations, lawyers were in high demand.

It also meant that anyone trying to do anything on Peyla faced not just a variety of regulations, but an even greater variety of lawyers willing to parse those regulations for exorbitant fees.

Fortunately, Gallen's research had two corporate sponsors. She liked to think of herself as an independent scientist, but in truth she wasn't. One corporation had built her habitat—not out of the goodness of its heart, but because she gave it a chance to test the habitat in the harshest of Peyla conditions (which, by human standards, was incredibly harsh).

The other sponsor got the fruits of her research. Early studies of Peyla—before the Peyti and the others on the planet joined the Earth Alliance—showed some trace minerals and organic compounds not found anywhere else. Some of those compounds, in particular, might have properties useful in the medical field—and not just in human medicine, but in Disty medicine as well.

Since the humans and the Disty didn't share a lot of diseases in common, the fact that such material could be used for both made the corporations sit up and notice. Their scientists figured that those compounds might have uses beyond humans and Disty, with other alien groups that shared some of those common traits.

Privately, Gallen called that magic science. Or simple wish-fulfillment. The corporations saw tons of money.

Gallen used that monetary fantasy to fund research into the Peyla landscape. She wanted to know how this particular world bred its varied and unusual species. She believed that the organic compounds making up the soil, water, and air were the proper place to start.

Outside, the landscape of Peyla was a goldish green. She had grown used to the landscape, both harsh and beautiful at the same time. The habitat sat on a cleared patch of land, and had its own landing strip for the hovercraft that she used to get here (courtesy of the first corporation). Beyond that, tree-like plants rose above a tangle of other plants. In the distance, mountains covered in red snow glowed in the half light.

She loved it here, even though the atmosphere was toxic to her. Toxic to all humans. When she went out into it, she had to wear an environmental suit. The air burned human skin, even though the atmosphere was not hot.

That was different from the Peyti reaction to an oxygen-rich environment that humans needed to survive. The Peyti only needed a mask to function in a human environment. The mask covered their faces so profoundly that Gallen spent her first few months on Peyla staring at Peyti mouths when the Peyti spoke. The mouths were square and moved inward when the Peyti said something.

Without the mask, the Peyti also looked less delicate. They had twig-like arms and legs, a slender body, and elongated faces. But without the mask, the mouth dominated those faces, and whenever a Peyti spoke, double rows of very powerful teeth glimmered gold.

The color gold—not the element gold—threaded through everything here. The dark soil had a goldish tinge. The plants, all of which were specific to Peyti, had some of that gold threading through them. It wasn't chlorophyll and it wasn't anything else that human-based scientists recognized.

The Peyti had a word for it, and they claimed that the gold substance was the fountain of life. It might have been for them. For humans, who hadn't been allowed to test it early in their relations with the Peyti, the gold substance was a mystery, something they hadn't encountered before.

And because it was gold-colored, Gallen suspected, humans believed it had special properties. From time immemorial, humans believed anything that looked like gold brought value to them.

Gallen cared less about that than other components of the soil, which had not been studied from a human perspective. Before joining the Earth Alliance, the Peyti confined most outsiders to the cities. Only a select few ever made it to the countryside.

After Peyla joined the Earth Alliance, the Peyti insisted on having Peyti involved in any organization that tried to do business on Peyla. Often the Peyti would stop research or investigation into something new and interesting to humans by handing the organization Peyti information on that very thing.

Usually that Peyti information was enough, but it had become clearer and clearer—at least to Gallen—that the Peyti information obfuscated as much as it clarified.

She had managed to get this far into the Peyla countryside because she was operating as an individual. In fact, in her proposals for funding to the two corporations backing her, she sold her individual status as a plus. She would be able to find out things that no other human had discovered because she was working alone, without true affiliation. The Peyti requirement of having a Peyti representative on the team was void here.

And the Peyti saw it that way too, although she got a sense, after her research was approved, that they would close this loophole in the future. They had seemed annoyed that someone—a non-Peyti—had found a loophole in one of their own regulations.

She moved the soil sample into the storage cabinet behind her desk. She did most of her work using contemporary equipment, wands that went deep into the soil and took readings as they went; chips on her gloves (that spoke to the chips on her fingers), which took readings from anything she touched; her environmental suit, which monitored the atmosphere and its changes around her; and the lab equipment she had inside the habitat, which took each microparticle of soil and explored it thoroughly without destroying it.

She was learning a lot, although she wasn't sure how useful it would be to anyone besides her. That was the one thing she hadn't told the corporations when she applied for her help: She believed she had a 95% chance of failing to discover anything new.

That didn't bother her, but it would have upset them, considering how much money they had spent to fund her.

She didn't mind. She didn't have to pay any of it back. And she got a three-year-long commitment from them. Three years in which she didn't have to see anyone if she didn't want to. She could study her little patch of Peyla and maybe learn something about another planet that pleased her, even if it didn't please anyone else.

She sat in her chair, ready to focus on the analysis of several grains of dirt, when something squealed outside. The squeal was high and piercing, almost painful to her ears.

She looked up, saw a Peyti in the air several meters outside her building. The Peyti was going backward, almost as if it had been catapulted out of a machine or dropped from great height and blown backward by a wind. Only there was no wind. And the Peyti didn't fly.

The Peyti was the source of the noise. It flailed its arms, head tilted back, eyes even wider than usual.

And then it turned bright orange, revealing its twig-like skeleton, and vanished. Bits of glowing orange fell to the ground, lighting up the dirt around it.

Gallen put her hand over her mouth. Had that been some kind of projection? Or was it a vision of some kind?

Or had she actually seen it? Had a Peyti died in front of her in a particularly horrible way?

Her heart was pounding. She moved her fingers across the desk, accessing the security feeds. Only she shut off the sound. She didn't want to hear that scream ever again.

The exterior cameras had picked up something flying at her, and that something resolved into the Peyti she had seen. The security feeds told her that the Peyti was male. She tapped the screen for more information when she heard the scream again.

She cursed. She didn't want to hear that, so she punched off the sound. The desktop sent up a warning to stop trying to shut off sound that wasn't on.

Which meant that the sound was coming from outside—again. She looked up in time to see another Peyti propelled backward. That Peyti was screaming too, but not flailing. Instead, it was looking around, trying to see if it could grab onto something.

It looked identical to the other Peyti, but she knew that was just a trick of the eyes. She had never been able to tell individual Peyti apart at first glance.

This Peyti's scream got more concentrated, then an orange beam appeared briefly. It enveloped the Peyti, showing its skeleton just like the last one, before this Peyti literally exploded.

Charred orange bits of Peyti fell to the ground, just like the previous Peyti.

Gallen's stomach turned. She crouched, afraid whatever was doing this could see her. She grabbed a pad and slid under the desk, breathing so hard she had to caution herself against hyperventilating.

Peyla was one of the safest places in the known universe. The Peyti believed in laws, not violence. They hadn't had war here in nearly a century. They were known as the most peace-loving species in the entire Alliance.

They even conformed their laws to Earth Alliance-preferred laws— at least for resident aliens, so that people like Gallen wouldn't make a mistake and subject themselves to something culturally inexplicable.

Another scream began. She glanced at the pad, at the images from the cameras on that side of her habitat, saw another Peyti sailing toward her.

Something awful was happening, right outside her windows. Something terrible and terrifying.

She sent an emergency message through her links, coding it for humans only. She didn't want any Peyti outside to know she was here. She didn't even hit her emergency beacon.

She needed to stay hidden. But she had to stay safe.

She wasn't sure how she could do both.

7

THE WALK TO ABBONDIADO PROPER WAS SHORTER THAN ZAGRANDO had expected. The city looked far away when he left the landing area, but he hadn't realized that Whiteley had landed the ship on the flat top of a hill.

The bulk of Abbondiado was down that hill and in a bowl-shaped area. And it wasn't ruined like he had expected. Most of the buildings remained intact, if changed, by their current residents.

Murals covered everything, most of them non-representational. That surprised Zagrando the most because the Fahhl'd decorated nothing except their own bodies.

The Fahhl'd were greenish creatures, no wider than his left arm. They were made up of thread-like fibers that wrapped around a central core. He'd never seen the actual core, although he'd seen pictures of it. It was clear, the size of a strand of hair, and it held everything from their internal organs to their brains. They did not have obvious eyes, which always unnerved him. Instead, they saw through their outer fibers. Sometimes, when they were intrigued, they raised their outer fibers and brought them close to whatever they were studying.

Because of their interesting build, they could adapt to almost any living situation. They rarely built their own homes; they just modified what they found.

But they didn't paint. Humans did. Other species did as well, but he hadn't realized those species lived here.

Nor did he realize that the Disty had once had a presence here—not until he saw the ruins of a Disty colony in the center of Abbondiado, near the river. Whiteley explained to him that the Disty had found this place first. But PierLuigi Frémont drove them off—or so the legend went.

Zagrando wondered if the Disty—who believed that a dead body contaminated all it touched—had heard of Frémont and thought it the better part of valor to vacate this small colony than to live in proximity to him. But Zagrando didn't ask Whiteley. Zagrando didn't want to seem too learned about anything other than weapons.

The Disty ruins didn't just sit like an abandoned lump in the middle of town. Instead, they had become some kind of artist sculpture. More murals decorated the walls, using zigzag patterns to accent the haphazardness of Disty architecture.

Some of the murals were quite faded, as if they had existed since the Disty left, but others had fresh colors, including a vibrant red that caught the eye. Someone was restoring the murals with great love and care.

"No one lives there," Whiteley said. Apparently he had noticed Zagrando's glance at the Disty ruins.

"I figured," Zagrando said. "The artwork surprised me, that's all."

"There's some kind of renovation going on here. Restoring the good stuff, getting rid of the bad stuff, that kind of thing." Whiteley stopped and peered in the direction of the Disty ruins. Then he shook his head. "Waste of time, if you ask me."

Anything that failed to make obvious money—and a lot of it—was a waste of time to Whiteley.

"It does seem odd for the Fahhl'd to be doing this," Zagrando said.

Whiteley gave him a how-dumb-are-you look, which Zagrando both wanted and expected. Just like Whiteley played dumb with the people around him, Zagrando often played dumb with Whiteley.

It usually worked, too. Whiteley couldn't help telling Zagrando when he had made a major mistake.

"The Fahhl'd don't do stuff like this," Whiteley said. "Abbondiado is a major artist colony. Human artists. The kind who are avoiding all the corporate crap from the Alliance and trying to make it on their own."

Zagrando felt a fissure of discomfort. He had thought humans had long ago abandoned this place. He should have known that humans lived here. Someone should have told him or it should have been in the information he accessed on the public links. That it wasn't disturbed him greatly.

But he couldn't let his discomfort show. "These artists figured they can 'make it' by rehabbing Abbondiado?"

"Other historical sites make tons of money off tourists. Why not Abbondiado?" Whiteley said, adjusting the pack on his back. The adjustment was the only sign that he found the pack heavy.

"You're the mainstream businessman," Zagrando said. "You tell me."

"I think it's long-term smart and short-term stupid," Whiteley said. "*Someone* will make money off this place, just not these idiots. They'll fix it all nice, open it up, and no one will come here. Then some corporation will come in, chase out the Fahhl'd—pay them to leave or something—package the place just right, and stupid Earth Alliance tourists will swarm here. Tell me that I'm wrong."

He wasn't wrong. Zagrando could actually envision it, particularly now that he had seen this community. It certainly wasn't what he expected. He hadn't expected the charm or the beauty.

But that feeling of unease he had noted when he got off the ship remained. He couldn't quite recall ever feeling like this before—extremely pleased with the beauty of a place and at the same time possessed with the urge to get the hell out of here right now.

Some of it might have been the river. It was the source of the impending rain smell. It also was a brownish orange that reminded Zagrando of puke. He couldn't tell the source of the river's color—the nearby hillside was an earth-like green—and that bothered him, too.

Whiteley led him around a corner, and suddenly the entire sense of the community changed. A humming sound, like a constantly vibrating violin string, grew.

Maybe that was the source of Zagrando's unease. He must have been hearing that sound before he was actually aware of it. He made himself take a deep calming breath and go farther forward.

This entire section of the city was a gigantic public market. Only the Fahhl'd ran it, not humans, so at first, it looked impenetrable. Bright threads in gold, red, silver, and blue wrapped the market in a web.

Zagrando had been around the Fahhl'd long enough to know that those threads weren't actual fabric, but Fahhl'd performance artists making some kind of political statement.

He'd never tried to figure out Fahhl'd politics, since they were always regional and always arcane, but he did know better than to barrel into the market without permission.

Apparently Whiteley did as well. He made a sharp left into a building not covered in thread and hurried down a flight of stairs.

Zagrando followed. The rain smell slowly changed into a mildew odor combined with something else, almost like a salty, pasty smell. It made Zagrando want to sneeze.

But the discomfort was leaving him, and he realized that he could no longer hear that hum. He suspected it was gone on the subconscious level as well.

The stairs went down a long way. The air grew cool. Someone had stuck transportable ship lights against the walls, which told Zagrando that no power came to this building. Whether that meant that the Fahhl'd hadn't restored power to Abbondiado or whether that meant this building was supposed to be uninhabited, Zagrando didn't know.

That was one of the many things he hated about the job he did now. When he was on Valhalla Basin, he could tell just by the way a building looked whether or not something was going wrong there.

Here—and everywhere he went now—he had no way of knowing if what he saw was normal or abnormal, safe or threatening. He felt constantly off balance, and no matter how long he did this job, he didn't get used to it.

His handlers would argue that was a good thing. He needed to stay off balance to do his job. But a person who was off balance was a person who expended too much energy, even when doing nothing. It was no wonder he had lost weight in the past few years. At least he had retrained all of his muscles. Now, at least, he was in fighting shape.

He just never knew when or where he might fight.

He certainly hoped it wasn't here. Escaping from whatever place he ended up might mean running back up this ridiculous flight of stairs.

Finally, Whiteley reached the bottom. He waited there for Zagrando to catch up. Down here, the walls had been carved out of the dirt and slapped with a substance that colonists used to make sure the dirt didn't collapse. That substance had turned a sickly orange, which now told Zagrando why the river had its unusual color.

It was probably too toxic to drink as well.

Frémont really had come close to destroying Abbondiado. Zagrando wondered where the locals got their fresh water, then decided it was none of his business.

"You let me do the talking," Whiteley said. "He wanted to meet you, but that's as far as it goes."

Zagrando hated it when the rules changed just before a meeting. "I need to do my own negotiating."

"Then you can go back up those stairs all by yourself," Whiteley said. "You have to be sanctioned to talk to this guy, and you're not."

"Why didn't you get me sanctioned before we got here?" Zagrando asked.

"This is how you get sanctioned, dumbass," Whiteley said. "He doesn't do anything without a meet. But there's protocol. He will ask you questions directly. Even if you understand them, you will answer through me. Got that?"

"He doesn't speak Standard?" Zagrando asked. He didn't think there was a human in the sector who didn't speak Standard.

"Oh, he speaks it," Whiteley said. "Just not well enough for anyone to understand. You'll see."

He pushed open the door, and the mildew smell turned into a full-blown stench. Zagrando's eyes watered. He hadn't been assaulted by a smell like that in a long, long time. He could taste it, and he knew he would never ever get this smell out of his clothing.

If he had been anywhere else, he would have snidely thanked Whiteley for the warning. But Zagrando knew better than to speak.

He wasn't looking at a human enclave. Whiteley had led him to an Emzada Lair.

Zagrando had never actually seen or smelled an Emzada Lair before. He'd always heard that it was an overwhelming sensual experience, and it was. His skin itched, and he kept swallowing so that he wouldn't gag on the odor.

The Lair itself was lighter than the stairwell, but the light seemed gray, mostly because of the skin cells coating everything. The Emzada itself sat in the center of the room like a gigantic slug. It needed the cool air to slow down the rate of sloughing. It lost one-quarter of its skin every day in an oxygen-rich environment. Since the skin regenerated, the Emzada really didn't care, but it had to be careful that it didn't lose too much.

Its skin had medicinal properties for the Ilidio and other species, which made the skin cells very valuable. As a result, the Emzaden stayed in areas where the Ilidio weren't common.

In fact, Zagrando had never actually seen an Emzada before. He had heard about them, particularly about how foul their lairs were, but he had never known anyone who had encountered one. The Emzaden rarely traveled far from their native land. They established Lairs on planets not affiliated with the Earth Alliance, like this one, and even when they were in such a place, they kept to themselves.

Even though Whiteley had called the Emzada "he," Zagrando wasn't so certain about the Emzada's gender. He remembered hearing somewhere that Emzaden kept their gender quiet. But Zagrando didn't want to rely on what he remembered, however, so he was just going to follow Whiteley's lead.

Not that he had any choice.

They were stuck in this foul room.

Whiteley folded his hands together and bowed. "Great One," he said in Standard. "This is the man I told you about. This is Zag."

Great One? Zagrando didn't know the protocol for addressing an Emzada, but he certainly didn't like the implications of the term.

"Bow," Whiteley whispered.

Zagrando felt flustered. He had a persona with Whiteley—a tough arms dealer persona—and for the first time, Zagrando wasn't sure how that tough arms dealer would act.

He hesitated for a moment, and then he bowed. But he didn't quite mimic Whiteley's position. Zagrando didn't press his hands together and he didn't bow deeply.

"So," the Emzada said, "this is the man in need of dedicated, thinking weapons."

The Emzada's Standard was excellent, his accent perfect. Whiteley had misrepresented the situation—again.

Zagrando swallowed hard. Some of that was nerves, but the bulk of it was his gag reflex. The stench—and the fact that the air felt coated with skin cells—bothered him. His stomach was doing a slow roll that he hoped he could keep under control.

"It is that man, Great One," Whiteley said.

"He should speak for himself," the Emzada said.

Zagrando debated doing so, despite Whiteley's warning. He opened his mouth, then closed it again, glancing at Whiteley. Whiteley would have to tell him when he could speak.

Zagrando had to trust that Whiteley wouldn't bring him all this way to screw up a deal.

"He is following protocol, Great One," Whiteley said. "He has not been sanctioned to speak to the Emzaden."

"I can sanction him," the Emzada said.

"He is aware," Whiteley said. "He is also aware that a single Emzada sanction holds less force than a sanction from the Emzaden Assembly. He would prefer the wider sanction if he is going to do business with the Emzaden."

"Wise man," the Emzada said.

And Zagrando let out a small breath. His silence had been important after all.

The Emzada was still speaking to Whiteley. "You will vouch for him."

"Yes," Whiteley said.

The Emzada straightened. Skin cells fell around it like rain. They even made soft little pelting noises as they hit the floor.

"You have answered too quickly," it said. "You must listen to my questions before vouching for this creature."

"I am sorry, Great One," Whiteley said with actual remorse in his tone.

"You will vouch that this man is not a spy?" the Emzada asked.

Zagrando kept his face expressionless. He still couldn't stop the slow roll in his stomach, but he willed himself not to feel it. Nor did he want to think about how trapped he was.

The Emzaden were supposed to have three supple limbs that could catch a man before he even took a step. Zagrando didn't see where the Emzada hid those limbs, but then everything in this Lair was covered in grayish skin cells, so what Zagrando thought was a part of the wall might actually be part of the Emzada itself.

"What man knows another man's heart?" Whiteley said.

Zagrando gave him a surprised sideways look. He had expected Whiteley to deny that Zagrando was a spy.

"Yet you bring him here," the Emzada said.

"I do," Whiteley said, "because I have known him for two years, and in that time, he has not made a wrong move. He has done exactly what he said he would do. He has kept his promises, paid his debts on time, and has not interfered with the Black Fleet's business. That is all I know of him and all I want to know."

It seemed like a fair assessment, but Zagrando didn't know what the Emzada was listening for.

"You trust him," the Emzada said.

"I trust no man," Whiteley said.

It felt like they kept taking one step forward and two back. Zagrando continued to look at Whiteley, trying to assess what the man was actually doing.

"Then why should I trust him?" the Emzada said.

"I have not said that you should," Whiteley said. "I believe you should do business with him, however."

"Business, for the Emzaden, is based on trust," the Emzada said.

Zagrando swallowed again, hating that gag reflex. It got in the way of his attempt to seem calm.

"You don't trust me," Whiteley said. "You don't trust anyone who is not Emzaden. That's why you have a vouching system."

The Emzada straightened even more, releasing another flurry of skin cells. The stench grew. Zagrando wanted to cover his nose.

The Emzada turned its black eyes on Zagrando. "What do you need assassins for?"

Zagrando glanced at Whiteley.

Whiteley raised his eyebrows and shrugged. "If I knew the answer to that question, I'd speak for you."

Now Zagrando was in a tough position. He had to answer, and yet not answer directly.

"Please tell our kind host that I am shopping for a client, and I make it a practice of mine to never ask what the weapons will be used for." Zagrando made a point of speaking directly to Whiteley.

The baseboard moved upward. It took Zagrando a moment to realize that moving gray thing was actually part of the Emzada. Apparently it was making some kind of gesture or getting comfortable or something, because Whiteley did not seem disturbed.

"Your friend is quite wise," the Emzada said again, directing its comments to Whiteley. "We prefer not to know what our clients need either. Only in this case, it is necessary. Our dedicated, thinking weapons are each a particular type. And we must know what sort of work they will do to match weapon type with job type."

Whiteley turned toward Zagrando. Zagrando took a deep breath. He felt the need to cut through the euphemisms.

"My client," he said to Whiteley, "wants human weapons, not some kind of robotic weapon that also 'thinks.' My client wants something that can pass for normal in human worlds, but has either a program or a script to follow. Before we go any further, I need to know if our gracious host and I are discussing the same kind of weapon."

Whiteley looked a little pale. Apparently frank talk was frowned upon, even in a private meeting like this.

"Great One," Whiteley said, "my friend—"

"I heard," the Emzada said, its tone dry. It sounded human, even though it was not. It even managed to get a weariness into its voice that Zagrando thought specific to humans.

The Emzada moved its bulk so that its small eyes focused on Zagrando. The movement sent a storm of cells into the air, clouding it. Zagrando felt some of the skin cells land on his cheeks and forehead. The cells felt like drops of jelly that wouldn't come off.

"Yes, human," the Emzada said to Zagrando, speaking slowly as if he were stupid. "We are speaking of clones. Human clones. Fast-grow or slow-grow, bred for certain behaviors or bred to blend into a population over time. I have DNA from multiple historical personages, from murderers and thieves—*successful* murderers and thieves— who can be turned to something greater than their biology allows. My people can train them to become whatever you want or you can have them from conception forward to do with them what you need. The cost varies as to the type of job you want, the amount of care you need, and the kind of package you chose. Are we clear now?"

Zagrando swallowed a third time. His skin smelled like the Emzada's—or maybe those cells had gotten inside his nose. But, he realized, that wasn't the only thing making his stomach turn.

He kept seeing his own image overlaid on the Emzada. Not his actual image, but an imperfect one—or perhaps a more perfect one. His cloned image. Younger. Trimmer. Fighting for his life, even though he didn't understand why or what he could do to save himself.

Zagrando hoped the illness that he felt didn't show on his face.

"Please tell our gracious host that we are clear," Zagrando said.

But Whiteley didn't say anything to the Emzada. Instead he spoke to Zagrando. "Does that mean you want to keep going?"

No. Of course not. What kind of person trafficked in this?

"Yes," Zagrando said. "I have money, and I'm ready to make a deal."

8

FLINT WAS BEGINNING TO THINK TALIA GOT IN TROUBLE JUST TO annoy him. She wanted out of school. She believed she should be helping him research the Anniversary Day cases. She was helping him with that, after she was done with her homework and with her school day. He didn't want her deeply in the middle of everything. He wanted her safe, and he knew Aristotle Academy was safe.

But Talia had different ideas. So when he got notice through his links that she had, yet again, gotten into trouble, he had to brace himself for the worst. Everyone might want her to take time away from school—everyone except him.

He drove into the protected parking garage underneath the Armstrong Wing of the Aristotle Academy. The Academy was the best school on the Moon, and part of the best school system in the sector. Over two hundred Aristotle Academies existed and the Armstrong Wing consistently took first place in the rankings of both the academics and in the security itself.

The security was even tighter now. He didn't know if it was better— he always worried about the addition of human security guards—but it was certainly more prevalent. Flint used to have to go through six layers of security just to get into the parking structure. Now he went through ten, and two of those had a human component.

He parked his aircar in its usual spot, got out, and headed toward the main door. The parking garage was full of expensive vehicles—probably other parents arriving to take care of their recalcitrant children. Apparently there had been an actual fight in the lunch room, something Flint didn't think possible, given all the protections this place had.

Of course, there had been fights in lunch rooms and on school grounds when he was a kid too, especially when everyone hit Talia's age group. Teenage hormones were teenage hormones. Kids acted impulsively, based on their chemistry as much as their brains.

In fact, there was still some argument about whether kids should have links installed before the age of twenty-one, or even thirty. The male brain didn't finish its development until sometime in young adulthood, which these kids were far from.

"Mr. Flint."

The sound of his name made Flint stop. His heart rate went up. He hadn't seen anyone in the parking structure, which was unusual for him. If someone was here, he should have seen him. Flint always took in his entire environment.

Except that he was focused on Talia. This was the reason he had decided to retire from his Retrieval Artist business. When he worried about Talia, he couldn't think about anything else.

A man approached Flint from one of the cars. The car itself was high-end and worth fifteen times Flint's rather utilitarian vehicle. The car also had a parking space, which meant that it belonged here.

The man wore a long black coat that flapped open as he walked. His hair was dark, his features square. He was taller than Flint, with broader shoulders, and the kind of walk that only older athletes had.

It took a moment for Flint to place the face.

Luc Deshin.

"Mr. Deshin," Flint said, keeping his voice neutral. He had crossed paths with Deshin nine months before in a case involving both Aristotle Academy and Deshin's son, Paavo.

Flint had mixed feelings about Deshin. Deshin was one of Armstrong's most notorious criminals. Although he'd never been charged with anything, everyone knew that Deshin ran Armstrong's largest crime syndicate.

He also adored his young, difficult son, and would do anything to protect him. Flint respected Deshin for that. That respect made Flint feel uncomfortable, given everything else he knew about Deshin.

Deshin reached his side. As far as Flint could tell, Deshin was alone. But Flint never trusted appearances.

"I need to talk with you," Deshin said.

"I need to go to my daughter," Flint said. "The discussion can wait."

Deshin put a light hand on Flint's arm. "Your daughter got caught in a melee in the lunch room. She defended two kids who were being bullied. She's tough, that daughter of yours."

Flint didn't like the fact that Deshin knew about Talia. He also didn't like the fact that Deshin knew more about the lunch room incident than Flint did.

Flint looked down at Deshin's hand. Deshin removed it.

"What's this about, Mr. Deshin?" Flint asked, keeping his voice neutral. He wanted to end this little discussion as quickly as possible.

"I owe you a favor," Deshin said.

Flint sighed. After the events with his son, Deshin had tracked Flint down and promised him a favor for the work Flint had done on Paavo's behalf. Flint had argued that he was well paid by his clients, but Deshin had none of it.

He promised the favor—"as big a favor as you need," he had said—and then clapped Flint on the shoulder like they were old friends.

Maybe in Deshin's world, they were.

"We've had this discussion, Mr. Deshin," Flint said. "I was just doing my job."

"You weren't and we both know it," Deshin said. "You defended me."

Flint started to speak, but Deshin waved his hand as he continued.

"Which is neither here nor there. This is not the favor. But I know you'll at least listen to me, and no one else will."

Flint stiffened. "What are we discussing, Mr. Deshin?"

"The lunch room incident, it's something you have to take care of. Family, right?" Deshin seemed uncomfortable. That alone caught Flint's attention.

"Yes," Flint said, "and my daughter's waiting for me."

"My son's waiting for me, even though his class isn't involved. All the parents are being called in. It's because of what happened six months ago."

Everyone knew what happened six months ago. "Anniversary Day," Flint said.

"Anniversary Day," Deshin said in agreement. "That awful day."

"I'm sure the school will tell me—"

"You work with the authorities, right? You're trying to find out what happened?" Deshin spoke fast, as if he were trying to get it out.

That had Flint's attention. "Yes. I'm helping with the investigation."

"I got information that can help, and I got people all over the Alliance and beyond who can find us even more information, but I don't got contacts in the government here or with the investigation, and I don't got time—we don't got time—to go through lawyers and channels. You understand?"

Flint did. Suddenly this odd meeting made sense. "What do you have, Mr. Deshin?"

"You got people trying to find out where all the bomb components came from. That I know, not just the final suppliers, but where a lot of this stuff originated."

Deshin probably knew it because he used the same suppliers. Flint must have looked hesitant, because Deshin said,

"Look, I lost people too in those bombings. Good people. Family, friends. What happened, this is all wrong. You don't indiscriminately kill people for some political end."

"Is that what you think this is?" Flint asked. "A political end?"

"That's what the news is saying," Deshin said. "Because of the Frémont connection. Is that wrong?"

Flint shrugged. "We don't know. We don't know why this happened or who did it or what they wanted."

Deshin's entire expression changed just for a moment, and Flint finally saw the steely man beneath the somewhat charming exterior, the man that most of his colleagues probably knew and feared.

"I was hoping you were farther along than this," he said. Then he took a deep breath. "I got a lot of contacts in places your people probably never heard of. I can get information you can't. I just want to make sure it gets used, you know."

"I'm sure the authorities will want this information to be obtained in legal ways," Flint said.

Deshin laughed. "Yeah, I'm sure they say that. But they wouldn't have hired you if that was true, now would they?"

Flint couldn't help himself. He smiled.

"Listen," Deshin said. "Just be upfront with me, okay? I like plain speakers. I know you can't always do that, but do it with me. You're worried that we're going to give you torture information, aren't you?"

"Or worse," Flint said, "that you might kill for the information."

"It's friends and family we're talking about," Deshin said.

"It's six months in the past," Flint said.

"I think something bigger's coming," Deshin said.

They stared at each other.

"Honest, plain speaking," Deshin said after a moment. "You think so too, don't you?"

Flint wasn't sure he wanted to be honest with this man, that he wanted to be on "plain-speaking" terms with him. But he also didn't think he had a choice. What Deshin offered him was too good to pass up.

"There's a theory," Flint said slowly, "that the first bombing more than four years ago now was a practice run. It correlates that these bombings and assassinations might also be a practice run."

Deshin shook his head. "You don't practice on a different target."

"Meaning what?" Flint asked.

"Your theory might be right about the first bombing. Or maybe a little off. That first bombing might've been inspiration, you know? It might've given someone an idea."

Flint nodded. He'd thought of that too.

"But this second event, it's too big to be practice. It's more like notice. For that something big."

"We're thinking they might be trying to take down the Earth Alliance," Flint said.

"That'd be hard," Deshin said. "It's got too many tentacles in too many places. But they might be trying to shake it up or change it."

His answer was quick and a bit unnerving. He had clearly given this a lot of thought.

"Or they could be going after something else," Deshin said. "Some organization or corporation or something. Don't get locked into thinking the Alliance is the beginning and end of the universe."

Good advice. Flint hadn't really thought of that at all. Deshin was already proving useful. Flint still wasn't sure if he liked that, but he couldn't ignore it.

"Listen, this isn't the best place to talk," Deshin said. "Besides, we got kids to fetch. How about we meet in neutral ground?"

Flint smiled. "What's that?"

He wasn't sure what his neighbors would say if Deshin came to his office. And he certainly wasn't going to Deshin's office.

"We got a lawyer in common," Deshin said. "Celestine Gonzalez. She said she did some work for you a while back."

She had. Gonzalez had also handled Deshin's adoption of his son. Flint had seen her in court that day. So she had been the one to tell Deshin who Flint was.

"Yes, she did," Flint said. "She was good."

"She saved my butt, with some help from you and the folks here," Deshin said. "I'm sure she'll give us a private room, no questions asked."

This was the moment when Flint could turn away from the offer. He could thank Deshin and walk away.

But then he would always wonder what Deshin could provide besides a fresh perspective.

"All right," Flint said. "Tell me when and I'll be there. You also need to give me a way to contact you."

"Tonight, seven," Deshin said. "And I'm sending you my private business link now. You can reach me at any point. You got something more private than the public nets?"

"I do," Flint said, and sent it back just as he received Deshin's information. No turning back now.

They headed toward the door. As they reached it, Deshin touched his arm again.

"If I were you," he said softly, "I'd be looking to see where else people have been practicing."

And then he let himself into the school. He was halfway down the corridor when Flint stepped inside.

So obvious and he had missed it. Of course. If they had a practice bombing here in Armstrong for their Moon attacks, then they might be running a practice bombing—or attack—somewhere else.

But the universe was a very big place. He had no idea how he would even find another practice attack or if he would recognize it if he saw it.

Still, something to think about.

And then he set it aside, as he headed to the Office of the Headmistress to collect his daughter yet again.

9

THE OFFICE OF THE HEADMISTRESS WASN'T BIG ENOUGH TO HOLD everyone. Students sat on the floor outside the office, some with legs splayed, others with their heads leaning back, eyes closed.

Talia had pulled her knees up to her chin. She watched everyone else, her breath shallow. She felt exposed now, as if they had discovered her secret, when in reality no one had.

The Chinar twins sat beside her, looking as frightened as she felt. They were good kids, those twins. They felt like this entire mess was their fault, when in reality, they were the ones being bullied.

Talia wanted to explain that to them, but the security guards enforced the no-talking rules.

Since Anniversary Day, the security guards at the school had changed. In the past, the school had a mixture of human guards, androids, and an amazing security system that Talia's dad had upgraded after a little kid got stalked.

But Anniversary Day changed everyone's attitudes toward everything (otherwise, she wouldn't be sitting here) and especially toward security. The android guards worked only at night now, and then as a backup to the human guards. The human guards changed too, from the friendly folks who greeted the kids every morning with a smile to these military-type goons who stood with their backs to the wall, arms crossed, and faces turned outward.

They never responded to a hello. A few of the older kids got in trouble for harassing the guards, by standing near them and saying things like "Hello" or "Why aren't you answering me?" or "You could at least look me in the face, you know."

Talia had watched the whole thing, privately cheering them on, but in accordance with her no-calling-attention-to-herself policy, she hadn't joined in.

Not that her policy worked anymore. Not that she had followed it today.

Of course, if she had followed it, then Kaleb Lamber and his friends would have completely terrorized the twins, and they would have gotten even quieter. There was some old Earth quote that her dad liked, something about evil flourishing when good people did nothing.

She believed that.

And look where that belief had gotten her. On this cold floor with stupid security guards standing beside her, arms crossed, ready to enforce some stupid silence rule so that the kids wouldn't run amok again.

What she hated the most was that she'd had to contact her dad. She had kept the links on audio only when she reached him so she wouldn't see his face. She knew he would have this expression of disbelief, disappointment, and sadness. She'd seen it too much before, like he always expected better of her and she always failed him.

Maybe if he expected less, he'd think she was a better person.

She sighed, and leaned her head back, resisting the temptation to bang her skull against the wall just to make some noise. She felt trapped, both here on this floor and at this stupid school. She should be working with her dad, not dealing with some kid who couldn't keep his bigoted mouth shut.

She looked over at him. Kaleb Lamber sat cross-legged, hands upward on his knees, in one of those "relaxation" positions. His cheeks were red, either from exertion or emotion, and one of his gorgeous eyes had swollen closed.

The headmistress, Ms. Rutledge, wouldn't let the kids fix their bruises. (No one had been hurt worse than that.) She wanted the parents to see the results of the melee, as she called it.

She'd been furious. She was a short woman, at least by Talia's standards, but she had a big personality. She was one of the toughest women that Talia knew, and Talia knew her dad's friend Noelle DeRicci, who was super tough.

Still, Ms. Rutledge scared Talia. Ms. Rutledge had gotten really angry, not just at the fight, but also at what the fight was about.

"We didn't bring you here to train you to bully," she had said. "You don't pick on people for what they look like or who they are. We are going to have a school assembly about this and it looks like we're going to have to change some policies, yet again. For right now, though, I'm going to send you all home. I can't stand to look at you. I'm ashamed that you're all a part of Aristotle Academy."

That had gotten to Talia. How come she didn't get credit for standing up to a bully? How come the Chinar twins had to go home? They were the ones bullied.

But she hadn't asked any of that, even though one of the kids next to her had nudged her, like he expected her to say something. Or maybe he was just adding a "yeah, right," to Ms. Rutledge's comments with his elbow.

Kaleb saw Talia looking at him. He sneered, but it was clear that his heart wasn't in it. If anything, he seemed a little scared.

You're an idiot, she sent through her links on the in-school network. She didn't know his private link. The school was probably monitoring all of this, but she didn't care. She was mad, and she had to take it out on someone before her dad got here.

Besides, what could they do to her? Send her home? They were already doing that.

You're a self-righteous prig, Kaleb sent back. *If you had minded your own business, everything would be okay.*

Yeah, for you maybe. What's wrong with you? Why do you like picking on people?

His eyes narrowed. *I think certain things—*

And then the communication cut off. A bunch of kids looked startled, so she and Kaleb weren't the only ones who had been using their links.

His cheeks got darker. *Later,* he mouthed.

Screw you, she mouthed back.

You wish. At least, that was what it looked like he said. She couldn't tell for sure. She leaned her head back and closed her eyes.

Her dad was taking forever to get here. He usually could almost teleport when he thought she was in danger. But she wasn't in danger, and they both knew it. Except maybe from the school. Her dad would think it an issue if they didn't want her here anymore. For some stupid reason, he thought school was important.

She sighed. She could learn all this stuff on her own and more, and she wouldn't have to deal with idiots like Kaleb. She would be able to look up stuff and learn stuff and work with her dad on important things.

Then she bowed her head. That's what was taking him so long. He was working on all the Anniversary Day stuff at the Security Building, and something truly important happened. He wouldn't be happy that she had pulled him from his work.

"Talia?"

She opened her eyes. There he was, standing over her, looking— perplexed? Why would he look perplexed? Didn't anyone tell him what happened?

He held out his hand, and she took it, letting him pull her up. Everyone else watched. She hated it when they stared. She knew that her dad looked different—there weren't a lot of blonds with pale skin and blue eyes—and people sometimes commented on that. Usually the sideways comments were mean, too, like her dad's family had done something weird to preserve its recessive gene pool.

She had the same hair (slightly darker) and the blue eyes, but her skin was copper like her mom's, which made her not nearly as exotic as her dad. Except when they stood somewhere side by side, like right now.

"Ms. Rutledge is going to see us now," he said, and he wasn't yelling at her. Not that he would yell at her in front of anyone anyway, but still. He didn't look like he wanted to yell at her either.

Talia held onto his hand—she knew that was baby stuff, but she didn't care; she never got to be a baby with him—and they walked into the Office of the Headmistress.

The front part of the office was big. Plants and desks and furniture arrangements subdivided it into sections. Ms. Rutledge didn't have secretaries or anything—the desks were smart desks that did a lot of the work without being told, plus they recorded nearby conversations, no matter how soft.

A lot of kids had convicted themselves of whatever they'd been accused of by talking to another kid in what they thought was an empty room.

Ms. Rutledge had another office off to the side that was her personal sanctuary. Talia had never been in there. No one had, so far as she knew.

Ms. Rutledge stood in the doorway of it now. She looked tired, which surprised Talia, since Ms. Rutledge was always this tower of strength. Her dark hair was pulled back without any loose strands like it had earlier, so she had redone her appearance. She wasn't even wearing her trademark cape (which Talia thought was kinda creepy—the cape, not the fact that she wasn't wearing it). She had on a white blouse with the school's logo on the left, and a dark skirt that went to her knees.

"We'll meet in here," she said, and stepped away from the door.

Talia looked at her dad in surprise. He had done some work for the school, so maybe he had gone back there before.

He wound around the desks, still holding Talia's hand, and she followed, her heart pounding. She had no idea why she was nervous, except that this was all weird, and she didn't like weird.

Talia's dad put his hand on her back and propelled her into Ms. Rutledge's office first. She wished he hadn't. She always felt awkward in a strange place. She never knew where to sit or what to do or how to behave.

The office smelled like vanilla. Talia had read that vanilla was a soothing smell, but at the moment, it wasn't soothing her at all. Some real plants sat on the windowsill, their vines and leaves trailing all the way to the floor. Three chairs formed a semi-circle in front of the desk, and behind it, a huge couch took up the entire back wall.

The couch looked used, like Ms. Rutledge slept on it or something. There was even a blanket folded neatly across the top, and a gigantic pillow pushed to one side.

Ms. Rutledge sat in the huge chair behind her desk. She kept her hands clasped on the chair's arms as if it held her up.

"Miles," she said to Talia's dad. "I don't know if you know what happened today—"

"I only know what you sent to us," Talia's dad said.

Talia's stomach clenched. What had Ms. Rutledge sent?

"Let me show you," Ms. Rutledge said.

A holographic security image rose on her desk. A fight had already started near the table where Kaleb Lamber stood. Students ran toward that fight, as if they were being encouraged to do so.

The image had no sound, but it didn't need any. Talia winced as she watched friends get punched, people fall, and one kid pick up a chair to hit someone else. Fortunately, one of the lunch room workers grabbed the chair just in time.

"I don't see Talia," her dad said.

"I'm afraid Talia started this," Ms. Rutledge said. "She—"

"I did not," Talia said. She hated being falsely accused. "Kaleb Lamber started it. He was calling the Chinar twins names, and I couldn't take it anymore. Kaleb is one mean kid and he hurts people and you don't do anything about it."

Talia's dad put a hand on her arm. It was his shut-up-and-let-me-handle-this gesture.

Ms. Rutledge sighed. "I haven't interviewed everyone, but Talia is correct. She was defending the Chinar twins."

"Thank you," Talia said with sarcastic emphasis. Her dad's grip tightened on her arm. She didn't care. If Ms. Rutledge wanted to expel her, then Ms. Rutledge could expel her. She could do important stuff then.

"Nonetheless," Ms. Rutledge said to Talia's dad as if Talia hadn't spoken, "her actions caught the attention of the entire lunch room, and the entire fight escalated from there."

"Talia's not fighting anyone," her dad said. "I don't even see her here."

"I got the Chinar twins out," Talia said. "Kinda. Security grabbed us."

Her dad's grip tightened again. Then she realized that he had been defending her. Maybe she should shut up, after all.

"Talia's actions in the lunch room are not the reason I brought you in here," Ms. Rutledge said. "What happened today pointed out to me a problem in the school that I really hadn't acknowledged until now."

Talia sat very still. So did her dad. He loosened his grip slightly. Her arm was sore; he might have bruised her. He never did that. He had to be really tense, which was weird all by itself. Her dad never got tense like that.

"The problem is cloning," Ms. Rutledge said.

Talia froze. Her dad's hand didn't move and neither did his expression. She wondered if hers had.

"Not cloning itself per se," Ms. Rutledge added, "but the prejudice toward clones."

Talia felt her cheeks heat. Damn, she was blushing. She didn't want to be blushing. It felt like a confession.

She hoped Ms. Rutledge wouldn't see it that way. She hoped Ms. Rutledge would think it a reaction to the fight in the cafeteria, not to the facts of Talia's birth.

"The prejudice has become rampant," Ms. Rutledge said. She seemed to be talking to Talia's dad, not Talia. Ms. Rutledge hadn't met her eyes once. "I'm concerned. If the children are reacting this forcefully and violently to the presence of clones in their world, then what are the parents saying?"

"I'm afraid I'm not following," Talia's dad said. "The presence of clones?"

"Ever since Anniversary Day, clones have been in the news. People overreact. If one group of clones attacked the Moon, then all clones are going to be evil." Ms. Rutledge frowned. "I thought you understood how people can be, Miles."

"I've been in my own bubble," he said, but there was something off in his tone. Talia didn't want to look at him—she didn't want to distract him. It sounded like he had poked Ms. Rutledge to see what her beliefs were.

"I understand that you're working with the Security Office. This is something they should be aware of as well. Today's events frightened me," Ms. Rutledge said.

"In what way?" he asked in that strange tone.

"If the students realize they have an actual clone in their midst, I don't know what they'll do." Ms. Rutledge looked directly at Talia.

Talia held her breath. She was trembling. Her dad's hand rested on her arm, but he didn't grip anymore.

"Why are you telling us this?" Talia's dad said. "It sounds like my daughter tried to prevent the bigotry, not add to it."

Ms. Rutledge's glance went from Talia to her father.

"Miles," she said softly. "I have looked at student entrance papers for decades. Talia's are irregular, and you never did present her birth certificate. Does she have one? Or does she have a day of creation certificate?"

Talia swallowed. She couldn't help it. How did Ms. Rutledge know?

"We've had this discussion," Talia's dad said. "My daughter's documents come from Valhalla Basin. Her mother died in rather horrible circumstances, and my daughter was not allowed to return to her home. We're missing many important documents from Talia's life. You waved some of the restrictions when you approved her application. Have you changed your mind now?"

Talia didn't move. Her dad was really good. He hadn't answered the question at all, but turned it on Ms. Rutledge.

"All I'm saying, Miles," Ms. Rutledge said slowly, "is that you and Talia need to be very careful. I've never seen children erupt like this. I've learned in my decades here that children learn their prejudices and their fears from their parents. So if children are on such tenterhooks, then the parents must be even more volatile. I will do my best to quash this. Children Talia's age make their own decisions once they have the right information, and I will do my best to make sure the children here at Aristotle Academy have the right information."

Talia swallowed again. She couldn't control that reaction. She was terrified, and she was sure Ms. Rutledge could see it.

Just like she was sure Ms. Rutledge could see Talia's clone mark.

Talia really had to hold still to make certain she didn't touch that mark.

"I will do my best to make certain everyone in Aristotle Academy is safe," Ms. Rutledge said, looking briefly at Talia.

Talia's cheeks heated again.

"But," Ms. Rutledge said, "I can't control Armstrong or the reactions here on the Moon. And what these children have taught me today is that right now, the Moon itself is a very dangerous place for clones. And for anyone else who might be mistaken for a clone."

"Like twins," Talia's dad said.

Ms. Rutledge looked a little sad. Then she nodded.

"Like twins," she said.

"Is that all?" Talia's dad asked.

"For now. Take Talia home. Take care of her." Ms. Rutledge turned to Talia. "You have good instincts, my girl. But sometimes yelling at someone will not make a difference."

"He was saying crap," Talia said. "I couldn't let him do that."

Ms. Rutledge smiled at her. "I know."

Ms. Rutledge was being kind to her. Talia hadn't expected that. Talia's dad stood. He took Talia's hand again, and pulled her toward the door. When he reached it, he stopped and looked back at Ms. Rutledge.

"Thanks, Selah," he said.

Then he put his hand on Talia's back and propelled her outside the room. He didn't say another word, and neither did Talia.

She wanted to cry, but she wasn't going to.

She wasn't going to let any of this get to her.

She didn't dare.

10

THEY ESCAPED THE ROOM LIKE REFUGEES FROM A WAR. ZAGRANDO wanted to take a deep breath as he closed the door behind himself, but he knew better. The Emzada's skin cells followed him, rising off him as if in that hour, he had become Emzada himself.

Whiteley had started up the stairs, leaving a gray cloud behind. Whiteley was covered in gray. He looked like he had been dipped in some grayish gel and told not to remove it.

Zagrando knew he looked no better.

He wanted to ask if there was a place to shower nearby, but he didn't. He didn't know what kind of security the Emzada had.

Still, they had managed to make an exchange. Zagrando had paid half of the upfront fee for delivery of the clones. He and the Emzada, using Whiteley as an intermediary, had set up a meeting place to work with the clone provider.

Zagrando was supposed to bring his client. He might need assistance with that, because he suspected he was going to meet with another intermediary. He wasn't quite sure how to go about this.

He would have to talk with Whiteley.

They climbed the stairs, both men breathing shallowly on purpose.

When they were halfway up, Zagrando said through his teeth, "You could have warned me."

"I wasn't sure you'd go into an Emzada Lair," Whiteley said. He didn't try to keep the conversation quiet.

Either that meant they had moved past the surveillance or Whiteley didn't care if the Emzada knew about this conversation.

If Zagrando had known about the Lair, he would have dressed for it. He might even have worn a nearly invisible environmental suit to prevent this kind of contamination.

"You should have asked," Zagrando said.

"And spoil the fun?" Whiteley asked.

"How come you didn't wear some kind of protection?" Zagrando asked.

"It insults them," Whiteley said, looking up this time. So the surveillance continued. Whiteley simply hadn't cared until now.

Whiteley was very familiar with this place and he didn't seem bothered by the skin-cell sloughing. Which meant he had experienced it enough to have developed an internal coping mechanism.

"You got a finder's fee for this meeting, didn't you?" Zagrando asked.

"You didn't expect that?" Whiteley increased his pace on the stairs. He clearly didn't like having this part of the conversation here.

"I expected you to get a finder's fee when we met with the dealers, not their broker."

Whiteley shrugged. "I make my money in a variety of ways."

Meaning he was going to get even more fees as this transaction went on.

If this transaction went on.

"So you're going to cart me to the meeting with the brokers?" Zagrando asked.

"Someone has to," Whiteley said.

"I know where it is, and in theory, I'm bringing my client. I'd prefer it if you don't accompany us."

Jealousy among arms broker wasn't just a formality, it was a survival skill. If Zagrando had been a true arms broker, he would worry that Whiteley would poach his clients. So Zagrando needed to act as if he did worry about it.

"Yeah, I figured you wouldn't want me along." Whiteley reached a landing and stopped. He looked down at Zagrando. "But, in the spirit of honesty, I know where the meeting is, so I'm going to be there whether you want me or not."

And maybe with a few of his friends.

Zagrando's stomach, which had settled slightly, rolled again. A real arms broker would kill Whiteley for making that statement. And Whiteley probably knew it.

Was this some kind of test? If so, it was a stupid one, because it would cost Whiteley his life.

Unless he knew that the Emzada would protect him.

Whiteley had already made it clear that the Emzada was watching some kind of security feed.

Zagrando reached the top of the stairs, then clapped a hand on Whiteley's shoulder, wincing at the gooey feel of his shirt. Whiteley was gambling that Zagrando would do nothing, afraid of screwing up the meet. But Zagrando had to do something, or the Emzada would not take him seriously.

He wondered if Whiteley had thought of that.

"In the spirit of honesty," Zagrando said loud enough that his voice would appear on any security feed, "I should kill you for that."

Whiteley grinned at him, apparently satisfied that Zagrando understood. "You should," Whiteley said. "But you won't."

"You really do trust me," Zagrando said with just a touch of surprise.

"Naw," Whiteley said. "I've watched you. Killing's something you let someone else do."

With one quick move, Zagrando slid his hand down the side of the pack that Whiteley carried, and pulled out the laser pistol that Whiteley always had in the outside pocket.

He shot Whiteley in the right leg. Whiteley screamed, so Zagrando shot him in the left leg for good measure.

Then he wrenched the pack off Whiteley's back.

Zagrando made himself smile.

"Nice to know you're right, isn't it?" he asked Whiteley, who was rolling and grabbing his legs in extreme pain. "I always let someone else do the killing. Unless, of course, there is no one else. And even then, I prefer the maiming method to the death method. I use it as a warning. People should know better than to screw with me."

Zagrando ran up a few steps, then turned.

"I hope for your sake that the Emzada doesn't mind you fouling his Lair or attempting to screw up such a lucrative deal. I also hope he doesn't realize that he can get his finder's fee back if he just lets you die."

"Hey!" Whiteley moaned. "Hey. You—me—we're friends."

"What man can know what's in another man's heart?" Zagrando said and continued up the stairs.

As he rounded the next corner, he heard Whiteley shout, "You'll never get the ship started. It's coded to me."

"I disabled that part of your ship when I dropped off my supplies," Zagrando said. He had always made it a policy to travel only on ships that he could pilot in an emergency. And if the ship's owner wasn't willing to make that easy for him, he always did it for himself.

Then he hurried the rest of the way up the stairs, not sure if he would run into some resistance. Whiteley yelled behind him, voice growing fainter as Zagrando reached the top of the stairs and the outer doors.

He pushed them open and stepped into what passed for daylight in Abbondiado. It felt like he had been below ground for days.

That hum had returned, but it didn't unsettle him. His adrenaline was pumping; nothing could unsettle him at the moment.

He adjusted the pack on his back, hoped that no one noticed or cared about the thin film of gray goo coating him, and made his way—as cautiously as he could—back to Whiteley's ship.

And onto the next stage of this rather horrible journey.

11

MILES FLINT ARRIVED AT THE LAW OFFICES OF OBERHOLTZ, MARTINEZ & Mlsnavek a few minutes late. If pressed, he wouldn't have been able to say that he arrived late accidentally or by design. He had had second thoughts about this meeting with Luc Deshin all afternoon, but he hadn't canceled it.

Flint simply wished he could avoid it. But he felt that way about almost everything to do with his post-Anniversary Day work.

He had left Talia at the Security Building mostly because he didn't want her to get into trouble. He knew she would research the bombings; she had been working hard on various theories. He wanted her to do it from a safe computer system.

No matter how many times he explained to her that even the simplest search from an open network put her (and others) in danger, she didn't quite understand it. She felt if she looked up something that seemed unrelated, no one would flag the search.

She had gotten into trouble a year or so ago doing the same thing, so now, rather than take the lesson that she had to avoid open networks, she simply believed she could do only obscure searches from a public place. He had mentioned that to DeRicci once, and she had laughed at him.

You have a teenage daughter, Miles. She'll be smart one minute and stupid the next. Deal with it.

He had thought DeRicci a bit cynical until he talked with parents of teenagers, particularly girls. He used to think that he understood teenagers—after all, he had been one once—but now he believed that either he had been the best-behaved teenager ever or he misremembered almost everything about that period of time. His parents were no longer around to ask, even though he had a hunch what their answer would be.

At least Popova was at the Security Office to watch Talia, and if something went wrong, an entire security force could guard her.

He couldn't ask for anything else.

He certainly couldn't bring her here.

Oberholtz, Martinez & Mlsnavek was one of the richest law firms on the Moon, with branches all over the Earth Alliance. Oberholtz, Martinez & Mlsnavek was not the most prestigious firm: it handled too many known criminals for that. But the firm was known for winning the bulk of its cases.

It was not only one of the wealthier firms in the Alliance, but it was also one of the most powerful.

Flint preferred working with Maxine Van Alen, but he had ended up with Celestine Gonzalez of Oberholtz, Martinez & Mlsnavek during Talia's adoption proceedings. Talia's mother—Flint's ex-wife Rhonda—had hired Oberholtz, Martinez & Mlsnavek to handle her criminal case, and had instructed Talia to contact them should anything bad happen.

Then Rhonda got kidnapped and Talia had followed her mother's instructions. By the time Flint came on the scene, Gonzalez already had the case well in hand.

Flint liked her. She was honest and smart, just not quite as crafty as Van Alen was. Gonzalez had done good work for her firm in the past few years. She was now a partner, with a bigger office and a lot more clout.

Still, she had made time for this meeting. But Flint wasn't certain if she had done so because of Flint or because of Luc Deshin.

Gonzalez had a corner office on the fifteenth floor of the Ober-holtz, Martinez & Mlsnavek Building. She had spent a small fortune decorating the room with imported silk rugs and matching silk drapes, clearly not made on the Moon. The desk, though, was old and scuffed, and made of faux wood like so much Moon-based furniture.

Flint suspected the desk had sentimental value. He had never seen Gonzalez behind it. She liked to conduct her work from an overstuffed chair positioned with its back to the corner where the windows met. She used a handheld pad to record the meeting and to make her notes.

Although on this day, she wasn't doing that. Instead, she was stand-ing in the center of the room with Deshin himself. She wore silver plat-form shoes that made her almost as tall as Deshin. The shoes matched her silver-and-black suit, but even it couldn't hide the fact that she had put on weight in the intervening years. She now looked matronly instead of young and eager.

Flint liked the new look, not because of her size, but because of what it suggested. It suggested that she cared more about the work than she did about looking like some kind of feminine ideal. Besides, looking like a strong woman gave her a lot more power in the court-room than any kind of youthful beauty would.

"Sorry I'm late," Flint said as he came in. He started to shut the door, but Gonzalez waved him off.

"Actually," she said, "I'm giving you the office for an hour or two. I'm late for dinner. I want you both to know that all recording devices are off and that you don't need to worry about me or the firm knowing what you have discussed. I'm assuming you will leave shortly after I do. If you end up talking, then that's your issue, but there's no one else on this floor. So you needn't worry that anyone will see you both together."

Her words made Flint's breath catch. She had given this some thought. Plus, it seemed like she was used to doing these things.

For Deshin? Or for other clients?

Deshin didn't seem as uncomfortable as Flint was. Deshin prob-ably did things like this all the time.

"Thank you, Celestine," Deshin said, then put his hands on her shoulder and bussed her cheek. "I appreciate the fact you set this up on such short notice."

"The dinner date precedes the meeting. You just picked a good time," she said. Then she wiggled two fingers at Flint, grinned at him as she passed, then went out the door, pulling it closed behind her.

"You're going out of your way not to be seen with me," Flint said as he moved away from the door.

Deshin nodded. "Believe me, that benefits you more than it benefits me."

Flint actually didn't think it mattered. He had no real reputation that could be harmed, not the kind Deshin was thinking of. Either Deshin didn't understand that, or he tended toward the grandiose.

But his comments did signal that the meeting had started in earnest.

"Before you tell me anything," Flint said, "remember that I used to be a police officer and I'm working with the Security Office."

Deshin smiled. "You're a Retrieval Artist now, Mr. Flint. We both walk on the wrong side of the law when it's convenient."

Flint didn't like that characterization. Yes, Retrieval Artists sometimes worked outside the law, but he didn't avoid the law when it was convenient. He had enforced the law when he worked for both Space Traffic Control and for the Armstrong Police Department. There he had learned that he didn't like turning children over to other species to satisfy some law that made no sense in human terms.

That wasn't convenient. That was damned inconvenient, at least in Flint's opinion.

"You disagree with me," Deshin said.

Flint realized he had been quiet too long.

"We're not going to get into a philosophical argument about how we characterize our work," Flint said.

"Believe me," Deshin said, "I consider myself a businessman, and as such, I don't view business as philosophy. The difference between me and the corporations you used to have to defend when you worked for the Armstrong Police Department is that I run a small organization. Instead of tens of thousands of lawyers and a shell company Disappearance service, I have a handful of lawyers and I try to avoid working with other species whenever possible."

Deshin was trying to justify himself to Flint? That made Flint more uncomfortable than the characterization of his work as a Retrieval Artist.

"I am a former police officer for a reason," Flint said. "I don't like how the corporations or the Earth Alliance do their business."

"Neither do I," said Deshin. "But that's not important. Like you said, we don't need to have a philosophical argument. Instead, I'd like to help you."

Flint still had trouble with that. He believed there was a catch.

"You want to help me," Flint repeated. "Out of the goodness of your heart?"

"I told you," Deshin said. "I lost friends and family on Anniversary Day."

"The fact that you lost people on Anniversary Day," Flint said, knowing he had to be ruthless to get his answers, "that makes you think I'll believe you're a good guy now?"

Deshin tilted his head slightly. His eyes had grown cold. Flint finally saw the man who controlled the largest criminal empire in the city.

"Of course not," Deshin said. "You're not naïve, Mr. Flint. These attacks happened in *my* city, on *my* turf, to *my* people."

"I didn't think you cared about the mayor," Flint said, knowing he was probably pushing Deshin too hard. "Or did someone else close to you die in Armstrong that day?"

Armstrong had had very few casualties, and only two had made the news: Mayor Arek Soseki and his assassin.

Deshin opened his mouth, then closed it. His eyes grew even colder.

"Fair enough," he said. "You want honesty? Here's honesty. It disturbs me that this investigation had gone on for six months with no obvious leads. It bothers me that no one knows what, exactly, happened

94

that day. It really upsets me that we don't know why, because if we don't know why, then the attack could happen again, and this time, we might lose the entire Moon."

If Deshin thought he was going to insult Flint, he was wrong.

"I worry about the same things," Flint said.

Deshin nodded. "Then I will tell you what you need to know to stop this. I will tell you about things I know, things legal and illegal. You will probably assume I know these things because you people believe that I run a criminal organization—"

"You people?" Flint asked.

"You still have a police attitude, Mr. Flint. You're working for the security office at the moment. You may break the law when it suits you, but you tell yourself that you do it because you're following some higher morality. You're not following a higher morality. You just assume that the human way is the best way. Frankly, Mr. Flint, that's bigotry."

Flint's breath caught. He'd heard the argument before. It was an argument against Disappearance Services, and had been around since the first human used a service to disappear. It was, oddly enough, an Earth Alliance argument.

But no one had ever said it to Flint's face before. It surprised him that the statement stung. He didn't think of himself as a bigot, merely a man who had the welfare of other human beings at stake. He never did anything that would deliberately harm another species, although he had occasionally done things that had circumvented their legal process.

Deshin shoved his hands in his pockets. The movement made his entire body seem tense.

"So," he said, "I figure you're here because you believe that I can tell you things you don't know. I figure you're here because you're stuck. Am I wrong?"

Flint knew that Deshin was trying to provoke him like he had been trying to provoke Deshin.

"Unfortunately," Flint said, "the investigation of a crime is harder than the commission of it. Sometimes it takes years to know what happened. And we're hampered by the loss of authority in various communities, by inadequate law enforcement organizations in others, and by the fact that a lot of the evidence got obliterated in the dome destructions and in the bombings. So, no, we're not stuck, but we're certainly not moving as quickly as any of us would like."

Deshin nodded, the movement of a man in charge giving up a point to an inferior. Flint had pushed him; now Flint saw the real man.

"All right," Deshin said, "I'll give you that. I have a personal and financial stake in getting the Moon back to normal. Because of that, and because you people can't seem to find your asses with a detailed map, I'll tell you things that would probably get me arrested if you were still with the Armstrong Police Department."

That second part was a warning, and Flint knew it. It was his cue to leave if he didn't want to hear the information.

"Of course," Deshin said, "you're no longer with the APD, and if you believe you can somehow take the information from this meeting to the authorities and get me arrested, you'll get a brief victory. The arrest might happen, but if we go to court, I will deny the meeting ever took place. I had a confidential meeting with my attorney. You came for a meeting with your attorney. We'd met before. We said hello. That's all."

Flint could see how that would play out. He had known that Deshin was a smart man; this was simply more evidence of it.

"All right," Flint said. "Then answer me this. If discovering what is going on is so important to you personally and financially, and you possess information that solves the crimes, why haven't you gone after the perpetrators?"

Deshin let out a small laugh, then shook his head. "Assuming that I have a criminal organization. Assuming that I would take extralegal methods to settle a score."

"Assuming that you're a patriot and you would want to ensure that these possible future attacks that you're speaking of would never happen," Flint said.

Deshin smiled. Those cold eyes had warmed. They twinkled. "You are a fascinating man, Mr. Flint."

"Not really," Flint said. "I'm a serious man. And I want an answer to that question before we go further."

"Assuming facts not in evidence," Deshin said, using a legal term, "which are that I am capable of taking out someone or something big enough to cause these attacks, why haven't I? The answer is truly simple, Mr. Flint, and you know what it is."

Flint suspected he knew. "I want to hear it from you."

"Fair enough. Like you, I have only bits of the puzzle. Only I have different bits than you do, I'm sure, and a greater knowledge of the darker world we're operating in."

Flint doubted that part, but he didn't contradict Deshin.

"What I have found leads me to the underbelly of the Earth Alliance," Deshin said, "as well as points outside of the Alliance. It leads me to places with more money than I have, more clout than I have, more weaponry than I have, and more ruthlessness than I ever imagined."

That answer took Flint's breath away. He had expected part of it, but not all of it.

"You're afraid of these people," Flint said.

"You're assuming that we're dealing with people," Deshin said.

Flint blinked. He had made that assumption from the first.

"Don't worry," Deshin said. "It's part of your ethnocentrism."

"Not bigotry?" Flint asked, with a bit of a smile.

"Call it what you want," Deshin said. "We're working together, so I was being polite."

"Now," Flint said.

"Now that you are being polite as well," Deshin said, and his own smile took the childish edge off the words.

"You know that we're not dealing with humans?" Flint asked, returning the conversation to its original direction.

"I know that some of the players aren't human," Deshin said. "Whether or not they're the instigators, I have no idea."

He sighed and walked to the window, his fingers brushing against that faux wood desk. He looked out over the city.

Flint didn't move. He had no idea if Deshin's restlessness was normal or if it was because this topic made Deshin so uncomfortable.

"We live in a fragile environment," Deshin said. "Not just because the dome is the only thing that protects us from the harshness of the Moon's surface, but because we are trying to keep hundreds of species allied in an organization that's deeply flawed and deeply necessary."

Flint had heard a similar version of this speech from DeRicci. He'd heard it from her as recently as a week ago. She lamented the fact that the Moon had allowed a haphazard group of local governments to function instead of an overall government, that the haphazardness infected the entire Earth Alliance and threatened it from within.

"It deeply disturbs me," Deshin said, "that I don't know what the motive is behind these attacks. Something this orchestrated, something that took *decades* to accomplish, has a set agenda behind it, and it doesn't matter how hard I look, I can't find that agenda."

"So you came to me," Flint said.

Deshin nodded, his back still to Flint. "I came to you. I hoped that in exchange for information I give you, you'll give me information in return."

"What kind of information?" Flint asked.

"The component parts of the various bombs used all over the Moon on that day. I know you're keeping them quiet."

Flint sighed. "That's the one thing we aren't keeping quiet. They're all different. They were all built with local materials, and often brought in by the stooges that the assassins found in each city. Somehow, these people knew what material was available, and they were able to move it to the right place, and activate it at the right time."

"Still," Deshin said. "Get me a list."

"In exchange for?" Flint asked, not promising anything.

"Two rather large things that, from what I can tell, your people don't know," Deshin said. "First, most of the zoodeh used to kill the various mayors and heads of state did not come from that quarantined ship, like you believe."

Flint didn't move, although his heart rate increased. While the media reported that zoodeh had killed the mayors, no one reported that the zoodeh had come from quarantined ships inside Armstrong's Port. DeRicci didn't want anyone else to learn that hazardous materials were stored inside ships in the Port. Even now, even though they'd learned what a danger those ships were, no one knew what to do with them or their hazardous cargo.

After the attacks, DeRicci had increased the security around the quarantined ship area of the Port, but hadn't done anything else. She figured the ships had been there for years, so they weren't the pressing problem like so many other issues raised by Anniversary Day.

She was probably right.

But Flint was unnerved that Deshin knew this, and knew that other quarantined ships existed.

Flint also didn't know how to respond to Deshin. The easiest way to confirm information you were uncertain about was to speak about it with certainty. That way, the person you were speaking to would tell you what you needed to know, while assuming you already knew it.

Flint had used that technique hundreds of times himself.

"You don't have to confirm or deny the existence of the ships," Deshin said. It was uncanny the way that this man seemed to know what Flint was thinking. "I know you want to keep the existence of the quarantine area in the Port secret. Unfortunately for you, a number of my current and former clients have ships locked away there, with a mountain of money in inventory and no hope of ever getting those ships out."

Flint tried to think of a response to that, but couldn't. Apparently, he didn't need to because Deshin turned around, his mouth a thin line.

"You're going to say they broke the law trying to smuggle that stuff into the Port," Deshin said. "I agree. That's why I've never offered support or legal representation in trying to get those ships out of quarantine. But that doesn't stop the clients from complaining. It's quite a list."

Flint moved to one of the chairs and sat down. He was tired of standing, tired of working hard to control the reaction of each muscle in his body. So far as he could tell, Deshin wasn't playing any games—or, at least, any *obvious* games.

Deshin took the chair opposite him. Neither man sat in Gonzalez's chair, which Flint found privately amusing.

"All that stuff about the quarantined ships aside," Deshin said, "has anyone in any of the police forces, the security office, or the crime scene laboratories done an analysis of the amount of zoodeh it took to pull off all of these assassinations?"

Flint felt his cheeks warm. Looking at the weapon, where it came from, and how it could be obtained was standard in any murder investigation. The thing was, it felt like they had done it here. They identified the zoodeh, saw that it was a banned substance, and figured it had come from the quarantined ships.

That led to Ursula Palmette, who then tried to blow up Armstrong's Port, using yet another quarantined ship.

No one did any deeper analysis. No one felt the need.

"You've done the analysis," Flint said.

"Yes, I have," Deshin said. "Zoodeh is very unstable, and it would have been hard to transport, especially for twenty young men, even if they were specially trained. So not only did they need the zoodeh, they needed a special case to keep the tiny needle in until the moment they could use that needle."

The heat in Flint's cheek rose. He wasn't really blushing; he was too angry at himself for that. They had missed it. They had all missed it, and it was obvious.

No wonder Deshin was feeling dissatisfied with this investigation. It had started haphazard and had grown more so rather than less so as the months went on.

"Plus," Deshin said, "even if they handled the needle right, there was no guarantee that they wouldn't scratch themselves first. So they had to have some kind of protection there too. Whether it was some kind of breakthrough on the weapon itself—some kind of protection developed that we don't know about—or whether it was some immunity built into the clones themselves, I have no idea. But nevertheless, they had some protection or they wouldn't have been able to carry the zoodeh all over the Moon, and then use it so casually."

"The immunity wasn't built into the clones," Flint said. He figured he could give Deshin that much.

Deshin looked at him, surprised. "How do you know?"

"Because the assassin in Glenn Station didn't follow the plan. He was supposed to take out as many as he could with him, like the other assassins tried to do, and instead, someone evacuated the building he was in. He died alone in a room he had run to, after using the zoodeh on himself."

Deshin took a deep breath. "I hadn't realized that. All right. That's actually an important piece of information."

"Why?" Flint asked.

"The clones mean something," Deshin said. "They weren't fast-grow. They developed over twenty or more years. Which means that they were grown special for this task."

Flint had thought that as well, but he didn't want to tell Deshin that—at least, not yet. "We have no proof of that."

"You might not," Deshin said. "But I do."

Now Flint knew why he was in this meeting. "How could you know that?"

"Because," Deshin said, "designer criminal clones are a problem that the Earth Alliance has never acknowledged."

Flint felt cold. "I have never seen anything about designer criminal clones and in all the jobs I did for the local authorities, I would have seen something."

Besides, he would have looked because of Talia. He knew a lot more about clones because of Talia. He had made it a point to learn everything about clones. Or so he thought.

Deshin let out a small chuckle. "It's amazing what the police don't see," he said, leaning back in the chair. "Designer clones, used for criminal purposes, are a big business. Generally, they get used for petty crimes or family crimes, regional crimes, things that stay beneath the Earth Alliance's notice."

Flint wanted to ask Deshin if he had used such clones, but he knew better. It would derail Deshin, and at the moment, Flint didn't want to do that.

"Let me get this straight," Flint said. "People buy specific clones for a specific crime."

"Yes," Deshin said.

"And not just fast-grow clones, but clones that can think for themselves. Clones raised for a specific purpose. Clones who are, in reality, human beings with free will." Flint tried not to let too much passion in his voice here.

Deshin's eyes narrowed. "You can breed humans just like you can breed animals. You can select for certain traits. And then you train them, like you would anyone. You train them from birth to do a certain kind of job, to learn a certain kind of morality."

"That's a big gamble," Flint said. "You're hoping that your designer clone won't rebel."

"That's why designer slow-grow clones are raised in bulk," Deshin said. "You cull from the group the ones in which the indoctrination doesn't take."

Flint shuddered. "You're kidding me, right?"

"No," Deshin said.

Flint shook his head. "And people actually pay for this? It would seem a lot of work and financial outlay for something that's not guaranteed."

"That's what I think," Deshin said. "Not to mention the moral side of this. I believe that slow-grow clones are human. It sounds like you do as well."

"All clones are human," Flint said. "Some have simply less of an opportunity for life than others."

"Again, a philosophical argument. Although I don't traffic in clones, slow-growth or otherwise. I think it takes a particularly cold human to do so," Deshin said.

"But other people do," Flint said.

"People, yes," Deshin said. "Alien groups as well. As I said, it's big business."

"If you don't do this," Flint said, "how do you know about it?"

"I get offers," Deshin said, suddenly coy. "People want to sell me everything. They think I will buy anything, have need of all kinds of items, and am willing to pay for a variety of rather disgusting things. I came across designer criminal clones a few years back when it became clear that some wealthy friends were being targeted by the Black Fleet. The Black Fleet was installing nannies inside wealthy households, and the nannies were legit. It made no sense, frankly, until I found out that the nannies were taking DNA from every member of the household."

Flint blinked, frowned, and then his chill grew. "If they were going to put in a cloned family member," he said, "then they'd have to remove the original family member."

Deshin nodded. "That's what I thought initially. The cloned member would inherit or whatever. But it's more complicated than that. Especially since most families have wills that specifically state that no clone can inherit, to prevent just this type of scenario."

"So what are they doing?" Flint asked.

"Installing a low-level spy into the household. With the right links to send information back to the Fleet. The spy doesn't even know what it's doing. It becomes—it *is*—for all intents and purposes, a member of the family."

"And what happens to the original?" Flint asked.

Deshin shook his head, his mouth a thin line. "I have no idea. I really don't want to know."

And that was the difference between them. Flint would want to know. Flint would want to do whatever he could to stop the practice.

But for now, he had to keep the focus on Deshin and the information he was getting about Anniversary Day.

"So these clones who attacked the Moon, you believe they were designed for the attack," Flint said.

"Yes," Deshin said. "And if they were created by the company that originally contacted me—or if they were created along the same lines that the company used—then these clones were the successful ones. There have to be unsuccessful clones from the same line."

"You don't think they'd kill the unsuccessful clones?" Flint hated Deshin's language. It was so impersonal. But it served the purpose of this conversation.

In fact, Flint didn't want to think about all the implications of everything Deshin told him. Not yet, anyway.

"I'm sure they do kill the unsuccessful clones," Deshin said. "But someone would have to notice, wouldn't they?"

This time, Flint shook his head. "It's a big universe. You can do a lot without being noticed."

"They wanted to be noticed," Deshin said. "They arrived in a group. They could have arrived separately."

"That crossed my mind as well," Flint said. "They got off transport in the Port and separated here in Armstrong, in front of surveillance, rather than arriving at different times on different ships. I figured they were sending a message."

"What do you think the message was?" Deshin asked. The question seemed sincere. He didn't seem to know.

"I think they wanted us to be distracted by PierLuigi Frémont," Flint said. "I think it was a diversion."

"PierLuigi Frémont was a ruthless cold-blooded killer," Deshin said. "If you wanted ruthless cold-blooded assassins, he's a great place to start."

"Sorry to say this," Flint said, "but there are and have been millions of ruthless, cold-blooded killers in the known universe. Frémont was a famous one. If you wanted to do this and not get noticed, you would have chosen someone other than Frémont."

"So Frémont was a message," Deshin said slowly.

Flint nodded.

"The question is," Deshin said, "who was the message for?"

"You don't think it was just for propaganda value? Distraction?" Flint asked.

"These bombings were well thought out," Deshin said. "I think nothing had been left to chance. I think that if something could have done double- or triple-duty, then it would have."

"You think the message was for you?" Flint asked.

"I'm not that arrogant," Deshin said. "But you already said that designer criminal clones have not been a police focus. It's pretty well known that the Earth Alliance either avoids thinking about such clones or hasn't noticed them at all. So that message is—hey! The clones exist! And look, we can clone evil bastards like PierLuigi Frémont."

"But you knew the clones existed," Flint said, beginning to see where Deshin was going.

"I know, and others know. A lot of others," Deshin said. "As I mentioned, it's a big business."

"What kind of message would they be sending to you?" Flint asked.

Deshin pushed himself out of the chair. He paced back to the window, looked out, then turned around again. It was as if the cityscape calmed him.

"I had a weird reaction when I saw the footage of those clones for the first time," he said. "My reaction was shock. Shock that someone would actually pay for and use designer clones for crimes this big. Shock that it worked. Because I always thought that things like this sounded better in theory, for the very reasons you mentioned. The idea that most humans in their twenties would have lives of their own, would make decisions on their own, that they couldn't be sustained as a weapon for this long."

"A weapon," Flint said.

Deshin nodded. "That's how they were initially advertised to me," he said. "As weapons."

"My God," Flint said. He couldn't tell Talia about this. He wasn't sure he wanted to tell anyone about this, even though he would have to. DeRicci had to know. "You will give me the names of the sellers who approached you."

"And you'll give me all the bomb components," Deshin said.

"Yeah," Flint said. Deshin had given him something they hadn't had. Deshin had been right; they needed each other on this.

Flint would trust Deshin at least a little.

"We got sidetracked on the clones," Flint said. "You were going to tell me something about zoodeh."

Deshin smiled. "Something I'm sure you've thought of. But it's better to be safe."

"All right," Flint said, sure he wouldn't have thought of it. It was beginning to seem like he hadn't thought of anything. "What is it?"

"The Earth Alliance banned zoodeh when it became clear that zoodeh was a great weapon for assassinations," Deshin said.

"Yes," Flint said. He knew that.

"But the Earth Alliance didn't force people to turn in whatever zoodeh they had. The zoodeh the Alliance knew about got quarantined, but there was a lot of zoodeh the Alliance didn't know about."

"Is it still being sold?" Flint asked.

Deshin shook his head. "That's the quickest way to get the Alliance to notice you. The Alliance watches weapons sales—at least those inside its borders. You need to look at who ordered zoodeh back when it was legal."

"Or who made it," Flint muttered. He suppressed a curse. They had missed that as well. "Do you have a list?"

"On zoodeh?" Deshin gave Flint a half-smile. "No. I don't sponsor assassinations. I'm not in the business of killing. But I do know that death is a big business. A lot of money gets made not just on weapons, but on finding the right targets, and manipulating the right events."

"You know who does this?" Flint asked.

"No more than you do," Deshin said. "This kind of stuff is always in the news. We just don't pay attention to things outside of our little sphere. Until those things try to blow up our sphere."

"Or succeed in blowing it up," Flint said.

"Yeah," Deshin said. "I've done a lot of thinking these past few months. That's why I'm talking to you."

Flint stood and extended his hand, something he hadn't thought he'd do at the beginning of the conversation.

"I'm glad you did," Flint said. "I'm very glad you did."

12

NOELLE DERICCI KICKED OFF HER SHOES, MOVED THE GIFT BASKET OFF the top of the bar at the far end of her hotel suite, and reached for the whiskey on the bar's top shelf. Earth-made whiskey in a bottle covered in dust. She didn't care.

She wanted a drink. She *deserved* a drink, and by God, she was going to have one.

She poured three fingers worth into the real glass tumbler near the mirror, and looked at herself as she did so. She wanted this moment burned in her memory.

This was the moment when she started drinking alone.

Which wasn't actually true. She had done the same thing after the bombing of Armstrong four years ago. And about at the same place in the timeframe. Six months after the actual event, when she realized she would never ever catch the damn bomber.

When she realized she might never have answers.

She set the tumbler down without taking a sip. Then she sighed.

You don't understand, Dominic Hanrahan, the mayor of Tycho Crater, had said to her just a few hours ago.

The problem was that she understood too well. *He* didn't understand. He had no idea what kind of pressure she was under. It was the same pressure he felt, magnified one million times. Each death that he allowed himself to think about matched one thousand deaths she couldn't allow herself to think about—particularly as individuals.

If she thought about all of those people as individuals, she'd crack.

She looked up. A thin-faced woman with large eyes looked back at her, her once-dark hair now almost completely gray. She had never been thin, never looked thin, never was incredibly thin, not even when she was in her best shape as a police officer.

Now she wasn't eating enough because she wasn't sitting down long enough to have a meal, and when she did sit down for a meal it was often in a high-stress situation with someone like Hanrahan. What great way to kill an appetite. Then when she got to her hotel room or her office or home, she didn't want to eat or she just plain forgot.

She was forgetting a lot of things, which her assistants kept telling her was normal for someone under the kind of stress she felt. Her forgetfulness was another reason she had staff shadowing her at all times.

Or at most times. Fortunately, at the moment, those shadows were in their own hotel rooms, probably contemplating their own liquor cabinets.

Long damn day. And tomorrow would be more of the same. Hanrahan promised to have the rebuilding plans in her hands by breakfast.

She wondered where he would find an architect who could design a working model of an entire dome section on such short notice.

She grinned at that thought. Hanrahan was so transparent. She had defeated him verbally at the disaster site, and now he was afraid of her. Now he would do what she wanted.

She only wished he would do it without intense supervision.

She wished a lot of things. None of them would ever come true. She wished she had known what life would be like now back when she had agreed to take this job. She wished she knew that life was this way because the change was inevitable, not because it was her fault.

She wished she had someone to talk to, someone who would truly understand what she was going through.

Noelle? At first, she thought the voice coming through her links was her imagination.

She turned away from the mirror. *Miles?*

A small holographic image of him appeared on the bar. The gift basket dwarfed him. She moved so that she wouldn't see both in the same frame.

I wasn't sure I'd reach you, he sent. *I know that sometimes you're unavailable when you're touring the scenes.*

That was earlier. She pulled over one of the bar stools and sat down. She hoped he couldn't see the drink sitting untouched near the mirror.

You look tired.

He was clearly being polite. She looked exhausted.

He looked—what? Energized? Animated? Something was different about him. Something she recognized, but something she hadn't seen in a long time, since before Anniversary Day.

I had the most extraordinary meetings today, he sent.

With who? She wished she could say her meetings had been extraordinary. They weren't. They had been like every meeting she'd had since Anniversary Day.

I'll get to that in a minute, he sent. *But I've got some information, about the clones, about the zoodeh, and about the way we're approaching the investigation.*

What about the investigation? she asked.

We're going about it wrong, he sent.

Of course they were. She rubbed her eyes, noting that even her thoughts were sarcastic or cynical. She *was* tired. She didn't want to contemplate the idea that they had done something wrong, let alone conducted the investigation wrong.

What's wrong with it? Just asking that question took more strength than she had anticipated.

We're assuming that Anniversary Day was a practice run, just like that first bombing in Armstrong. Flint practically vibrated as he sent that. Wherever he had gotten this idea, he liked it. No, it was more than that. He *believed* it.

It isn't?

110

He shook his head. *We need to search for other smaller bombings elsewhere in the Earth Alliance. There will be more attacks, but probably not here.*

Who told you this? DeRicci asked.

This part is just a theory, Flint sent, *but it makes sense to me.*

Her brain hurt. The theory didn't make sense to her. But then, little had of late.

Look, Noelle, Flint sent, *the only reason I'm telling you this is so that we can move the investigation wider. We'll need Earth Alliance help.*

We already have Earth Alliance help, she sent.

Looking at internal records of other cultures, he sent. *I suspect the practice runs on some of them have already happened.*

And you want me to contact someone, she sent. She was feeling more and more tired with each idea. She didn't want the Earth Alliance involved any more than it already was. She certainly didn't want those investigators to interfere with the way things were going on the Moon.

He shrugged. *Maybe you should contact someone. If we find anything. First, I need your permission to look.*

I'm not in charge of you, Miles.

I know, he sent. *But you're in charge of the investigation, and I can't give orders without your authority. In fact, I need you to tell Rudra that my theory is worth pursuing.*

She disagrees? If Popova disagreed, then DeRicci would too. After a difficult period just after Anniversary Day, DeRicci could trust Popova again.

She doesn't know, he sent. *She doesn't like the Earth Alliance investigators already in your office.*

DeRicci didn't like them either. But maybe this was a sign that DeRicci needed a real assistant. Not shadows, not a glorified secretary like Popova. Someone who could make decisions for her. Someone she trusted one-hundred percent.

The problem was that she didn't trust anyone one-hundred percent, not Miles, not anyone.

DeRicci sighed. *Looking in a new direction won't hurt. I'll let her know. But I don't want her to involve the Earth Alliance investigators. I think they're here to take over my investigation.*

At that moment, she sent Popova a private message. In it, she warned that whatever direction Flint wanted to take the investigation was all right with her, but that the Earth Alliance investigators should be kept in the dark.

Flint had his arms crossed. Something was bothering him.

Anything else? DeRicci sent.

Zoodeh and the clones, Flint sent. He was frowning now, as if he couldn't believe she had forgotten that.

She could believe it. She really needed something to eat. Or some sleep. She wasn't sure which was more important.

What about them? she sent.

He told her about the zoodeh, the fact that a lot of it remained in the Earth Alliance after the ban.

We should have thought of that, she sent. *The Alliance is so disorganized.*

Flint nodded. *So we're going to investigate that too.*

Good, she sent. *And the clones? Did you find who made them?*

No, he sent, *but I did find out how they came to be. They're designer clones, Noelle. Someone is selling clones for specific activities, as thieves or assassins. As* weapons.

DeRicci closed her eyes and tilted her head back. There it was. Someone from the Alliance had finally talked to Flint.

I know, she sent.

You know? he sent and she could feel his disbelief. She knew what he would say next. This was something she should have told him.

It's classified. I couldn't have told you if I wanted to, she sent.

Don't you think it would have helped the investigation if I knew?

No, she sent, even though she did think it might have helped. *The Earth Alliance already has people investigating this.*

And they haven't done anything in years, Flint sent.

They have, she sent. *They're on the trail. They've moved even more personnel to this task since the bombings.*

His little holographic self stared at her. She was glad she was seeing him in miniature, because if he were across from her, she wasn't sure she could defend his lack of knowledge on this.

Who told you about this? she sent. *Those lackeys from the Earth Alliance that Popova's been messaging me about?*

Luc Deshin, Flint sent—and severed their connection.

DeRicci sat down. She wasn't sure if she was more surprised that Flint had cut her off or that he had been talking with Armstrong's most notorious criminal boss.

Luc Deshin. He had probably been the source of all of the information that Flint got. She wondered what Deshin got out of pushing the investigation in this direction.

Flint wasn't easily manipulated. In fact, he had a stronger spine than she did. So Deshin couldn't push him in a direction he didn't want to go.

Still, Deshin's presence in this investigation made her wary.

Everything made her wary.

And the conversation with Flint left her unsettled.

She thought of contacting him again, and then she changed her mind. She needed food. She needed rest.

She needed to think about something else for a while.

She turned around, and without giving herself a chance to change her mind, she downed the tumbler of whiskey.

It burned and it didn't make her feel any different. Not more relaxed, not happier, not anything.

It didn't make her forget either.

Nothing ever would.

13

WHITELEY'S SHIP STARTED THE MOMENT ZAGRANDO TOUCHED THE controls, just like it would have with Whiteley at the helm. The ship rose easily, and all of the monitors—from the automated ones to the visual ones—showed no one following him.

This ship was huge, and it felt empty. Zagrando had hated it from the first moment he'd seen it, and he hated it more now. It looked more like a battleship than a businessman's yacht, with all the weaponry up front and the utilitarian cockpit.

Zagrando's stomach ached. He was both tense and queasy. He had to get off this ship quickly, and he really didn't have a plan for that. He figured the Black Fleet would know within hours that Whiteley no longer piloted his own ship.

And Zagrando did not want to be on board when they figured it out. He suspected they would do nothing to him because Whiteley had been the one who had been incautious, but Whiteley was part of the Black Fleet family and Zagrando was not. Therefore, predicting what the Black Fleet would do to him was a fool's game.

Even though he had disabled the ship's coded command system before boarding, he had not expected to steal the thing. Now he was in an unfamiliar region of space in a stolen ship, after he had shot its owner, who was an integral part of the Black Fleet.

He didn't dare contact the Earth Alliance. He didn't dare contact anyone for help.

He had to figure this out on his own.

But first, he had to get the Emzada's skin cells off him. He had no idea what that goo would do to him after a day or so of contact, and he really didn't want to find out.

He clicked into the ship's navigation system, looking for nearby starbases. He didn't want anything affiliated with the Earth Alliance. Nor did he want a place frequented by the Black Fleet.

He needed some place that would allow him to dump this ship and purchase another. Then he would have to dump that ship somewhere along the way—after changing its identification codes—and find yet another.

At some point he would have to stop leaving a trail—both physically and metaphorically. He needed a destination, but his desire for one warred with his desire to get this crap off his skin.

His nose twitched, and his throat felt thick with Emzada cells. How many of those damn things had he swallowed anyway?

He would have to use one of the nanocleansers from Whiteley's medical stock, just to make sure this stuff hadn't permanently become part of his system.

It would be brilliant, wouldn't it, if those cells turned into some kind of tracking device.

Three years ago, he would have considered that thought paranoid. Now he worried that he wasn't paranoid enough.

The navigation system pinged. It had located several stops not too far away. Most were human-based. One was Disty-owned, and his already tortured skin crawled at the thought. He hated the warrens that the Disty built everywhere, but he'd use them if he had to.

The other belonged to the J'Slik. His already upset stomach twisted even more at the thought of going there. The J'Slik refused to join the Earth Alliance because of all the legal requirements. Like the Black Fleet, the J'Slik had a criminal culture. Unlike the Black Fleet, the J'Slik believed the individual primary, so anything any J'Slik individual did took precedence over any group activity.

He had studied the J'Slik and had run into a few of them, but he had never deliberately gone to one of their bases.

But the Black Fleet tried to avoid them as well. And that, more than anything, was a point in the J'Slik's favor.

Besides, the J'Slik loved trades and money—of all types. Zagrando had something to trade and, failing that, he had enough money to buy his way out of there.

The trick would be to leave shortly after he arrived.

He programmed the coordinates into the navigation system, then sighed. He had a hunch that just by programming those coordinates, he guaranteed some Black Fleet ships would head his way.

He hoped he could get to the starbase before they did.

But he wasn't going to worry about it at the moment. He was going to think about it all after he had cleaned the Emzada out of his system.

Before he left the cockpit, he activated one more automatic control. He wanted the ship's cleaning system to get rid of any trace of the Emzada as well.

He didn't want to get reinfected when he stepped out of that shower. He needed to be clean, even though he wondered if he would ever feel clean again.

14

MILES FLINT BOWED HIS HEAD. HE WAS IN HIS CAR OUTSIDE OF CELESTINE Gonzalez's office. Luc Deshin had left fifteen minutes before, and had smiled at Flint as he had gone by.

Flint had waited until Deshin was gone before contacting DeRicci.

And then she had told him that she had known about the designer clones.

He had severed the connection with her so that he wouldn't yell at her. Then he shut down all but his emergency links. He needed a moment.

He hadn't been this furious in a long, long time.

Not since he had found out about Talia.

The car felt too small. He didn't feel exposed, though. No one else was on the street. He was probably visible on some surveillance cameras, but what would anyone see? A man in his car, clearly communicating with someone, and then bowing his head afterward as if he had received bad news.

Had he received bad news?

Yes and no. He was relieved that the Earth Alliance had someone pursuing the designer clones, but he was furious that he had been kept in the dark. Because of Talia, and because of a few cases he had helped on, he knew a great deal about clones, cloning companies, and cloning laws throughout the Alliance.

He also knew how to track clones, maybe better than anyone else on the Moon.

Of course, Flint's expertise in this area was something he hadn't talked about.

Still, the lack of trust astounded him. He thought DeRicci had brought him onto this case because she trusted him wholeheartedly.

Instead, she had been using him to help the investigation, but she hadn't done everything she could for that investigation.

The feeling he'd had of late, the feeling that investigation had slowed because of something outside of the investigation, turned out to be true.

And that something was politics.

By the person he believed did not have a political bone in her body.

Of course, if he really thought about it, DeRicci had more politics in her soul than he ever had. She had grown in this job, helped the Moon through the Disty crisis, and had been an advisor to Governor-General Celia Alfreda before the governor-general became one of the Anniversary Day victims.

Since then, DeRicci had held the Moon together, in part because of her political skills.

He had seen that, but he hadn't really *seen* it. He still viewed DeRicci as the woman he had met all those years ago when he had first partnered with her in the detective division. Back then, she'd been an insecure but excellent cop who dressed poorly, wasn't sure how she was perceived, and was likely to say whatever was on her mind, even if it got her in trouble.

But she had never mishandled the victims or the suspects. She had ignored the brass because she thought them unimportant.

She had thought justice was important.

That was the DeRicci Flint had known. That was the DeRicci Flint still believed he had been working with.

But he hadn't been. Not for a long time.

This DeRicci dressed well, kept important people in the loop, and let other people investigate. He hadn't seen her finesse a victim or a suspect in years.

But he had seen her finesse other people, including him.

The changes in her had been so gradual that he hadn't really registered them. And now he was faced with the truth of it all: This DeRicci, the woman she had become, was a lot more secure in herself. She had stepped into the role as the Chief Security Office for the Moon. She had actually overstepped at times, taking on more authority than she actually had by law, to save the Moon itself.

She had done it in the Disty crisis. She was doing it now.

Her heart was still in the right place. Flint had to believe that. He didn't think she had changed so much as to be unrecognizable.

But he did think she wasn't the woman he thought she was.

She no longer believed in justice.

She was more concerned with the politics.

And that meant that she no longer had the victims or the investigation at heart.

He did. He wanted this solved, and he didn't care who or what got in the way.

That was why he met with Luc Deshin. Flint would continue to use people like Deshin if it got him to the perpetrators of this horrible crime. Especially if he got there before they attacked again.

And if he had to break a few alliances, betray some political pipe dream, hurt a long-forged understanding, he would do that.

If it cost DeRicci the goodwill she had from the Alliance and the people of the Moon, he would still do it.

He closed his eyes and took a deep breath.

A long time ago, his mentor, Paloma, had told him that friends and family were a liability. She told him to have neither. He ignored the advice, just like she had. She had spoken out of experience: Her friends and her family, in particular, had cost her a great deal. And she had betrayed almost everyone.

That advice bubbled more than Flint wanted it to. He wanted to dismiss it because of all the secrets he had learned about Paloma, all the disillusioning secrets.

But the advice kept coming up.

Like tonight. How far would he be on this investigation now if he hadn't trusted DeRicci? If he had followed his own path, making his own rules, ignoring some of the niceties that everyone insisted on?

Would he be farther ahead?

On one hand, he would have a lot more freedom, but on the other, he wouldn't have access to certain databases, wouldn't know who was doing what in some other jurisdictions.

Not that he knew all of that now. The Earth Alliance betrayal taught him that much.

He let out a small breath.

He couldn't wait for DeRicci to come to her senses. For all he knew, she had come to her senses and had arrived at a different conclusion as to what was important.

If she wanted to toss him out of the investigation, so be it. He had enough contacts. He could still get any information he found to the right people.

The thing he had to think about was whether or not he wanted to continue working out of the Security Building. Maybe he was making excuses for being there. Maybe he should up the security protocols in his office, and work from there.

But that twisted his stomach. He couldn't leave Talia there alone. The Security Building, at least, was the safest building in Armstrong.

And there it was again. A compromise decision because of someone he cared about.

But when he came to Talia, he was never going to do something deliberately to harm her.

He would work in the Security Building as long as he could. He might have to take a few trips to some outside networks to look up information that DeRicci might not approve of him knowing. But he could do that.

He probably would have done that in his office anyway.

He sighed, rubbed his eyes, and tilted his head back. He couldn't quit now. He just had to change his focus.

He had to take control of the investigation.

DeRicci had given him permission to control the zoodeh part of the investigation.

If she caught him working on the clones lead, he'd tell her that he had misunderstood her: that he thought, since these clones were weapons, he could include them in his search.

He started the car.

He had a lot of work to do, an entire investigation to reorganize.

And he needed to get started, right now.

15

JIN RASTIGAN HAD NEVER SEEN THE PEYTI INVESTIGATIVE GUARD IN action. They swarmed over the forested area near Sunbeam Gallen's habitat. Rastigan had spent eight years on Peyla, most of them as the head of human-based security for the Earth Alliance at the Alliance's headquarters, and not once had she seen anything like this.

The Peyti moved as if they were in a panic. Usually Peyti walked upright, their stick-figure bodies almost comical in their awkwardness.

But now, half of them crouched, running on all fours, stopping and plunging their long twig-like fingers into the dirt where Gallen had said she had seen bits of bodies fall, burning, to the ground.

Rastigan stood inside Gallen's habitat, along with one Earth Alliance diplomat, a lawyer, and a mental-health counselor, all from the human-based section of the Alliance headquarters. Gallen had sent for help through her human contacts. The Alliance, in turn, contacted the Peyti, and Peyti help had arrived first.

But the Peyti did not have the kind of equipment that allowed them inside the habitat. In addition to permission, they needed breathing apparatus.

The Peyti hadn't seen the habitat as the issue. They'd found something on the grounds, something that had disturbed them so greatly that they weren't talking about it.

Rastigan wanted to know what that something was.

She had arrived shortly after the first Peyti officials had, along with her team. She had no idea what she would find, or even if she would find Gallen alive.

Rastigan had come in first, laser pistols in both hands, only to find Gallen cowering under one of the tables. No one—and nothing—else was in the habitat, so Rastigan had beckoned her team to come inside.

She had gotten the story from Gallen in bits and pieces. Gallen was both scared and afraid she'd be banned from this part of Peyla. Rastigan got her to focus on what actually happened—and what actually happened sounded strange.

Peyti flying backward through the air as if catapulted? Peyti hit with some kind of weapon, glowing, and disintegrating?

Rastigan hadn't heard anything like it before.

She finally managed to palm Gallen off on the other three, letting them deal with the woman's worries. She'd already sent them a private message, letting them know that Gallen wouldn't be able to stay here. She was going to have to go back to headquarters, at least for the short term, maybe longer.

It all depended on what the Peyti decided. This was their land, after all, and their problem.

Rastigan informed the others that the moment they could get Gallen out of here, they should. They shouldn't wait for Rastigan.

She needed to download the security vids. Gallen wanted her research as well, and while Rastigan let her take all of the computerized information, Gallen also wanted dirt and beakers and stuff in some kind of frozen unit. Until Rastigan knew exactly what happened here, she wasn't bringing any part of the soil or anything else physical to headquarters.

She wasn't going to explain that, either. That was why she had brought a counselor as well as a lawyer. Initially she had figured the lawyer would deal with everything, but it was becoming clearer that the mental-health professional was the important one here.

Rastigan wasn't sure if Gallen was just at the edge of her very short rope or if she was slightly crazy.

Considering how far away from everything Gallen actually was, Rastigan was voting for crazy, and maybe not so slightly.

Rastigan had long ago shut out the conversation, filled as it was with Gallen's sobbing and terrors. Instead, Rastigan had gone to the nearest desk and examined the computer setup. The science part of the setup had been added, and looked awfully complicated. But anything to do with the habitat was standard issue and easy to understand. Rastigan had worked with systems like this her entire life.

She tapped a few icons, and had the security feeds sent to her links. Then she stood near the window where Gallen had seen the so-called attack and watched the feeds superimposed over her left eye.

It was a strange experience. One eye saw Peyti swarming the ground in front of her, investigating in crouches, their long fingers deep in the dirt, and the other saw Peyti propelled backward, hands open in panic, then turning orange and dissolving.

Gallen had said they screamed as they died. Rastigan shuddered. She understood why.

She turned around to ask Gallen a question, and realized that her entire team had left. Somehow they had gotten Gallen out of the habitat.

Rastigan was relieved about that. She had thought it would be harder.

She sighed and was about to leave when a Peyti came into the habitat. The Peyti held a mask over her features with one long-fingered hand.

Most humans had trouble recognizing individual Peyti, but Rastigan didn't. She could see the subtle differences around the eyes, the changing patterns of gray in the skin tone, all of the things that Peyti saw when they looked at each other.

Even with the mask, she knew that the Peyti before her was Uzvot, who had come from Alliance headquarters to act as both liaison and as translator if need be.

Rastigan spoke Peytin fluently, but sometimes—particularly in moments of stress—the Peyti preferred to talk with their own. That was why Rastigan always brought a translator with her to any event that might later become important.

"You have to see this," she said to Uzvot.

Uzvot, to her credit, didn't say a word. She just moved closer to Rastigan.

Uzvot was tall for a Peyti, but still shorter than Rastigan. Rastigan always felt large around the Peyti, even though she was considered delicate by human standards. She used her delicacy to her advantage with humans; they rarely saw her as a threat. The Peyti were more willing to accept her because of her slight frame and large eyes. More than once, she'd been told she was as close to Peyti as a human could get.

Uzvot had never said those things, however. Uzvot and Rastigan had an understanding. They didn't need to explain much to each other.

Rastigan tapped a few places on the desk and called up the security feed, this time as a miniature hologram that she ran near the only solid wall.

Uzvot turned a slight blue—a sign of distress among the Peyti.

"This went on until your people arrived," Rastigan said.

The Peyti had responded to the distress call quickly. But, because Gallen had gone through human channels instead of Peyti ones, the arrival had taken three times longer than normal.

Still, Rastigan felt that Gallen's decision to contact the humans through her links was the smartest thing Gallen had done. Gallen had no way of knowing if whatever—whomever—was murdering the Peyti monitored Peyti emergency links. By avoiding those links, Gallen had protected herself in a very difficult situation. More importantly, she— and her habitat—hadn't been noticed.

Rastigan didn't watch the killings again—at least, not closely. Instead, she looked at that bare ground through the windows. How long had this type of killing been going on? Once the bodies disintegrated, there was no evidence that they had even existed.

Or did the Peyti have a way of figuring that out? Was that what the hands in the dirt signified? Or were there chips on those Peyti's fingertips that read something in the soil's composition?

Even though Rastigan was an expert on the Peyti and the Peyti culture, there was a lot she didn't know.

Uzvot waved her free hand. "Shut it off."

The area near her right eye had turned turquoise, something Rastigan had heard about but had never seen in all of her years on Peyla.

That turquoise color, she had been told, was the Peyti equivalent of tears. Unlike human tears, which served many functions, the turquoise color showed up only in moments of great distress.

Uzvot bowed her head and adjusted her mask so that she didn't have to hold it in place.

"Give me a minute," she said.

Rastigan would have preferred to leave the hologram frozen, but she shut it off like Uzvot requested.

"We will need that," Uzvot said.

"I know," Rastigan said. "I'll make copies."

"It would be best if copies did not get out." Uzvot raised her head. The turquoise had faded, but her skin remained a light blue.

"I won't let any copies out," Rastigan said.

"I know, but this is important. It could cause unrest."

Rastigan's breath caught. "Among the Peyti?"

"Yes, among the Peyti," Uzvot said.

Rastigan shook her head. "I didn't think such a thing was possible."

Until a few moments ago, Rastigan had thought the Peyti had all the difficult emotions under control. Within the Earth Alliance, the Peyti were known as the most peaceful of the species. They never had civil unrest, hadn't had a war in more than a century, and always—always—preferred negotiation to violence.

It was a private joke among diplomats: If you wanted war, don't let the Peyti into a planning session.

Of course, the flip side remained true as well. If someone wanted peace, the Peyti were the best allies to have.

"We have our history, like you have yours," Uzvot said. "Only unlike you, whenever we are faced with the violent among us, we do not shrug and say that it is part of our character. We believe that with thought and self-control all things can be conquered, even the dark impulses."

Rastigan knew that. She also knew that the Peyti all struggled with what they called their dark impulses. But she had thought—apparently mistakenly—that they had conquered one dark impulse almost completely. She thought that the Peyti had weeded out the violent among them so long ago that they had bred themselves into pacifists.

Apparently not.

"I'm confused," Rastigan said. "I've been in here investigating. Your people have been dealing with everything outside. The death of these Peyti—it was caused by other Peyti?"

That turquoise color returned, but this time Uzvot did not turn away. She brought her head down, and then back up, the Peyti equivalent of a nod, learned only by the Peyti who had interactions with humans.

"Yes," she said simply.

"They were using each other as *target practice*?" Rastigan raised her voice, not because she was angry, but because she couldn't quite believe this.

Peyti didn't behave like that.

"Your phrase 'target practice' is simplistic. We do not know what has happened here. Only that we have many dead, a true tragedy."

"Caused by Peyti," Rastigan said, feeling surprised. Somehow she had believed that some other group had caused this, or something had malfunctioned.

"Yes," Uzvot said.

"And you consider this murder," Rastigan said.

Uzvot bowed her head. "It is murder, yes."

"Wow," Rastigan said softly. "Wow. I didn't think such things happened here any longer."

"They don't," Uzvot said with emphasis.

"And yet this has," Rastigan said. "Is that why you don't want the information leaked?"

"No," Uzvot said.

Rastigan glanced outside, feeling horribly off balance. She hadn't contemplated any of this before.

The Peyti still crouched in the dirt seemed frantic, their movements quick and forceful. Two Peyti stood to one side, conferring.

"I'm confused," Rastigan said. "Are you asking me to bury this vid?"

"Yes," Uzvot said.

"Because of the murders," Rastigan said.

"No," Uzvot said.

Rastigan sighed. She couldn't destroy the vid even if she wanted to. She was being foolish to consider it. But she was curious. She had no real idea what was happening here.

She turned. The color in Uzvot's face had receded to a light blue.

"You do realize that parts of this are out of my hands, right?" Rastigan said. "The Earth Alliance has already been notified. We've been involved from the start. We got the distress call. We don't silence our people, no matter what species they belong to. Any crime here will be prosecuted by Peyti law because this happened on Peyla, but the Earth Alliance will be involved. Gallen ensured that just by being here. This is not a strictly Peyti matter."

"Can't we do something to fix that?" Uzvot asked. The blue in her skin seemed darker. "Perhaps tell the Earth Alliance that there was a mistake?"

Rastigan shook her head. If she got caught lying to the Alliance about something this important, she would lose her job.

For a brief second, she thought of lying to Uzvot. The lie was easy: She could say that security information from all habitats got uploaded onto a special network. But that was too easy to check.

She supposed she could also lie and say that she would tell the Earth Alliance it was all a mistake. While that would work with some species who contacted the Alliance as little as possible, it wouldn't work with the Peyti, who followed the minutia of all Earth Alliance activities.

"You know we can't," Rastigan said. "I'm sorry. This is on the record."

Uzvot tilted her head back. A hand went to her mask to hold it in place. But Rastigan could still see that the turquoise color had returned.

"Forgive me," Rastigan said, lapsing into diplomatic speak, "but why don't you want this out?"

Uzvot shook her head. She turned away slightly, as if she were embarrassed by her emotional reaction.

"Then what?"

"You did not notice anything strange about that incident?" Uzvot asked.

"I think the deaths are strange," Rastigan said. "I honestly did not think that was possible here."

Uzvot tilted her head slightly, the human equivalent of a sad smile. "Not all of us control our dark impulses every moment of every day."

In other words, murder did happen here, and the Peyti did not discuss it with outsiders.

Which was fine. Outsiders didn't need to know anything about Peyti-to-Peyti relationships.

"You're referring to something specific, aren't you?" Rastigan asked. "You saw something in particular."

"I did." Uzvot walked to one of the side windows.

Rastigan joined her. On a far hillside, another swarm of Peyti were barely visible. Rastigan squinted. They seemed to be encircling some buildings.

"We are different," Uzvot said, and Rastigan waited. Of course the two species were different. It was obvious on more levels than Rastigan wanted to consider.

"I know," Rastigan said.

"No," Uzvot said sharply, "you do not know. Your people think we know nothing about the jokes, about how difficult it is to tell a Peyti from a twig, let alone a Peyti from each other. But we are *different*. Each of us—like each of you—is unique."

Rastigan's face warmed. She hadn't realized—she doubted anyone had realized—that the Peyti were aware of the jokes. But of course they were. It should have been obvious from the beginning. The Peyti paid attention to the smallest of Earth Alliance details. Of course they would notice something as prevalent as a joke.

But Rastigan didn't say anything. She didn't want to derail Uzvot.

"The Peyti out there," Uzvot waved an arm toward the window they had abandoned, "the ones who died. They were not unique."

Rastigan frowned. She wondered if she had understood properly. She repeated the same sentence in Peytin, repeating the Peyti word for "unique."

"Yes," Uzvot said in Standard. "Your eyes did not deceive you. Those Peyti *did* look the same."

Honestly, Rastigan hadn't noticed. She had been so shocked by the deaths that she hadn't looked at the faces of the individual Peyti, except to see their sheer terror.

"What do you mean?" she asked.

"Unlike so many other species, we do not have the phenomenon of twins or naturally occurring duplicates. Those Peyti, they were cloned."

Rastigan frowned. "Cloned?"

Uzvot nodded.

"So someone was killing off its own clones?" Rastigan asked.

"I don't think so," Uzvot said, her turquoise color nearly neon now, "since the original has been dead for more than a century."

"You *recognized* the clones?" Rastigan said.

"No Peyti could have missed it," Uzvot said. "We have our Pier-Luigi Frémonts as well. Only we teach about them, tell children how horrible they are, what monsters they were—monsters that lurk in our own skin, monsters that we must always control. And we use faces of real monsters to illustrate our point."

"So this is—?"

"Uzvekmt," Uzvot said, "destroyer of the Qavle."

The worst genocide on Peyla in the last three hundred years. Maybe the worst genocide on Peyla ever. Rastigan had learned that, just like she had learned that it was in response to Uzvekmt that the Peyti had developed the program they now used to get rid of the so-called "dark impulses."

"So someone is killing clones of Uzvekmt?" Rastigan asked.

"Let us hope that is all which is occurring," Uzvot said, "because it could be so much more."

16

THE J'SLIK CALLED THEIR STARBASE SOME UNPRONOUNCEABLE combination of symbols that Zagrando couldn't quite grasp, even with a phonetic translation. On human-made charts, however, someone had labeled the J'Slik base "Hellhole," and the name had stuck.

Zagrando had expected some ancient and decaying starbase, dark and dingy and impossible to navigate. Instead, he found a colorful, modern starbase with a docking system so easy that he wondered why places in the Earth Alliance hadn't adopted it.

When he disembarked, all he had to remove from the stolen Black Fleet ship were his own bag and that bag that Whiteley had been carrying (cleaned of the Emzada goo). He had sent the clothes he had worn to Abbondiado through the airlock long before landing, putting on a pair of black pants and a matching black shirt. The rest of the clothes he had brought with him were in his own bag, along with some weapons he had found in the ship.

Before he took the weapons, he removed all the tracking devices from them.

The docking ring's exterior was a bright orange. Its interior was an equally shocking kelly green. The door leading into the main part of the base was a neon purple.

All of the colors in the Hellhole were so clearly defined that they hurt his eyes. He was so distracted by the brightness that it took him a moment to realize no one had checked him for weapons, nor had he gone through a decontamination chamber.

Apparently, a person entered Hellhole at his own risk.

He did, however, have to stop in front of a J'Slik guard positioned in front of three ornate gold doors. At least, Zagrando assumed he was looking at a guard. The J'Slik had a pad of Earth Alliance design in one meaty paw and tapped on the surface with a curved claw.

Every J'Slik that Zagrando had ever seen had a triangular head with matching triangular eyes and a nose that was little more than nostrils against a curved mouth. The ears stuck straight up like antennae. J'Slik had very flat feet the length of a human leg, and seemed to get most of their balance from a short tail that touched the ground when they weren't walking.

They hid their gender under scarves and multicolored markings, although doubted he would recognize what gender they were even if he could see the genitalia. The identification came from the number of hairs in the belly fur—two hundred or more belonged to a female of the species, less than two hundred strands indicated a male.

He supposed if he saw little or no belly fur at all, he would know he was looking at a male. Otherwise, he figured determining gender would be impossible.

The J'Slik could change color at will, and this one had chosen to clothe itself in a muted forest green. It wore a gold scarf that matched the ornate doors.

"State the purpose for your visit," it said in a flat tone.

"I would like a new ship," Zagrando said. All of the information he had seen about J'Slik territory warned him to give away as little as possible when being questioned.

"Use the door on the far right," the J'Slik said.

Zagrando did, and it wasn't until he went through the door that he realized he had not been asked to identify himself in any way. Nor had his very sophisticated chips told him that surveillance had surreptitiously looked for his identification.

He glanced back to see if he had missed some kind of security, but he hadn't—at least none visible to the human eye.

He was in a neutral area, like an airlock, between doors. He had to push open a gray door to go farther. He did, stepping into a wide atrium with a design that appeared to show the stars around the base. The ceiling design almost vanished in the shock of the rest of the atrium.

Everything was hot pink, from the floor to the walls to the doorways. The only way he could even see the doors was that they were outlined in a bold, almost clashing, red.

Maybe Hellhole was a more accurate name than he had initially thought. The colors—at first bold and refreshing—had already become unsettling. He could imagine how they might turn nightmarish over time.

At least the smells were better than those in the Emzada Lair. This place had the faint odor of oranges, which also caused a sensory disconnect with that hot pink. Dozens of J'Slik stood before him, gathered in small groups, talking, gesturing with their paws, and tapping on various pads. Some J'Slik sat at tables at what seemed to be the exteriors of restaurants.

He saw no humans at all, and very few aliens of other types.

He took a deep breath and slipped into the crowd. He didn't read J'Slik, so he had to set his links to translate signs for him. He saw nothing that told him where he could get another ship.

Finally, he found an information booth. A pale yellow J'Slik stood in the center of the booth, resting its chin on its paws.

He stopped in front of the booth, but the J'Slik did not look up. Other J'Slik, however, glanced over at him, and several stopped their nearby conversations.

Rather than speak out loud, Zagrando decided to use his links. That way his query would get translated immediately, and it would be harder for the nearby J'Slik to overhear him.

Excuse me, he sent. *I need some information.*

The yellow J'Slik did not raise its head. Zagrando wondered if he needed to tap on something or do something to get the J'Slik's attention. He felt uncomfortable doing so; he had no idea what this culture considered rude—or worse, some kind of legal offense.

Although, if he thought about it, a legal offense seemed a lot less likely, considering how much the J'Slik opposed the Earth Alliance legalities.

Then he realized that the yellow J'Slik's eyes were open. They were yellow as well, their pupils slitted and dark.

What? it sent back.

The question had arrived in Standard, but Zagrando had no idea if that was a translation or if the J'Slik had actually sent the response in Standard.

I'm in the market for a ship, Zagrando sent. *I was sent through the door that led me here. Is there someplace—*

The J'Slik actually sighed, shook itself as if it were getting cobwebs off its fur, and then sat up. It extended its right paw and curved all but one of its claws downward. The remaining claw pointed toward the right.

"That way," it said out loud in Standard. "Talk to H'Jith."

Then it crossed its paws again, and put its head back down, closing its eyes.

Zagrando sent, *Thank you,* mostly out of fear. He still didn't want to seem rude and he figured being on his best human behavior would help.

The J'Slik to his right had parted to form a corridor. They watched him pass. At the end of their makeshift corridor was another J'Slik. Its fur was a patchwork of oranges that clashed with the hot pink around it. Its eyes were blue, and—Zagrando thought—seemed to be twinkling.

But he didn't dare assume that twinkling eyes meant a kinder, gentler J'Slik, or even an amused one. He was beginning to regret his decision to come here. He had no obvious allies, and no one knew where he was.

"A ship, eh?" the J'Slik said in Standard. "But you just arrived in a cruiser. How can I improve on that?"

Zagrando's still-sensitive stomach turned. But he had to look at all of this logically. With so few humans here (if there were any others at all), he would be conspicuous. And they would know what he arrived in.

He suspected it would take very little for them to track the ship itself.

The J'Slik tilted its head. Its lips curled upward in what Zagrando would call a smile, even though he wasn't sure if that was correct either.

"You are Whiteley?" it asked.

So they had checked the ship's ownership. They probably knew it was a Black Fleet vessel.

"Unfortunately, Whiteley is dead," Zagrando lied. He figured that the lie was a better explanation than the truth. Besides, the lie kept up with the do-not-over-explain rule. And, all by itself, it gave a reason for Zagrando's presence here with someone else's ship.

"That is unfortunate," the J'Slik said. "I take it that you do not like his ship?"

Games. It was all about games.

"I would like one of my own," Zagrando said. "I was told to talk with H'Jith about that. Are you H'Jith?"

The J'Slik's mouth opened just a little, then closed. Its tail twitched, then it bowed its head slightly. "I am. And you were told correctly."

"I do not know your customs very well," Zagrando said, "so forgive me if I'm hurrying you, but I am due to meet a friend and have little time."

He deliberately did not specify where he was meeting that friend. Perhaps H'Jith would believe that he was meeting the friend in Hellhole.

"With paying customers," H'Jith said, "we follow their timeline. What sort of vessel are you searching for?"

Good question. If he said something fast, it sounded like he was in trouble. If he said something large, it sounded like he had money.

"I would like to see your ship," Zagrando said, remembering a trick an old trader had once taught him.

H'Jith's tail twitched again, but the movement was different. Zagrando would like to think that the question surprised it. Perhaps it did.

"I will not sell my own ship," H'Jith said.

"I understand," Zagrando said. "But if I see what you consider to be quality, then I can better communicate my needs to you."

H'Jith's eyes slitted and it tilted its head toward Zagrando. "Just so. Let us repair to my section of the docking ring then."

H'Jith had its own section of the docking ring? Either it bought and sold a lot of ships, or something else was going on here.

Or both.

Zagrando had a large knot in his stomach. He always had an acute sense of danger, and this place had more danger than he had expected.

He needed to be smart, and he needed to be quick.

He also had a hunch money might not solve his problems.

But he didn't want to trade the Black Fleet ship for any old ship that H'Jith gave him. Nor did he want to leave behind a trail.

He needed some kind of plan, and he needed it quickly.

17

NOELLE DERICCI SAT ON ONE OF THE BAR STOOLS IN HER HOTEL ROOM for the longest time, staring at her empty whiskey glass. All the damn stuff had done was give her heartburn.

Or maybe Flint had done that, the way he had disconnected their link. Or the mention of Luc Deshin, which disturbed her greatly.

Or maybe the whiskey had nothing to do with the heartburn. Maybe the heartburn had come from the walk that she had taken earlier through Tycho Crater.

She had done so many of these just on this trip alone that they blurred. The twisted rubble, the cautious mayors who believed their tragedy was the real tragedy. The lives, not just lost, but evaporated.

She swallowed hard. Her mouth tasted sour. The whiskey had been the exact wrong thing. Drinking never got her anywhere. If she wanted to be anesthetized, she could find a better way to do so. There were a whole pile of drugs that could shut off her emotions while leaving her reasoning intact.

Theoretically.

It was the "theoretically" that she didn't like.

Any more than she liked her schedule. Three more cities, three more dome repairs to see, three more craters in the middle of a once-thriving district.

All those lives.

She reached into the gift basket, annoyed that it even existed. Who gave a gift basket on an occasion like this?

A mayor who wanted to suck up to the woman who was, in reality, in charge of the Moon? Or someone on the mayor's staff who wanted the prominent visitor to be comfortable?

Or both?

DeRicci didn't know, and she didn't entirely care.

She opened the wrapping, found some locally grown produce—purple apples (why purple? What was wrong with red or green, for that matter?), purple grapes, and some kind of fruit she couldn't identify. She also found an orange with an Earth Alliance label in the peel. She took that instead of the local stuff.

With her heartburn, the last thing she needed was some weird-tasting apple that didn't agree with her.

She clutched the orange and stared at the apples for a moment. If the bad guys (as her office had started to call the unknown people behind the attacks) wanted to truly disrupt life on the Moon, they shouldn't have taken out the center of the domes. They should have taken out all the Growing Pits and agri-habitats outside the various domes.

They should have knocked out the food supply.

She supposed that would have been harder because all of those greenhouses and grow-plants and hydroponic warehouses were so well guarded.

And fewer people would have died.

She stood up, playing catch with that orange. Fewer people would have died *in the short term*. In the long term, everyone would have suffered. But they would have trusted the governments to take care of it. And it wouldn't have taken more than a few days to get relief supplies from Earth or Mars or both.

Still, the disruption would have been profound. And long-lasting. It would have taken years to rebuild the food supply, costing the domes millions.

Not that these attacks wouldn't cost millions. They would. But the surviving populations still ate well, and in the smaller cities and towns, they went about their lives as if nothing had happened.

No, what had happened on Anniversary Day was designed to murder as many people as possible.

The attacks on the mayors and on Celia Alfreda showed what the true intent was: It was to disrupt the governments down to their core.

To make the Moon completely non-functional. And to keep fear alive.

To make people do rash things, like consult with known criminals.

"Damn it, Miles," she muttered. She hated it when he went around her. He had done it more often than she liked to think about.

She set the orange on the bar.

What was she accomplishing here? What would she accomplish in those other cities besides making her heartburn worse, making her guilt worse?

She needed to appoint someone to handle the cleanup Moonwide. She needed a coordinator, someone who would glad-handle the surviving mayors and the interim-mayors, someone who was better at fielding sob stories and combining those with real action, getting plans approved, getting the rebuilding started.

The sooner the rebuilding got underway, the better for everyone.

She picked up the orange and put it back in the gift basket. She was going to go down to the hotel restaurant for dinner. She would have a good, warm, healthy meal, with no alcohol, and then she would have her travel assistant change her plans.

Tomorrow morning, she was heading home.

And then she would deal with Miles Flint.

18

SHE WASN'T SUPPOSED TO LEAVE HER DAD'S OFFICE, BUT SHE WAS HUNGRY. Talia regretted turning down her dad's offer of dinner before he left on his mysterious errands. She had been mad at him—he hadn't really taken her side in that whole school-fight thing. He said he admired her for standing up for friends, but maybe she should have thought twice about the time and the venue. After all, things were dicey for everyone right now.

She knew what he meant: He worried that in the heat of the moment, she would reveal her own status as a clone.

He had left it all up to her. She could tell everyone who she was or not, what her life had been like back in Valhalla Basin or not, that she was adopted *and* her dad's biological child or not.

So far, she had chosen to keep her background quiet. In fact, she couldn't see a time when she would reveal it, especially now, when tempers were so high. Since she couldn't imagine ever telling anyone who she was, she couldn't imagine letting the information slip in the heat of the moment either.

But she didn't reassure her dad about that. It irritated her that he worried about it, that he didn't trust her on this thing.

She had draped herself over her favorite chair, niggling at her homework. Ms. Rutledge had assigned everyone a written essay about bigotry and violence, due the following morning.

Talia hated writing. She saw no point in it. She always did vid essays whenever possible. But this time, Ms. Rutledge had said there'd been too much talking. She wanted everyone to quietly reflect on all that had happened, and perhaps learn from their mistakes.

Yeah, right. Like an essay would do that.

Talia had done some research, not that it helped. Her brain really wasn't on the science of bigotry. She wanted to keep looking for information about PierLuigi Frémont, or learn something new about Anniversary Day to prevent the new attacks.

Only her dad had told her she couldn't do anything without him present. He was afraid she'd leave a trail.

If she were honest with herself, she was afraid of that too. She'd left one before, when she was looking for her sister clones. She'd found several of them living very different lives from her, and then her dad told her about the risk she had put them under.

He had helped her bury her tracks, but too late. She had set off a different kind of investigation—not into the cloning her mother had done, but into one of the cloning companies.

She had learned her lesson then, although her dad was afraid that all she had learned was how to cover her tracks better.

On the small stuff, he was right; she did cover her tracks better. But now she left the big stuff for him.

And anything to do with Anniversary Day was the big stuff.

She sighed and set down the pad she'd been noodling on. What she really wanted to do was write a history of Kaleb Lamber's family, with a focus on their bigotry. But she knew that Ms. Rutledge wouldn't allow it.

This was one of those moments when Talia wished she had really good friends so she could at least share the idea with someone who would appreciate it, someone who wouldn't tell on her.

She stood, and debated for a brief moment. Her dad wanted her to stay in the room, but he couldn't regulate bodily functions like that. She had to leave for the bathroom, so it followed that she could head to the in-house kitchen area too, just to make herself a snack.

She supposed she could ask Rudra Popova to bring her something, but as her dad had told her repeatedly, Popova wasn't her assistant. She was Noelle DeRicci's assistant and as such, she had a really important job, more important than running errands for teenage girls.

She pulled open the door and looked around her. No one in the corridors. Of course, she couldn't tell if someone was monitoring the surveillance cameras. Someone probably was, but she wasn't going to do anything technically wrong—at least not by Security Building standards. She was only going to do something wrong by her dad's standards, and then only if she couldn't argue her way out of it.

The kitchen was to her left. She made a detour into the bathroom so that she could use it as an excuse (and just plain use it), then she headed to heat up something good. She'd learned over the past few months that there was always something yummy here, which her dad (and Detective Nyquist) said was unusual for a government building.

The kitchen was a small room, almost an afterthought, to the right of one of the other offices. A large refrigerator held a lot of fresh foods, the kind that were really expensive elsewhere in Armstrong. A cook-to-order unit had a basic menu, but right next to it stood an actual stove with a warning that flashed whenever someone touched it. The warning informed the user that they had to know how to operate the stove before trying anything.

Talia knew how to operate a stove—she'd learned from her mother years ago—but that warning on this stove always scared her silly. She opened the refrigerator door to see if someone had left something prepared, something she could reheat.

"Your father works here, doesn't he?"

Talia jumped. She hadn't realized that anyone else had come into the room.

She closed the door and turned around. A slender woman with wedge-cut black hair leaned against the wall, arms crossed. Her hair had reddish purple highlights that matched the trim on her black suit.

The woman smiled, then leaned forward, hand extended. "I'm Wilma Goudkins."

Talia stared at the outstretched hand, like she had seen her father do when he didn't approve of the person who owned it.

Goudkins finally pulled her hand back, then smiled again, softly. She probably thought the smile was conciliatory. Instead, it seemed embarrassed. "And you are?"

"I've never seen you before," Talia said coldly. She wasn't about to tell any stranger who she was.

"I haven't been here long," Goudkins said.

"Obviously." Talia looked her over carefully, didn't see any weapons, and so turned around. She opened the refrigerator door again.

"There's a leftover meat pie," Goudkins said.

The meat pie did look good, but Talia wasn't about to take it now. She removed an orange, then closed the door. She leaned over to the cook-to-order unit, punched in the number for the only thing that tasted remotely like food, and hoped it wouldn't take long.

She wasn't fond of the cook-to-order taquitos, but they were better than nothing.

"So you're here often enough that you don't have to put an ID into the cook-to-order unit," Goudkins said.

Talia rolled her eyes, happy her back was still to the woman. No one had set up the identification part of the cook-to-order unit because everyone figured that only authorized personnel would be on this floor. But again, she wasn't going to say that.

The unit beeped. Talia opened the drawer and removed six steaming taquitos. They smelled good, which told her just how hungry she was. Normally those things smelled like dirty socks.

"Are they any good?" Goudkins asked.

"Why would I make something that isn't good?" Talia asked. She put the taquitos on a tray and then added the orange. She grabbed a bottle of water, and carried it all to the door.

Instead of saying "excuse me" or politely asking Goudkins to move, Talia just waited. Finally, Goudkins smiled that uncertain smile again, and stepped to one side.

Talia walked past her and headed straight to Popova's desk. Goudkins probably had a reason to be here, but Talia was hoping she was unauthorized. The woman had annoyed her so much that Talia wanted to see an arrest.

Popova sat at her desk, her long black hair pulled back. She had big circles under her eyes, and she'd lost so much weight that she looked like she might break.

Talia's dad never said anything about the changes in Popova over the past few months, but Talia had noticed. One of the guards here said that Popova had been in love with the mayor and the mayor's death nearly broke her.

Talia had offered condolences when she found out. Popova had thanked her, teared up, and left the room. Later, DeRicci made Talia promise not to speak of Popova's relationship again.

"Hey," Talia said. "I got some crummy taquitos. You want one?"

Popova lifted her head and smiled. Unlike Goudkins' smile, this one was filled with good humor. "What an offer. Did they come from the cook-to-order unit?"

"How'd you guess?"

"Why don't you let me order you something edible from one of the restaurants around here?"

Talia smiled. "Then who would we palm these taquitos off on? That Goudkins woman?"

All the humor left Popova's face. "Did she talk to you?"

"Yeah," Talia said. "Is that a problem?"

Popova's mouth thinned. "What did she want to know?"

"If my dad worked here," Talia said. "I didn't answer her. Who is she?"

"One of the investigators the Earth Alliance keeps sending. She's the most annoying person." Popova stood, and handed Talia a small pad. "Here's a list of restaurants that we order from. Just get yourself something."

"Where are you going?" Talia asked.

"I'm going to tell that woman not to bother us," Popova said.

"Can I watch?"

Popova frowned at her. "I thought you were hungry."

"I am, but if she leaves the kitchen, I can heat up something from the fridge."

Popova laughed. "Come on then. Let's take care of this problem once and for all."

19

H'JITH TOOK A DIFFERENT ROUTE TO THE DOCKING BAY. ZAGRANDO HAD a hunch that the section H'Jith took him to was nowhere near the section where he had initially docked. If he hadn't already been on alert, he would have become so now.

He had no quick and obvious escape route, and if he hadn't had a map of the station on his links, he would have been lost. Even so, some of the passages that H'Jith took him through were not on the map.

All of the passages were brightly colored, however, and the colors seemed to have no relation to anything that Zagrando could tell. The earlier passages, through one of the storefronts (if, indeed, that's what it was) and through a back area, were a deep, rich brown. Then, within the pace of a single step, it became a vibrant lime, followed by a stunning fuchsia. Sometimes the colors accented each other, but most often they clashed. And all of them made H'Jith's multicolored orange look garish and loud.

Three doors led to the docking ring, but they were a different three doors according to Zagrando's map. They were a shiny silver with black etchings. He ran the etchings through his universal translation unit (not that it really translated everything, but it knew thousands of languages—ancient and modern), and got no translation at all. Either the etchings were decorative or they belonged to a language the program did not know.

H'Jith took him through the middle door, and they were in the docking area. Unlike most starbases, the docking area did not form a ring, but jutted out of certain sections, like a child's pouting lower lip.

Like the other docking area, this one had an airlock design as well, but Zagrando saw no guard or anyone who could be mistaken for a guard. He wondered, then, if the other section was for non-sanctioned or non-J'Slik vessels.

H'Jith stopped as they encountered another series of doors.

"I owe you honesty," H'Jith said. "I do not sell my personal vessels. I only sell certain ships. I do not even have for sale a vessel like my own."

"That's all right," Zagrando said. "I would still like to see yours."

H'Jith's tail, which had been slightly off the ground as they walked, settled on the floor with an audible thump.

"Let me at least show you my inventory," H'Jith said. "You might reconsider once you see the vast selection."

"I will not buy a ship until I see yours," Zagrando said.

"I understand," H'Jith said in a tone that implied it did not understand. "Still, look here."

It shoved against one of the doors with its left paw, and the door banged open, revealing a gigantic docking bay. Ships of all kinds and sizes extended off into the distance.

Zagrando remained at the door, staring at them. He noted some excellent—if dated—vessels up front, but farther back, he saw models so old he wondered if they could fly.

That sense he'd had from the moment he arrived, that sense of impending doom, finally became clear. He understood now that the risk wasn't of dying on Hellhole, but dying outside of it.

If he left Whiteley's ship here, then that ship would become the property of someone like H'Jith—probably of anyone who wanted to take on the Black Fleet. If he then bought a ship from H'Jith, H'Jith would know more about that ship than Zagrando. For all Zagrando could tell, the ships here all had flaws that might cause them to stall or break down not too far from Hellhole. Or perhaps they didn't move quickly and could be easily tracked.

One ship, even with up-to-date weaponry, couldn't outgun an organized group of ships from Hellhole. And he doubted that the ships for sale here, no matter what their model specifications were, actually had the highest speed range.

He could lose Whiteley's ship, pay out a small fortune for another ship, and then lose either that ship, all of his funds, or his life as he left Hellhole.

And contacting the Alliance wouldn't help him. Nor would contacting his handlers, because his handlers wouldn't be able to get him help quickly enough.

Zagrando wondered if H'Jith had purchased all of the ships here or if they had been stolen from people passing through. Zagrando had a hunch that most of them had been abandoned, like he was about to do with Whiteley's ship, or stolen according to one of the scenarios he had just come up with.

"You are right," Zagrando said. He needed to keep control of this meeting. "You have an amazing amount of inventory. But I have a personal policy. I like to see how a ship broker keeps his own ship before deciding to buy something from his inventory."

"You are a cautious human," H'Jith said. "Most humans are not that way."

Zagrando smiled. "I would assume most humans aren't comfortable on this place and would like to leave quickly."

That twinkle had returned to H'Jith's eyes. "You are also a wise human."

Zagrando bent his head slowly in mock nod, as if flattered by the compliment.

"But," H'Jith said, "you have made it clear that you have a meeting and must make this decision quickly. As you can see from my inventory, just inspecting the ships will take time. If you would like to leave quickly, then we should look at the ships available for purchase."

H'Jith was clearly beginning to think of this as a sales game. Fortunately, H'Jith enjoyed the process as much as human salespeople seemed to.

Zagrando knew he had to keep H'Jith focused on the sales part of the game to win this encounter.

So he kept his voice calm as he said, "I am in a hurry, but I can always have my meeting and then return. I have time to consider my purchase."

H'Jith made a small grunting sound. Zagrando wondered if that was the J'Slik sound of surprise.

"And if I don't like your inventory," Zagrando added, "I can always take the ship I came in. I at least know what its flaws are."

H'Jith's tail twitched in what Zagrando was beginning to see as displeasure. His human friends would call that a tell.

But Zagrando was not going to rely on it too much, because he had met other salespeople who had deliberately set up tells to mislead clients. Zagrando needed to remain focused on his own mission, so that he wouldn't be distracted by H'Jith.

Or by his need to get out of Hellhole as fast as possible.

"I assure you," H'Jith said, "my ships are as flawless as I can make them."

So the mention of "flaws" bothered him. Did that hit too close to home, perhaps? Was Zagrando sounding too canny? He didn't dare, for this plan to continue.

"I believe you," Zagrando said—and he did. He figured the ships were as flawless as they needed to be for whatever purpose H'Jith needed them for. "However, I will stick to my personal policy. I would like to see your own ship."

"I do not have one ship," H'Jith said.

"Then I would like to see your favorite ship," Zagrando said. H'Jith looked like it was about to say something, so Zagrando added, "and if you do not have a favorite, then I would like to see the ship you use the most for distance travel."

H'Jith sighed and its tail did not move. "I cannot talk you out of this."

"You can talk me out of it," Zagrando said. "But you are also talking yourself out of a sale."

H'Jith folded its front paws in front of its multicolored chest. For humans that was a serene pose, but not for H'Jith. Zagrando had the sense that H'Jith was very agitated.

"You are the first human I have encountered who strikes such a hard bargain," H'Jith said.

"Really?" Zagrando asked. "Because my species is known for tough deliberating."

H'Jith's mouth opened just a bit, the second time it had made that movement in a situation when a human would have smiled reassuringly. Zagrando wondered if H'Jith was trying to mimic the human smile and failing, or if this open-mouth movement was the J'Slik equivalent of a cold smile in the middle of a negotiation.

"Humans are not known for their toughness on Hellhole," H'Jith said, using the human name for the starbase.

"Surely, you do not call this place 'Hellhole' among yourselves," Zagrando said.

"We do not," H'Jith said. "We like it here. Humans never do."

"Well," Zagrando said, keeping his tone light. "That explains why there are so few of us here."

"It is your first time to Hellhole?" H'Jith asked, clearly trying to take the attention off their wrangle for just a moment.

"It is my first time to…" and then Zagrando tried to pronounce the J'Slik name. He knew he had mangled the name from H'Jith's small shudder, but H'Jith tilted its head again, apparently in surprise.

"And you do not want to flee?" H'Jith asked this with something like compassion. Apparently, it had decided it would become Zagrando's friend. And friends apparently understood how terrifying Hellhole was for humans.

"I would prefer to finish my business," Zagrando said calmly, "but it would seem that you're not interested in selling me a ship. So I'm sorry that I wasted your time."

He turned, hating that airlock-thing. He hoped that it wouldn't be like a real airlock, the kind of place that changed atmosphere with the touch of a button, because he was certain he was making H'Jith angry.

"Wait," H'Jith said. "I will show you my ship."

Zagrando stood for a moment, deliberately keeping his back to H'Jith. He knew how dangerous that maneuver was, but he used it as a gesture of either trust or naïveté. Or both. At least, that was how he hoped H'Jith would respond to it.

"Which ship?" he asked, as if he were no longer sure he would take H'Jith up on the offer. "Your favorite, or the one you use for distance travel?"

"I do not travel long distances," H'Jith said.

"Then how do you get your inventory?" Zagrando asked.

"I am a broker," H'Jith said. "Others come to me."

So most of the ships were stolen or abandoned, as Zagrando suspected.

"All right then," Zagrando said, and he slowly turned around. H'Jith stood with its upper paws pressed together, that nervous gesture that Zagrando had noted before. "Show me the ship you use the most."

"For travel," H'Jith said. "I will show you the one I use the most for travel."

"You live on your ship," Zagrando said with some surprise. "That's why you didn't want to show it to me."

"It is not fair to my family," H'Jith said, and Zagrando got the sense that it was finally speaking the truth. It kept its family on a ship because it didn't trust life here on Hellhole? Because it needed to escape quickly? Because it wanted its family to have an escape route?

Zagrando stared at it for a long moment. H'Jith shifted slightly, clearly uncomfortable. If Zagrando were truly the man he was portraying, he would have visited H'Jith's family ship.

But he couldn't be quite that ruthless, particularly with the idea floating in the back of his mind. He didn't want to put H'Jith's family at risk, either.

"All right," Zagrando said with as much reluctance as he could muster. "Take me to the ship you use for travel. Quickly. This negotiation has already taken too much of my time."

"It is my pleasure." H'Jith bowed slightly. But something flashed across its eyes. Taking Zagrando to the ship was not pleasure. Taking Zagrando there was coercion. H'Jith wanted the money.

And, Zagrando knew, H'Jith would make sure that Zagrando paid for this perceived slight.

Zagrando had to make sure that would never ever happen.

20

FLINT PICKED UP BURGERS AND CARRIED THEM INTO THE FIRST Unit of the Armstrong Police Department's Detective Unit like he still worked there. The office looked different than it had when he left. It had more cubicles because more officers had moved up to the unit—not because more officers deserved promotion, but because Chief Andrea Gumiela had decided that she needed more investigators after Anniversary Day.

He had never thought of Gumiela as visionary or even a good leader, but she had been right about that. And she had increased the call for more police officers. Somehow she had convinced the city to give her more money for scholarships and loans to the police academy.

It helped that she knew the temporary mayor.

He wound his way around the cubicles. The greasy scent of the burgers made his stomach growl. He'd splurged for real meat, from one of the cow farms in the center of the Moon. Expensive stuff, but not as expensive as the beef imported from Earth, brought on very speedy ships with tight schedules, delivering outrageously priced "real" food for the food snobs who thought anything Moon-grown or developed wasn't good enough.

It took him a few minutes to find Bartholomew Nyquist's office, even though Flint had been there a number of times before. Flint had contacted Nyquist about half an hour earlier, promising him dinner in exchange for a discussion.

Nyquist was the one who suggested the precinct.

Either Nyquist was extremely busy with work, or he didn't want to be seen with Flint. Or both.

They had an uneasy relationship. It was based on respect: Flint knew Nyquist was one of the best detectives on the Moon and Nyquist knew that Flint could find anything. But Nyquist did not approve of the fact that Flint had left the legal side of the job to brush against the shady side. Nor was Nyquist comfortable with the fact that Flint had paid Nyquist's medical bills after a Bixian assassination attempt. The city's health plan wouldn't provide the funding for the kind of rebuild and rehab that Nyquist needed to remain a functioning member of society. Besides, Flint always felt a bit guilty about that attack. He should have seen it coming.

Both men also had DeRicci between them. Nyquist was involved with her, but she often turned to Flint first in professional matters. It made both of them uncomfortable.

But DeRicci was her own woman and she was going to make her own choices, no matter what each man said to her.

No matter how senseless her choices were.

That last thought came with a surge of anger, which Flint tamped down. If he were giving advice to Talia, he would tell her to wait to make a decision until her emotions receded.

But Flint had a hunch these emotions wouldn't pass. Besides, he felt the press of time.

He peered into Nyquist's office. It looked like the man had been sleeping there—and smelled like it, too. Nyquist was sitting behind a desk littered with food wrappers, old coffee cups, and a pile of pads. A crumpled blanket covered one end of a sagging couch, and a group of shirts had been balled up in an approximation of a pillow.

Nyquist looked up at Flint, the circles under his eyes so deep that the scars from the attempted assassination—the ones that Nyquist refused to have removed—shone whitely against his skin.

Flint held up the bag of burgers. "Let's go to an interrogation room," he said. "It has to smell better than this place."

Nyquist smiled, then stood up. He carefully made his way around the desk, apparently not wanting to dislodge the mounds of anything, and came to Flint's side.

"What couldn't wait?" he asked.

To the point, as usual.

"I got some new information," Flint said. "Noelle said I could tell everyone about it and run the investigation if I wanted to."

That much was true. Whether or not he would imply to Nyquist that DeRicci wanted Nyquist to investigate the clones was another matter entirely.

"Wow, aren't we becoming the most important man in the room," Nyquist said.

He didn't sound bitter, although his words could be taken that way. Flint was glad they were discussing this in person rather than through links. He would have taken offense without the light tone Nyquist had in his voice.

"Are you on the payroll yet?" Nyquist asked, and this time, the tone wasn't light.

Flint smiled. "You know I don't need the money."

"Yeah," Nyquist said, "although I don't like being reminded of that."

Flint's money, and the way he had gotten it, was at the heart of the disapproval Nyquist felt toward him.

"But I wasn't asking about money," Nyquist said. "Payroll means you work for them. Have you taken the plunge?"

Even though he knew Nyquist was brilliant, Flint was always surprised at how intuitive the man was. Nyquist had gotten to the heart of why Flint had arrived, without Flint saying a word.

"No," Flint said. "I'm never going to work for anyone again."

"Yet Noelle put you in charge of the investigation." Nyquist pushed open the door to an interrogation room. It was one of the all-white rooms, which had nanoscrubbers to keep the filth off the walls. Someone somewhere had figured that sensory deprivation made criminals talk faster.

It probably wasn't true, but it sounded true. And people liked to do things that sounded true more than they liked to do things that were true.

"It's not that straightforward." Flint put the bag on the table. He propped the door open, not because he minded the room, but because he knew that most of the surveillance systems kicked in only when the door was closed.

Nyquist opened the bag and pulled out the wrapped burgers, along with the gigantic cups of coffee that Flint had insisted on. He'd survived on precinct coffee for too many years to ever drink it again.

"You're creepy, you know that," Nyquist said as he unwrapped the burger. "You remember how I like my burger."

Flint smiled and took his. "I don't remember. Talia taught me to keep a log of the things people like. She got mad every time I forgot."

Nyquist sat in one of the chairs. "That kid of yours has changed you."

"In a good way, I hope," Flint said.

"Jury's still out." Nyquist kicked one of the chairs toward Flint. "Sit down. I promise I won't arrest you."

"I'd like to see you try," Flint said with a smile. He sat down. He was surprisingly nervous. He made his decision to go around DeRicci and the first thing he did was talk to her lover.

But Flint needed Nyquist. Flint needed Nyquist to move the police investigation in the right direction. Even though Nyquist wasn't officially in charge, he had a lot of clout both by virtue of his personality and his closure rate. He struggled against authority—something he used to have in common with DeRicci—but he was popular among his fellow detectives.

Flint unwrapped his burger. Juice flowed off it and onto the wrapper. Even if he spilled, the scent of the burger would not remain in this room. Unlike Nyquist's office, this room smelled fresh, as if it had been recently scrubbed. It probably had—more of that sensory deprivation thing.

"The reason I wanted to talk to you," Flint said, "is that I found out something rather startling about zoodeh. The quarantined vessels aren't the only source of it in the Earth Alliance."

He explained what Luc Deshin told him. Nyquist's eyes widened, but he didn't say anything. He simply listened as he devoured his burger.

When Flint finished, Nyquist said, "We shouldn't have missed that."

"I know," Flint said. "I feel the same way."

Nyquist nodded, his cheeks just a bit red. He seemed furious at himself. He took a deep breath, crumpled the wrapper, and set it aside for the recycler. Clearly, he was gathering himself, setting his emotions aside, forcing himself to concentrate on the investigation now, not on the mistakes of the past.

"You still have informants," he said, surprising Flint. Unlike De-Ricci, who had demanded that Flint tell him the source, Nyquist knew the source wasn't exactly legal, and didn't seem to mind.

"Yeah," Flint said.

"You keeping this one close to the vest?" Nyquist asked.

"For the moment," Flint said. "But I will tell you this: My informant has access to a lot of information. He wants to know the bomb components, because he think he can trace them through his networks."

Nyquist smiled slowly. "He wants to know the bomb components, does he?"

Flint didn't smile in return. He wondered if Nyquist thought the request naïve, if Nyquist thought that Flint's informant would then use that information to build his own bomb. Flint was about to say something when Nyquist added,

"We'd love to know the components, too."

"You don't know?" Flint asked.

"No," Nyquist said. "We think all the bombers did what Ursula did. We think they attached something to easy-to-convert something or other, something that would become a bomb with the right trigger."

158

Flint nodded. He had heard some of that, but he figured he'd leave the bomb details to the bomb squads. "I'm sure the dome collapses didn't help."

"We have no idea what we're looking at." Nyquist leaned back. "I even went back to the old warehouse from the first bombing four years ago to see if we missed anything."

"Had you?"

"Hell if I know. What I do know is this: We're never going to know what caused that bomb to blow, and we're never going to know about the others. I think that's deliberate. I think the Etaen issues around the first bombing and the appearance of those clones of PierLuigi Frémont were deliberate distractions, so we'd look the wrong direction. We looked in the wrong direction after the first bombing, and we've been chasing our tails with this one."

Flint raised his eyebrows. "And you think that's deliberate."

"So do you," Nyquist said, "or you wouldn't be here. What do you really want, Miles?"

Here it was: the opportunity to tell Nyquist everything. Flint had to decide right now if he should trust the man completely or not.

"We've been working on the clones, and honestly, getting nowhere," Flint said. "We thought they were about PierLuigi Frémont, about someone using him to scare us all or to make this worse somehow."

"It's not?" Nyquist asked.

"Are you familiar with designer criminal clones? Order up your favorite criminal, the perfect one for the crime at hand?" Flint's heart was pounding. Here was his gamble: Had DeRicci talked to Nyquist and sworn him to secrecy?

Flint couldn't quite imagine that. DeRicci kept secrets, exactly the way she was instructed to keep them. If she could tell no one, she told no one.

End of story.

"Designer clones have been around since cloning started," Nyquist said. He was clearly thinking out loud. "Mostly it's illegal. Not just because people try to pick parts and glue them together as if a clone is some kind of robot, but also because the truly famous people, the ones everyone wants to clone, own their own DNA. If they sell their DNA, the designer clone is legal. But most famous people never sell their DNA."

"Yeah," Flint said. "And people like PierLuigi Frémont cannot be cloned. That's an Earth Alliance law as well. If the criminal has not been rehabilitated, then he or his heirs cannot sell his DNA."

"Yet you're saying someone is doing it, that this DNA did not come from the heirs." Nyquist set his coffee down. "That it's some kind of racket."

"Yes," Flint said, waiting for Nyquist to catch up to him.

"I should have gotten notification. All legal and security entities inside the Earth Alliance should have gotten notification," Nyquist said.

"I don't think the cloning or the sales are happening inside the Earth Alliance," Flint said.

Nyquist turned gray. He rubbed his fingers across his mouth, then swore softly. "Because all you need is one," he said. "Slow grown. Trained."

Flint nodded. "Who is going to notice a thief with a vague resemblance to one of the more famous thieves in the Alliance? Especially if he's younger, dressed differently, and speaking current slang?"

"There's no guarantee here, though," Nyquist said. "You can't be sure that because a clone shares the DNA with his famous originator, the clone will act in the same way. Sorry, Miles, I'm a big believer in environment."

"Me, too," Flint said. "But look at it. These clones are made in bulk."

"Raised in bulk," Nyquist said.

"And not human." Flint hated saying that. Because they were human. He'd always known it intellectually, but Talia had proven it to him. "Under the law, anyway."

"You're talking Earth Alliance law," Nyquist said.

"Do you know anywhere that gives clones the same rights as the original?" Flint asked.

"Not without a lot of legal mumbo jumbo," Nyquist said. "And the Earth Alliance is the most progressive place I know for the legal mumbo jumbo side of things."

"Yeah," Flint said.

Nyquist stood up. "You're saying they raise clones in bulk, like cattle, kill the ones that won't go with the program, and sell the rest."

"I'm guessing," Flint said, "but that's the only way this all makes sense. At least to me."

"Given the information from your informant," Nyquist said.

"That too," Flint said.

Nyquist shook his head. "That seems like a lot of work to me. Why not build an android or use something else to do your big theft?"

"Androids won't work," Flint said. "No one can seem to make them sophisticated enough."

He'd studied their systems in the past, and he'd found that there was still some kind of limitation in artificial intelligence that made some humans nervous.

"I liked it better when we thought one nutcase created the clones specifically for this job." Nyquist grabbed his coffee cup and swirled it. "What you're telling me is that there is a nutjob who wanted the clones for this job—"

"And waited more than twenty years for them," Flint said.

"That's what I don't get," Nyquist said. "You have to be one cold S.O.B. And now you're telling me there are enough cold S.O.Bs to make designer criminal clones into some kind of market category."

Flint shrugged. "I suspect most of them are used for other things, like creating your own team of pickpockets."

"Fagan for the modern era," Nyquist said.

Flint actually had to reference the word "Fagan," and he realized then that Nyquist was referring to an ancient Earth novel, one still taught in schools. "Yeah, I guess."

But Nyquist had moved on. "That one nutjob and then whoever—whatever—is making the clones. Of all the things you could have told me, Miles, this scares me more than anything."

"It scares me too," Flint said. "Someone has designed these clones as weapons."

Nyquist looked at Flint over the cup. Flint tried to hold off a blush. His pale skin betrayed him more than he wanted it to, particularly when someone like Nyquist, who could see things clearly, looked at him with that level of speculation.

"You made that point earlier, without saying it," Nyquist said. "There's something you're not telling me here."

Yes, Flint imagined himself saying. *Noelle told me that you could handle the case, but the clones were something classified. I'm just bending the rules a little.*

"Yes, there's something I'm not telling you," Flint said. "And for now, I'd like to keep it that way."

Nyquist set the coffee cup down without drinking anything. "You want me to look into the designer criminal clones, don't you?"

"In a specific way," Flint said. "I want you to look at past investigations here on the Moon, in particular. See if any arrests have led back to some kind of organization or ring."

"What if that organization belongs to your informant friend?" Nyquist asked.

"Nothing would surprise me." Flint sighed, then decided to add one more layer of honesty. "I'm tired of the way this investigation is going nowhere, Bartholomew. Some of that is our fault, but a lot of it isn't. And I'm done playing nice. I'm going to piss off a lot of people in the next few weeks. If you don't want to be part of that, say so now."

Nyquist smiled slowly. "'Piss off a lot of people,'" he repeated. "Like your informant friend."

"Possibly," Flint said.

"And Noelle."

Damn that man was perceptive. "Yes."

"Aren't you worried that I'll tell Noelle something you don't want her to hear?"

"No," Flint said.

"Because you're not worried about me?" Nyquist asked.

"Because she already knows I'm mad at her. If something she doesn't like comes at her from the investigative side, she'll know it comes from me."

"You're positive?" Nyquist asked.

"Oh, yeah," Flint said. "And if she doesn't like it, well then, too bad. I don't work for her."

Nyquist leaned back. His expression had become unreadable. "I don't work for her either, Miles."

"I know," Flint said. "But you're close."

"I have no idea if we're close," Nyquist said. "I suspect you're closer to her than I am."

It was a night for honesty. "Noelle and I have never been involved."

"That's not what I mean," Nyquist said.

Flint didn't know how to respond to that. He never had known how to deal with that undercurrent between him and Nyquist. It had started before Nyquist started seeing DeRicci. He and Nyquist hadn't entirely trusted each other then either, but they had respected each other.

Apparently, they still did.

"No one has really taken charge of this investigation," Flint said. "I've been given a dozen reasons why, most of them coming down to the way that this agency can't do something without that agency's approval. I'm tired of it. I don't belong to any agency. So I'm going to run the investigation. If people don't like it, then fine. They can ignore me."

"Or arrest you," Nyquist said.

"If I do something illegal," Flint said. "I don't plan to."

"Yet you've done illegal things before," Nyquist said.

Flint looked at him, purposely keeping his expression neutral. "Have I?"

This time, Nyquist didn't respond directly.

"It doesn't matter, Miles," Nyquist said. "I guess that's what I'm trying to say in my own inept fashion. I'm going to help you. If it costs my job, so be it. I can't live this way either."

"And if it costs your relationship with Noelle?" Flint asked.

Nyquist shrugged. "You get older, you realize that things change."

"That's a rather bloodless way to look at life," Flint said.

"I prefer to think of it as realistic," Nyquist said.

"Does Noelle know about your realistic point of view?" Flint asked.

"She's not at issue here," Nyquist said. "What's going on outside us, the fact that we can't catch these criminals, that's the issue. I'm with you, Miles, all the way to the end if need be. We will catch them."

Flint smiled. He was more relieved than he realized. "And we will make them pay," he said.

21

Uzvot took Rastigan to the site where the attacks against the Peyti originated. Uzvot didn't have to take Rastigan there; in fact, Rastigan had the sense that Uzvot was jeopardizing her position with her own people.

But it was Uzvot's decision to make. Besides, Rastigan wanted to see this.

She suited up so that she could handle Peyla's toxic atmosphere, and trudged more than a kilometer to the origin site. There was no way to hide her presence. The suit alone, with the creaks and the groans it made in the strange air, made her conspicuous.

Uzvot stayed at her side, not leading the way. Since the Peyti were all about small details, Rastigan wondered if Uzvot's decision to walk beside her had a subtlety to it—a silent complaint that her fellow Peyti would understand: *The human insisted on seeing the site; I do not approve, that is why I am not leading her here, but merely accompanying her.*

Rastigan did not ask because it was none of her business. Uzvot was doing her a favor—again, for a reason that Rastigan did not entirely understand—and she was going to take advantage of it.

The suit was bulky. She should have been used to wearing one by now, since she wore one everywhere she went. But Uzvot insisted that

Rastigan wear a full environmental suit instead of a thin one that provided minimal protection while allowing for freedom of motion.

As she walked, Rastigan had the suit run a continual diagnostic, in case the atmosphere around her shifted composition. She suspected it might, just because of Uzvot's insistence on the suit, but she didn't compulsively watch the numbers.

Instead, she monitored everything around her.

The franticness she had noted among the Peyti investigators had lessened up here. They did not crouch and examine the soil. Instead they touched things like tree trunks and had soft discussions that Rastigan could only catch bits of.

Mostly, they were talking about weapon range and power. Somehow, that chilled her.

Then she crested the last rise and felt even colder. She saw a weapon she had only seen in histories, something native to Peyti. She had once explained it to a student as a catapult crossed with a dedicated laser.

In other words, the impression she had had—that the Peyti had been catapulted from something and then shot—was correct. They had been strapped into that thing, then flung forward with incredible force as the weapon itself fired on them.

Even if the weapon hadn't fired, the Peyti would have died. Their physiology was delicate: They broke bones when a human shook their hands with a normal (human) grip. Crashing against a wall or a tree, or just plain landing too hard, would probably have killed them.

The laser itself was deliberate overkill.

She glanced at Uzvot. Uzvot did not look at her, but stared at the weapon, her mouth flat. She carried her mask, useless in this atmosphere, in her right hand. And because she did, the full range of her expression became visible to Rastigan.

Her entire face was threaded with soft blue. Much as Uzvot tried to hide her emotional reaction, this entire scene broke her heart.

On the crest of the next hill were the buildings that Rastigan had seen earlier. Unlike most Peyti buildings, these were quite utilitarian, with no obvious design at all. They looked like buildings copied from early human colonies, made with limited materials, designed only to house the colonists and to do little else.

In the valley between the two hills, Peyti gathered. It took Rastigan a moment to realize that half of the Peyti had corralled the other half.

I don't want to take you closer, Uzvot sent. *Does your visor have magnifying capability?*

It took Rastigan a moment to understand. Uzvot meant the helmet of the environmental suit.

Yes, she sent as she stopped. She switched the helmet to a scope lens and looked into the valley.

She almost asked what she was looking for, then realized she didn't have to. It was quite obvious.

All of the Peyti acting as security wore various versions of a dark suit and each carried a single handheld weapon that Rastigan had seen before.

But the others surprised her. The others did look the same. They were the same height and weight. They had the same posture and even held their hands in the same position.

The most shocking thing, however, was their faces. The expressions differed—a few seemed downcast, others neutral, and one or two had turquoise lines throughout their skin—but the faces themselves were identical.

More clones? Rastigan sent.

Exactly the same type, Uzvot sent. *Young adult versions of Uzvekmt.*

They were the ones doing the killing? Rastigan sent, feeling a little shaky.

Yes, Uzvot sent.

What were they doing, just lining up and killing each other? Rastigan's heart rate had increased. She was more upset than she realized.

We don't think so, Uzvot sent. *We believe the ones killed were undesirable.*

Which means what? Rastigan sent.

We will find that out, Uzvot sent.

They're young, Rastigan sent. *Were they unsupervised?*

We do not think so, Uzvot sent. *A ship left the area shortly after Gallen contacted the Earth Alliance by emergency link.*

And you believe the supervisors were on that ship. Rastigan scanned the faces. They did not look evil. But then, she didn't know what evil, insane Peyti looked like.

We do not know. It seems likely.

Which also means they were monitoring all link channels. Rastigan frowned. She was trying to remember if the emergency message had come through a secure link, and she couldn't recall.

She supposed it didn't, since the message had routed through the habitat's emergency links.

You're going to track this ship, right? Rastigan sent.

I don't know, Uzvot sent. *I am not in charge of this investigation.*

Rastigan nodded. Now it was her turn to be deeply unsettled. Uzvot had been unsettled when she recognized the clones as clones of Uzvekmt.

But this, this mass killing in a people not known for any kind of violence, was disturbing enough. The fact that she saw before her young adult clones of the Peyti's most notorious mass murderer had sent alarm bells through her head.

Back in the habitat, Rastigan sent, *you mentioned PierLuigi Frémont. You realize there is a parallel here.*

Uzvot did not respond. So Rastigan turned toward her and saw Uzvot slowly moving her head up and down. A nod. Most Peyti did not know what a nod was, and Uzvot knew that.

She was communicating in a way that would not get her in trouble.

You have warned your people, right? Rastigan sent.

They know, Uzvot said.

Rastigan stared at the identical faces more than a kilometer away from her. Then she looked up at the compound. It looked lived in. Fresh dirt surrounded the buildings, remains of meals sat on outdoor tables.

She was cold, and she shouldn't have been, given that she was wearing an environmental suit.

I have to go back to Alliance headquarters, Rastigan sent.

I understand, Uzvot sent. She did not move. She was not happy about the way the information would escape, but she seemed to know why it was necessary.

Uzvekmt, clones. I cannot assume that this is a coincidence, Rastigan sent.

We Peyti do not believe in assuming anything, Uzvot sent. She did not look at Rastigan.

Rastigan placed a gentle gloved hand on Uzvot's shoulder, and then pivoted. She would follow their footsteps back the way they had come.

Nor, Uzvot added through a different link, *do we believe in coincidence.*

Rastigan glanced back at Uzvot. Uzvot hadn't moved.

Yet she had given Rastigan her blessing.

Something horrible was going on. They both knew it, and now they had to let the Alliance know.

Because if it had happened among the Peyti and among the humans, it might be happening elsewhere in the Alliance.

And Rastigan had no idea exactly what that meant.

22

H'JITH TOOK ZAGRANDO THROUGH A FEW MORE SIDE PASSAGES AND an odd little door that both had to duck through to get inside. This section of the docking bay had an entirely different feel than the other sections Zagrando had seen. The colors—while still bright—blended into each other as if an artist had swirled them together with a brush.

The effect was softer, and not as jarring. Zagrando had the sense that he had entered a section of Hellhole that most outsiders never saw.

Oddly, knowing that made him feel calmer.

H'Jith led him along some twisty paths that went past several vessels of a type that Zagrando had never seen before. He hoped that H'Jith's vessel was at least familiar. If not, Zagrando's troubles would grow worse.

Then H'Jith stopped in front of an extremely expensive space yacht. Zagrando hadn't seen anything that elaborate in person. He'd heard of them, of course, but hadn't known anyone rich enough to own one.

He certainly doubted H'Jith was that rich as well, although, given the number of ships it had for sale, it might have been.

The yacht was half the size of Whiteley's cruiser, but had a sleeker form and was probably faster. Which was good.

The yacht was also hot pink, which was, apparently, a favorite color of the J'Slik. The yacht shone, and looked like it hadn't been used much.

Or, at least, it hadn't been used much since its color had changed. Zagrando couldn't imagine that hot pink being standard issue.

"Now you've seen it," H'Jith said. "Let us return to my inventory."

Zagrando ignored H'Jith and walked around the yacht until he found the entry. He put his hand on it. Of course, it did not open to his touch.

"When I said I wanted to see your ship," Zagrando said, "I didn't mean the exterior. I want to see how well you keep up your personal ship. Plus I want to see the cockpit, so that I know what kind of additions and modifications you prefer."

H'Jith's head tilted backward slightly, its wide mouth thinning. Then it sighed.

"All right," H'Jith said. It put its three right claws into a small, three-pronged opening on the side.

Zagrando cursed silently. He would either need H'Jith's claws to open the ship on his own or he would have to get H'Jith to continue opening it for him. He didn't like either option.

The door slid open with a hiss, revealing a glowing red interior.

"You first," Zagrando said, as if he were being generous. He just wanted to make certain there were no booby traps for strangers inside this vessel.

The yacht had no steps. H'Jith put its upper paws on either side of the door, then used its tail to lever itself inside.

Zagrando placed both hands on the floor, then lifted himself with his arms, clambering into the ship like a man pulling himself out of a swimming pool.

H'Jith waited at the airlock door, tapping it with a claw. It opened as Zagrando stood.

The interior of the ship was dark. Lights came on as H'Jith led the way.

"Crew quarters first? Cabins? Or the cockpit?" it asked.

"The cockpit will tell me more than anything," Zagrando said. "So if you want to close this deal quickly, then we start with the cockpit and if I need more information, we visit other sections."

He touched the middle finger of his left hand to his right wrist, activating a chip sensor. He usually didn't use internal sensors because they could alert a system monitoring for such things, but he wanted to do it here.

He needed to know if anyone else was on board.

H'Jith's signature showed up in the right corner of Zagrando's right eye as, appropriately enough, an orange blob. Zagrando's signature followed, a fuzzy purple. Long ago, he had set the colors to reflect not just body heat, but species as well.

He expanded the signal area to include the entire ship, and saw no other blobs. He would try to confirm that inside the cockpit.

As they walked through the corridor, though, he shut down the chip. Cockpits often had more technology than the rest of a ship. And a ship like this would have the latest gadgets, even if H'Jith chose not to use them.

The cockpit was in the nose of the ship, which Zagrando always believed to be a dangerous design. He preferred ships with cockpits buried in the interior. That way no weapon could take out the cockpit with a single shot.

Clearly, this yacht was not designed for battle, but for leisure.

All the better.

The cockpit itself was huge. A crew of ten could fly this thing. But a small console blinked up front, between two open portals. Right now, they showed the interior of the docking bay. No other ships were close to this one. Either H'Jith paid for privacy or no one else had the money (or the permission) to dock in this area.

Or, perhaps, there weren't enough ships to fill the entire bay.

Zagrando didn't know and he hoped he wouldn't find out.

"Big," he said. "Clean."

It was clean. In fact, much of the cockpit looked like it had never been used. That worked in Zagrando's favor.

"Do you fly this yourself?" he asked.

"Usually I hire a pilot," H'Jith said. "I prefer to broker ships, not fly them."

Even better.

"Does your pilot fly from this console?" Zagrando asked, standing in front of the main console.

"No," H'Jith said. "This one."

It touched the small console, and the entire thing lit up. So did the console that Zagrando was standing in front of. He recognized all of the symbols on it: This yacht had been built to Earth Alliance specs.

He tapped the pilot lock, which had not been activated. H'Jith hadn't lied. Anyone could fly this yacht.

"Shame to waste such a lovely console," Zagrando said. He slid his fingers across as if he were admiring it when in fact, he had opened the controls. He tapped his fingertips over the locks, engaging them so he was the only person who could run this ship.

"We do not need something that big," H'Jith said, apparently unaware of what Zagrando was doing. H'Jith did not look at the console beside it, which had jumped to life, nor did it come over to Zagrando's side to monitor him.

"Still," Zagrando said, "this is quite an amazing ship, and quite well designed. With very little training, anyone could run it."

"I have no interest," H'Jith said. "I hire pilots. It is a perk of my job."

"I'm sure it is," Zagrando said. He tapped a few more controls, locking down the ship. Now no one could enter—or leave—without Zagrando's permission.

Then he tapped the emergency bar. It flared up, just like he expected it to. The cockpit defense controls were the same on all Earth Alliance ships. He hit *miniprison* and directed it at the other life form.

Bars of light appeared around H'Jith.

"Hey!" H'Jith grabbed at the bars, then moved its paws away, clearly in pain. "What are you doing?"

"Stealing your ship," Zagrando said. "It shouldn't be that hard to figure out. I know you've done the same thing to hundreds of others over the years."

"I've never stolen a ship from anyone in my life!" H'Jith said, reaching for the bars again and, again, pulling its paws away in pain.

"You know," Zagrando said, "I can make those bars even closer together so that you won't be able to move at all."

"You wouldn't do that," H'Jith said.

"And you wouldn't lie, either, would you?" Zagrando asked. He shut the door to the cockpit and sealed it. Then he set up the automated system so that the ship would make the usual requests to leave Hellhole. That way, he would get the commands correct.

"I don't pilot," H'Jith said. "How could I steal?"

"You already told me," Zagrando said, studying the navigational maps. "You hire someone to do the flying for you."

"I don't. I never would. I'm a broker!"

"And how many of those ships you showed me were stolen, H'Jith?"

"I don't know," H'Jith said and then tilted its head back in obvious distress. The moment it said those words, it knew it had made a mistake. "I'm a broker. The ships get brought to me."

"And you don't check the license or registration, do you? You don't care." Zagrando found a nearby resort that catered to humans. The Black Fleet would follow him to Hellhole, but it would take them a while to figure out how he left the place and even longer to figure out which ship he actually took.

He would get a few hours of advantage.

But then, a few hours was all he needed.

"I do care, I do," H'Jith said. "None of the ships I sell have valid registrations."

"For the J'Slik," Zagrando said. "They lack valid J'Slik registrations, which are all that matter here. You never check for Earth Alliance registrations."

"I'm not a member of the Earth Alliance," H'Jith said. "Why would I check for that? I only do business here."

"And by 'business,' you mean you sell ships to unsuspecting customers, then follow them off Hellhole and rob them blind."

"I do not!" H'Jith shuddered, then looked—wild-eyed—at the bars around it. "I don't."

The ship rose. Zagrando shut all the portals then monitored the departure on the console itself. The jutting lip of this part of the docking bay slid open and the ship eased into space.

"That's right," Zagrando said. "You stay here. You just give the name and the make of the ship to some friends of yours, and they do what they want with your former client, most likely killing him. Then they bring the ship back to you, the ship broker, and you pay them their fee."

H'Jith's shuddering got worse. It tried to make itself smaller by holding its paws against its side.

"What do you want?" It asked, no longer denying how it ran its business.

"I want your help," Zagrando said, looking up from the console.

H'Jith's frightened gaze met his. "This is a stupid way to ask for it."

"And calling a person who holds you prisoner stupid isn't one of the smarter moves in the universe, either," Zagrando said.

H'Jith closed its eyes. The shuddering didn't stop, but it slowed down a bit. Then H'Jith opened its eyes.

"How can I help?" it asked in its business voice.

"Ah," Zagrando said with a smile, "I thought you would never ask."

23

THE ELEVATOR DOORS OPENED ONTO DERICCI'S FLOOR IN THE SECURITY Building. Flint stepped out, feeling tired. Not physically tired. Discouraged. He had wasted too much time pursuing this investigation in the wrong direction, and he had done so without the correct information.

If he had known about designer criminal clones, then he could have made a lot of connections faster. If he had thought the entire zoodeh mess through, he would have found the other sources of zoodeh in the Earth Alliance quicker and maybe made some connections.

Flint had tried to keep that discouragement out of his meeting with Nyquist. Nyquist was one of the best detectives on the Moon, and he had contacts no one else did.

But he was also involved with DeRicci, and Flint didn't want Nyquist to tell DeRicci about Flint's mood.

Flint actually felt betrayed. He wondered how much other information—important information—DeRicci had withheld from him, citing some kind of stupid need-to-know basis.

She used to be a detective. She knew that the more information an investigator had, the better the investigation. The fact that she had withheld something as important as the clones disturbed Flint deeply.

And made him realize how far DeRicci had gone, from detective to Chief Security Officer for the Moon, to a politician fighting to survive.

In the past, she would have ignored the confidentiality requests. She would have seen how important it was to find whoever had done this.

Now, she was weighing Earth Alliance secrets against the good of the Moon. The good of Armstrong.

He didn't like it.

Flint turned a corner, expecting to see a few staffers, busy at work. Instead, he found Popova still at her desk, Talia sitting across from her. The remains of a meal covered the desktop, and they both were laughing.

He wasn't sure what shocked him more: that Popova had eaten a meal at her desk or that she was laughing.

And then he remembered that he had told Talia to stay in his office.

"What are you doing?" he asked.

Talia jumped, and he understood why. All of the frustration and disappointment he felt with DeRicci and the stalled investigation had come out in his tone. He couldn't call the words back, and he wasn't sure he wanted to.

He at least wanted his daughter to listen to him.

"Um," Talia said. "I got hungry."

"I gave you a chance to eat before I left." He couldn't quite set the irritation aside. Not that he really wanted to.

"I got hungry later," she said.

"I'm the one who invited her here," Popova said.

"I don't need you making excuses for my daughter," Flint said. "She's been acting up all day."

Even though that was entirely true, she had done the right thing at school. But she had done it in the wrong environment, endangering herself. He worried about her more than he wanted to.

"Go to my office," he said to Talia.

She got up, her mouth open slightly, as if she'd never heard him talk like that before. Maybe he never had, not in this way.

She walked past him, head held high. In spite of himself, he felt admiration. It was hard to tame this girl's spirit, no matter what she faced.

Still, he didn't watch her make her way to his office. Instead, he glared at Popova.

"I don't need you circumventing orders I've given my daughter," he snapped at her.

Popova stood. She piled the dishes onto each other. "I don't think you should be yelling at her."

"The way I treat her is none of your business."

"She handled herself really well tonight," Popova said as if he hadn't spoken. "She left the office to use the restroom, and got approached by one of the Earth Alliance investigators. She didn't answer any questions."

"She got approached in the restroom?" Flint asked.

"I don't know," Popova said primly, which convinced him that she was lying for Talia.

"So she got approached in the kitchen," he said, and he didn't make it a question. Popova bent her head and gathered the silverware. Her movements were as good as a yes. He would deal with Talia on that later. "What did the investigator want?"

"She wanted to know if you worked here," Popova said. "And honestly, if she heard you a few minutes ago, she would know that you do. 'Get to my office' indeed."

"I don't work here," Flint snapped. "You provided me with space."

"And you decorated it," Popova said.

"If I work here, then someone should damn well pay me." He took a deep breath. He wasn't angry at Popova. He was angry at DeRicci.

Logically, he should take Talia home. But he wasn't quite ready to do that.

"So," he said, "that Earth Alliance investigator is still here."

"They will be until the chief comes back," Popova said.

"That's why you're still here," he said.

"Fortunately, I don't have a life." That sounded bitter. And considering the depth of the mourning she had experienced, she had the right to sound that way. "And there's a couch in this room."

In spite of himself, Flint glanced at it. "You're going to spend the night?"

She shrugged. "I don't want them to snoop."

"I'm pretty sure I can prevent that," he said. "Where are they?"

"You're not authorized to talk to them," Popova said, her voice rising.

"I'm not authorized to do anything," Flint said. "I don't work for you, remember?"

Then he pivoted and walked down the hallway. If Popova wouldn't tell him where the Earth Alliance investigators were, then he would just have to find them on his own.

Maybe DeRicci didn't want to work with them, but he did. This looming threat was too important for politics.

If someone else could solve it, then he was all for it.

He was tired of living in fear. He suspected everyone else was too.

24

DeRicci sat alone in the dining room of the hotel, at a table that overlooked the edge of the crater. Before she came here, she would have thought it weird to stare at Moon rock throughout her meal, but it wasn't.

It was beautiful.

The crater's side had multicolored mineral deposits running through the strata. The restaurant's windows and lighting accented the colors, but didn't add to them.

The information in the little restaurant audio links told her that the original colonists decided to leave the crater walls intact, and mine for the minerals in other parts of the crater, digging the ground a little deeper so that the housing could actually have a foundation.

DeRicci got the sense that she was looking at a small fortune that the city founders—and by extension, the current government—decided not to touch.

The meal proved both relaxing and an antidote to her heartburn. She did not order any alcohol, not even a local wine made from those same purple grapes, nor did she allow any of her assistants to sit with her. She dined alone on chicken cooked with those purple apples (they were spicy), local potatoes, and a soup that she couldn't identify.

She was just considering dessert when Popova contacted her through their secure links.

Forgive me, sir, Popova sent, always formal. *I hope I'm not waking you.*

DeRicci sometimes doubted that she would ever sleep—really sleep—again, but of course she didn't let Popova know that.

I'm having a late dinner, she sent. *Are there problems?*

It was an unnecessary question, since Popova wouldn't have contacted her this late otherwise.

I just had the strangest interaction with Flint, Popova sent.

DeRicci felt cold. She pushed her plate aside, then waved off the waiter walking over with a dessert tray.

When was this? DeRicci sent.

Not five minutes ago, Popova sent.

DeRicci nodded. She should have expected something. Flint had acted strange after DeRicci told him the information on the clones had been classified. It was almost as if she had offended him somehow.

What happened? DeRicci sent.

Talia was here, Popova sent, *and one of the damn Earth Alliance investigators cornered her, trying to get information out of her.*

I hope you told them she was off-limits, DeRicci sent, knowing how crazy Flint could get about his daughter.

I didn't have a chance, Popova sent. *Talia did just fine, by the way. She wouldn't be interrogated. She refused to answer questions, and then she walked away.*

DeRicci wished she could see Popova. She almost put the link on visual, but the restaurant felt unprotected, even though she was alone here. It was harder to keep a holographic image secure than it was an internal link. She didn't know the technical reasons, just that her security team had warned her more than once to keep the most confidential conversations link-only.

Then she came to me, Popova sent. *I got dinner for us, and I calmed her down. I planned to talk to the Earth Alliance investigators when we finished eating, but Flint came in before that. He got mad at Talia—*

He what? He never got mad at his daughter. DeRicci thought that was a failing. Kids needed discipline, and as smart and precocious as

181

Talia was, she also walked that fine line between brilliant and impossible. Flint saw almost everything she did as brilliant, but DeRicci would have labeled a lot of Talia's behavior as impossible.

He got mad at her, Popova sent. *I thought it weird, too. He seemed like he was angry when he got here.*

DeRicci sighed. Of course he was. He had been angry at DeRicci when he cut the connection.

Then, Popova sent, *after he got angry with her, he went to see the Earth Alliance Investigators.*

To yell at them, DeRicci sent. *That's completely in character. I think—*

No, Popova sent. *Normally I would have thought that, too. But I got the sense that something else was going on. He seemed less angry at them than he was with me.*

You sensed this? DeRicci asked. *Or you know it?*

It was what he said to me, Popova sent. *He said that he didn't work for us, that he could do what he wanted.*

Technically, Flint was right. He was a private citizen. He was also a member of the Earth Alliance. He could talk with the investigators, and neither she nor Popova could stop him.

No matter how much they wanted to.

The meal DeRicci had eaten turned into a lump in her stomach.

He was going to talk with them about the clones. She had no idea why that upset him so. Of course the investigations had different branches. Of course some aspects of the investigation were confidential.

He used to work for the police. He knew that.

She had no idea why he had expected anything else.

Has he met with them? DeRicci sent.

He's meeting with them now, Popova sent. *You want me to break it up?*

I want you to join them, DeRicci sent. *I want to know exactly what's going on.*

He's not going to like that, Popova sent.

DeRicci finally had enough. She didn't care what Miles Flint did or didn't like. He didn't work for her, but she didn't work for him, either. And she wasn't his partner any longer.

I really don't give a damn, DeRicci sent. *He's in my office. He does things my way or he leaves.*

She didn't get an immediate response from Popova, and for a moment, DeRicci thought the link had been severed.

Am I authorized to say that? Popova sent.

You are, DeRicci sent.

Again, that moment of silence. Then Popova sent, *He contacted you earlier, right?*

Yes, DeRicci sent.

Did something go wrong in that conversation?

DeRicci closed her eyes. She had no idea how to answer that. Did something go wrong? Not until Flint confessed he was working with Luc Deshin. Or maybe not even until Flint severed their link.

I didn't think so, DeRicci sent, and it wasn't entirely a lie. She hadn't thought so until Flint overreacted. *But it seems that he does.*

You want me to get to the bottom of it? Popova sent.

No, DeRicci sent. *Just listen in on their conversation. I'll take care of it when I get back.*

Whatever "it" was. Whatever needed taking care of. She would do it, like she'd been doing everything else these past few months.

Somehow, she would do it all.

25

ZAGRANDO PILOTED H'JITH'S SPACE YACHT AWAY FROM HELLHOLE, moving slowly so as not to attract suspicion. H'Jith stood inside a clear prison made of bars of light, shuddering uncontrollably. Apparently, H'Jith didn't mind toying with others, but hated to be toyed with itself.

Zagrando ignored H'Jith until he was certain no one had followed him. No one had sent distress messages, no one had tried to contact the ship. He set the coordinates for the resort he had found, then sat in the pilot's chair.

"Here's what I want," Zagrando said. "When we get to our destination, I want you to buy me a ship. Then I will leave, and you are free to go home."

"I can't pilot anything," H'Jith wailed.

Zagrando shrugged. "Hire someone."

H'Jith was silent for a moment. Then it tilted its head. Its tail twitched just slightly. That lovely tell. Apparently it *was* involuntary.

"You will have to set me free when we arrive," H'Jith said. "I must be able to see the ships to act as broker."

Zagrando sighed. "I am really tired of the way you lie, H'Jith. Is that something all J'Slik do? Or is that simply the way J'Slik criminals behave?"

"I am not a criminal," H'Jith said sullenly.

"That's right, you're not," Zagrando said. "You're a ship broker. And as such, you have other people buy ships for you, which you then re-sell. So I'm now one of your suppliers. You're going to give me your account information so that I can buy my next ship."

"No," H'Jith said.

Zagrando reached across the console, tapped the miniprison controls and moved the bars just a little closer. H'Jith watched them move and tried, in vain, to make its body smaller.

"I'm sorry," Zagrando said. "I didn't hear you."

"Please," H'Jith said. "Just let me go."

"I already told you that I would let you go after you've helped me," Zagrando said, keeping his fingers poised over the prison controls. "I also know you have dozens of accounts. Someone like you would have to. So make sure I have one of your fattest accounts. I don't need the others. When we arrive, I'll go out, buy a new ship, and then set you free. You can find your pilot and your way home."

"You won't do that," H'Jith said. "You'll let me die in here."

Zagrando made a face.

"I'm not that kind of man," he said, although he really needed to portray that kind of man in his role as an arms broker. He was failing the ruthlessness test all over this part of the sector. "But if I were, you'd still be all right. Someone would find you. I'm sure there are ship brokers at every port, and I'm sure they all would love to take on a ship like this. They'll break in eventually. They'll take the ship, and then they'll find you."

"It could take weeks," H'Jith said, voice trembling.

"Ah," Zagrando said. "Really? Hmmm. That would be too bad. I would think, then, it would be better to work with me on this."

"I've never met a human like you," H'Jith said.

"Yeah," Zagrando said, wiggling his fingers, but careful to keep them away from the controls. "Apparently, you've only met victims."

H'Jith shifted just a little. It was clearly getting uncomfortable.

"I have not victimized anyone," it said.

"I'm sure they all volunteered for your special brand of commerce," Zagrando said.

"They did," H'Jith said. "They were in such a hurry—"

"That they allowed themselves to be victimized," Zagrando said in an even voice.

H'Jith blinked at him, clearly confused by Zagrando's tone.

"I didn't hurt them," H'Jith said after a moment.

"Keep believing that," Zagrando said. "The more you deny it, the more I'm thinking I'm going to just use this ship to continue on my way."

"Everyone would know it was stolen," H'Jith said.

"I'm sure it is." Zagrando leaned forward and pretended to study the controls. Then he looked over at H'Jith with a fake look of surprise. "Oh, you mean, stolen from you, not from the original owner."

"Please," H'Jith said, "have some pity."

"I have," Zagrando said. "I told you. Give me your account. I'll buy a ship, and you can forget you ever met me."

H'Jith bowed its head. A violent shudder, almost a spasm, ran through it.

"I hate you," H'Jith said softly.

"I don't know why," Zagrando said. "We've only just met."

H'Jith stared at him. Zagrando stared back.

Then H'Jith shook its head. "All right," it said. "One account if you promise you'll never bother me again."

"That's going to be an easy promise to keep," Zagrando said. "I promise. I won't bother you."

"All right, then," H'Jith said. "I'm going to give you an account."

"And, before you do," Zagrando said, "realize one thing: If you screw me in any way, you'll die, standing up in the middle of this stolen space yacht. Your family won't know what happened to you for months, maybe years."

The shuddering had grown so bad that H'Jith could barely stand. "One account," it said, "and then we're done."

"I'm waiting," Zagrando said.

"You'll have to let me link to you," H'Jith said.

"I'm sure the information is in your console here," Zagrando said. "Ships like this back everything up. Just tell me how to access it."

So H'Jith did.

26

The Earth Alliance investigators had taken over the central conference room. Popova had probably banned them from the area around her desk, thinking that would make them leave.

Instead, they had taken over the conference area that had clear windows on all four sides, with corridors around it. In truth, it should have been Popova's office because she was the center of this floor, but the conference room wasn't close enough to the elevator for her to monitor all the arrivals and departures. Rather than letting security do that, she preferred to do that herself.

In that way, she reminded Flint of DeRicci.

And himself.

He could feel Popova's gaze on his back as he made his way to the conference room. He had shut her up when he told her that he didn't work for her, but he had a hunch she was contacting DeRicci.

And DeRicci wasn't going to be happy with him.

He didn't care as long as he managed to move forward on this investigation.

The two Earth Alliance investigators weren't sitting around waiting for someone to talk with them. They had attached some equipment to the long table in the conference room, and were doing some investigating of their own.

Fortunately, the conference room table wasn't networked into any of the systems in the Security Office, so the investigators couldn't access any proprietary information.

He wondered if they had tried.

He pulled open the door. The woman looked up at him first. She had wedge-cut black hair. It had purple highlights that matched the highlights on her clothing. She had tinted her lips purple as well, and the lids above her eyes had a faint purple tinge.

While he had learned to accept that level of fashion detail in some professionals without judging them, he found it odd that an investigator, whose job was often to blend in, would bother taking that kind of care.

The man sitting next to her looked more like the average investigator to Flint. That man had on a rumpled black suit, and his brown hair was tinged with gray. He had lines under his eyes and some extra pounds around his middle.

After a moment, the man looked up, too.

They watched Flint as if they were wary of what he was going to say or do.

"I'm Miles Flint," he said, letting the door close behind him. "I'm a retired Retrieval Artist. I've been consulting on this investigation."

"Hm," the woman said as she stood. "And here I thought you were actually doing some of the investigating. I'm Wilma Goudkins."

She extended her hand. Flint took it, noting the softness of her skin. She'd either had enhancements or had spent a lot of money to have treatments.

"And I'm Lawrence Ostaka," the man said, extending his hand. "Forgive my partner. We're a bit frustrated. The Earth Alliance sent us here to work with you folks to make certain that the investigation has all the resources it needs, and we've been frozen out."

Flint shook Ostaka's hand as well.

"I understand," Flint said. "Secrecy is important up here. There's a lot I don't know, either."

Somehow he managed to keep that from sounding bitter. He was angrier at DeRicci than he thought he was.

"But they finally sent you in here to talk with us," the woman—Goudkins—said.

"Actually," Flint said, "Rudra Popova just tried to stop me."

Ostaka moved his head back just a little, as if he were surprised. "You came on your own?"

"We have to be clear," Flint said. "I am not working for the Security Office, the City of Armstrong, or any Moon-based organization. I'm consulting, yes, but I'm doing this part on my own."

"This meeting," Goudkins said. Her dark eyes glittered. "That's what you're doing on your own. Not the investigation."

Her questions irritated him. He was beginning to understand why Popova didn't like them.

"The investigation," he said, "has so many branches that it's impossible to keep track of. Each bombed city has its own investigation. Then there are separate investigations into the assassinations. The Earth Alliance wants its own investigation, and Security Chief DeRicci is trying to find out what happened Moon-wide, so that she can prevent another attack."

"You sound critical," Goudkins said.

"If you continue to question me like you would question a suspect, Ms. Goudkins," Flint said, "I will leave this room. And for the record, I don't like the fact that you approached my underage daughter, trying to get information that Rudra Popova would not give you. You talk to my daughter again, and I will go to your superiors with a complaint."

"They know I have to conduct this investigation—"

"They know inappropriate behavior as well," Flint said. "I worked with the Earth Alliance dozens of times back when I was with the Armstrong Police Department. I'm not telling you anything new. You've looked at my records. But what you might not know is that I've developed some of the computer systems that the Alliance still uses. I don't just have police contacts, I have contacts with the upper echelon of the Alliance. I will not hesitate to use those contacts if you persist in involving my daughter. Are we clear?"

Ostaka leaned back and crossed his arms. His expression didn't change, but Flint got the sense that the man was amused.

Goudkins sat up just a little straighter. "We're clear. Although I must say that threatening someone is not the best way to begin a co-operative relationship."

Flint couldn't take it any longer. "Is she always like this?" he asked Ostaka.

"Actually," he said with a bit of a drawl, "her blunt doggedness usu-ally gets us exactly what we want, which always surprises me. I would expect people to push back like you and your daughter have. But they generally don't."

Goudkins glared at her partner. He shrugged and gave her an al-most impish smile.

"It's true," he said.

Flint knew the good cop, bad cop routine. It annoyed him.

"If we're going to cooperate," he said to them, "then I will be an equal partner or this conversation is over now. I want to know what you know—all of it, even the classified stuff. I don't care if you tell your bosses. I certainly won't. In fact, I won't compromise much of any-thing. I know how to search for information without leaving a trace. And if you tell me information, I don't have to seek it out on my own. If I do that, there's the risk that I will blunder into your investigation and ruin it."

"A threat, Mr. Flint?" Goudkins asked.

"The truth," he said. "If you think you're going to get cooperation when Security Chief DeRicci gets back, think again. She is the one who ordered Rudra Popova to ignore you. She doesn't like you, and she's worried that you'll take over the investigation with no *quid pro quo*."

"So why are you here?" Ostaka asked. "Are you going to feel us out?"

"I know this investigation has stalled. I also know that parts of the government have information the rest of the government doesn't have.

I talked with a few people tonight who have even more information." Flint crossed his arms. "The problem here is that we have too much information. We don't have enough people to process it, and we have no central clearinghouse for that information."

"You propose to be the central clearinghouse?" Ostaka asked.

"I'm going to act that way whether you cooperate or not," Flint said. "I will go to anyone I can to get information from and I will do my best to put that information together. I don't care what organization gets stung in the process, whether it's the Earth Alliance or some Moon government. I prefer to work in cooperation with everyone, but if that's not possible, I will work alone."

"Why are you so vigilant, Mr. Flint?" Goudkins asked. "What makes you so special?"

"I have special skills," he said. "I can solve this thing if I have the right information. But that's not what you're asking, since you know who I am. You want to know why I care so much. You met the reason I care. My daughter has to grow up in this new world we find ourselves in. I prefer that she concentrate on her schoolwork instead of spending her free time looking for bombers. I want her to spend her days making friends instead of worrying about what threat lurks around the next corner. That's why I'm working so damn hard. I'm kind of amazed no one else is."

"No one else, Mr. Flint?" Goudkins asked. "We're here. No one in this office will work with us."

"Because we've all worked with the Earth Alliance before. I've had cases that you people took over and then forbade me from working on. I know that Noelle has, too. I'm sure every major law enforcement agency has had the same experience."

Ostaka's amused expression slowly changed to something more serious. He sat up a bit straighter as well.

Goudkins hadn't changed her position at all.

"As to why you're here," Flint said, "I assume you're here because someone ordered you to be here. Otherwise, you'd be investigating some other crime in some other portion of the known universe."

Goudkins looked down. Then she sighed.

"You assume we don't have a personal stake," Ostaka said.

"You probably work at Earth Alliance Headquarters on Earth," Flint said. "The Moon can be very far away from there."

"Wilma's sister lived in Tycho Crater," Ostaka said.

"Shut up," Goudkins snapped.

"She contacted Wilma the minute the crisis started at the Top of the Dome."

"*Shut up*," Goudkins said.

"She was sending information through their private links all day—"

"He doesn't care." Goudkins turned toward her partner. "He's going to think you made this up."

"Actually, it's easy to check," Flint said. He was feeling sympathetic despite himself.

"Then you can check," Goudkins said. "My sister stayed inside the center of the dome to help with the rescue efforts. When the Top of the Dome blew, she was right there."

Goudkins looked like she was going to say more. Then she shook her head, as if saying more wasn't worth her time.

"She heard her sister die," Ostaka said softly.

"I did not." Goudkins stood up and walked to the other side of the conference room. "The link severed when the dome blew open."

If she was acting, she was doing a terrific job. Flint could feel her upset, even though she had tamped it down.

She had walked to a corner of the conference room where the light hit the windows just right. He could see shadows of her face, but not a reflection of her face.

That movement, more than any other, convinced him she was telling the truth.

"You people here on the Moon," she said, her voice steady but just a bit too soft, "you think you're the only ones hurt by this crisis. You forget that families get spread all over the Alliance. You forget that we all watched what happened, just like some of you did. You forget that analysts agree with your Security Chief. This attack was something big, something that's aimed at a large goal we don't understand. And until we do understand it, we won't know what's going to happen next or who it will happen to."

"I haven't forgotten," Flint said quietly. "That's why I'm here, even though I know my old partner Noelle DeRicci will be quite angry at me for talking with you."

"You're here for the children," Ostaka said drily.

"No," Flint said. "I'm here for one child. Mine. If other people get helped, then that's all well and good. But in this case, I'm being one selfish son of a bitch. This crisis has gone on too long. I want it to end. And I'll do what I can to end it, even if it means disagreeing with good friends."

Ostaka studied him for a minute, as if he'd never quite seen anything like Flint before.

Then he asked, "How do you know you can trust us, Mr. Flint?"

"I don't," Flint said. "But I'm willing to work with all kinds of people I don't trust. I'm willing to look at all the information and see what fits. I want to stop this thing. Am I the only one?"

His words echoed in the overly large room. Ostaka watched him.

But Goudkins was the one who moved. She turned around. Her eyes were sad, her mouth turned down. She looked like she had aged a year in the past few minutes.

"No," she said. "You're not the only one. I volunteered for this assignment. I'm here because I want this solved, too. I'll help you, Mr. Flint. No matter what it takes."

27

THE EARTH ALLIANCE HEADQUARTERS IN HENATAN, THE LARGEST PEYTI city on Peyla, sprawled across half a kilometer of land. The headquarters had several buildings, attached by what could only be called airlocks. Since the Peyti built the headquarters and they were housed in the Peyti's largest city, the main areas all had a Peyti-safe atmosphere.

However, an Earth-type environment worked better for the bulk of Alliance members, so over the years, the oxygen-rich parts of the headquarters had grown to nearly fifty percent of the available space.

Rastigan stood in what the humans privately called the true office complex of the Earth Alliance Headquarters. In most ways, the layout was identical to the layout in the Peyti section. The conference rooms in this section were bigger since they got used more often, and the offices were smaller.

Rastigan stood in the Office of the Director of the Peyti Earth Alliance Headquarters, which was, in Rastigan's opinion, a fancy way of saying that the Director had no real power outside of this building, a problem that Rastigan was butting her head against at this very moment.

The Director, a slight human man named Cyril Connab, stood in the center of his office, watching the habitat security vid for the third time. He stood with his hands clasped behind his back. His brown hair needed a trim, and he looked like he hadn't eaten in a long time.

Granted, the food on Peyla left a lot to be desired, but people generally got used to it.

"Here's my problem," he said, still watching the cloned Peyti sail through the air, turn orange, and dissolve. "The Peyti haven't contacted us. And this is their jurisdiction. Peyti-against-Peyti crime. I don't think I have the authority to even comment on this."

Rastigan felt a frustration so deep that she could only sigh. "Sir, Uzvot went out of her way to let us know the facts here—"

"Those aren't facts, Jin," he said. "It's her speculation. We don't even know that these Peyti are cloned."

Rastigan resisted the urge to roll her eyes even though the director's back was turned. She had done that once before and had gotten reprimanded. Apparently, he watched the security vids of all of his office interactions.

"We do know they're cloned, sir," Rastigan said. "I've shown you the images from my suit. The Peyti in the center of that group are identical. And the Peyti do not have multiple matching offspring, like twins, so there is no possible way that these Peyti could be anything other than clones."

"I have to take your word for that, do I?" he asked, still not turning around.

"The Peyti reproductive capacities are in the database, sir," she said, hoping her irritation did not show in her voice. "But it would be easier if you took my word."

He turned around. "Why do you care so much about this? The Peyti are taking care of it."

"It mirrors the Moon's Anniversary Day, sir," she said.

"I don't see how," he said. "No leaders have died. No bombs have gone off."

"The clones are of a mass murderer, sir, and they are young adults. They were produced en masse, and they're clearly training in murder." She cut off the ends of all of her words. She couldn't help it. He was a transfer here, and saw the post as a stepping stone to a better

Earth Alliance position. Even though he'd been here nearly two years, he hadn't bothered to learn much about the Peyti at all.

"Yes, but what kind of murder? We have no idea. We don't know that they're going to go kill Peyti leaders." He raised his chin slightly. It still left him half a head shorter than she was. "And even if they do, Jin, it's a Peyti matter. If they believe there's a threat to the Alliance, then they have a duty to contact us. They haven't, so they do not believe there is a threat."

She wanted to shake him, but she knew that wouldn't help her cause. Although it would make her feel better.

"Beg pardon, sir," she said, "but the Peyti are very rule-oriented. They do things subtlely and when they do break a rule, as Uzvot did today, we have to pay attention. The Peyti do not do such things lightly."

"I don't know what you're telling me," he said.

"I'm telling you," she said slowly so that she wouldn't add *you idiot* each time she took a breath, "that Uzvot told me these things with the full knowledge that I work here, in Earth Alliance headquarters, and absent your presence at that habitat today, I was the top Earth Alliance official on site. Everything she said, she said with the full knowledge of my rank and position. I told her repeatedly that I would have to go to the Earth Alliance with this, and while she said she wished things could be different, she continued to tell me details about the deaths, the clones, and about the parallels between Uzvekmt and PierLuigi Frémont."

The director studied her for a moment. She could almost hear his calculations. How much risk was he taking if he contacted the Earth alliance with this? Would he offend the Peyti? Would he have to leave Peyla in disgrace, sidelining his diplomatic career?

Careers had been destroyed for less.

"Sir," she said, "if you fail to provide the Earth Alliance with this information and this is an important piece of the Anniversary Day puzzle, if this incident actually shows what direction the next attacks will move in, then your career will be over."

He blinked at her. Clearly he hadn't considered that side of the argument. He turned away from her and looked at that vid for the fourth time, his expression unchanging.

She had no idea how anyone could watch that repeatedly without becoming at least a little upset. But she had long suspected that Connab had a human bias, and that all other members of the Alliance were just not as important to him as humans were.

Apparently, he didn't see them as individuals who could suffer and feel pain.

Or maybe this reaction of his came because they were clones, and not because they were Peyti.

Or perhaps it came from both.

He turned back to her. "If you believe this is so important," he said, "then you have my permission to contact the Investigative Arm of the Alliance."

"Your permission?" she asked.

"Yes," he said.

He was distancing himself from the information in case it was tainted. He would blame her then.

"I think it would be better coming from you," she said, "and I think it should go to the council."

"If the investigative arm agrees, they will contact the council."

"It'll slow down the release of information," she said.

"Which you have already told me the Peyti do not want," he said.

Her breath caught. Damn him for using her words against her. He had missed the point, again.

Or maybe she had. At least she had gotten permission to contact the main branch of the Alliance.

If she didn't know how to do it properly, if she accidentally included the council in her notification to the investigative arm, well then, it would be his fault, wouldn't it, because he didn't do it himself.

"I could rethink my entire position," Connab said.

"No need, sir," she said. "I would be happy to let the investigative arm know what happened here. Then they can deal with it as they see fit."

"Exactly, Jin," he said. Then he waved a hand at the holographic image. "Now, get this thing out of my office."

"Yes, sir," she said. She would gladly get this issue out of his office. And she would make sure it went to the people who needed to know about it.

The people who could follow up on it.

The people who might make sense of yet another group of clones with a sinister historic origin. A group of clones who killed and, unless she missed her guess, reveled in it.

Just like their originals had.

28

It took only a few hours to reach the resort that Zagrando had programmed into the navigation system. H'Jith stood for half of that, but then its complaints got to Zagrando. He didn't want to listen to the whining for the rest of the trip. So he expanded the bars on H'Jith's little prison to allow H'Jith to sit down.

Then H'Jith complained about sitting on the floor instead of a chair. Zagrando didn't give in any further, and, by the end of the journey, had added a sound barrier in addition to a light barrier on H'Jith's private prison.

He probably should have listened to H'Jith. H'Jith had been in and out of the resort dozens of times. But Zagrando had had enough.

Besides, he wanted this little detour to end. He needed to contact his handler. He needed a ship. He needed to control his own destiny again.

He hadn't given the resort much thought, so when he arrived, it surprised him. It was much more upscale than he had expected. If he had gone in as a civil servant, he wouldn't have been able to afford the docking fees alone. Fortunately, paying to dock was the first test of the account that H'Jith had given him. The fee got paid with no problem.

If Zagrando hadn't received the reminder to pay the docking fee, he would have forgotten to turn on the sound in H'Jith's little prison.

As it was, he had to make sure the account had enough money to handle all the expenses of the resort plus a ship purchase.

"How much money is in this account?" Zagrando asked.

"It's not my fault you chose to go to Goldene Zuflucht," H'Jith said.

That was the name of the resort, which apparently should have been some kind of clue. Zagrando hadn't heard of it, but then, he hadn't heard of most places in this part of the sector.

"Answer the question," Zagrando said.

"Take me with you," H'Jith said. "We can forget that our little misunderstanding ever happened. I can broker the ship purchase—"

"Answer my question," Zagrando said.

H'Jith had sighed heavily, then said, "There's more than enough."

"To handle the fees and a ship purchase?" Zagrando asked.

"And bribes if need be," H'Jith said.

Zagrando glared it. "There better be."

Then he left the cockpit. The door closed to sound of H'Jith cursing him. Zagrando had smiled, hoping he would never have to see H'Jith again.

His backup plan was simple: If he couldn't get a ship in a short period of time, he would take H'Jith's space yacht to another port and make his decisions from there.

Of course, H'Jith would have to tag along, until Zagrando abandoned the ship completely.

The interior of Goldene Zuflucht was as golden as the name implied. The walls looked like they were made of gold leaf, even though Zagrando knew they couldn't be or the place wouldn't still be standing.

He had gone through a significant amount of security to enter, and his arms' dealer identity had held up. The identity had some dicey entries on purpose, to make him more palatable to the Black Fleet, but it also made him unwelcome at more law-abiding places.

Either Goldene Zuflucht was not law-abiding or it didn't care about anyone who broke Earth Alliance laws.

More likely, the security had checked his fake identity's bank accounts and determined that Zagrando had more than enough money to purchase anything he needed on this resort.

Resorts like this, which were starbases with a limited clientele, catered to the very rich. Most everyone that rich had some kind of shady background, whether it was obvious or not. The most important thing at a place like this wasn't how someone looked or his species, but how much money he could spend—and whether or not he would interfere with the other "guests."

Since Zagrando's alias's past had shady business practices, but had no murders or violent crimes on his record, he was one of the criminal class that places like this liked.

At least, he hoped that was the case.

He also hoped they wouldn't discover that he had stolen the space yacht he'd brought to Goldene Zuflucht, and that the owner (or at least the purported owner) was being held prisoner inside.

The interior of the station couldn't have been more different than the interior of Hellhole. From the moment he entered the resort proper, he felt wrapped in luxury. The air smelled like mint. The lighting was soft. Well-dressed humans went from place to place, moving with purpose. His public links activated, filling with ads that he could delete if he wanted to. He shut off the audio—he preferred to hear what was going on around him rather than ads inside his own head—but he kept the visuals running as a tiny image on the upper left of his left eye. He purposely made the image hard to see, but he could see its movements, and he tracked it as if it were a suspect he was trying to ignore. He wanted to see what the resort offered him. It provided yet another clue as to the amount of money in his accounts.

The corridor into this part of the resort looked like a path in a park on Earth. The path, made of multicolored stone, had flowering plants growing on either side. The ceiling above was a pale blue that clearly changed color with the time of day. At the moment, some wispy clouds drifted overhead.

Restaurants and shops had windows that overlooked this part of the resort, and each door bore the name of the establishment in a florid gold script. In fact, everything in the interior had a faint gold tinge, which was, in Zagrando's opinion, the only tacky thing about the place.

He didn't have to ask for directions this time. Instead, he linked into the information network that the station provided and searched for shops that specialized in ships.

He thought he would have to settle for shops that specialized in ship design, but he didn't. At least three stores near the dock sold ships, most of them focusing on Earth Alliance luxury brands. One shop specialized in racing vessels, and Zagrando toyed with that. He would need speed.

But he would probably have to dump this ship as well, and he was tired. He really wanted some place he could sleep before he had his big meeting.

If he had his big meeting. He hadn't even had time to think about it.

He selected the largest of the luxury ship stores, and followed the lights that appeared on the path. He was the only one who could see those lights, of course, but he appreciated them all the same.

In fact, he appreciated this place more than he wanted to. Given his druthers, he would stay here for a few days, get the rest he needed, and move on.

He was burning out. Not that long ago, he would have loved this entire mission, Emzada Lair and all. He would have seen it as a challenge. He would have enjoyed the survival aspects of the game he played now, and he would have taken real pleasure in beating H'Jith, not to mention managing to outrun the Black Fleet (at least so far) and he would have done his best to figure out as much as he could about the people he was meeting before he met them.

Now he hadn't even given them a single thought.

He wanted to quit, move on, become someone else for real.

He wondered if Earth Alliance Intelligence would let him do that, or if they'd threaten to kill him again, like they had done on Valhalla Basin.

It didn't take him long to find the storefront for the luxury ships. The store's name was in German, just like the resort's was, and it meant—surprise, surprise—best luxury ships. (Why didn't every place just default to Standard, so he didn't have to use a translation program?)

The door stood open, and he stepped inside.

The place smelled of fresh-cut wood. The interior had polished wood walls with brass trim. Even the sales counter matched. Windows along the sides looked like portholes. It took Zagrando a moment to realize the place had been designed to look like a sailing ship—the kind that traversed seas, instead of ships that flew between planets.

He was about to leave when a woman came through a side door he hadn't even noticed.

"Good afternoon," she said. "May I help you?"

"I think I'm in the wrong place," he said. "Sorry to bother you."

"You're looking for a spaceship, right?" she asked. She had reddish brown hair and dark eyes.

"Yes," he said.

She smiled, and he realized she was older than he had initially thought. "The design here was my father's. He loved old sailing ships and probably would have been happier selling them. I used to hate the way this place looked, but since he passed on, I can't bear to change it."

Zagrando nodded, uncertain what to say.

"As if that matters to you," she said, her smile changing slightly. It was sadder. "I'm Ruth."

"Zag," he said, using his alias's nickname. "I'm sorry about your father."

She shrugged. "People who knew him really aren't. All except me. And again, I'm sharing much more than you need to hear. He's only been gone a month. So it's still new to me."

"I understand," Zagrando said, even though he didn't. His parents had passed away long ago and he hadn't had a close relationship since he started with Earth Alliance Intelligence. No one would miss him when he was gone.

She squared her shoulders as if donning her salesperson identity. "What brings you here today?"

"I lost my ship just outside Hellhole," he said. "A friend brought me here. I'm supposed to be on the other side of the sector right now, and I need a way to get there."

It wasn't all a lie. He had lost his ship, and he'd left Whiteley's ship behind. H'Jith wasn't a friend, but anyone checking on Zagrando would see that he had come in one of H'Jith's ships. Besides, the friend story only had to hold until he got away from this resort. Then he'd set H'Jith free, and H'Jith could say whatever it wanted about him.

"Sounds like a dilemma," Ruth said. She didn't seem as eager to sell him anything as H'Jith had been.

Zagrando didn't know if that was her sales style or if she really didn't care if she sold another ship. Or maybe she was just muted because she was still in mourning.

He thought that both odd and admirable. Usually people with money got mood enhancements so that the unpleasant emotions, like grief, passed by with barely a notice.

"Are you looking for a long-term vessel or a short-term one?" she asked.

He was just looking for a quick way off Goldene Zuflucht, but he didn't want to say that. "Long-term."

"Luxury with or without defensive capabilities?"

Since he had already said long-term, he needed to go all the way with the ruse. "With."

She smiled again, but this time the smile was businesslike. She moved to a podium near the center of the room, and tapped the surface. Holograms of ships surrounded him.

Large ships, small ships, mostly black with a few that were as rich a brown as the walls of the store. None of them had prices, but all of them looked expensive.

"I'm going to some dicey parts of the sector," he said. "I'm not sure something that luxurious would—"

"They all have masking capabilities," she said, and by that she meant that the ships could appear less than they were. The size was always impossible to hide, but the exterior could change just enough to look like a ship that was a cheap imitation of something like this.

"Good." He knew better than to ask about price. Someone who could buy ships like this cared less about price than about features. "I don't need a large ship. I will never carry many passengers and not all that much cargo."

Five of the ships faded away.

"And I'd prefer ships with a bit of speed," he said.

Six more ships vanished.

That left seven ships, all of which looked just fine to him.

"Which do you prefer?" he asked.

She made one of the images grow. "This one has the best captain's quarters I've ever seen. You'd be traveling in luxury. Plus, it has a secondary cockpit. Not just the ability to pull the controls to a different part of the ship, but a whole secondary unit so that you can shut off one cockpit and use the other. It's especially nice if the ship gets boarded, and since we do have a pirate problem in this part of the sector, you can lock them off and save yourself all at the same time."

He had to repress a smile. He'd already locked someone out of a cockpit today, but, he had to admit, capturing H'Jith was unbelievably easy, especially when compared with taking on the Black Fleet.

"Let me see that one, then," he said.

"My pleasure," she said. "Follow me."

She tapped the podium and all of the ship images disappeared. Then she walked to the back of the shop, and pushed open a door he hadn't even seen. He followed her as she requested, and saw that the door led to another docking bay.

This one was probably part of Goldene Zuflucht's docking ring, but the bay had been walled off. It looked private. It didn't extend forever like H'Jith's seemed to. Instead, it only had two dozen or so ships, which was still more than the eye could take in at one time.

She led him around a corner and up a small flight of stairs. The ship he had expressed interest in was on the same level as the other ships, but its entrance was in a non-standard location.

"This ship was built outside the Earth Alliance," he said.

She smiled at him over her shoulder. "We're standing outside of the Earth Alliance."

He smiled back, feeling like she had put him gently in his place. "So many ships are built to Earth Alliance specs that I'm not used to seeing one built on a different model."

She nodded. "Earth Alliance specs make ships easier to board. Out here, we prefer non-standard luxury ships. They're safer."

That made a lot of sense. If the layout of a ship was unusual, then it would be harder to attack. She led him into the ship, showed him the dual cockpits as well as the captain's quarters, which were, indeed, luxurious. He wanted to fall on the bed and sleep now.

He wasn't sure when he'd last had a good sleep; it had probably been years.

As he walked through, he had his links ping for any obvious tracking devices. He didn't get any. He knew the ship had some tracking material built in, but he could deal with that when he purchased it.

"So," he said, "can I buy the ship and take it off Goldene Zuflucht today?"

They had just gone through the corridor to the large cargo area. Ruth stopped, a little frown of concern on her forehead.

"It's irregular," she said.

He shrugged. "I have business away from Goldene Zuflucht, and I need to leave as soon as I can."

"I didn't say it couldn't be done," she said. "The problem is not with payment—we have systems for that—but with registration. The ship won't receive your registration for at least two days. You won't be able to take it to any Earth Alliance venues until that registration comes in."

"That's not a problem," he said. In fact, it benefitted him. He didn't say that. "I can even return to Goldene Zuflucht if I need to after my meetings to make sure all of the registration happens."

"Oh, no," she said. "You won't have to do that. We run into this a lot. We're far away from anything, and often if someone has a problem with a ship, they leave it here in trade for a new ship. So we have dealt with this situation before."

He nodded. "All right, then," he said. "I like the ship, and I'll take it."

She smiled. "Then let's finalize everything and get you to your business as quickly as possible."

He smiled, too. Finally, something had gone his way. He hoped the trend continued as the day progressed.

29

FLINT PULLED OUT A CHAIR IN THE CONFERENCE ROOM AND SAT DOWN. Ostaka watched him. Goudkins still stood by the windows, looking at the city beyond.

"I'll tell you part of what I have," Flint said, "but I expect information in return. I know the Earth Alliance sent you here to both monitor us, and to augment what we do. You also have information that they sent with you, that you may or may not share, depending on how you feel about us."

Ostaka's eyebrows twitched ever so slightly. Apparently, he was surprised that Flint knew that much.

"I'll start," Flint said. "I think the key to finding out what happened is weapons."

Goudkins turned around. She glanced at Ostaka, who pointedly did not look back at her. So either the Earth Alliance agreed with Flint on weapons, or something else was going on.

Maybe they had even more information on the weapons systems than he did.

"I'm looking at more than one kind of weapon here," Flint said.

"Each dome was different?" Ostaka asked.

"We don't know," Flint said. "That's part of the problem. I'm taking this from a strictly Armstrong perspective. I've discovered, just today, that the amount of zoodeh used for the assassinations is more than the amount the supplier we caught had access to."

"What does that mean?" Goudkins came back to the table. She pulled out her chair, but didn't sit, her hands fluttering nervously over the chair's back.

"It means we missed something. The Earth Alliance banned zoodeh a long time ago, but never shipped the zoodeh here out."

"Actually, that's not true," Ostaka said.

Flint glanced at him, a little appalled that the Earth Alliance investigators were already looking into the zoodeh side of things.

"The Earth Alliance had a give-back program, but assumes that there was only one-third compliance. Everyone who had zoodeh was supposed to turn it in, and they could do so anonymously. But the records don't match. The amount of zoodeh turned in was much less than the amount shipped throughout the Alliance in the previous five years alone. If you compound that number by decades that zoodeh could be sold here, then the amount loose in the Alliance is staggering."

Flint felt cold. "You knew that and said nothing?"

Ostaka shrugged. "We assumed you people knew it as well."

Goudkins' fingers played across the back of the chair. She wasn't trying to hide her nerves.

"We honestly didn't realize how disorganized the criminal justice systems are here on the Moon until we got here," she said. "Usually we deal with only one jurisdiction, you know, Armstrong or Gagarin Dome or some place like that. The systems seem fine when you do that, but the overall system here—well, it doesn't exist."

"It's starting to," Flint said because he couldn't just let DeRicci hang. "That's what Noelle's been trying to set up."

"Yes, at the urging of Celia Alfreda," Ostaka said. "But she's dead now, and there's no guarantee that this system will work."

It wasn't working right now.

"Right now, twenty jurisdictions are trying to solve the same crime," Goudkins said. "It's terribly inefficient."

"I know," Flint said. He'd already told them that. That was why he was here.

"We've made all kinds of assumptions that aren't valid," Goudkins said. "You want to know why the Earth Alliance takes over your investigations? It's because you people don't have the resources—"

"Stop," Flint said. "I'm not 'you people' and this won't get us anywhere. You knew about the zoodeh. We didn't. We do now. Can we track it?"

They looked at each other again, and there was a long pause.

"We've done some tracking," Ostaka said after a moment. "But the information we have is old. It takes us to the usual groups—the crime organizations that work in this area, the corporations that initially thought they could use zoodeh, and all of the quarantine areas run by places like the Port of Armstrong. It's going to take a lot of old-fashioned legwork to see if the zoodeh came from any of those places, and even then, we might never know."

Flint let out a sigh. He thought he'd had a good lead here. He leaned back in his chair, and as he did, he saw a movement behind him. Popova stood outside the room, a frown on her face.

"She been out there long?" he asked.

"Almost as long as you've been in here," Goudkins said. "Do you want me to yell at you so she doesn't think you're cooperating?"

"Am I cooperating?" he asked.

Goudkins smiled and looked down just a moment too late. So much for yelling.

Flint got up and pushed the door open. "You're welcome to join us, Rudra."

"The chief wants to deal with them," Popova said.

"I know." Flint continued to hold the door open. "You're her eyes and ears. Join us."

Popova bit her lower lip. "She wants me to."

"Noelle does?" Flint asked.

Popova nodded.

Flint swept his hand back. "Then come on in."

"What are you doing?" she whispered. "Just stop."

He shook his head. "I already told you what I'm doing."

Popova nodded. Then she leaned forward. "She's going to be furious with you."

"I know," Flint said. "Coming?"

"No," she said.

"No need hover, then," he said, and let the door close.

Ostaka and Goudkins hadn't moved. Nor had they said anything out loud. He wondered what they'd been sharing on their links.

"All right," he said. "I gave you what little I had."

Which wasn't entirely true. He held back on the clones, at least for the moment.

"Now, tell me why my discussion of weapons made you two share not just a glance but some information across your links."

Ostaka moved slightly. Goudkins's fingers gripped the top of the chair.

"Full disclosure, remember?" Flint said. "We're working together now."

Ostaka's gaze met Goudkins and he shook his head so minutely that Flint almost missed it.

She raised her chin. "We've been ordered away from the weapons."

Flint frowned. "Ordered away? By whom?"

Her gaze moved toward Ostaka, and then she blinked. He was still sending messages along her links, probably warning her off.

"The Earth Alliance doesn't want us to look at the weapons," she said.

Ostaka spun his chair away in frustration.

"The zoodeh?" Flint asked. "Why? They didn't want us to know how much was loose?"

"No." Ostaka stood. His voice was flat. He shot Goudkins a long look.

"Stop using the links," she snapped at Ostaka. "You can leave and talk to that horrible woman watching us if you want to. You can report me or do what you want. But I want to solve this. Mr. Flint is right; we can't do it without cooperating. So make your choice."

Flint knew better than to say anything. He needed to let this play out.

Ostaka glanced at the door. Popova still stood outside, arms crossed, watching, as if through the force of her will, she could stop Flint from talking to the Earth Alliance investigators.

Ostaka rubbed a hand over his mouth, sighed, and then let his hand drop. "We're not supposed to follow the clones."

Flint's breath caught. "The clones as weapons," he said, deciding not to play dumb. "You weren't supposed to figure out who sent them?"

"Who made them, who trained them, who sent them," Ostaka said. "It's all of a piece."

"Why weren't you supposed to follow those leads?"

"Supposedly," Goudkins said, the word sharp with emphasis, "someone else is doing it."

She was standing rigidly straight, her dark eyes flashing with anger.

"You don't believe that," Flint said. It wasn't a question; it was a statement.

"No," she said, "I don't."

"Why not?" he asked.

"Because I think the clones are blowback, Mr. Flint," she said, "and I think the Earth Alliance doesn't want anyone to know."

30

Meetings conducted by secure holographic link sucked. Jin Rastigan hated them and now she remembered why.

She stood in the center of a small office in the Earth Alliance headquarters in Henatan, the only place in the headquarters that a human could use a secure link without wearing an environmental suit. She felt crowded even though she was alone.

The images of a dozen Earth Alliance investigators littered the floor, the desk, and the shelves. A few actually rested on the back of chairs. Some of the holograms fuzzed in and out, leading her to believe that the investigators watched from different parts of the Alliance.

Most of them hadn't identified themselves. A few kept their faces obscured. Some used a vocal scrambler. She suspected even more investigators watched through a non-holographic link, but she had no way to prove that.

She had already explained—or tried to—why her boss, Cyril Connab, wasn't contacting them. She had to use diplomatic language, too. She couldn't tell the gathered investigators that Connab was a self-absorbed jerk who only wanted credit if something worked. He didn't care about saving lives.

She did, and she made that clear.

She sent the security vid from the Peyti murders. She sent images of the Peyti mass murderer on whom the clones were based. She even sent an affidavit from Uzvot that the information Rastigan was presenting was correct.

The investigators listened, but she had a sense that they didn't understand.

"You're saying that there will be an Anniversary Day-style attack on Peyla?" the head investigator asked. Like so many of the others, he hadn't identified himself. She thought of him as Chubby Guy because he had a roundish face and he wore loose clothing. She couldn't imagine him working undercover, but what did she know about that stuff?

"Or against the Peyti," she said. "It's only a matter of time."

"Based on the clones," Chubby Guy repeated.

"Yes," she said. Why was it so hard for everyone else to take this leap? Why could she see it and no one else could?

"Not anything else?" he asked. "No evidence, no threats, no missing bomb materials?"

"Was there evidence or threats on the Moon before the attacks?" she asked. "No, there wasn't. It was a *surprise* attack."

She could feel the frustration yearning to take over her voice.

"You say the clones are based on a Peyti mass murderer?" Chubby Guy asked.

"*Yes.*" Jeez. How stupid were these guys? They were supposed to be investigators. They were supposed to understand information when it came to them.

"And that's your evidence?"

"Why do you keep asking this?" she asked. "Yes."

Some of the other investigators shifted. She realized that as this exchange continued, a few of the investigators had left the meeting. They didn't see this as important.

"Do the Peyti believe this will result in an Anniversary Day-style attack?" Chubby Guy asked.

"You have Uzvot's statement," Rastigan said. "She wouldn't have made this claim if she wasn't worried."

"About such an attack or about criminal activity?" Chubby Guy asked.

She bit back, *What the hell is your problem?* and took a breath before continuing.

"She wanted me to get this information to the Earth Alliance," Rastigan said. "The Peyti are subtle, as you well know."

Even though this idiot probably didn't know. He watched her, but he didn't seem all that interested.

"She wouldn't have presented this to the Earth Alliance if she thought it strictly a Peyti matter."

"But it wasn't strictly a Peyti matter, was it, Rastigan?" another investigator—who hadn't identified himself either—asked. He had his face obscured, but not his voice. He sounded familiar. Did she know him? She wasn't sure.

God, she hated politics.

"That's right," another investigator said. "A human was involved from the beginning. Don't you think that's why the Peyti wanted the Earth Alliance to know about this? The Peyti are rules-followers. They'd want every detail seen to. I don't read anything sinister into this at all. I think it's a Peyti matter, and they're doing us the courtesy of keeping us informed."

"I think your boss feels that way as well," Chubby Guy said. "Otherwise he would have presented this himself to someone higher up."

Rastigan's face warmed.

"Did he speak to you about this?" she asked, because she couldn't keep the question to herself.

"Of course not," Chubby Guy said, a bit too quickly. "It's just the way procedure works. You want us to pay attention to the details of Peyti procedure. Perhaps you should look at ours as well. This really isn't unusual."

"Clones based on mass murderers aren't unusual? We just suffered a major attack—"

"And it's being investigated," Chubby Guy said. "We will look into this incident as well. Thank you for bringing it to our attention."

He signed off. The holograms of the other investigators vanished as well. Her skin crawled. She felt weirdly alone and yet watched.

What the hell was wrong with these people? Didn't they understand the implications here? Something was happening, something important.

And she didn't even have their names. When the actual attacks happened—and she believed they would—she wouldn't be able to report these people for ignoring her warning.

"Jin?"

She whirled.

One image remained. It stood on her desk, but she had to squint to see it. A youngish human man, muscular and trim, or so it seemed from the image. His face was obscured, but not as darkly as some of the others. It looked like someone had placed a gray sheet over his features.

"Have they seen anything like this on Peyla before?" he asked.

His voice was altered too, but she was convinced she knew him. He called her "Jin," and wasn't doing it in a derogatory way, in an attempt to put her down. He was doing it because he was comfortable with her, because they had worked together.

She hit one of the chips on her hand to record this part of the conversation. She should have done this before, but she hadn't expected the investigators to ignore her warnings.

"Do you mean the killings?" she asked. "Because the mass murderer—"

"No," he said. "The clones. Have they seen clones based on major criminals before?"

Her breath caught. He knew something.

"No, I don't think so," she said.

"But you don't know," he said.

"Uzvot wouldn't have reacted like this if they had. She wouldn't have worked with me. She would have dismissed me." Rastigan was convinced of that. She knew Uzvot well enough. But, as Chubby Guy would have said, this was a hunch, not actual facts.

"That's what I thought," he said. "I think you're right. I think this is important."

"Can you convince the others?" she asked.

"No," he said. "But I will investigate. I'll let you know if I find anything."

"If I find something," she said, "how do I contact…."

He had vanished. Dammit. All the secrecy. All the hiding. It didn't help.

She felt an urgency and no one else seemed to. They seemed to think they had a lot of time before something else happened—if something else was going to happen.

But she thought it might happen soon, and then where would they all be?

She sank into one of the chairs. Maybe Uzvot could get someone higher up to contact the Earth Alliance. Maybe then they'd listen.

Because they weren't listening to Rastigan—not in the way that she wanted. Not in the way they needed to listen.

She had to take matters into her own hands, but she wasn't quite sure how.

31

THE SHIP FLEW BEAUTIFULLY. ZAGRANDO HAD NEVER HAD A SHIP THIS new, this expensive, or this well-made. He had used H'Jith's account, and the transaction had gone through without a blip.

He hadn't freed H'Jith before he left. Instead, he sent an anonymous message to Goldene Zuflucht's security that H'Jith was being held prisoner in his own ship. The anonymous message went through dozens of systems so that it couldn't be traced, and Zagrando timed it so that the message would arrive an hour after he left.

He needed the head start.

He also made sure to file a travel plan with Goldene Zuflucht, like the average traveler would. It made most travelers easy to find. Zagrando submitted detailed travel plans that set up routes for the next week.

When he got on board the ship, he followed the first part of the route until he had established the ship's new identity. Then he sent one of the life pods with a built-in navigation system out on the route he had registered. He cloned the pod's navigation system so that it registered as the ship. That would lead someone on a merry chase if they decided to track him, and by then, they wouldn't be able to find his ship.

He changed the ship's identity three times in the next hour, and followed a meandering path until he had checked the entire ship for tracking devices to make sure no one could tail him.

He didn't trust his own systems—they weren't sophisticated enough to detect some new kind of technology—but they were good enough to get him to the meeting.

First, however, he had to contact his handler. And he had to trust that he had blocked enough of the tracking devices that it would take a lot of work to figure out who he was talking to.

Even so, he went into the large kitchen. Most people would never send important messages from a kitchen, particularly in a luxury ship. The kitchen had been designed to hold a chef and a staff, most of whom would be outside hires. They wouldn't have clearance to listen to important messages.

Zagrando leaned against one of the wood counters. It was smooth and warm against his back. Then he sent a message along his secure link to his handler.

Ike Jarvis's face appeared above the grill. Slowly the image rose so that Jarvis's face would be directly across from Zagrando's, unlike real life, where Zagrando towered over the bastard.

Generally, Zagrando tried to use other handlers to deal with small matters. Zagrando had done his best to limit contact with Jarvis since Jarvis moved him off Valhalla Basin. Zagrando tried not to think of that day often because it so infuriated him.

Unfortunately, this was not a small matter.

"I have a lead," Zagrando said, "but I also have a problem."

Jarvis's image didn't extend to his neck. The head was three-dimensional, but clear, so Zagrando could see expensive tile through Jarvis's skin. It made him look tattooed.

"Problem first," Jarvis said in his gravelly voice.

"Lead first," Zagrando said. "I have put a down payment on weapons, but the seller insists on meeting the buyer. He knows I'm just a broker."

"That's unusual," Jarvis said.

"No kidding," Zagrando said. "But it actually makes sense with these weapons. They're individually designed."

Jarvis's head moved slightly, but Zagrando couldn't tell if that was deliberate or if the man had shifted in his chair. Zagrando hated it when someone let only their head show and nothing else.

"You sure this is a big enough fish, then?" Jarvis asked. "Individually designed seems like small weaponry."

"Oh, this isn't small," Zagrando said. "This might actually lead us to the Anniversary Day attackers."

Jarvis blinked, as if surprised. Of course, he could just be reacting to something else being sent across links or maybe he always blinked like that. Zagrando stopped trying to read the man long ago.

"You're sure?" Jarvis asked.

"Yeah," Zagrando said. "I think I found the source of the clones."

Jarvis nodded, his chin dipping in and out of the grill. The tile tattoos slid eerily along his face.

"How come you didn't just follow through?" he asked. "You need more cash?"

Zagrando slipped his hands behind his back so that he could clench his fists. No surprise, no thank-you, no reaction at all. He had expected a reaction.

"I need a buyer," Zagrando said.

"Find one," Jarvis said.

"Within a few hours," Zagrando said. "I'm heading to the meet now."

"It doesn't look like you're in your ship."

"My ship is blown," Zagrando said.

Jarvis frowned, clearly irritated. "A buyer would never show at this kind of meet."

"Well, I don't get the sale without one," Zagrando said. "I don't get a sale, I can't follow the money or the source of the weapons. I can't follow anything, I can't catch anyone."

"Where's the meet?" Jarvis asked.

Zagrando knew better than to answer that. "This isn't an open line, *boss*, but I'm not sure how secure this new vehicle is either. How about I meet you somewhere?"

"Me?" Jarvis asked. "I can't pose as anything. I haven't been undercover in a generation."

"Send me someone," Zagrando said.

Jarvis glanced off to the side. Something reflected in his eyes, and Zagrando realized Jarvis was looking at an exterior screen.

"Where are you?" he asked.

"I can meet someone at Javier's Corner," Zagrando said. Javier's Corner was a space station, but a small one. The folks who stopped there needed something from fuel to a meal to a quick-and-dirty hire. "Get him there in two hours."

"That's not a lot of time," Jarvis said.

"It's what I've got," Zagrando said. "And make sure this is someone impeccable. I may only get one shot at this."

"I don't like threats, Iniko," Jarvis said.

"Not a threat," Zagrando said. "Fact. We blow this one, we lose a lot of opportunities."

He severed the link, mostly because he didn't want to hear Jarvis's complaints. And Jarvis would complain. The man was never satisfied. It took Zagrando too long to find contacts, or Zagrando wasn't working hard enough or Zagrando was moving too quickly on something.

Zagrando had actually put in for a new handler every six months or so, but he never got one. He was told that handlers needed to have a long-term relationship with their operatives.

A long-term relationship was one thing; a long-term hatred was another.

But he couldn't say that, because if he did, then someone would see that as the reason for his complaints, not because Jarvis had killed him.

Not that anyone in Earth Alliance Intelligence saw Jarvis's actions as anything close to murder. Killing a clone was different from killing the original.

Supposedly, Zagrando understood that.

But in truth, he didn't. He didn't understand any of it. He tried not to think about it. But his brain kept returning to that day on Valhalla Basin, the day he had to leave his old job forever.

Someday Jarvis would pay for the cruelty he showed that day. Not just to Zagrando, making him watch his own clone die. But to the clone himself.

Zagrando had a hunch Jarvis liked watching things like that. He also had a hunch that Jarvis refused to step aside as his handler because Jarvis thrived on the hatred.

But Zagrando couldn't prove any of that.

It wasn't his job. Just like dealing with the Earth Alliance wasn't really his job.

His job was tracking weapons back to the biggest suppliers and, with luck, hooking them up to the corporations who funded those suppliers.

He was on a good track for the first time in years.

Maybe if he succeeded, he could get a new assignment—one that took him far away from Jarvis.

One he might actually enjoy.

32

"Blowback," Flint repeated. He hadn't heard that term in years. It referred to weapons created by one group for one purpose, only to have those weapons eventually used against that group by someone else.

Corporations that dealt in arms manufacture sometimes suffered from blowback, but mostly, blowback happened against countries that sold or gave weapons to other countries—to prop up a government, say, or to defend a country in a war. Eventually those weapons would get used against—or would blow back to—the country that invented them.

"Blowback." He ran a hand over his face. "We don't develop weapons on the Moon, at least, not those kind."

That he knew of. He didn't know what all of the corporations were doing.

"Not the Moon, Mr. Flint," Goudkins said gently. "The Earth Alliance."

Flint closed his eyes. The Earth Alliance. Of course. He had known this was big. He couldn't quite wrap his brain around this.

He opened his eyes. Goudkins was staring at him. Ostaka had looked over his shoulder at Popova who was, apparently, still standing outside.

"Why would the Earth Alliance develop clones from known criminals?" Flint asked.

"Thieves, mostly," Goudkins said. "Plants, to insert into the Black Fleet."

Flint bowed his head. "Using real live people as the originals, not dead people, right? So that these clones could go undercover?"

"More or less," Goudkins said. "We're not allowed to investigate, so it's only what we've heard before."

"Son of a bitch." Flint stood up. He had to move. He couldn't remain sitting with this information. "The Earth Alliance isn't involved now, is it?"

"No," Ostaka said quickly. "Definitely not."

Goudkins gave her partner a withering look. "We don't know that. We don't know anything. We're not allowed to investigate it. Someone else is supposedly doing that."

"But you don't believe it," Flint said.

She shook her head.

"The Earth Alliance wants this part of the investigation dropped." Flint walked away from the table and went to the windows. The city spread before him, intact, the damage from four years ago impossible to see.

So many other cities weren't intact. So many were ruined, so many lives destroyed, and the Earth Alliance didn't want all of this investigated?

And DeRicci knew?

He couldn't believe that of her. He knew she followed orders she didn't like—that was why she stayed with the police after he left—but she had ethics, just like everyone else.

She couldn't know.

Could she?

"I'm sure the Alliance doesn't want to be embarrassed," Ostaka said.

Flint bit back a curse. Embarrassed. That was more important than preventing other attacks.

"Do you think the Earth Alliance knows who launched this attack, then?" he asked.

"No," Ostaka said.

Flint turned. His gaze met Goudkins'.

"I don't know," she said.

Flint gathered himself. He had to think clearly. "You know I'm going to investigate this."

"I do," Goudkins said.

"If you help me, you could lose your jobs over this." He made sure he looked at Ostaka, who had turned slightly gray. "If you don't want to be part of the investigation, leave now. We'll say you had nothing to do with our conversation."

Ostaka tapped his fingers against his mouth. Then he looked at Goudkins.

"If I leave now, the Earth Alliance will know something is up."

"Not right away," she said.

"They'll shut you down," he said.

Flint watched. They could have carried this part of the conversation to their links. They weren't. He wasn't sure why. So that he would be witness to it, obviously, but why have the personal part in front of him?

"Not right away," she repeated.

Ostaka glanced at Popova. She still had her arms crossed, and she was watching intently, swaying slightly as if she wanted to keep herself focused.

Focus. Flint let out a small breath.

They were having this conversation out loud so that he would volunteer his systems. So that he could look up this information without implicating them.

Was it altruism? Or was it a way of tracking him?

God, he didn't trust anyone anymore.

They looked at him, as if they expected him to say something. But he wouldn't.

He didn't need them, not really. Not having their access would slow him down, but not enough to risk his work, his systems, or the solution to this case.

"It's your decision," he said.

Something changed behind Goudkins' eyes. He was going to double-check her story about her sister's death.

"But," Flint said, and this time he was talking to Ostaka, "there are still other facets of this investigation that need coordination. It would be better to have Earth Alliance investigators working with the Alliance instead of detached from it."

Ostaka's eyebrows made that slight twitch. They had hoped Flint would jump on this. He wasn't going to, not in the way they wanted.

"He's right," Goudkins said. "You can leave the room when we talk about weapons if you want."

"I'm sure Noelle will join you," Flint said, partly because he was feeling bitter, but partly to make it easier for Ostaka to stay. Flint almost added, *She likes following orders, too,* but he didn't.

He wasn't being fair.

Not that anything about this investigation was fair.

"You think she'll cooperate with us now?" Ostaka asked.

"I don't know what she'll do." Flint nodded toward Popova. "But, I suspect, I have given her no choice."

"You're a complicated man, Mr. Flint," Ostaka said, and Flint wondered if that comment came because he hadn't acted as they had hoped.

"Not really," Flint said. "I didn't lie to you when I came in this room. All I want to do is prevent another attack, so my daughter doesn't live in fear. It's really that simple."

Goudkins' eyes narrowed.

"Nothing is that simple," she said, and sat down. "Should we see what else we don't know about each other's investigations?"

"Yeah," Flint said, and sat too, knowing that he would share only what he had to. He hadn't lied about the other part either. He was going to coordinate this entire investigation, even if no one else would.

33

THE HOTEL ROOM HAD BEEN BEAUTIFUL, BUT DERICCI COULDN'T STAY in Tycho Crater any longer. Not with Flint acting strangely. It felt like the investigation was spiraling out of her hands and she wasn't quite sure how to stop it.

Not that the investigation had been going well.

She sat in a private train car, the curtains down. Even though the bullet train went faster than any other Moon-based vehicle, it still took hours to return to Armstrong. She should have been sleeping—in fact, her annoying assistants all thought she was.

This car had three different rooms, including the bedroom. She sat cross-legged on the bed, the covers pooled around her legs. Even though the bed had shaped itself to her preferences, it felt uncomfortable. Some of that was the movement of the train, but most of it was in her head.

She couldn't forget Flint's curtness. He'd judged her harshly before, back when they were still partners in the Armstrong Police. She had been willing to comply with some of the Earth Alliance laws; he hadn't.

Although she would argue that the word *comply* was too harsh. She wanted to find every legal solution that she could. She was willing to bend the rules; she just hadn't been willing to break them.

Flint had broken them.

She had looked away. She had considered looking away as far as she could go. She couldn't break the laws along with him, or so she had thought at the time.

Chief? The voice belonged to Popova.

DeRicci frowned. Popova rarely used her voice through the links. If she used her voice, she usually used visuals as well.

I didn't go in.

Was it DeRicci's imagination or did Popova sound tentative? *In where?* DeRicci sent.

The room with Flint and the investigators, Popova said.

Why not? DeRicci sent. *I ordered you to.*

I know, Popova said. *He invited me in. I just couldn't bring myself to go. I did record it, though.*

Flint got everyone to do what he wanted. DeRicci didn't know how, but he always managed it. And he would probably find a way to destroy that recording if he had to.

If it's any consolation, Popova said, *it looked like they were fighting.*

No, it's not, DeRicci sent. *I gave you a direct order.*

Yes, sir. I'm sorry, sir.

Go home, Rudra, DeRicci sent. *It's late.*

I just figured I'd wait for you, Popova said.

No need, DeRicci sent, and signed off.

Not even Popova was listening to her anymore. Had DeRicci become that ineffective? She certainly hadn't gotten as much done as she would have expected from herself. She had thought this entire investigation would be wrapped up by now, or at least on the right track.

She couldn't even get the cities to cooperate with her.

She needed Celia Alfreda, but the Governor-General was dead. The best leaders on Armstrong were gone, and she was alone. Even her friends had stepped away from her.

Flint always had his own sense of right and wrong. She had used that in the past. She had let him do stuff she would never have done. Not that she could control him.

She closed her eyes, and felt the train sway around her. Maybe she should resign. There really wasn't much of a government any more anyway. She was trying to hold together something that hadn't had much stability in the first place.

And why was she doing it? Because it was her job? Or because Celia Alfreda had asked her, and she felt guilty that she survived while Alfreda died?

Or was it because DeRicci felt like she could have prevented all of this if only she had solved that first bombing four years ago?

She didn't know the answer to any of that.

Or maybe she didn't like the answers that she did have.

She sighed and scrunched down in the bed. When she got back, she'd have a long talk with Popova and Flint. DeRicci would make decisions she needed to make—not for Armstrong or the United Domes of the Moon—but for herself.

And maybe by making those decisions for herself, she would be doing what was best for everyone around her.

Because right now, she had a hunch she wasn't doing anything good for anyone.

34

THEY WERE RELYING ON OLD-FASHIONED TRADECRAFT: EYESIGHT recognition, a verbal cue, a passphrase, a gesture. Zagrando had requested this, not Jarvis. Zagrando didn't want to risk using his Earth Alliance identification anywhere in this sector.

His cover was too deep, and too many people knew him by his undercover name.

Jarvis didn't like the decision, but Jarvis didn't work here. Besides, what Jarvis liked or didn't like didn't matter.

Zagrando had picked Javier's Corner because of its size and terrible reputation. The space station was barely larger than some battleships he'd seen. Most people came here because it was the only free place to stop in this part of the sector. Every other place had docking fees or arrival fees or some other kind of fees.

Of course, anyone who stopped here paid in other ways, from the exorbitant prices in the two terrible restaurants to the price of supplies.

Two restaurants and six bars, all of them different. Zagrando didn't choose the exact location of the hookup because he didn't want that going over the secure link, but he knew the person his partner sent wouldn't have a lot of places to hide.

He landed and coded the luxury ship to his DNA, a nice feature that most ships didn't have. He was beginning to fall in love with this vehicle, and he didn't like that. He hadn't been in love with anything, from a person to a location, in a very long time.

He came in dressed well—he had to look worthy of that ship—and decided to walk through Javier's Corner first, just to see if he knew anyone here. Then he would scope out the bars.

He had just started his first pass through the narrow, tube-like corridor when a woman said, "Jarvis told me you'd be taller."

Zagrando smiled. A combination of two passphrases: *Jarvis told me you would be here,* and *Somehow I imagined you would be taller.* Good agents did that. In fact, combining passphrases was a recommended, if old-fashioned procedure that many outside the Agency didn't know.

Still, he didn't turn, but continued forward. He heard heels behind him, the heavy step of a woman in the wrong shoes.

He went into one of the bars—the only one he knew that served halfway decent alcohol—and sat at the farthest table. The woman following him was wearing a formfitting dress, her black hair piled on the top of her head. She had great legs and, like he expected, terribly impractical shoes.

Had she gotten a room from the awful hotel near the docking ring, or had she left her ship dressed like that?

She leaned across the bar, slipped some kind of payment card into one of the machines, then picked up two honey ales, the bar's specialty.

So she'd been here before. He found that even more interesting.

"I don't know if you drink alcohol," she said as she brought the ales to his table, "but I'd recommend it here at least. The booze'll kill whatever germs are thriving in this place."

A third passcode. The one about the booze. The least reliable of all the passcodes just because it was about the booze.

He took one of the ales. "Thanks," he said, but didn't offer any passphrases in return. Instead he ran his hand over the place hers had just been. He had a DNA coder chip in his thumb, with more storage than he thought possible.

If she had her DNA on file with the Alliance or if she ran with the Black Fleet, he would know.

An identification appeared over his right eye in black, which meant she worked for the Alliance. He had set up the color coding, not anyone else, so no one would know where she worked, even if they somehow got their hands on his chip.

Her name was listed as on file, but he couldn't get it from the simple DNA. He could get any one of sixteen aliases if he chose.

Instead, he extended his hand. "Zag."

"Elise," she said.

The chip double-checked her DNA and confirmed the name as one of her aliases.

"I understand you're coming with me on the meet," he said.

She shrugged one shoulder. "Apparently, the person we work for is too far away, and feels that he shouldn't be there, anyhow. It was a dangerous suggestion."

Zagrando didn't know if she were role-playing or telling the truth. The negativity sounded like pure Jarvis, but Zagrando couldn't be sure. After all, they had agreed that the so-called buyer wouldn't arrive with Zagrando to do the meet.

"You have the instructions, I take it?" Zagrando said.

"As much as I'm privy to," she said. "I'm amazed you couldn't do this yourself."

"No more amazed than I am," Zagrando said. "This is what the seller wants. You realize this entire thing could be dangerous."

She smiled. "I may be here as our client's attorney, but I can handle myself in a crisis."

He bet she could.

"We should take my ship," she said.

"But we're not going to," Zagrando said. "I'm taking you there."

He'd learned his lesson. He wasn't going to let anyone ferry him anywhere ever again. He needed to have a ship that responded to his commands and no one else's.

"Why don't we meet there?" she asked.

He smiled. "Either you come on my terms or you stay behind."

"You're the one who needs a second," she said.

"I need my client," he said. "No one else."

She stared at him for a moment. "It's going to be like that, is it?"

"Yeah," he said with a cold smile. "It's going to be like that."

35

THE APARTMENT WAS QUIET. THE ONLY LIGHT STREAMED FROM FLINT'S home office, but he didn't sit in there. He sat on the uncomfortable couch in the living room, in the very center of the apartment, and held his breath.

He had learned the sounds of Talia sleeping, and he had learned that he could hear them from here. When she first arrived, he would peer into her room like the anxious parent he was, but then she would say, *I'm not a baby,* a phrase designed to both hurt and push him away.

Her original, Emmeline, had died as a baby. That day had broken Flint's heart, changed his life, and, he thought at the time, destroyed his marriage. Only later, only after he found Talia, did he realize the marriage he thought he had might never have existed.

He still hadn't dealt with his feelings about Rhonda. He set them aside, just like he set aside the fact that Talia was only one of several clones of Emmeline, clones—girls, children, *his* children who were growing up without him.

It disturbed him that Selah Rutledge, the Aristotle Academy headmistress, knew—or at least suspected—that Talia was a clone. Secrets had a way of coming out, no matter how closely held they were. And right now was not the time to expose Talia as anything other than Flint's natural-born child.

He ran a hand over his face.

No sound came from Talia's room. Not rustling, not shifting, not the creak of the floor. Try as she might, she always made noise when she was awake.

She had finally dropped off, and he had to repress the urge to check on her. He didn't want her to know how worried that incident at the school made him. If anything, it made him even more determined to solve the entire Anniversary Day mystery.

If he could call it that.

He stood up and sighed. He was solving this for Talia, and because of Talia, he couldn't work the way he wanted to. He wanted to work until he found out all the information he could, no sleep except for a cat nap here and there, meals caught on the fly.

But he didn't dare do that. He needed to take care of his daughter as well, and he needed to remain alert. Plus he couldn't investigate everything from his home computers. As sophisticated as they were, as many protections as he had placed on them, he would never do dicey work on them. He didn't want to anger someone by accidentally (or intentionally) probing a dangerous organization, and then have that organization target him.

Finding where he lived was easy enough, but he didn't want to invite someone here, particularly when he was doing an anonymous search.

So he couldn't do a lot of the investigating he wanted to do.

He'd already tried to see which corporations worked on weapons systems for the Earth Alliance, figuring that the search was the kind a journalist or a school student might do.

He immediately ran into a wall. He got a list of corporations, but they were subcorporations of other subcorporations, and the farther he went down into them, the less information he got. He couldn't even tell what some of their primary businesses were.

He had figured he would be able to see a corporation that specialized in cloning, for example, on that list, but he didn't find any.

The corporations that specialized in cloning, like the one that created Talia, did most of their work with consumers or with scientific laboratories, not with the government.

At least that he could find.

He went into the kitchen, more as a force of habit than because he was hungry. Talia had helped him pick out this apartment. He had made a fortune after he left the Armstrong Police Department, and until he found Talia, he had spent almost none of it.

This apartment was the most expensive thing he had ever purchased in his life. It was a penthouse apartment, the most secure place in a brand-new building. Flint had watched the thing go up, and knew it had been built to the highest possible standards.

The building had top-notch security, and the penthouse apartment even more so. Plus he had added features of his own.

Initially he had planned on buying a house, but Talia didn't want one. Her mother had been kidnapped out of their house in Valhalla Basin; Talia had been held prisoner in her own closet for hours until she figured out how to escape.

She felt that she could have gotten rescued sooner if she'd been in an apartment. Someone would have heard her pound on the floor or scream or something.

Flint didn't have the heart to tell her that the floors in this very secure building had a secondary floor beneath, so that no one on the floors below could hear anything. The rest of the apartment—in fact, the entire building—was soundproofed, so that the residents couldn't hear anything anyone else did. They couldn't hear street noise, either.

It was as close to a self-contained environment that an apartment building could have.

The kitchen was large, with shiny cabinets and the most up-to-date appliances. Talia had chosen this place not for its size or its views of the city, but because of its kitchen and its unbelievably ornate bathrooms. Most apartments they'd looked at together had a great master bath, but the rest of the bathrooms were pedestrian.

Not here. Flint could have lived in one of the bathrooms, and probably had had apartments smaller than Talia's bathroom suite.

He felt awkward showing his wealth like this, but Talia convinced him they needed the comfort. He believed they needed the security.

If anything, the arrival of Talia into his life had made him more paranoid, not less. And he had been pretty paranoid to begin with.

He touched the pantry/cooler door to see what kind of foods he had in here. He wasn't that hungry, but he wasn't tired either, and he needed something to distract himself from the investigation.

He pulled out some real beef—Talia had also convinced him to buy the best-tasting food, not the least expensive—and some freshly baked bread from the deli downstairs, and started to assemble a sandwich.

A notice pinged against his right eye. It was a subtle notice that he had a contact, as if the sender had not wanted to disturb him in case he was sleeping.

Flint tapped the secure link access on the pantry/cooler door, put the sound on low, and stepped back.

"Why doesn't it surprise me that you're awake?" Nyquist peered at him. If anything, the man looked even more rumpled than he had earlier, and the parts of his office visible behind him even messier. "Although I gotta say, that's some fancy digs behind you."

Flint made himself smile, even though he inwardly cringed. The expensive nature of this place was visible in the cabinet materials, the high-end tile, the countertops. He should have left Nyquist on a private link, but hadn't thought it through.

"You got something?" Flint asked, not really willing to discuss his apartment.

"I got a lotta somethings," Nyquist said. "None of them any good."

He ran a hand over his face, a sign of exhaustion. He actually looked a bit gray. Flint wondered if Nyquist's health was breaking down. The man had nearly died a few years ago, and even though his systems got rebuilt, rebuilt systems were never entirely the same.

"Designer criminal clones," Nyquist said, "do not exist."

"Um," Flint said, about to argue. "But—"

"At least, as far as the Armstrong Police Department is concerned." Nyquist sighed. "I can't search for that phrase. I find myself catapulted out of our information systems when I even try. This is what happens when something is classified."

When it was ostentatiously classified. Flint knew because he designed the system. If someone had to know that the inquiry was not allowed, the system spit the inquiry back. If the inquiry was quietly classified, the questioner would get sent to similar ideas or concepts and might never ever know that their original inquiry got bounced.

"Which you probably know," Nyquist said. "Sorry. Tired. Forgot who I'm talking to."

"It's all right," Flint said.

"So I just looked for multiple arrests of similar clones and yeah, there are a few on Armstrong, but it's small stuff, not the kind of thing you're talking about. Clones of criminals manufactured in large numbers never made it here. There are some older cases on Earth, of all places, but they're political—someone cloned old historical figures and tried to have them speak on the current situation, stuff like that. Nothing like what we saw on Anniversary Day."

Flint sighed. He should have expected that.

"But here's the thing," Nyquist said. "If I look outside the Earth Alliance, I find a lot of these cases, often involving Earth Alliance corporations. I can't investigate far, mostly because some outside agency steps in and shuts down the inquiry or because the corporation decided to investigate in-house, but your rumor from your friend isn't a rumor. It's something the Earth Alliance knows about, has classified, and is really touchy about. Which I don't like at all. Because that means, well, what it means is something I'm not going to say even on a secure link."

"I know," Flint said. "I found out more this evening, and you're right to be cautious. Look up the term *blowback*."

Nyquist cursed. "I know the term. And yeah, I was beginning to suspect as much."

"I've been trying to figure out who made these weapons systems," Flint said, "but I'm not working in a secure area at the moment."

Nyquist's eyebrows went up. "That's your kitchen? Hell, man—"

"I keep getting stuck by the same things that are interfering with your investigation," Flint said quickly, so that neither man would focus on Flint's kitchen.

Nyquist gave him a small grin, clearly aware of what Flint had just done.

"Here's what I'm thinking," Nyquist said. "I'm thinking this all fits, even the blowback. Particularly the blowback. If you really consider it, what Ursula Palmette and all the others like her, the ones that opened doors for these cloned killers, as you call them, or provided them with weapons or whatever, what these folks did was a form of blowback. They used systems designed for one purpose against the designer. It's like a signature of the entire attack."

Flint felt lighter, the way he did when pieces he had seen came together into a realization. Then he shuddered. "This means whoever—whatever—is behind these attacks has a real solid knowledge of the way that systems within the Alliance work."

"Which gives us a clue as to who they are," Nyquist said.

"More a clue as to who they aren't," Flint said. "They aren't outsiders."

"Or if they are," Nyquist said, "they were inside once."

Flint nodded. He felt breathless. He felt like they had made more progress in one day than they had made since the attacks.

"It probably gives us a clue as to motive as well," he said.

"Probably," Nyquist said. "But we won't figure that out until we have a name."

"Or at least a suspect," Flint said.

"Yeah." Nyquist picked up a coffee cup that looked like the same cup he had used at dinner, hours ago. "It also means our investigation needs at least two prongs. We have to work within the system to back trace what they did, but we also need to go outside the system to find out what happened."

"Because they know that we can't research the clones," Flint said.

"And they probably know lots of other things too." Nyquist leaned back in his chair. The little squeak it made carried through the link. "But here's the thing I realized as I was researching all of this stuff. If these clones were designed for use *outside* the Earth Alliance—not the PierLuigi Frémont clones that attacked us, but the weapons system— then there is no reason to use someone famous like PierLuigi Frémont as the original. You just find someone less famous, someone who was probably more efficient at whatever you believe he did, and then use the so-called inherent abilities of these clones as your basis for whatever was done. Or you use clones of someone famous in the place you were going to attack, not famous in the Earth Alliance."

Flint had been looking at the fame as a clue to the reaction the orchestrators of the attack wanted, and he knew tracing the clones might bring him to the attacks, but he hadn't thought of the fame being a clue in and of itself.

He let out a small whistle. "Brilliant."

"Nah," Nyquist said. "Just something to consider. It doesn't make sense to have a famous original unless you want to make a point with that original. If you're designing these things to infiltrate somewhere, you pick the best one for the job."

"And the best ones for this job made us focus on Frémont," Flint said, "not on what they actually did."

"Precisely," Nyquist said. "I mean, if you look at Frémont himself, he was more a cult guy who happened to commit mass murder rather than a mass murderer on some kind of rampage. If you wanted efficient killers, you wouldn't recreate Frémont."

Nyquist was right. Again, whoever was doing this understood the system, almost better than the investigators.

Although that wasn't entirely true. Whoever designed these attacks knew how investigators worked, how fragmented the law enforcement system was, and how information didn't come in large pieces. The designer also knew that a lot of information would get lost or never found and that everyone would focus on the most obvious connection—PierLuigi Frémont and the statement—not on actually tracking the designer.

Which meant that the attacks had another, larger purpose, one Flint hadn't seen yet—no one could see—because they didn't know how or what caused all of this mayhem.

Or what they got out of it.

Who benefitted from mayhem? And how would they benefit?

Flint felt an answer tantalizingly out of reach.

"So here's the thing that I can't investigate because it's outside of my jurisdiction," Nyquist said. "Who provided the DNA from PierLuigi Frémont? I checked the family. They had no access to his DNA and most of them wanted nothing to do with him. He was in a maximum security Earth Alliance prison until he died, and his DNA was closely monitored, just like all of those people's DNA is, particularly the famous ones or the culty ones."

"Did he distribute DNA before he got captured?" Flint asked. "Sperm, maybe, or something else?"

"All of it destroyed," Nyquist said. "Or at least, that's what the records tell us. The fires in Abbondiado destroyed his compound, then the arresting officers did a search, double-checked by Earth Alliance officials, to make sure no one was keeping anything—including DNA—for Frémont."

"That would be hard to track," Flint said.

"The Alliance has bots that can look at the smallest skin cell for its origin, and those bots get used in cases like this, cases where the Alliance believes the alleged criminal might become or already is a cult figure. No bit of that person's actual DNA leaves an area. Theoretically."

"You sound like you believe that," Flint said.

"I do, actually." Nyquist sounded surprised at himself. "I worked on one of those investigations once. It was scarily complete. You'd be amazed at how much DNA you shed, and how much can be collected and theoretically disposed of."

"You keep using the word 'theoretically,'" Flint said.

"Yeah," Nyquist said. "I'm an old-fashioned, cautious kinda guy. I don't believe anything happens unless I do it myself."

Flint grinned in recognition. People often saw that as a can't-play-well-with-others trait, but Flint liked that perfectionism. It actually made him more comfortable to work with someone like Nyquist, rather than less.

It also explained why, despite their prickly relationship, he liked the guy.

"So you're thinking the DNA came from the prison," Flint said.

"Yeah, and if so, there's some coordinated activity going on. I would wager that someone is selling DNA or something," Nyquist said.

Flint sighed. "Are there enough major criminals with the right reputations to do that? Or did someone get approached?"

"I don't know the answer to that. You're going to have to find out."

Flint glanced out the kitchen door. He had no idea how he would find out. In the past, he would have gone to the prison himself.

"Can't someone take care of the kid?" Nyquist asked, ever prescient.

"Theoretically," Flint said.

Nyquist let out a small laugh. "Okay. Point made. We'll have to see what we can come up with."

"I have few ideas," Flint said. "I'm not sure you're going to want to know what they are."

"If they violate Armstrong law, it's better if I don't," Nyquist said. "No matter how committed I am to this cause."

Flint nodded. "Let me know if you find anything else."

"Oh, believe me, I will," Nyquist said, and signed off.

Flint stared at the pantry/cooler door. Now all it showed were the foods inside along with their expiration dates and a request to see if he wanted recipe suggestions.

He shut down the door entirely and went back to building his sandwich.

It seemed to him there were three kinds of designer criminal clones: the ones designed by the Earth Alliance to infiltrate troublesome crime syndicates like the Black Fleet; the ones designed to help organizations like the Black Fleet pull off a particular kind of crime (usually theft); and the kind designed to both commit the crime and scare the non-victims into some kind of compliance.

The Moon had just experienced the third. He had no idea if any other place had. He wasn't even sure there were enough famous criminals of the PierLuigi Frémont stripe to make this kind of designer criminal clone a viable business option.

He opened the cooler and got some Armstrong-grown lettuce, along with a chutney that Talia had made. He spread that on the bread, then assembled the sandwich, and put all the ingredients away.

He carried the sandwich across the stupidly large apartment, all the way to his office. He paused in the living room. He still didn't hear Talia, which was a good thing.

He went to his desk. Even though he wouldn't let himself search for things on this particular network, he liked sitting here. He did some of his best thinking in front of an active screen.

He couldn't go to the prison. He couldn't leave Talia here, even with a trusted friend. He simply wouldn't be able to concentrate properly if he did that. He also couldn't bring her to the prison.

He would have to find someone else who could get this information for him.

Maybe Goudkins and Ostaka could, but if they reported the wrong thing, it might filter its way through the Earth Alliance. He didn't trust them enough.

He needed a reporter. He needed someone like Ki Bowles who gave up everything for the story. But he no longer knew anyone like that, now that Bowles was dead.

That left only one person, whom Flint shouldn't trust at all. Luc Deshin. Deshin would be credible to whomever started this scheme. And Deshin would have the contacts that could get him to that prison fast.

But Flint couldn't trust Deshin. No one could.

Yet the man had seemed sincere. Flint actually believed Deshin when he said he wanted to do something about preventing more Anniversary Day-type attacks.

Flint could either rely on a man he didn't trust to find out this information, or he could get it himself while compromising a promise he'd made to himself to keep Talia safe.

Two terrible choices. And yet it felt like an easy decision.

He'd contact Deshin—and hope to God that Deshin really did want to do the right thing.

36

AFTER HER DISCUSSIONS WITH HALF A DOZEN EARTH ALLIANCE officials, Jin Rastigan started to believe she didn't know anything about Anniversary Day. So she went to her office in the Earth Alliance headquarters on Peyla and spent an hour watching the crisis unfold. Then she scanned through half a dozen sites that told her all about the investigation.

Her office was aggressively Earth-centric. Much as she loved Peyla, she missed her home. Sometimes she got tired of the poisonous atmosphere here, the unfamiliar plants, the strange customs. Her office had hard-to-tend orchids and dozens of different species of violets under soft grow-lights. The ceiling had a sky-show program based on her Iowa hometown, and she often had the scent of fresh-mowed grass pumped into the environmental system.

None of that comforted her today. Her meetings had upset her, although not as much as the security vid or Uzvot's willingness to give up Peyti secrets.

Something was happening here, and no one outside of Peyla seemed to care.

Plus, they all seemed to be feeding her misinformation.

Each site she went to—and the damn vids—all had the same image of the clones arriving in the Port of Armstrong, talking with each other like old friends, and then going their separate ways.

She hadn't misremembered that at all. But someone—a lot of some-ones—in the Earth Alliance wanted to downplay that part.

Rastigan didn't care about the politics of the situation—or any situation, for that matter. If lives were at stake, then someone had to do something.

She just kept getting the sense from the Earth Alliance officials she had contacted that human lives were worth a lot more than Peyti lives.

Of course, because of her status in the Alliance, she had to either work through Peyti representatives or through human ones. The Peyti expected her to handle the humans on this potential conflict; the humans expected the Peyti to come to them if there was some kind of Peyti problem.

She was stuck, and worse, she was beginning to feel like the worst kind of whistleblower—the kind that continually and fruitlessly pissed into the wind until something awful happened, and she was seen as the poor sap everyone should have listened to.

It wasn't until she was deep into yet another vid that she realized there was one person she could talk to without going through the Earth Alli-ance: Chief of Security for the United Domes of the Moon Noelle DeRicci.

All of the reports mentioned DeRicci and her unorthodox meth-ods that had saved the Moon, not just this time, but during a crisis with the Disty some years back. Apparently DeRicci knew when to take things into her own hands and when to let the system take charge.

Right now, Rastigan needed that kind of advice. Even if DeRicci couldn't help her with the Earth Alliance, the woman might give her a touchstone, a way of approaching the problem from a completely dif-ferent angle, one that might save Rastigan time and grief.

And maybe, just maybe, DeRicci would understand the signifi-cance of Uzvot's fear and everything Rastigan had seen today.

Rastigan started digging through all her Earth Alliance contacts and protocols. There had to be an easy way to contact someone on the Moon without involving the Earth Alliance.

Rastigan just had to find it.

37

ZAGRANDO SAT IN THE CABIN OF HIS SHIP. THE CABIN WAS, AS advertised, the most spectacular cabin he had ever seen. The bed alone could have accommodated four huge people. And the mattress, which he had only touched with his hand, was sinfully soft.

He had coded the entire ship to his DNA so that most of the rooms were off-limits to anyone but him. The ship did not inform other travelers how they got locked out of certain areas, only that they were. He imagined it was frustrating.

He hadn't discussed the frustration with his first passenger, who was calling herself Elise. He had verified—again—that she worked for the Earth Alliance, but she made him nervous. He had a small screen open on his wall, and instructions to follow her. She sat in the lounge, a tablet on her lap, and tapped away at things he didn't understand. He supposed he could zoom in on her work, but he chose not to. Instead, he let the system keep a record of what she was doing, in case he needed to know later.

She hadn't moved since they got onboard the ship.

He had. He had programmed their flight path into the navigational system, then moved it all to the secondary cockpit, which was in a room just off the captain's suite. He would fly from there, but he locked off the main cockpit just to be safe.

Then he had come here to find out who she really was. The cabin had its own dedicated network, one that didn't interface with the rest of the ship. He had tracked it on his way to Jarvis's Corner to see what nets it logged onto, and he found that it used systems he hadn't seen in a long time. Most of them charged for the privilege. He still had money from H'Jith, so he used H'Jith's account to log into one of the networks and used facial recognition to track Elise.

She had a long and varied history, mostly with the aliases he'd found. No one had placed obvious warnings on her nor had they flagged her.

When he logged off that system, he piggybacked on several others, looking again, and finding nothing.

Finally he logged off entirely and used one of his secure links to interface with the Earth Alliance system. He didn't contact the system itself, just the downloads he carried with him. She was in there, along with her date of hire. Her real name took access to the network itself, and he decided not to look for it.

He had as much confirmation as he needed.

But he still felt awkward, forced to trust someone in a potentially dicey situation, and he knew nothing about her.

He had known more about Whiteley than he would ever know about her.

The ship pinged him. They neared their destination. Either he went for this or he didn't. But he was the one who had requested her. He was the one who had set up this meet.

He would go through with it, even though he had his doubts. Once he got the information the Earth Alliance believed it needed, he would decide what to do next.

Without their help.

38

THE CONTACT STARTLED HER AWAKE.

DeRicci had fallen asleep propped against the wall of the train, pillows scrunched around her neck and back. She had been dreaming about the Moon Marathon all those years ago, when she had to deal with dying runners and Frieda Tey. Only this time, Tey ran away from her and no one would let DeRicci run after her.

She awoke with her heart pounding and a blinking signal in front of her left eye, one that wouldn't go away.

The signal came from the Earth Alliance headquarters on Peyla, of all places. She didn't know anyone there. She decided to ignore it, but as she blinked it away, it flared a bright red, with the word *Please* embedded into the image.

Someone knew DeRicci would ignore the signal and wanted to prevent her from doing that.

Her curiosity piqued, she answered the signal. She left the privacy settings on so that whomever contacted her couldn't see her.

I'm sorry to bother you, Chief DeRicci, the message said, *but my name is Jin Rastigan and I'm with the Earth Alliance on Peyla. I've worked with the Peyti for years and have encountered a situation that has the Peyti spooked, but the Alliance itself won't listen to me. I was wondering if I could get advice from you.*

The message was a canned one, just like that *Please* was. DeRicci blinked, and smoothed a hand over her tangled hair. In spite of herself, she was intrigued.

She sent a message back: *Make it quick.*

Then she hooked Rastigan's link so that a visual would appear when Rastigan got back to her. DeRicci swung her legs over the side of the bed—no more sleeping this night—and decided to take a shower before finding out exactly where the train was. They couldn't be too far from Armstrong by now.

She'd barely had the thought when Rastigan's image appeared in front of her, startling her. She had expected Rastigan to take a while to get back to her.

Rastigan was a middle-aged woman with lines beside her delicate mouth. Her light brown skin looked bruised, and deep shadows had formed beneath her almond-shaped green eyes.

"Thank you for this," she said.

DeRicci left the visuals off. She didn't want to appear like someone who had just woken up, even though she was. Instead, she used a still shot where the visual would be.

"What do you need?" she asked.

"Advice," Rastigan said. She appeared to be sitting on something in a small office, shelves behind her. "Let me explain what happened here today."

She told DeRicci about the killings, how she got called in, how upset it made the Peyti. That they had found a compound with clones.

"Cloning is frowned upon here," Rastigan said. "And seen as really unusual. The Peyti don't have anything like identical twins or triplets. Each individual has a certain look."

DeRicci's stomach clenched. She didn't like the way this was going.

"Don't tell me," she said. "The clones are of someone famous."

"Yes." Rastigan sounded relieved.

"Someone famous and awful," DeRicci said.

"Yes," Rastigan said. "The most famous mass murderer in Peyti history. This whole thing so disturbed one of my Peyti cohorts that she wanted me to contact the Earth Alliance, but no one in the Alliance will listen to me. My boss won't contact his superiors. He had me talk to the investigative unit, who just shut me down. Only one member of the unit even thought I had a reason to worry."

DeRicci closed her eyes and let out a small breath, thankful she hadn't put her image on visual. Not because of how she was dressed, but because she had actually felt the blood leave her face when she heard who these clones were.

"Tell me why you're worried," she said, mostly as a stall. She needed to think.

"Isn't this how the Anniversary Day attacks started?" Rastigan asked. "With clones of a mass murderer?"

"But they didn't kill each other," DeRicci said. Or did they? She really didn't know what they had done before they came to Armstrong. They had been slow-grow clones, which meant they had a life before they came here.

The Earth Alliance had told her they would investigate the clones' history, but she hadn't received any updates on anything. And the history should be the easy part.

"So you don't think it's anything to worry about?" Rastigan asked. She sounded almost hurt.

DeRicci made herself look at the woman. She recognized Rastigan's face, not because she'd met her before, but because she used to be her—a woman who got frustrated by bureaucratic inactivity. A woman who hated hitting walls in an investigation. A woman who knew something was wrong in her gut, but lacked proof.

She clicked off the still shot, revealing herself in all her sleep-rumpled glory.

"No," she said. "I didn't say that. I think you have great cause to worry. You and the Peyti. I think we all have something to worry about."

It couldn't be a coincidence that there was another group of famous clones involved in crimes. It had to mean something.

"What do you think I should do? The Alliance won't listen to me." Rastigan sounded panicked.

"But the Peyti are investigating this," DeRicci said.

"As a crime of murder," Rastigan said. "They're leaving the possibility of a bigger attack to me."

"Because they don't believe in it?" DeRicci asked.

"I don't think some of them believe it could happen here," Rastigan said. "Uzvot—she's the one I'm working with—does, but she has less clout than I do."

"We didn't believe anything like this could happen here, either," DeRicci said. "And we had warning."

That earlier explosion, the one that had made her career. It had saved lives here on the Moon only because she had learned the value of fast action. But it hadn't prevented any attacks.

What if Rastigan's information could prevent attacks?

DeRicci ran her hand through her hair again, hoping she didn't look too crazed. "Can you get the Peyti to help you?"

"Do what?" Rastigan asked.

"I don't know enough about the Peyti," DeRicci said. "I've only worked with them here, and they're always wearing those damn masks. Does facial recognition work with them?"

"Of course," Rastigan said, and then her cheeks flushed. She must have realized that her answer was a bit abrupt.

The abruptness didn't bother DeRicci. She was all about abruptness—or she used to be.

"Then you have to do the biggest search of your life," DeRicci said. "You need to use facial recognition to search all over Peyla, and find out if more of these clones exist. If they do exist, what are they doing? If you find a bunch of them, go back through old security footage and see if you can figure out what they're up to."

A small frown had formed between Rastigan's eyebrows. She was concentrating, hard.

"The clones that ended up attacking the Moon looked innocent enough," DeRicci said. "They arrived in a group at the Port of Armstrong, laughed and joked with each other, and then they went off in their separate directions, just like any family would. Not too many people noticed how similar they looked, and no one noticed until after the attacks that they resembled PierLuigi Frémont. Only in hindsight did their actions look sinister. When they arrived, they looked like any other group traveling together. Do you understand what I mean?"

"Yeah," Rastigan said, sounding both tired and frightened. "I do."

"Is there going to be a problem with the Peyti on this?" DeRicci asked.

"No," Rastigan said. "They're already upset about what's happening, and as a group, they're very law abiding. They have security everywhere. We should be able to track anything on Peyla."

"What about other parts of the Alliance?" DeRicci asked. "I know that a lot of Peyti work in the justice system. Are they spread out all over the Alliance or just in certain parts?"

"All over," Rastigan said. "They mingle well with other groups."

So many alien groups didn't. They preferred their own groups. "They're like humans, then," DeRicci said.

"Even more outgoing, if you can believe it," Rastigan said. "No Peyti minds being the only one in a university or a town or even in a region. They don't get that sense of being an outsider that can drive humans nuts."

DeRicci had noticed that, but it hadn't registered until now. How often had she seen a single Peyti going about his business? She'd seen dozens of them on this trip alone. Peyti were common; they blended in.

"That makes things harder, not easier," DeRicci said. "How old are your clones?"

"I don't know," Rastigan said.

"Ours were slow-grown, and by the time they got here, they were in their late twenties. That means there's a twenty-year trail that we have to follow to figure out who and what they are."

And she hadn't been following it. She had trusted the Earth Alliance to do it. No wonder Flint was mad at her.

"I don't know anything about Peyti, or Peyti lifespans," DeRicci said. "But you need to figure all this stuff out. The more assistance you can get on this project, the better off you'll be. Let's just hope this is some weird coincidence, something that means absolutely nothing."

Rastigan's mouth thinned. "Do you think it is?"

"No," DeRicci said. "I think the problem is even bigger than we originally thought, and that has me worried."

"For us here on Peyla?"

"For everyone in the Earth Alliance." DeRicci let out a small sigh, then shook her head. In trying to do the jobs of a dozen people, she had lost track of who she was. She wasn't Celia Alfreda or Arek Soseki. She didn't run a city or even the United Domes of the Moon.

She ran the Security Office, and she should have kept that as her focus and nothing else.

Not Earth Alliance rules, not Earth Alliance promises. Not re-building, not even being mourner-in-chief like she had been. She had to drop the guilt, drop the sense of responsibility, and remember who she was.

She was Chief of Security for the United Domes of the Moon. Nothing more and nothing less.

"Send me the image, would you?" DeRicci asked. "Is there anyway to modify it so that I can have some different images? I need the young clones' image, the images of the mass murderer throughout his life, and images of all of them with a mask they might wear in the human parts of the Earth Alliance. Can you send me that?"

"You're going to search, too?" Rastigan asked.

"I'm searching the Moon," DeRicci said. "And I'll send the information to the Earth Alliance through the channels your boss refused to contact. I'll flag everything."

Rastigan put a hand over her mouth and closed her eyes. She looked like a woman not used to being overwhelmed with emotion trying to hold back tears. Then she opened her eyes, let her hand drop, and nodded once.

"Thank you," she said. "I can't thank you enough."

"Me?" DeRicci said. "You're the one who deserves the thanks. You may have saved countless lives."

"Everyone tells me 'may' is the operative word."

"I don't know about them," DeRicci said, "but I like to make decisions that err on the side of saving lives, rather than wait to have some bomber or killer prove my suppositions for me. Even if no one is planning an attack, you may have given us the kind of clue we need to solve our problems here on the Moon. I can't tell you how much I appreciate that. Keep me posted on what you find."

"I will," Rastigan said. "I promise."

And then, after an exchange of basic information, she signed off.

DeRicci sat on the side of the bed. The train leaned into a series of curves.

She believed Rastigan. The attackers were still out there, and they were planning something else. They had a larger plan in mind, and it wasn't what DeRicci had guessed it to be. She would never have thought of Peyti involvement, not ever. The Peyti were peaceful people. And that was probably one of the reasons to use them, for whatever this was.

She got up and made her way to the small shower. She felt refreshed. Not because she had finally gotten some sleep, but because Rastigan had given her some clarity.

DeRicci remembered who she was and what she needed to do.

She would leave the tasks of governing to people who actually had a talent for it.

She knew how to keep people safe. She had done it countless times. And even though she had lost a lot on Anniversary Day, she had saved millions of lives by thinking quickly. *Millions*, just by sectioning the domes.

She had to take credit for what she had done in a surprising, impossible situation.

The situation wasn't surprising any more. She had to act differently because the criminals who had instigated these attacks expected her to be on alert.

She needed to find them, she needed to figure out what they wanted, and she needed to surprise them.

She needed to take the offensive.

As soon as she figured out what, exactly, that was.

39

"I DON'T WANT TO GO," TALIA SAID, HER HEAD TILTED BACK AGAINST the passenger seat. She'd been saying some version of that sentence ever since they left home.

Flint stuck his hand out the window for the sixth and final layer of security he had to undergo for the private underground parking facility attached to Aristotle Academy. The system approved him, and he brought his hand inside. The window closed.

"Dad, please," Talia said. "Let me help you out. I know you're working on something—"

"Are you scared to go in today?" Flint asked, without really looking at her. "Or are you just embarrassed?"

She sat up. "Why would I be embarrassed?"

"Whether you like it or not, you helped precipitate that fight yesterday."

"I did not." Talia flounced in her seat, facing him. She bumped against the automated controls, but they didn't acknowledge her. She wasn't registered on this car.

He kept his hands on the controls even though he wasn't driving. He wanted Talia to think he had shut off the automation. He didn't want her to see the full range of his expressions.

He understood her desire to help him.

He also knew that she didn't handle social situations well with kids her own age. She had to face the results of her own actions yesterday.

She had to learn that even the right response had consequences.

"You did," Flint said. "And people will bring it up today. Does that bother you?"

"No," she said, and looked out the windows as the car headed to its designated parking space.

Flint could feel her anger and her frustration. He wondered if she felt just a bit of fear, too. After all, Selah Rutledge had hinted at Talia's clone status. That had to make her feel threatened.

It certainly bothered him.

"Oh, crap," Talia said, and sighed. "Look at that."

Flint glanced toward the interior doors. Five people dressed in suits flanked a man that Flint barely recognized, and one of the kids who had been sitting out in the hall with Talia the day before. People with suits weren't unusual. The fact that they flanked the man and the boy suggested they were either security or legal.

"Who is that?" Flint asked.

"Kaleb Lamber." Talia sounded sullen. "His dad thinks he's important."

It took Flint a moment to parse that sentence. He believed she meant that Lamber senior thought a great deal of himself, not that he thought his kid was important.

"Is he?" Flint asked.

"I don't know," Talia said. "He has less money than we do."

Flint glanced at her. She was chewing on her lower lip. She clearly hadn't meant to say that.

"You investigated their finances?" Flint was trying hard not to sound accusatory. "What made you investigate their finances?"

She shrugged. "Kaleb's always talking about how important his dad is. And he's always talking about how much money they have. But they don't, really. They just have a lot of property, which lost tons of value after Anniversary Day. They can barely afford the tuition."

"Talia." It was Flint's turn to face her. "You didn't confront him about that, did you?"

"No," she said, frowning. "I'm saving it for when he's a total jackass."

Flint let out a small sigh. "You can't say anything. You're not supposed to know about other people's finances. It's not legal to hack into their personal information."

She rolled her eyes. "I *know* that."

"Then why did you do it?"

"He's a jerk, Dad," she said.

"If he's a jerk, then why do you pay attention to him?" Flint asked.

She glanced at Kaleb, who had opened the door to the Academy. Flint had never seen that expression on her face before. It wasn't angry, but it wasn't kind, either. It was almost as if she couldn't stop herself from looking at him.

"You're not attracted to him, are you?" Flint asked.

"No. *No.* God. Dad. *No.* Ick. He's mean."

And she was denying it a bit too much.

"But handsome," Flint said.

"No," she said again. Then she glanced at Kaleb one last time, almost as if she couldn't help herself. "Nobody can be attractive when they're a jerk."

"You seem very focused on him," Flint said.

"Because he's *mean*," Talia said. "Someone has to take him down."

"Not you," Flint said. "If you have any more trouble with him, report him to Ms. Rutledge."

"Yeah, because everyone loves a tattler," Talia said.

"They don't like being thrown out of school for fighting, either," Flint said.

"It's better than telling on someone," Talia said.

"Really?" Flint asked. "Kids could have gotten hurt yesterday."

The car pulled into its parking space and shut off, surprising Flint. He had stopped paying attention to the vehicle somewhere along the way.

"Do you want me to come in with you?" Flint asked, wondering if maybe he should talk to Selah Rutledge again.

"No," Talia said. "That's the last thing I want you to do."

Then she let herself out of the car.

He braced himself for a slam of the door. Instead, she peered in.

"I don't want you to pick me up, either. I'll find another way home."

"No, you won't," Flint said. "I'll be here—"

She slammed the door and the car rocked. She stalked toward the entrance as if he were chasing her.

He wasn't going to, even though he wanted to. Every now and then, he couldn't wait for her to grow up. Most of the time, she seemed like a smart, reasonable person, and then she'd have days like this that reminded him just how crazy teenagers could be.

Still, he watched as the entrance opened for her and she slipped inside.

He felt unsettled. He hated leaving her like this. He too would have liked her to come to the security office with him, if only so that he could protect her.

But he had to let her go, even when he knew she was having a bad day. Even when he knew she could do the wrong thing.

It was her life, and her decisions. All he could do was advise and clean up the mess.

Not that he wanted to. He wanted her life to be mess-free. And it wouldn't be.

No one's was.

40

ZAGRANDO STUDIED THE HOLOMAPS ALL THE WAY TO THE MEET, BUT still felt out of his depth. The meet site was a villa on a small island in the middle of the Xandrian Sea. The Xandrian Sea covered most of the planet Jan, which had only two rather small continents, both of which might have been called large islands on most planets.

Jan had a series of actual islands, most owned by non-natives and used for nefarious purposes—or so the Earth Alliance thought. And now Zagrando could confirm it.

Or at least, he could as soon as he finished the meet.

If he finished it alive.

He rode in an actual water yacht—the kind that Ruth's father would rather have sold. It smelled faintly of teak mixed with cinnamon, which was probably the scent of some native wood here, and it was automated.

He did his best to make sure it was safe: He examined the entire cockpit to make sure no one had rigged the system to operate remotely, and then he rented the ship. He wanted to buy, but he didn't dare. He wasn't quite sure how much money he would need for the rest of the transaction this afternoon.

The Emzada had quoted him one amount, which he had paid half of, but he had already paid nearly that much in bribes and tips since he'd landed on Jan.

There were no space ports anywhere close to the villa. He had to take that hour-long yacht ride to get there, which made him nervous (and vaguely queasy). The sea was greenish black and calm, the sky a slightly darker green, and air so fresh that it made him a bit lightheaded. The air was warm and a bit thick, but the splash of the water as the yacht moved rapidly through it cooled him down.

He sat on a chair near the prow, watching the horizon. Elise sat beside him. She wore a black suit, carried a briefcase that doubled as a computer pad, and had on sensible shoes for once. She still had her black hair piled on top of her head, and Zagrando suspected—although he did not know—that she also had a camera chip in her left eye.

Since she was playing his client—or rather, the lawyer for his client—he wasn't going to complain. If she got herself killed, so be it. He wasn't going to be too upset about it.

He wanted this meeting done. He had tried to talk with her about it, and she reassured him she knew how the game was played. She also showed him her weapons, two small laser pistols, one up her left sleeve, and the other inside that briefcase.

She just had to describe what the clones would be used for—a series of targeted killings throughout the coming years in a place that she had to refuse to name. The killings needed to be timed, starting ten years from now, because her ethics did not allow her to kill children until they actually started in their chosen profession.

Other than that, she wasn't supposed to answer any questions at all unless Zagrando nodded to her. And the only other question he really wanted her to answer was why the client himself hadn't shown up. Of course, she would say he wouldn't expose himself like that. He worked closely with the families he was targeting and he didn't want them to know what he was doing.

Zagrando hoped that was enough.

He never quite understood the clones as killing machines—the thieves made more sense to him—but he had to work within the rules the Alliance had set up. They wanted to know where these clones had come from, and they wanted to make sure it was the assassin clones, not the thieving clones, assuming that they were sold by different manufacturers.

He didn't like assumptions, but then, he didn't like this job, and he didn't like Elise even more. Just her presence beside him, so calm and serene, bothered him. She should have shown more emotion, or at least have asked for more information.

That bothered him as well.

The island appeared on the horizon half an hour into their journey, but he couldn't see the villa until the yacht rounded black cliffs on the island's far side. Nearly hidden in a deep cove, the villa rose like the cliffs. In fact, if you weren't looking for the villa, you would think it part of the landscape.

The yacht turned into the cove, and a part of the hillside opened, revealing a harbor. Apparently that part of the hillside had been an illusion, or so Zagrando hoped.

He like places he could make quick escapes from.

As the yacht reached the dock, he saw a dozen young Emzada guards standing along the paths. Young Emzaden were reed-thin, their skin taut. They would add weight in their third decade, and in their fourth start sloughing skin. The older the Emzada, the more it shed.

Zagrando shuddered at the memory of that Emzada Lair, the one that had led him here.

The yacht attached itself to the dock, locked itself into position, then turned off. Zagrando had been warned it would do that, but that didn't mean he liked it. He had an emergency code to activate the yacht, but he wasn't sure how long the activation would take, nor did he know how long the code would last.

A human man stood in the middle of the Emzada guards. He wore black and had two different weapons slung across his back.

"Identification?" he said, extending a hand.

Zagrando touched the guard's palm with his thumb, using the chip that identified him as Zag the weapons broker.

"This is my client's lawyer," he said as he stepped out. "Elise Dumont."

She extended a hand as well. The guard brushed it, but didn't hold it the way he had held Zagrando's. The movement was subtle, but telling.

He glanced at her.

"I've done business here before," she said.

He felt cold. He hesitated just a moment. He wasn't sure if he should go in or not.

"I represent a lot of clients," she added.

She did have a cover here, and a history. But he didn't like it. He didn't like any of it.

He activated two emergency chips of his own, both weapons, one on each index finger. Both weapons had one small stun built in, and would shake him up as well. But if the guards here took Zagrando's weapons—and he expected they would—then he at least had a quiet and unpredictable way to defend himself.

The human guard led them up a stone path. The Emzada stood to one side, their fish-like eyes moving independently of each other as they watched. The fish eyes weren't visible on the older Emzada, a point in their favor.

It took several minutes to reach the end of the path. Zagrando was covered in sweat by the time he reached the top. No wonder Elise had worn sensible shoes; she had been here before.

He wondered what else she had failed to tell him. He wondered if he would live long enough to find out.

The path turned into a large patio with a built-in table in the very center—all made of the same black rock that covered the cliff sides. The table blended into the building behind it, visible mostly in outline and because of the five humans sitting around it.

All five were men. All five were fit. All five watched as Zagrando and Elise approached, saying nothing.

Zagrando didn't recognize any of them—and he was surprised that they were human. He expected more Emzaden.

The guard stopped in front of the table. "The identification checks out," he said. "This is the dealer Zag and the lawyer Dumont."

"You should have told us your client had Dumont for a lawyer," one of the men said, without standing. He was the oldest of them, with a fleshy face and mottled skin.

"I didn't know until today," Zagrando said.

"Such an excuse," said one of the other men. He had an elaborate black beard, but no mustache. It made his face seem longer than it was.

Zagrando shrugged. "I do not control the client. He pays me if he's satisfied with the work. At the moment, I doubt I'll make anything on this deal."

The Emzada guards in his line of vision moved closer. Zagrando didn't move. Elise gave him a startled glance, as if she couldn't believe he had spoken like that.

"We explained to you that the clones are personalized, yes?" asked the third man. He had skin so dark that he almost blended into the table. "That the client must let us know what they will be used for?"

"That's why Ms. Dumont is here," Zagrando said. "Apparently she knows."

All of the men nodded.

Zagrando's heart no longer pounded hard. He was calmer than he had been for a while. He had dealt with people like this before. They were businessmen, more concerned with money than power. They already felt they had enough power, and they assumed they had more than he did. He still knew there was a chance he might not get out alive, but the chance was less than it had been earlier.

"I still don't understand clones as weapons," Zagrando said. "There are more efficient ways of killing people."

"Not," Elise said, "that we need the high-priced assassin clones. My client wants thieves. He wants them customized for pickpocket work, particularly on space yachts."

Zagrando's breath caught. That bitch. Didn't she know that the entire point of this mission was the assassin clones?

He had to work to keep the surprise off his face.

"We were led to believe you need the assassin clones," the first man said. He leaned back just a little in his chair so that he could clearly see Elise's face.

Zagrando didn't look at her. "That's what I was told as well. That's what we put the down payment on."

"Well," she said, taking a step forward so that she stood nearer to the men than Zagrando did. "We heard the price and realized we could do that particular job simpler, quicker, and more efficiently with one of our own people. But we are intrigued by the thieves. It seems a better investment for slow-grow clones."

"It does work best," said the fourth man. He was small and redheaded. He looked younger than the others. "The training is more important. The assassins only work if you're dealing with a substitution for a real person or for a political mission."

"Or if you want to make a point," said the second man with a bit more glee than Zagrando liked. "It's always nice to scare someone with a figure from the past."

He was looking at Zagrando as he said that. Did he know that Zagrando was interested in the Anniversary Day attacks?

"Yes, we figured that out." Elise effectively blocked Zagrando with her body. Her posture, her attitude, everything about her told the men that Zagrando wasn't important.

He wasn't quite sure how a true weapons broker would handle this. A rogue lawyer? A client out of control? He didn't know. All he knew was that she had screwed him. He couldn't salvage this. And he really didn't want to do business with these men ever again.

He didn't want to do work for the Alliance ever again, either.

"The assassin clones are too elaborate for us," Elise was saying. "I have the specs. Who do I give them to?"

The fifth man, the one who hadn't spoken, extended a hand.

The other men watched Zagrando. Apparently, he was supposed to step in at this point. He made disgusted face and shook his head, as if to say he wasn't going to argue this point.

Apparently, Elise saw that. She gave him a small smile. "Don't worry. You'll get your money."

"I'm not worried," he said, although he was furious. "In fact, it's pretty clear that I'm useless here. You can finish the transaction and they can take you where you need to go."

He bowed slightly.

"Gentlemen," he said, then pivoted and walked back down the path.

She hurried after him and caught his arm. Her grip was firm, yanking him slightly.

"I came with you," she said. "I leave with you."

"It's clear your client no longer needs me," Zagrando said. "I have other, more important business. I'm sure your new friends will take care of you."

"But we work for the same man," she said, sounding just a little panicked.

"Not any more," Zagrando said. He shook her off.

Then he walked down the path, two guards following him. He didn't look at them as he headed toward the yacht.

If she continued to pursue him, she would blow her cover. She might have done so already. She had lost her advantage in the negotiation. By screwing him, and by his reaction to it, the five men knew they couldn't trust her.

She had, effectively, signed a death warrant if she didn't pay for the goods.

And he didn't care. He wasn't going to work like this any longer. He had thrown away a perfectly good investigation into the Black Fleet for this new one, only to have this woman destroy it. If she was as good as she thought she was, she could recover, and she could then follow the evidence to the thief clones who were, in Zagrando's opinion, not worth the Earth Alliance's time.

The assassin clones, on the other hand—they would lead to the killers on Anniversary Day.

And she had just made sure Zagrando's cover was ineffective. He couldn't work this case any longer. He probably would have to dump the identity, too.

He got into the yacht. From the dock, he couldn't see what was happening at the table.

He wasn't sure he cared.

Or rather, he did care, but in a curiosity kind of way. He wanted to know if she would make it out alive, the way that someone else might want to know how a story ended.

He walked the yacht and stepped inside. He glanced over his shoulder to make sure he was alone. The guards watched him from the top of the steps, but didn't do anything.

Apparently no one considered him important.

Good.

He left the yacht attached for just a few minutes while he made sure no one else had boarded it. Then he detached the yacht, got in the cockpit, and started it. As he did, the yacht reminded him that two passengers had arrived, and only one was leaving.

"The second passenger has other transportation," he said, so that it was on record, just in case he was in trouble.

Then he chuckled. Of course he was in trouble. He had left another operative with no money and no backup. She had a less than fifty percent chance of getting out alive.

He would report this to Jarvis first. He would report it as what it was: a betrayal.

If she worked alone, then Zagrando had just taken care of the problem.

If she didn't—well, he couldn't think about that. Not yet.

First he had to get away from this villa.

He commanded the yacht to hit top speed after it left the harbor. Then he sat down in the cockpit, which had actual defenses, unlike the prow of the ship, and hoped to hell Elise kept them all busy for at least an hour.

That was all the time he needed to reach his spaceship and get off this godforsaken planet.

One hour.

He hoped it wasn't too much to ask.

41

As DeRicci got off the elevator on the main floor of the security building, she had an odd, off-balance feeling. Usually, she felt like she had come home when she arrived here. She knew she belonged, and she knew how to behave.

But for the last six months, she hadn't had time to feel anything, and now, it seemed like she was returning from a long vacation or an even longer illness to a place she barely recognized.

Popova sat at her desk, one hand to her ear, meaning she was on a particularly loud link. Two security officers watched the conference room where, DeRicci supposed, the Earth Alliance investigators still camped.

She was going to ignore them for the moment.

She was going to ignore a lot of things as she prioritized. Time to take control of this investigation, do it her way, and make sure that every order she gave got fulfilled.

Time to start now.

"Rudra," she said. "I need you."

Popova looked up, clearly startled. She hadn't heard DeRicci come in, which was unusual enough for Popova. She was usually on top of everything.

She had deep bags under her eyes, and her clothes looked a little rumpled. DeRicci wondered if she had slept here. In fact, DeRicci wondered when Popova had last left the office.

It was time to pay attention to such things: time to make changes.

Popova stood and grabbed a pad. She rounded her desk and headed for DeRicci's office, pushing open the door.

The place was huge. It was the biggest office in the building, with floor-to-ceiling windows all around, something that Flint had commented on, something that he hated.

DeRicci couldn't work in a place without windows. She had done it as a young police officer, and she refused to do it again, even if it placed her in a bit of jeopardy.

She just needed to see her city. And by extension, her Moon.

Her Moon.

As she walked toward her desk, which looked terrifyingly clean, she said, "Have we heard anything from the Earth Alliance's investigation of the PierLuigi Frémont clones?"

"No, sir," Popova said. "I would have let you know."

DeRicci let out a small breath. She had wondered about that ever since she had spoken to Jin Rastigan on the train. DeRicci didn't like the fact that the Earth Alliance hadn't gotten back to her.

Or maybe they had, in the form of those investigators. She wouldn't be able to ignore them after all. She would talk to them when she was done here.

She made it to her desk, touched its clean surface, and wondered how she had let it get so sterile. Another thing to think about later.

She looked up at Popova, who had stopped in front of the desk.

"I had a disturbing contact from Peyla," DeRicci said.

"Peyla?" Popova asked.

"Yes," DeRicci said. "There's been an incident on Peyla that we wouldn't have known about if some Earth Alliance researcher hadn't been onsite. Even then, the Earth Alliance contact on Peyla couldn't get anyone in the investigative office to listen to her."

Popova frowned, then glanced over her shoulder. "Is something going on with the Alliance?"

"I think so," DeRicci said, "but what, I'm not sure. What I am sure of is this: We need to run facial recognition on three different files. They're all of the same face, but it's a Peyti face. These files are different ages and at least one of them has a standard Peyti mask. I want to know if we can find any hits here on the Moon."

"Faces of different ages?" Popova asked. "Of the same person?"

"Yes," DeRicci said. "I should have received the information from Peyla about ten minutes ago."

"Are we dealing with another clone problem?" Popova asked.

DeRicci sincerely hoped not. She wasn't willing to admit what she worried about, at least not yet. She didn't want Popova to know that DeRicci feared another Anniversary Day-type attack, only this time on Peyla.

"Something's happening," DeRicci said. "I'll explain it to you in a minute. And let's not discuss this yet with anyone else, all right?"

Popova's frown got deeper. "You mean the Earth Alliance investigators?"

"I mean anyone," DeRicci said. "I'm not sure if this facial-recognition thing is me helping a colleague, or something more."

"You're being very mysterious," Popova said.

"I suppose I am, but it can't be helped." DeRicci tapped her desktop screen. The files had arrived in a secure package, sent directly to her, avoiding all links. "The files *are* here. Let's start this process. And let me tell you what I learned from a woman named Jin Rastigan when she woke me up this morning."

42

THEY MET IN CELESTINE GONZALEZ'S OFFICE AGAIN. THIS TIME, FLINT arrived first. Gonzalez let him in herself. No secretary, no assistants, no one at all sat in the outer office.

"You know I can't keep doing this." She wore a powder blue suit that should have been too girlish for her, but somehow managed to accent her dark hair and eyes. The clothes made her look even older and tougher. "I don't rent office space."

"I know, Celestine," Flint said. "I appreciate this."

"You should." She held the door to her office open. "Fortunately for you both, I have court this morning. I'm trusting you to lock up. Close the door and double-tap the window when you leave."

"I will," he said.

"And I, to keep up appearances, will wait for our friend, Mr. Deshin."

"No need." Luc Deshin had entered the corridor. Flint hadn't heard him arrive. "I'll pay you for your time, Celestine."

"Of course you will, Luc." She smiled at him. "You get to pay for my office rental, too, even though I'll bill it as something else. You might want to share the cost with Mr. Flint. I know for a fact he can afford to chip in."

Flint grinned at her. "What ever happened to client confidentiality?"

"I never ran your financials, Miles," she said. "So I'm not giving away a client's secrets. But I do know where you're living now."

Flint let out a small grunt. People paid attention to the strangest things.

Gonzalez led them into her office. "My assistant arrives in an hour. No one else needs to be on this floor for another two hours. But I'd suggest you keep the meeting short if you don't want any questions."

She grabbed a pad and a briefcase. Then she locked down her desk. As she walked out of the room, she waggled her fingers at them. "Play nice, boys."

And then she was gone.

Flint looked at Deshin. The man seemed tired, his cheeks gaunt. That couldn't just be from this investigation. Flint wondered what else Deshin was working on, then decided he didn't want to ask.

"You said you wanted to be involved in the investigation," Flint said.

"I do," Deshin said.

"I need an assurance from you before we go any farther," Flint said.

"All right." Deshin pushed on the door, apparently seeing if Gonzalez had shut it tightly. "Did you scan the room to see if anyone is monitoring this?"

"No," Flint said. "I figure if there's a monitor, it's Celestine's and we shouldn't mess with it. Besides, what I'm asking you to do is not illegal."

"Just questionable?" Deshin returned to the center of the room. Both men stood there, as if they were afraid to sit down.

Flint shook his head. "I'm running out of people to trust."

Deshin's eyebrows went up. Then he inclined his head, just a little. He was clearly surprised that Flint had used the word "trust."

Flint wasn't going to explain that. "Before we go any further, I need a promise from you."

"What kind of promise?" Deshin asked. He didn't sound wary. He seemed intrigued.

"I'm going to need some investigation done, and I don't want it farmed out."

"You don't want my assistants doing it," Deshin said, as if he were clarifying.

"That's right," Flint said. "I'm trusting you, Luc, not anyone else."

He made sure to use Deshin's first name, even though the man had never given him permission to do so. Flint wanted this to be intimate, to be between them, as if they were friends.

"If I can do it, I will," Deshin said. "I swear to it."

That surprised Flint. He had expected more of an argument.

And his surprise must have showed, because Deshin smiled. "I understand the need for secrecy here. I'm not sure who is trustworthy when it comes to Anniversary Day, either."

Flint nodded once. Deshin was a smart man, something Flint would do well not to forget.

"All right," Flint said. "We're having trouble getting the Earth Alliance to investigate the assassin clones. We believe they're reluctant because there might be blowback."

Deshin's lips curved upward, but he didn't quite smile. "I wondered the same thing myself."

"Did you investigate?"

"No," Deshin said.

He did not explain, almost as if he were in a court of law. Maybe he felt like he was. He hadn't liked the possibility of being monitored here.

"My sources tell me that when PierLuigi Frémont was caught, all of his loose DNA was destroyed. A fire obliterated his compound, and any known DNA samples were demolished. One of my sources, whom I trust deeply, tells me that the Earth Alliance has a very complete system for getting rid of the most miniscule DNA samples."

"So," Deshin said, "the Frémont DNA came from a source the investigators know nothing about."

"That's possible," Flint said. "But I have a different idea. Generally weapons sales are about money, aren't they?"

"I would assume so," Deshin said with that curious half-smile.

"So someone could have made a lot of money selling PierLuigi Frémont's DNA."

"Including Frémont himself," Deshin said.

"Even though he was in one of the Alliance's maximum security prisons."

"Even though," Deshin said.

"You see my dilemma," Flint said. "I am unable to follow this lead from Armstrong, and because of my inability to trust anyone outside of my rather tight circle, I have no one to ask who can investigate this."

Deshin really did smile now. "Except me. Have the criminal investigate the criminal activity."

"I never said you were a criminal, Luc," Flint said.

"No, you haven't," Deshin said. "In fact, it could be argued that your business requires more criminal activity than mine."

Flint wasn't sure where that was going. Was it Deshin establishing a bit of power? Or simply an attempt on Deshin's part to make them colleagues?

"The problem with this part of the investigation," Flint said, "is that if I were to go in or send in another investigator, that investigator would have to be undercover—"

"I know this," Deshin said. "I already have what you call 'cover.' The problem is that no matter who runs this part of the investigation, it will take time. And I thought you wanted to resolve this quickly."

"That's why I came to you. Establishing an undercover persona can take years. We don't have years."

Deshin shook his head, that smile still on his face. "So you're operating on the *perception* of my criminality."

It didn't seem to bother him, but Flint had trouble reading Deshin easily. "I would have sent in Ki Bowles, the reporter, if she was still with us. But she's not."

It was a non-answer, but it was the safest thing he could think of saying.

"It's all right, Miles," Deshin said. "I play on the perception of my criminality all the time."

Flint smiled.

"So," Deshin said, "just to be clear. You want me to track Frémont's DNA. See how they got it, and maybe that will lead us to…what? The people who planned this?"

"It might lead us to the people who made the clones."

"Surely, if you know it's blowback, you know who made the clones."

Flint shook his head. "I might be able to find the company, but that doesn't mean it worked with whoever attacked the Moon. For all we know, there's a disgruntled employee who set up a shadow company to sell designer criminal clones."

"This, then, might be a major investigation," Deshin said.

"I think you were right initially," Flint said. "This part of the investigation will take time. I'll help as much as I can from Armstrong."

Deshin nodded. "I may have to bring in an assistant or two, but I will clear the information before I give it to you."

"I would prefer that no one else knows," Flint said.

"As would I," Deshin said. "But this sounds like a major investigation, and I may not be able to do it all on my own."

"Give it a shot," Flint said.

"Oh, I will." Deshin extended his hand. "Thank you for including me, Miles. I needed to do something, and I suspect this might be quite useful."

Flint took Deshin's hand. They were partners now, whether Flint liked it or not.

"I think it will be extremely useful," Flint said. "In fact, I think it might be the most important part of the investigation."

And he was trusting a known criminal to get it done. Ironic that he had no one else.

"We'll resolve this, Miles," Deshin said. "Whatever it takes."

Flint did not repeat that last. The *whatever it takes* worried him. He hoped that *whatever it takes* would be easy and legal.

He also knew that hopes like that were often in vain.

43

THE YACHT BOUNCED THROUGH THE WATER. ZAGRANDO FELT VAGUELY queasy. In fact, the queasiness was worse than it had been when he traveled to the island with Elise. And the queasiness wasn't caused by nerves or by remorse over leaving her behind.

Apparently, he got motion sickness on the water. Severe motion sickness. Because if it hadn't been severe, the stay-healthy nanobots would have alleviated all of it.

He needed to ride in the prow of the yacht, just so that he had an unimpeded vision of where he was going. But he didn't want to leave the security of the cockpit.

He monitored everything—the exterior, the water around him, the air above him. He worried that someone would come after him.

He was vaguely disappointed that no one had.

He really wanted to shoot someone. He hadn't been this angry in a long, long time. Maybe not since he had to stand in that room in the Port on Valhalla Basin, watching his own clone get murdered.

Murdered.

By the people he worked for.

Who had just screwed him again.

He'd been doing this a long time. He knew that Elise could have been working on her own. She could have made a back-door deal with one of the men on that island, and she needed to maintain her own cover.

But if that were the case, why hadn't she just killed Zagrando and taken over the meet herself?

He had a hunch—a strong hunch—that she was following orders. And orders usually didn't mean killing another agent. Usually orders superseded other orders, which sometimes led to the torpedoing of a case.

But courtesy between agents meant that she should have told him *before* they arrived on that damn island. Hell, before they traveled across this choppy water. Before they arrived on this stupid planet.

She hadn't said a word.

Maybe that was her style. Maybe she didn't share anything with anyone, just took matters into her own hands.

Or maybe she figured the men on that island—or their guards— would kill Zagrando for her.

There was only one thing she hadn't planned on: She hadn't planned on Zagrando walking away from her.

Leaving her behind.

Effectively signing her death warrant—if, indeed, she was still working for Earth Alliance Intelligence, and not working for herself.

He swallowed hard. Maybe this entire mess had made him sick. Maybe his body was just reacting to the betrayals. Over and over again, people in this business, this *intelligence* business, had screwed with him, lied to him, betrayed him.

He'd had enough.

He would contact Jarvis for the sake of his own conscience. Zagrando needed to find out if Jarvis had betrayed him, too.

If not, Zagrando had to let Jarvis know that Elise was tainted. Which meant that all her past work was tainted as well.

Zagrando glanced at the navigation equipment. He wasn't far from his ship now. Hopefully, no one waited for him there.

He needed to be cautious. He needed to stay on his game.

He needed to get the hell out of this place.

44

TALIA SLOUCHED IN THE BACK OF HER HISTORY OF EARTH CLASS. HISTORY of *Earth*. Like anybody cared. Most of the kids going to this school had never even been to Earth. Talia hadn't. And she certainly didn't care about its stupid history, which seemed to have gone on forever and ever and ever.

A security guard stood outside the door. Ms. Rutledge had increased the security on all of the rooms and in the hallways, not to prevent anyone from getting in, but to prevent the kids from rioting, which was her word. *Rioting*. If Ms. Rutledge had sat through a History of Earth class she would know what rioting really was. What had happened in the cafeteria yesterday was just a fight.

Most of the kids involved in the fight looked tired this morning. Their parents had probably yelled at them. Like that was a problem. The Chinar twins hadn't even come back to school, and Talia heard a rumor that they might not ever return.

The door opened, and Kaleb Lamber tried to sneak in. He hadn't been at the assembly this morning, and Talia had heard he was hiding out in the Office of the Headmistress with some lawyers. She had no idea who they would've been talking to, since Ms. Rutledge had conducted the assembly.

Kaleb looked smaller somehow. His right eye had closed completely and his face was a mass of bruises. Apparently, his parents hadn't let him get fixed up.

His friends said his dad was a nightmare, a bigger bully than Kaleb himself. No one went over to Kaleb's house because no one wanted his dad near them.

If Kaleb hadn't been so mean, Talia would have felt sorry for him. The fact that she felt a bit of sympathy now pissed her off. She didn't want to feel anything for him.

He glanced her way and caught her looking at him. Her cheeks flushed. She would've looked away, but that would've sent the wrong signal, like she was interested or something, like her dad had said. Sometimes her dad could be so clueless.

Instead of looking away, she sent, *So what's with the lawyers?*

None of your damn business, Kaleb sent back.

It's my business if you're siccing a lawyer on me, she sent, kinda proud of herself for doing it. After all, she was investigating, just like her dad did, and doing it without giving herself away too badly.

You're not important enough for lawyers, he sent, and headed to the only empty chair in the room.

"Mr. Lamber," the teacher, Ms. Schultze, said, her hand pausing over a 3-D replica of the population of Earth in something called the Middle Ages. "So nice of you to join us."

"Those Ages can't be Middle if they happened a million-zillion years ago," Kaleb said as he slipped into the chair. He was letting Ms. Schultze know that he was up to date on his homework.

"We don't name the eras," she said with a sigh. "We just teach them."

So what are the lawyers for? Talia sent, deciding to go with the direct approach after all.

If you must know, he sent, *the school instituted some kind of anti-bigotry policy thirty years ago, and Ms. Rutledge is thinking of expelling me, using that as her reason. I'm not a damn bigot.*

Could've fooled me, Talia sent. She felt a little better than she had just a few minutes ago. Ms. Rutledge was protecting kids against bigotry? Against bigotry against clones? Maybe it would be safe here after all.

What do you care, anyway? Kaleb sent. *You'd be happy if I get kicked out.*

Would she? She wasn't sure. He could be funny and entertaining and weirdly nice at times, although it'd been a while since she'd seen the nice.

I'd be happy if you just stopped picking on people, she sent back.

"My alarm has gone off," Ms. Schultze said. "Your links are too active. I will shut them down if I have to."

Kaleb bowed his head. Talia sighed, and leaned back even more. She wished she could go home.

She'd rather keep fighting with Kaleb about bigotry than think about smelly people with short lifespans on a planet she had never seen.

She wondered if it would set off the link-activation alarm if she did some research for her dad instead of listen to Ms. Schultze. It probably would.

An hour of hell, followed by another hour of hell, followed by at least six more. Then, maybe, she could do some real work at the security office, and think about things that actually were important, rather than stuff nobody cared about even back a million-zillion years ago.

What she needed to work on was an argument that would get *her* out of school for the rest of the year.

She needed to come up with something plausible, preferably in the next six hours. Because she didn't want to sit through any more stupid stuff while she missed out on all the important things.

She was too smart to waste her time on a million-zillion years ago. She needed to focus on *now*.

And so did everybody else.

45

JIN RASTIGAN STOOD IN UZVOT'S OFFICE, HANDS CLASPED BEHIND HER back. Rastigan wore her thin environmental suit which, theoretically, kept her at a comfortable temperature as well as provided her oxygen and protected her from the toxic atmosphere. But she was hot and sweaty anyway, and the suit couldn't seem to regulate that.

Which made her think the hot sweats came from nerves.

Or fear.

Uzvot's office looked surprisingly like a human office—desks, chairs, tables, and all kinds of technology, from screens to computers to pads. Most were Earth Alliance issue, but designed for the Peyti. Most Peyti had abandoned their traditional office customs for this setup, partly because they all went to Earth Alliance graduate schools, which taught them how to survive in an Earth Alliance environment. And the Earth Alliance started, as its name implied, with the humans, so most things that were Earth Alliance issue were human-centric.

The human-centric office didn't make Rastigan any more comfortable. In fact, it made her more uncomfortable. She liked Peyti designs, with their heavy cushions, thick draperies, and hidden surfaces. Uzvot had kept the oranges and reds of a standard Peyti design—apparently those colors were easiest on the Peyti eye—but the colors looked out of place here, rather like Rastigan felt.

Uzvot stood in the center of the room, her long fingers manipulating the 3-D images that floated around her. She kept shaking her head.

"It makes no sense," she said in her flawless Standard. "They've done this before."

She was referring to the murder of the Peyti clones. Rastigan had enlisted Uzvot's help using facial recognition to find out if there were other clones of the Peyti mass murderer Uzvekmt. They had found six compounds on Peyla so far, but most had been abandoned.

Before the abandonment, the majority of the clones had died—horribly—just like the clones that Gallen had seen the day before.

"Why make clones, grow them slowly, and then kill them?" Uzvot slowly moved the faces around. These Peyti faces were all the same, even though they had come from different parts of Peyla and different compounds. "If you wanted to use clones for target practice, wouldn't fast-grow clones make more sense?"

The Peyti desire for logic. It made them good lawyers and actually kept their governments stable. But it also gave them a coldness that a lot of humans didn't understand.

Rastigan understood it. She knew that beneath the logic, the Peyti were not cold. They used the logic to understand their world, to cope with its difficulties, and to keep their emotions in check. But the Peyti—when not surrounded by humans and when not doing their jobs—were an emotional people, who experienced great passion in their personal lives and with their families.

Rastigan loved the logic as well, although she was having a bit more trouble summoning it today. Some things defied logic, as far as she was concerned. This incident, for one.

She was monitoring her own screens, and she was seeing things she didn't like.

"Someone's developed these clones for years," she said.

"Indeed," Uzvot said. "Which is why I wondered at the slow-grow—"

285

"No," Rastigan said. "Look. The compounds you're watching emptied out six years to six months ago. These clones are all young, right? What we humans would call teenagers?"

"We do not have the same development cycle—"

"I know," Rastigan said. Sometimes Uzvot forgot who she was talking to. "I'm looking at the developmental age. These clones are between childhood and adulthood, but they have reached their full growth, right?"

Uzvot turned toward her, dark eyes glittering. She was clearly intrigued. "Yes."

"The murders occur at that age. We can probably assume that the compounds work like the one we found."

"We cannot make that kind of assumption without evidence," Uzvot said.

"Give me some latitude here," Rastigan said. "If the compounds work like the one we found, then not everyone got killed."

"We do not know what would have happened if we hadn't interrupted them," Uzvot said.

"We do too," Rastigan said. "There were no adults on site, at least that we found, which means that in the end, someone would have shot his companion, and then survived."

Uzvot shook her head. "It is only a theory."

"Yes, that's right," Rastigan said. "It's a theory. But if that theory is correct, and there are these compounds all over Peyla, then that means several of these clones—of various ages—are out in the universe, somewhere, doing something. And we don't know how old they are or how long this has been happening."

"You're saying our search is too narrow," Uzvot said.

"In both location and in time." Rastigan wished she could get authorities to help, but she couldn't. The Peyti were investigating the murders as an isolated crime. "How far back can we go with your programs here?"

"If we speed them up, we can go back decades," Uzvot said.

Rastigan swallowed hard. DeRicci had said that the clones that had attacked Armstrong were in their twenties.

"Can you search for the Peyti equivalent of a human in their twenties or thirties? Not a teenager. A fully formed adult, but without a lot of experiences yet."

"Yes," Uzvot said. "It will not be an accurate search because we cannot confirm ages, but we can get close."

She moved her hands and the images around her changed. Images also appeared on a screen along one wall. Rastigan watched, entranced. Faces over faces over faces, all Peyti, all the same.

"There are no clumps," Uzvot said. "But look at this."

She froze the images around her. Orange shawls, orange caps, hands up and fingers extended, a look of Peyti joy at some kind of celebration.

It took Rastigan a moment to understand what the celebration was. Graduation.

"They have all gone off-planet for their advanced education." Uzvot sounded relieved. "They are not here."

"Then where the hell are they?" Rastigan asked.

"That is a good question," Uzvot said. "I'm not sure we have the ability to find out. We will need Earth Alliance cooperation."

"Of course we will," Rastigan said tiredly. "Of course we will."

46

THE QUEASY FEELING REMAINED EVEN AFTER ZAGRANDO LEFT THE
yacht. If he never saw the Xandrian Sea again, it would be too soon. If
he never saw the sea again—any sea—it would be too soon. He hated
traveling on water, particularly inside a small box inside a boat.

He completed the return procedure for the rented yacht quickly.
He had a hunch that using the automated "fast-return" system had cost
him more money than he would have usually spent, but for the moment, this was all on the Earth Alliance's tab.

He bounded through the space port, heading to the terminal where
he had left his space yacht. He had all of his personal security systems
on full alert. Aleyd Corporation had developed the systems for the
police officers in Valhalla Basin, and Zagrando had modified them so
that they would never identify him as Iniko Zagrando again.

The systems gave him the ability to see around himself at 360-de-
grees. It made him dizzy (which didn't help the queasiness) but it protected him.

At least this way, he would know if he was being followed; he would
actually *see* whomever (or whatever) was behind him.

This spaceport was small compared to the standards he was used
to. He'd been told there was a larger port elsewhere on Jan, but it was
very far away from here.

This port clearly catered to the high-end customers. All of the shops displayed expensive items. Some shops even (obnoxiously) told him whether or not he could afford to shop there. He had no idea how they knew; he assumed they scanned available credit.

Zag, his alias, had no available credit. He was strictly a cash guy who used other people's accounts to pay his debts.

It took him only a few minutes to get from the water yacht rental place to the entrance to his ship's terminal. He slammed his fist with its temporary identification against the bulkhead door. It opened, greeting him via his links, and asked him if he had a nice stay.

Yeah, if you counted getting seasick, betrayed, and nearly murdered a nice stay. Then it was just one of the best trips he'd ever had.

He made himself slow down as he followed the path to his ship.

In his haste to leave that damn island, he hadn't recovered his weapons, so all he had were the chips in his hand. He had no real way to fight anyone who approached him here.

If he had been thinking, he would have left a few weapons on the water yacht, in case something went awry. But he hadn't—and besides, the Emzada guards on the island probably would have taken those weapons as well.

He was really and truly on his own here.

All he could do was hope that the port security was as good as the advertising claimed it was. And he had to hope that he could talk his way out of any problems—

If he had any problems at all.

He couldn't see anyone. This part of the damn port was curiously lacking in population, which he found suspicious.

Of course, he had no idea what *normal* was here. He had noted a lack of customers when he and Elise had arrived, and then he had attributed it to the fact that this port truly was at the ass-end of nowhere.

He rounded a corner.

There, looking like a significantly larger, classier, and more expensive version of the water yacht he had just left behind, was his new ship.

Damn, he loved that thing. He was happy to see it, as if it were a person in its own right.

No one stood around it. His heightened personal security didn't show anything, either. He seemed to be alone, and able to get off this horrible planet unimpeded.

He couldn't quite believe it.

But it made sense. The men on that island wanted a buyer for their wares. They had one, who, it seemed, might have betrayed them. They were more concerned with Elise at the moment than Zagrando.

Or they had been more concerned with Elise over an hour ago than they were with Zagrando.

Still, he had to get out of here. He also had to make certain they didn't find him, just in case.

He walked slowly toward the ship, his entire body tense. He kept expecting something to jump out at him, someone to tackle him, something try to take a shot at him.

But nothing happened.

He touched the side of the ship. It recognized his DNA, plus the temperature of his palm, along with the fact that blood still moved through his veins. No one had cut off his hand to gain access to the ship.

A stairway emerged from the side. He climbed it and entered the airlock, telling the ship to make certain to activate the major safety protocols.

Then he stepped inside, closing the door behind him.

He scanned the ship, using its own programs and his.

He was alone.

He shut his eyes, letting himself feel relief for just one moment. He wasn't done yet. He still had to leave here. He had to make sure that no one followed him, from those guards to Elise herself. He had to contact Jarvis.

But Zagrando had made it this far.

And, he was beginning to think, that had been a miracle in and of itself.

47

FLINT GOT OFF THE ELEVATOR IN THE SECURITY OFFICE AND immediately noticed that the place had changed. Activity everywhere, people scurrying down the halls, and Popova not at her desk like she had been for most of the past week.

DeRicci was back. That was the only explanation.

He paused at Popova's desk, wondering if he should talk to DeRicci first. But it probably wasn't wise. She would shut him down if she knew what he was doing.

Instead, he went into the conference room. The Earth Alliance investigators had made it their own little fiefdom. They had equipment, designated *secure,* on the large table.

Goudkins paced in the back corner of the room, where no windows revealed her to the rest of the office. She had changed clothes. She wore a blue shirt over blue pants, which were not Earth Alliance Official Regulation.

Ostaka still wore his suit, but the buttons were open around his neck and he had rolled up his sleeves.

Both investigators looked tired, but oddly, they seemed more relaxed at the same time.

Flint was a bit more relaxed as well. Goudkins' story about her sister checked out. Her sister had died, rather horribly, on Anniversary

Day, and Goudkins had taken a longer than normal leave to mourn. From what Flint could find—and he didn't dig as deep as he would have liked because he was at home—she had come to the Moon, taken care of her sister's affairs, and participated in the seemingly endless round of funerals that happened after the bombings.

He didn't know if that made her more trustworthy, but he found the information helpful. She hadn't lied. In fact, she had probably underplayed her reaction to Anniversary Day.

Weirdly enough, that made her part of the Moon, at least in Flint's mind.

He still wasn't sure what to make of Ostaka. Everything Flint found on him seemed to suggest he was a by-the-book investigator, which had never sat well with Flint.

Ostaka nodded at Flint as if they were colleagues. Flint wasn't willing to go that far.

"We're compiling a list of the companies that supply clones to the Earth Alliance," Ostaka said, without saying hello.

Goudkins turned. Apparently, she'd been so deeply engaged in the conversation she'd been having on her links she hadn't realized he had come into the room.

"I'm interested in the ones that supply the defense industry," Flint said.

"It's not easy to figure out which company is supplying for the defense industry and which just provides fodder for colonization," Ostaka said.

Fodder. The word made Flint bristle. His daughter wasn't fodder. No one was.

But he didn't want to say anything, or reveal himself as too involved with this. He had to remain quiet, for Talia's sake.

"What about companies that supply slow-grow clones to various industries?" Flint asked.

Goudkins shook her head, then turned her back on them. She was still having her conversation.

"The companies that provide slow-grow also provide the fast-grow clones that most organizations use," Ostaka said.

Flint tried not to think about the fast-grow clones. He'd seen a few. They were childlike because they were so young. Often they didn't understand what was happening to them.

He barely understood it, either. He never understood why anyone would use something that had human feelings and human reactions in a situation where 'bots or androids or other machines might do.

"I'm also trying to be careful as I make this search," Ostaka said. "I don't want to set off red flags too early."

"Makes sense," Flint said. "Are you finding anything of value?"

Goudkins turned around. Her eyes seemed clear now. They had lost that far-away look most people got when communicating through links.

"We've found some companies that the Alliance has stopped doing business with. The companies were flagged as dodgy, meaning they have ties to criminal organizations or have done business with other shady companies. *Not,*" she said, holding up a finger, "that that's any guarantee they're actually the companies we're looking for. I'm actually pretty certain they aren't."

"Why?" Flint asked.

"Most of them are out of business, for one thing," she said, "and from what I'm seeing, the loss of the government contracts pretty much devastated them financially."

"Which gives them incentive to find other money," Flint said.

"Yeah, it does," she said, "but they'd need it faster than they're getting it. I suspect they just had bad products, and that's why the Alliance got rid of them."

"*Suspect* isn't the same as *know,*" Flint said.

She smiled at him. He was beginning to like her in spite of himself. "I'm aware of that."

"We're also having trouble finding any evidence of blowback," Ostaka said. Then he held up both hands as if to forestall Flint's next comment. "Not that I expect to find such evidence easily. But I had hoped there'd be discussions or meetings or something about the problem."

He ran a hand over his mouth, then shook his head.

"I'm afraid the fact that I can't find anything like that means this problem has existed for a long time." He sounded disturbed by it.

"*Blowback* is an old term," Flint said. "I think it's been around as long as human governments built weapons."

Ostaka gave him a tired look. "I mean the problem with clones in the Alliance."

"Wouldn't we have seen something sooner?" Flint asked.

"I have no idea," Ostaka said. "This truly is above my pay grade."

A movement outside the room caught Flint's eye. DeRicci stood there, watching him. She looked too thin and exhausted. She didn't move at all, but he could tell that she wanted to talk with him—and she didn't want to come in here to do it.

"Can you two excuse me for a moment?" Flint didn't wait for an answer. He walked out of the conference room and almost—almost—asked DeRicci not to yell at him.

Apparently, he was feeling just a little guilty for going behind her back.

"Have they found anything?" she asked.

"You don't even know what they're looking for," Flint said.

"That's true," she said. "And I doubt they can help you."

"Why's that?" He felt wary. The entire conversation seemed off. Or maybe it was just his fury. He wanted to yell at her for that discussion they'd had the day before, but he didn't dare. He was too angry for that. He had to just deal with her right now. He could yell later.

"Because the Earth Alliance seems to be covering up important information," DeRicci said.

"I know," Flint said coldly.

She closed her eyes for a brief moment, then sighed. "Miles, I'm sorry I didn't let you—"

"Later, Noelle. We don't have time for this conversation."

"Actually, we need to have it," she said. "I need to apologize to you. I'm really naïve at times."

Whatever he had expected, that wasn't it. "Naïve?"

"I didn't tell you about the assassin clones because I legitimately thought the Alliance was investigating that side of things. Yes, they were confidential, and yes, I shouldn't even be talking to you about them right now, but I really thought that part of the investigation was being handled. I thought it was in all of our best interests to discover everything about this attack."

Flint frowned. Something had happened. "So did I. I still do."

"Me, too," DeRicci said.

"What changed your mind?" Flint asked. "Why are you talking to me about this now?"

"I've had some disturbing news," DeRicci said, "and it came through a source that shouldn't have spoken to me."

"Like Luc Deshin?"

She gave Flint a tired smile. "Actually, a more reputable source than Luc Deshin."

That was as close to an apology as Flint would get on the Deshin issue.

"This source," DeRicci said, "was a low-level Earth Alliance official on Peyla."

"Peyla?"

DeRicci nodded. "Come to my office. I have a lot to tell you. And, as always, I could use your help."

Flint glanced at the conference room. He wasn't getting anything from the two investigators in there, at least at the moment.

He still felt wary around DeRicci, but her apology had gone a long way to mitigating his anger.

Or maybe he had just gotten good at tamping it down.

"All right," he said. "But if I don't like the direction you're going, I'm going to continue on my own."

She nodded, that small smile still on her face. "I would expect no less of you, Miles," she said.

48

FLINT LOOKED FURIOUS. DERICCI RECOGNIZED THE EXPRESSION, although she had never seen it directed at her before. His features were flat, as if he were trying not to have any expression at all. She was a little offended that he was so angry. After all, she hadn't intended to slow down the investigation. She had honestly believed the Earth Alliance would do its job.

She didn't have the time to work things out with Flint, at least not more than the apology. She hoped that eventually he would forget his anger, or at least put it aside permanently.

Still, he followed her to her office, which she saw as a good sign.

She pushed open the door to find Popova standing in the center of the room, a deep frown on her face. Peyti faces with and without masks floated around her, and others appeared on various screens. Some had frozen. DeRicci recognized them as security images.

Her heart rate increased.

"I was just about to get you," Popova said without turning around. "Are you sure our system works for the Peyti?"

Flint came up beside DeRicci.

"What is this?" he asked.

Popova whirled. She clearly hadn't expected to find him in here. "Mr. Flint."

"Rudra." He bowed just a little. It almost felt mocking. Or maybe DeRicci was just being a bit too sensitive.

"This," DeRicci said, "is what I was telling you about. An Earth Alliance official on Peyla sent me images of clones made of a Peyti mass murderer."

"I didn't know there was such a thing," Flint said. But he didn't seem to be as interested in that as he was in those faces. He walked around a few of the holographic ones. "The Peyti are a non-violent people."

"Now." DeRicci's breathing had quickened. She was conducting the conversation with only one part of her brain. The rest of it was trying to absorb what she was seeing. "Where are these images from, Rudra?"

"I haven't touched anything, Sir," Popova said. "These are the settings you had me use."

The Moon. The images were from the Moon.

Popova was saying, "That's why I was wondering if the facial recognition works for Peyti. Because this just isn't possible."

This was dozens, maybe hundreds, of images, from all over the Moon. All Peyti faces, all of which looked the same to DeRicci.

"Okay," DeRicci said, trying to make sense out of what she was seeing. "These images span how many months?"

"That's just it," Popova said. "They're all from today."

DeRicci looked away from the images and directly at Popova. Her face had gone gray. "What?"

"They're from the past few hours. And if facial recognition *does* work on the Peyti, then something's really wrong."

"If you're using the system here," Flint said softly, "then yes, the facial recognition works on the Peyti, provided that you have images of them with and without the masks."

DeRicci felt just a little dizzy. "We do."

"Let me look at what you did," Flint said. "Just as a double-check. These faces are supposed to be of the clones of that Peyti mass murderer, right?"

"Yes," DeRicci said. She had already counted twenty images of clones, and she had just started.

Flint moved to DeRicci's desk. "You trust your source? You believe these images are of the clones?"

DeRicci hadn't thought of that. "I hadn't double-checked, no."

"What's the name of the mass murderer?" Flint said.

DeRicci's irritation rose. "I don't know. All Peyti names are Uz-something, and impossible to remember."

"Do you know when the murderer was active?" Flint asked.

DeRicci blinked. She made herself look away from the images for just a moment.

Flint's blank expression had left. A light red color had suffused his pale skin. He didn't look panicked—Flint rarely panicked—but he seemed alarmed.

"Um," DeRicci said, "she said he was the last mass murderer on Peyti, and the most famous."

"All right." Flint tapped her desk. Somehow he was in her system. Had she given him access to her desk's computer? She didn't remember doing it, but that meant nothing. Flint knew more about computers than anyone else she had ever met.

An image rose in front of the desk. An older three-dimensional image, with the 3-D showing some wear, the kind that came from files that were translated from old non-human programs.

It looked like the Peyti clones, but DeRicci couldn't tell. Not only could she not remember the damn Peyti names, but she couldn't tell them apart by anything except height and weight.

"Can you run some kind of scan to see if it's the same face?" Popova asked. Her voice shook.

"I just did." Flint raised his head, his blue eyes clouded. "It's the same face."

DeRicci did not want to hear that. She squared her shoulders and looked at all the images. Amazing that the software had caught them, considering the masks were an updated version from the image that Rastigan had sent her.

Then DeRicci's frown grew deeper. She had never seen that mask style before.

"I'm going to sort the images by location," Flint said, "and I'm only going to use the ones from the last five minutes."

He was tapping quickly. Popova watched him, as if staring at him would make the work go faster.

DeRicci kept track of him out of the corner of her eye. She was staring at the masks. They were all the same. A little fatter on the bottom. Not much fatter, though. An added piece about the size of a cupped human hand.

The images winked out, then reappeared. There were fewer images, but not many. Not many at all.

"That's got to be a hundred clones," Popova said.

"Two-hundred-and-fifty-seven," Flint said, his voice remarkably steady. "And that doesn't count the ones that weren't near a security camera five minutes ago."

"Two-hundred-and-fifty-seven?" Popova breathed. "We would have seen an influx on the Port security cameras, like those bombing clones, and I didn't see anything like that."

DeRicci now wished she had stayed for the program's initial sort. She could have double-checked everything herself. Instead, she had walked the hall. That was when she had seen Flint. And while she was walking, she had gotten a short message from Rastigan.

Make sure your search parameters are for different ages.

Different ages.

And of course, DeRicci hadn't done that since she got back. Flint had sidetracked her.

"We didn't see it," DeRicci said, "because they didn't come in together. Some of them have been here for years."

"You can't know that for sure," Popova said.

"No, I can't," DeRicci said. "But we can verify, right, Miles?"

"Yeah," he said. "I'll see what I can find."

"And as you do, see if they're always wearing these masks." She pointed at one of the floating faces. "These masks look strange to me."

"They're different any I've seen before," Popova said. "You want me to see if I can find out what that is?"

"No," DeRicci said. "I have to talk with Jin Rastigan. She's my source on Peyla. She'll know."

At least, DeRicci hoped she would know. Someone had to know. Because DeRicci didn't like what she was seeing. She wanted reassurance that she was overreacting.

Even though she had a hunch she wasn't.

49

ZAGRANDO SPENT THE FIRST PART OF HIS JOURNEY AWAY FROM JAN double-checking his space yacht. He'd kept it locked up tight while he'd been on the island, so he worried less about people attacking the interior, but he scoured the exterior for bugs and tracking devices.

So far, he had found nothing.

The highly sophisticated cockpit, with its state-of-the-art equipment—all of which was nonstandard—sensed no ships around him, and nothing monitoring him from the planet he had just left.

After he had checked all of that, he checked every part of the ship that Elise had been on to make sure she hadn't added her own surveillance devices. He used the security footage to follow her from place to place, then slowed it to a fraction of a second so that he could watch her every move.

When he had finished that, he laid out a map of the places she'd been and the moves she'd made, and physically followed them. He had to see for himself that she had done nothing.

He used a device he picked up from the Black Fleet to check for nanotrackers left by clothing.

Either Elise hadn't known about such things or hadn't thought them important. She probably figured she could use his DNA to get back onto the ship, and then fly it back.

Or maybe she had thought he would go along with her betrayal. She certainly had seemed surprised when he walked away.

He had set the ship on a random course, making sure it used evasive maneuvers. He had no place special to go, and as he traveled, he planned to reset his course a dozen times.

The smart move would have been to dump the ship, but he had become attached—which was probably a mistake. People who grew attached to anything were vulnerable, and that was the last thing he wanted to be.

Of course, going completely solo with no obvious vulnerabilities hadn't worked for him, either. Whiteley had betrayed him on Abbondiado, and then Elise had betrayed him on that island.

Zagrando let out a small sigh. Thinking of betrayal made him think of Jarvis. Zagrando needed to contact him. Jarvis needed to know that Elise had been compromised.

But Zagrando wasn't going to use any of the shipboard systems to make the contact. He was going to try a riskier link-to-link contact. If someone wanted to trace him, they'd be able to figure out where he'd been, but not what he was traveling in.

He'd toyed with going to some kind of a resort or a starbase, and then changed his mind. He didn't want anyone listening in on this conversation. And the risks of that on any kind of station were great.

So Zagrando went into the yacht's cargo bay. It didn't have great communications equipment here—nothing that could relay his signal outside the ship. The only way to communicate with this part of the cargo bay was to do so through the ship's internal system.

He stood in the empty area, feeling alone for the first time in weeks. He hadn't realized how much he had been through.

And he didn't want to think about it now.

He used his most secure link, and he sent a message to Jarvis.

He didn't expect to hear from Jarvis for a couple of hours, so he was extremely surprised when only a few minutes later, Jarvis pinged him back.

I didn't expect to hear from you for hours, Zagrando sent to Jarvis.

Zagrando was using his most secure links, which did not allow for holographic imagery. Those links filtered out all kinds of information, from location to ambient noise to anything that might reveal something about the user. The only thing that activated were the communication portion of the links themselves.

A small image appeared in the corner of his left eye. He could see Jarvis if he wanted to, but he didn't want to. For all Zagrando knew, making Jarvis visible might turn on all the security protocols that Zagrando had turned off.

I know you're on an op, Jarvis sent. *I stayed available.*

Which was a lie. Zagrando had been on ops before and had a hell of a time reaching Jarvis. Distance factored into all communication, even link communication. The fact that Jarvis answered meant he was in this sector and not, by Earth Alliance standards, very far away.

Zagrando walked back to the center of the bay. His mouth had gone dry, and his heart was pounding. Jarvis's proximity made him nervous. Or maybe the nerves from the entire operation had finally hit him.

I'm not on the op any longer, Zagrando sent. *Elise torpedoed it.*

She what? Jarvis sounded alarmed, although it was hard to tell via links.

She told the sellers we wanted thief clones, not assassin clones.

That was my order. Didn't I tell you? Jarvis asked. *Where is she now?*

You ordered the change? Zagrando had to clarify.

Yes. I told you. The op had to go a different direction.

I was on the trail of the assassin clones, the ones that bombed the Moon, and you felt it more important to go after thieves who don't have any impact on the Earth Alliance? Zagrando's hands were shaking. He had that same trapped feeling he'd had the day he watched his own clone get murdered.

I don't care about thieves, Jarvis sent. *It was just too late to cancel the op.*

It's never too late, Zagrando sent. *We risked our lives going in there, for nothing.*

I've been trying to ping Elise, Jarvis sent. *Is she around? Because she can explain this better than I can.*

I left her on that damn island. I made sure the sellers knew she had betrayed me. Zagrando remained motionless. If he moved, he would punch something. But the shaking had stopped. He finally knew who had really betrayed him.

Jarvis had.

You what? Jarvis sent. *Go back. Don't you realize she's in danger?*

Oh, Zagrando sent, *she's probably not in danger anymore.*

He let the words hang. He wanted Jarvis to know that he had set Elise up. Just like they had set Zagrando up.

You need to come in, Jarvis sent. *You might have caused an agent's death through your unwillingness to follow orders.*

Zagrando smiled. The smile felt cold, even to him. *I didn't have orders. As far as I was concerned, she failed to follow orders. I followed protocol for such situations, and saved my cover.*

You had new orders! Jarvis's agitation came through despite the layered links.

I did not have any new orders, Zagrando sent. *So under Earth Alliance Intelligence Department regulations, I'm in the clear. Someone botched this op, and it wasn't me.*

The silence after that comment went on so long that Zagrando did a short diagnostic to make sure the link was still open. It was.

Finally, he decided to end the silence.

Tell me one thing, Zagrando sent. *Did the orders to change the op come from you or from the Earth Alliance?*

I work for the Earth Alliance, Jarvis sent.

So do I, Zagrando sent. *So, theoretically, did Elise. I'm going to ask you again. Did the decision to change the op come from you or from a higher-up in the Earth Alliance?*

Are you asking me if I'm corrupt? Jarvis sent.

Interesting response. Zagrando started pacing. *You can review this conversation. You'll see I never once used the word "corrupt" until this moment. Until you introduced it.*

I work for the Earth Alliance, Jarvis sent.

Which was, apparently, the only answer Zagrando would get to that question. Which probably was enough. But he needed to find out more.

If the Earth Alliance wanted me dead, Zagrando sent, *why not just send someone to kill me? Why not cut off all my access to the Alliance? Why not leave me on my own? Why go through such an elaborate ruse?*

No one was supposed to die, Jarvis sent.

You could've canceled the op, Zagrando sent.

I changed it, Jarvis sent.

And didn't let me know, Zagrando sent.

I had trouble contacting you, Jarvis sent.

Not when Elise was with me, Zagrando sent. *You could have contacted me at any point.*

She outranked you, Jarvis sent. *I contacted her.*

I doubt that, Zagrando sent. *Here's what I know: Usually an operative who already had a cover with that organization would do the job, not someone like me. You had Elise. So therefore, the op I was supposedly on was unnecessary. The trail I was on was unnecessary.*

Then he froze. Unless someone wanted to know how easy it was to discover who developed assassin clones. Unless someone wanted to cover tracks.

The op wasn't tracking the clones. The op was seeing if the clones were trackable.

Zagrando hadn't been on a mission of discovery. He had been the dupe in an attempt to cover something up.

Come in, Iniko, Jarvis sent. *Your cover is probably blown. I'll protect you. We need to debrief.*

I'm sure you do, Zagrando sent. *Let's make it easy for you. I resign.*

What? Jarvis sent. *You can't resign.*

Too late, Zagrando sent. *I resign effective immediately.*

We still need a debrief, Iniko, and you'll need to fill out documentation. I need—

Zagrando severed the link. Then he scrubbed all contact information from that secure line so Jarvis couldn't contact him again.

Zagrando was going to have to remove all Earth Alliance Intelligence chips, which would mean he was going to have to go somewhere that could scrub him thoroughly. He couldn't do that in this sector because he had already screwed over the Black Fleet. He would have to go somewhere else.

Before he did that, however, he needed to do one more thing. He moved all the remaining money for the clone buy into a series of untraceable personal accounts.

The Alliance would claim he stole from them, if this was an on-the-books operation, which he doubted. They would probably write off the money as lost by Elise, on that island. No one would be able to prove that Zagrando had it.

He needed escape funds, and he didn't have enough from H'Jith. Besides, the Alliance owed him money for all those lost years. All those years where he sacrificed his entire life for them, his entire self for them.

They owed him.

And this was one way he was going to make them pay.

50

FLINT STOOD AT DERICCI'S DESK, OPERATING THE BUILT-IN COMPUTER. She had the most sophisticated computer network in Armstrong, and she had no idea how to use it. She also seemed to have no idea that this particular desk could be isolated from the network—and not hacked.

He couldn't remember if he had ever explained that to her, way back when she asked him to review the safety features of the Security Office's computer system. He suspected he had, but DeRicci probably hadn't paid attention.

She looked at computers as tools for her, not as communications systems that worked both ways. Someone could get in as easily as someone could get out.

At least, if someone was not careful.

DeRicci was still surrounded by the Peyti faces, but she had her back to both Popova and Flint. DeRicci was talking to her contact on Peyla, trying to get more information.

Popova kept refining the search parameters, trying to figure out how many of the Peyti clones were here.

Her searches interfered with Flint's. He had isolated the desk ten minutes before, so he wouldn't have to deal with Popova. He also ran an internal scan to make sure the desk hadn't been compromised. He didn't entirely trust the Security Office's network—not with the Earth Alliance investigators here.

He had to stay cautious, because something about this entire investigation bothered him, something he couldn't quite put his finger on.

Peyti clones of a mass murderer. Here.

It made no real sense, not like PierLuigi Frémont did. Humans were afraid or appalled by Frémont, even now, years after his death. Humans didn't care about a Peyti mass murderer. Humans had no idea such a thing existed.

But the numbers Flint was getting dwarfed the ones that Popova initially found. The system tracked at least five hundred of these clones, when adjusted for different ages, like DeRicci had asked.

No children, no Peyti equivalent of teenagers, very few young adults.

So far, Flint's system had found five hundred such Peyti scattered all over the Moon. He was having trouble setting the searches up so that he could prevent counting the same clone twice. He had to use a rather broad search, one that followed each of the five hundred clones to see if they interacted with each other.

So far they hadn't. And, as far as he could tell, they rarely interacted with other Peyti, either.

He wished he were dealing with humans. Humans would be easy. He could tell at a glance what he was looking at. Here, he had to trust the computer system, the facial recognition system, the information that DeRicci had gotten from her Earth Alliance contact.

"Okay." DeRicci turned around. "This was more confusing than helpful."

"You reached her?" Popova asked.

DeRicci nodded. "She's not familiar with the masks. She just wonders if it's a style thing. They do get redesigned on occasion. But remember, she lives on Peyla. She's usually the one in an environmental suit, and doesn't deal with many masked Peyti. She's going to check the databases."

Flint kept working on his, listening, and not really watching DeRicci. He could tell from her tone of voice that she was both perplexed and irritated. She always got irritated when she didn't understand something.

"She's sending more information on those clones," DeRicci said. "It's weird. She's finding those camps everywhere—"

"Camps?" Popova asked.

Flint looked up at that as well. He hadn't heard about camps.

DeRicci waved a hand. "It's a whole long story. Apparently, someone grew the clones in batches in camps. But I'll tell you the details later. Rastigan was looking to see if batches left Peyla together or arrived somewhere together, and she didn't find anything."

Flint's hands froze over the desktop.

"What she did find was graduation ceremonies. Dozens of them, maybe more."

"Graduation?" Popova sounded as confused as Flint felt.

"School is extremely important to the Peyti, at least that's what Rastigan said." DeRicci shrugged. "Everyone who had a graduation ceremony went off Peyla to a prestigious school. But none of them went to the same school or, rather, if they did, they went years apart from the previous Peyti."

Flint wasn't surprised by the Peyti desire to finish education. The Peyti he'd worked with over the years loved knowledge more than anything else, and weren't afraid to take classes here on Armstrong to get to know local laws or customs.

Of course, most of the Peyti he'd worked with had been lawyers, probably because of his involvement with law enforcement. He'd seen a lot of Peyti students in the law library and cafeteria at Dome University.

The Earth Alliance prized Peyti lawyers because of their brilliance, their ability to see through holes in cases, and their willingness to put in long hours.

"Lawyers," Flint said. "Most adult Peyti here on the Moon are lawyers."

"Lawyers have no power," DeRicci said. "They can't change the laws."

"The Peyti who want to do that are involved in Earth Alliance governments," Popova said. "We're not centralized enough for them. I don't think there are any Peyti in the United Domes of the Moon governments or in local ones. I'll check though."

"I'm still stuck on this school thing," DeRicci said. "Why would it matter?"

"It would get them to the Moon," Popova said.

Flint shook his head. That didn't feel right. He wasn't sure what was right. Whatever it was felt slightly out of reach.

"We don't prevent Peyti from coming here," DeRicci said. "They come all the time. They're one of our closest allies in the Earth Alliance. Everyone loves working with them."

DeRicci frowned. Then she tapped the holographic screen with several faces on it. "We should have gotten the graduation ceremony images from her by now."

"Don't open them," Flint said.

"You don't trust her?" DeRicci asked.

"I can find out how many educated Peyti are here by running the Earth Alliance bar registry," Flint said. "Then I'll cross-check the names against the employment records, and finally against our facial recognition software. These five hundred Peyti might not be lawyers. It might be an insignificant sidetrack."

"Five hundred?" Popova asked. "I didn't think we had that many from our scans."

"The Moon's a big place," DeRicci said. "Five hundred mixed in a population numbering in the millions is pretty insignificant."

It depended on where those five hundred were located, Flint thought, but did not say. He started the cross-checks.

"You initially didn't expect to find anything, did you, Noelle?" he asked DeRicci, mostly to distract her so that she wouldn't look at the graduation images.

"No," she said. "I was doing this so I could legitimately send information to the Earth Alliance because they weren't talking to Rastigan. I thought Rastigan would find a clump of the clones getting ready to attack some Peyti communities. I didn't expect to find any here."

"We don't know what stage this attack is at," Flint said. "For all we know, they could be training here."

"The Frémont clones weren't educated," Popova said.

"We don't know that," Flint said. "In fact, we don't know anything about them. That's part of the problem. We're working off assumptions, not knowledge."

DeRicci's gaze met his. "And that's always so dangerous. I'm sorry, Miles. That's my fault."

He shook his head. "It's mine, too. We approached this investigation wrong. We got overwhelmed by the size and scope, and made mistakes. Now we have to repair those mistakes and conduct the best investigation we possibly can."

"Whatever that means," Popova muttered.

"I guess," DeRicci said, "at some point, we're going to find out."

51

When DeRicci contacted Rastigan, it helped that Rastigan was in Uzvot's office. Rastigan didn't want to go through channels to contact anyone. Nor did she want to use her equipment to check out those masks.

Something about them bothered her.

She still felt sweaty and nervous in her environmental suit. She had almost taken a break from the search when DeRicci reached her. De-Ricci's image was blocked because she was using an extremely secure link, but Rastigan still caught the edge of panic.

DeRicci admitted she had seen some of the clones on the Moon. Which made no sense, really, unless they had gone to school there.

And now the masks.

Rastigan did not put the images that DeRicci had sent her on any equipment. Instead, she sent the images to Uzvot by a different secure link, even though the two of them were standing in the same room, doing the same work.

Have you ever seen these before? Rastigan sent with the images.

Then she turned around. Uzvot's mouth was open and her skin had turned a pale blue.

"Why do you want to know?" Uzvot asked in Standard.

"I just got those images from the Moon," Rastigan said.

Uzvot shook her head. Rastigan still couldn't get used to that movement from a Peyti, even one as used to doing business with humans as Uzvot was.

"That is not possible," Uzvot said.

"Why?" Rastigan asked.

"I am not supposed to tell anyone," Uzvot said. The blue in her skin had deepened. She was upset, for the second time in twenty-four hours.

"Why not?" Rastigan asked, trying to keep the panic out of her voice.

Uzvot curled her long fingers against her mouth. Then she turned away, as if she were thinking or consulting with someone. Rastigan couldn't tell which, and wasn't sure if she should interrupt or not.

She waited, heart pounding, for Uzvot to speak again.

Finally Uzvot let out a small coo, the Peyti equivalent of a sigh. "Those masks," she said slowly, "they are not sold anywhere. Nor are they in use by civilians."

Rastigan turned cold. "Who uses them?"

"No one," Uzvot said. "They are prototypes. I should not tell you this. I translated on a confidential meeting between a supplier, the Earth Alliance, and some of our military."

"Military." The word stuck in Rastigan's mind. "What are these things used for?"

"Here." Uzvot called up an image of the mask. Rastigan hoped she was using the image that Rastigan sent and not something on the system.

Rastigan was beginning to believe just being in possession of this information could be dangerous.

"See this?" Uzvot touched the bottom portion of the mask.

It looked big compared to the other masks. Rastigan hoped that it merely stored enough material for a few more hours of breathing. She knew that the Peyti had hoped for better masks, longer-lasting masks, for quite a while now.

"It detaches," Uzvot said. "You pull here, and it does not disable the mask."

Clearly, then, it was not extra supplies.

"What's it for?" Rastigan asked.

"It is designed to go through all Earth Alliance security measures, and many in other sectors."

"Okay." Rastigan still wasn't sure what she was looking at. "And?"

"And nothing," Uzvot said. "It is clever. It detaches. It can be left behind."

The chill that Rastigan had a moment ago grew deeper. "It's a weapon?" she asked, hoping she was wrong.

"Yes," Uzvot said. "It is a bomb."

52

A BOMB. A PROTOTYPE. FIVE HUNDRED PROTOTYPES.

On the Moon.

DeRicci let out a small breath. She couldn't look at Flint or Popova. Not yet. Because if she looked at them, if she told them, then the horrible thing Jin Rastigan had just told her might be true.

There might be five hundred bombers walking around the streets of the Moon, in various domes, in small cities and large, able to do more damage individually than the Anniversary Day bombers did six months before.

Not again. A big part of her prayed to deities she didn't believe in, asking all of them, every one she could think of, not again. Please. Not again.

Then she took a deep breath and shook off the terror she felt.

As Flint would say, DeRicci was only taking Rastigan's word. And for all DeRicci knew, that mask she had seen was only on one face, only part of one Peyti, somewhere on the Moon.

"I need to see something," DeRicci said as calmly as she could.

She had control of her expression, she knew that. And her voice sounded normal. Flint didn't even look up. Popova did, but Popova had to. She worked for DeRicci.

"I need to look at yesterday's faces. Just yesterday's." DeRicci hoped that Popova wouldn't ask why. DeRicci didn't want to tell her why.

She wanted to be wrong. She wanted to tell them later how she had believed Rastigan for a brief moment, and it had been silly.

She wanted them to laugh about this.

Popova didn't ask why. Instead, all the Peyti faces floating around DeRicci's office winked out for a half second, and then came back, in different positions.

And wearing different masks.

The masks DeRicci was used to. The masks every Peyti had worn since they had come to the Moon, maybe since they had started interacting with humans.

"Now," DeRicci said, her voice still calm even though her nerves weren't, "show me today's."

Flint finally looked up, a small frown between his pale eyebrows. He clearly had no idea what she was up to, but he knew she was up to something.

The images winked out again and reappeared.

With the damn mask prototypes.

She couldn't contain it any longer. Five hundred Peyti. Clones of a mass murderer. Wearing masks, prototype masks, with bombs.

"What is it, Noelle?" Flint asked.

Too big to contain, that's what. If she captured one of them, just one, he would let the others know that she had figured it out. If she disabled one bomb, just one, the Peyti wearing that bomb would let the others know.

Five hundred bombers.

Five hundred.

On her Moon.

In places she couldn't always see.

"Give me just a minute to think," she said.

Because, she suspected, a minute was all the time that she had.

53

Kaleb met her outside class. Talia stiffened and tried to move away, but he was too quick. He caught her arm.

No one else seemed to notice. They all streamed to their next classes. Even the security guards were looking the other way.

"I know you don't like me," Kaleb said. "But can I talk to you for a second?"

"No," she said, and shook him off.

She started down the hall. She heard his footsteps behind her, his voice on her link.

Talia, please. Just one second. Please. It's important.

She turned around. He seemed smaller than he had before. She had always thought of Kaleb as a big guy, but he wasn't. He was beefy, but not tall. In fact, in the right shoes, she would be taller than he was.

She could pull over one of the security guards. She could contact someone on the school's links, saying that this was an emergency, that Kaleb wouldn't leave her alone.

But something in his face bothered her.

Talia, please, he sent again. Taking a risk, using the school links, stuff that could be traced.

If he was up to something bad.

She sighed. Rolled her eyes. Stopped. And turned around. "What?"

The puffiness in his face looked worse than it had that morning. The bruising went all the way down his chin. Kaleb clearly didn't like looking like that. He turned his head slightly, so that the bruised side wasn't in the main part of her field of vision.

He took her arm again, and she immediately regretted stopping.

"Touch me one more time, and I swear, I'll hurt you," she said.

He let her arm drop.

"Can we go over there?" He nodded toward a side corridor. No one stood in it. "Please? It's private."

"You try anything—"

"I won't," he said. "I promise."

She was going to make some snide comment about the quality of his promises, but she changed her mind. She wanted this conversation over fast, and taunting him would prolong it.

She followed him to the side corridor, and they stood near some large plant that Talia couldn't identify. Its blue leaves gave them a bit of cover from the kids still passing through the main hallway.

He lowered his head. "I know I'm a jerk. I know I'm an idiot. I know I've been really mean, and I'm sorry."

"You shouldn't be apologizing to me," Talia said. "It's the Chinar twins and all those other kids—"

"I know, but they're not here." Kaleb sighed. "My dad wants me to stay home. He wants to hire someone to tutor me there, and I can't, Talia. I just can't."

Something in his voice, something terrified, caught her. She looked at him, at the bruising, at the way his lower lip trembled.

He said, "If you say you've forgiven me, if you say that I'm not so bad after all, maybe they'll let me stay here."

He sounded desperate. She recognized desperate. But she didn't get this, not entirely.

"Why won't they just put you in a different school?" she asked.

"My mom." His voice broke. "My mom died last year, and she said school was important. My dad doesn't think it is, and he thinks if we hire someone or use one of those knowledge implants, I'll be just fine. And maybe I will, but I'd have to stay home."

And the way he looked, the way he said *home*, Talia got the idea that he wasn't objecting to leaving school so much as to being trapped.

"They're not going to listen to me," she said. "I'm just some kid."

"No, you're not," he said. "Your dad has juice with the headmistress."

Talia bristled, but didn't say anything.

"And besides, you and me, we're the ones who started everything yesterday."

"No, we didn't," Talia said.

He nodded. "Sorry. *I* started everything. You tried to stop it."

"That's better." She sounded mean. She felt mean. But why the hell would he think she'd do anything for him, considering how mean he'd been?

He'd been mean as long as she'd known him. He'd always picked on other kids, and he'd always laughed at them. She hated him, and she hated his pretty eyes, and his occasional really funny sense of humor. If he left school, no one would miss him except those dumb kids who banded around with him.

"Why don't you ask your buddies to talk to the headmistress?" she asked.

"No one'll believe them," Kaleb said. "Everybody knows they listen to me."

"And everybody knows I don't, is that it?" Talia asked. "So if I say you're okay, then you are, right?"

He shrugged.

She shook her head. "I'm not doing you any favors. You don't deserve favors."

She pushed past him and started down the hall, bracing for him to comment on her links. Bracing for more begging, bracing for him to try to manipulate her.

But he didn't say anything.

In spite of herself, she glanced over her shoulder. He was still standing behind that stupid plant, his head down, one fist covering his face.

He looked defeated.

That should have made her feel better.

Instead, it made her mad.

54

"NOELLE?" FLINT ASKED. THAT FROWN BETWEEN HIS EYES HAD GROWN. He clearly knew something was wrong.

So did Popova. She stared at DeRicci. DeRicci wasn't sure what to say.

The Peyti faces, with those awful masks, floated around DeRicci's office as if they haunted the place.

DeRicci held up a finger. She wasn't sure she could stop the Peyti bombers. She would have to mobilize all of the law enforcement on the Moon, officers she wasn't even—by law—in charge of, and she would have to make them move in unison.

Provided they all knew where the bombers were.

She would have to accept some casualties. Because she wasn't going to be able to contain all of this.

"Were you able to cross-check the faces with the Peyti members of the Earth Alliance bar?" DeRicci asked.

Flint's frown remained. "I did. I got a lot of matches, but only four-hundred-and-eighty are here on the Moon."

"We have more than four-hundred-and-eighty Peyti in our image database," she said, looking at those horrible faces.

"I'm cross-checking with law school students, and with interns," Flint said. "I'll find them. But I'm not sure I'll find all of them."

DeRicci nodded. Now she would have to let the Earth Alliance know about the Peyti threat. It seemed like days ago that she had learned about this Peyti mass murderer and his clones. All she had planned to do was let the Alliance know they existed—elsewhere.

She had thought the attack would be elsewhere.

It was going to be here. Again.

"All right," she said. She didn't have time for emotions. Not if she wanted to save the Moon. "I'm going to need some massive help. And somehow we're going to have to coordinate all of this, stealthily. We're not going to have room for error. And we're going to have to act really fast."

That frown disappeared from Flint's face. Popova moved just a little closer, her shoulders squared. Clearly both of them were ready.

DeRicci wished that were enough.

"What did you learn, Noelle?" Flint asked.

"You saw the different masks, right?" she asked.

Both Flint and Popova nodded.

"The new ones. They're a Peyti military prototype. They're bombs."

Popova cursed, but Flint didn't move. He always managed to set his emotions aside quickly. DeRicci envied that.

"They weren't wearing those prototypes yesterday," he said.

"That's right," DeRicci said. "This is another coordinated attack against the Moon, and it's going to happen today. Rudra, I need the head of every law enforcement agency on the Moon in a conference. I'll also need all of the surviving and acting mayors, and every member of the United Domes of the Moon council. I'll need to talk to them in ten minutes."

"What're you going to tell them?" Popova asked.

"We're going to send them the last known location of every one of those clones on the Moon," DeRicci said. "We're going to have to get eyes on those clones, and then we're going to have to arrest them all, somehow neutralizing those masks."

"How do we neutralize them?" Flint asked.

Thank God she had remembered to ask Rastigan that. Thank God Rastigan had had an answer.

"That thing we noticed on the mask, that extra piece? It comes out. It becomes a bomb when you activate it."

"How easy is it to set off?" Flint asked. Leave it to him to be practical.

"It depends on what you want to do," DeRicci said. "If you want to blow yourself up along with everything around you, you can click through two safeties and do it fast. If you want to escape, you need to put in a code and set a timer. It'll count down."

"How easy is it to deactivate?" Flint asked.

"It doesn't activate at all in a Peyti-only atmosphere," DeRicci said. "It's built to explode in any atmosphere *except* a Peyti-only atmosphere."

"These things were designed to kill humans?" Popova asked. "By the Peyti military?"

"Our environment isn't that unique. A number of aliens can thrive in it," DeRicci said. "The Peyti environment, on the other hand, only exists on Peyla."

That was the answer Rastigan had given DeRicci when she asked this question, and that was the answer she was going to share. Because she wasn't going to think about the implications of this. At all. She didn't want to think about the larger implications.

She had to solve this, and she had to solve it now.

"So we turn the environment from Earth Alliance Standard to Peyti Standard and the bombs are deactivated?" Flint asked.

"Actually," DeRicci said, "they simply won't work. They remain activated until we physically deactivate them. But they won't work in a Peyti environment. It's like a failsafe."

"It *is* a failsafe," Flint said, more to himself than to her, "and that's an easier solution than I had hoped for."

"Except that someone will have to deactivate that bomb in a Peyti atmosphere no matter what," Popova said.

"We can do that," Flint said. "We can send someone in wearing a suit."

"Or we can send in a Peyti after we've neutralized the bomb," De-Ricci said tiredly. "Not every Peyti is involved here."

Popova took a deep breath, as if that very thought disturbed her. Then she said, "If we switch to Peyti Standard, the atmosphere will kill everyone in the room except the Peyti."

"And if we go in wearing environmental suits before we change the atmosphere, they'll know something is up," DeRicci said. "See why we need to coordinate this?"

"If we have time," Flint said.

"We're going to pretend we have time," DeRicci said, "because that's all we can do."

55

Kaleb didn't show up for lunch. And Talia, weirdly, was watching for him.

Normally, she wouldn't be able to find him easily in the lunch area. The alcoves, the private spaces, the sheer size of the space meant she shouldn't have been able to see him at all.

But, she realized, he was always at lunch when she was, and he always hovered somewhere nearby. Every day, she had done her best to avoid him—and most days, she usually succeeded.

Of course, on the day she wanted to see him, she didn't. She even did a walk around the lunch area, just scanning. She wasn't sure what she wanted. She was kinda worried about him, and that bugged her because he was such an idiot.

But their conversation had disturbed her, and she thought about it during her entire next class.

Plus, she looked up his dad through the public nets. Not his dad's financials. Just reports about his dad's personality.

And she didn't like what she had seen.

Like most parents, Kaleb's dad had money. Mostly he used that money to make problems go away. She found the ghosts of some domestic violence complaints, erased when Kaleb's mom died, but remaining as gaps in the record.

Talia also found some complaints from former employees who worked with Kaleb's dad, saying he had behaved "unprofessionally," whatever that meant. And then a couple of those employees moved out of Armstrong, buying expensive property elsewhere on the Moon.

Talia didn't exactly want to talk to Kaleb about this, but it bothered her, just like his reaction bothered her.

And the fact that he wasn't here bothered her too.

She grabbed an apple and wandered out of the lunch area. The headmistress's office wasn't too far from here. Talia didn't exactly want to tell anyone that she had forgiven Kaleb—she hadn't—but she did want to know what was going on.

Her dad would tell her that curiosity could harm her. He had told her that a lot since she looked for her sister clones a while back. But he always seemed a little uncomfortable saying it, since he got overly curious too. Otherwise he wouldn't do the job that he did.

As she walked toward the headmistress's office, she saw a couple of security guards standing outside of one of the conference rooms. Talia stopped. They only did that when a meeting was going on.

No one had thought to opaque the walls of the conference area. Inside it, she could see the guys who'd come in with Kaleb that morning, plus some lawyers. She could tell who they were by their fancy suits and the Peyti sitting in the group. A larger version of Kaleb with a florid face and a downturned mouth and mean, tiny eyes sat in the middle of the lawyers. Ms. Rutledge also sat there, hands folded, with yet another lawyer beside her.

At least, Talia thought that guy was a lawyer. She'd seen him around a few times, so she figured he worked for the school.

Kaleb sat all by himself at the far end of the table, his head resting on his arms. He looked worse than he had an hour ago, and now, despite herself, Talia felt sorry for him.

He hadn't been lying to her. He didn't want to leave the school.

The question was, did she want him to leave? He was nasty and disruptive and unreasonable. She shouldn't have to defend him just because he wanted her to.

But maybe he acted tough here because he couldn't be tough at home. Or maybe he had learned it there.

She finished the apple and cupped the core in her hand. How come she was the one who had to make this decision? How come somebody else couldn't?

And she didn't know who would get hurt worse: the kids around her if Kaleb stayed in school or Kaleb if he had to leave.

Not that she was sure if it mattered.

She tried to figure out what her dad would do, and couldn't. She knew what he would say. He would say it was her choice.

Only she didn't know what choice to make.

56

It didn't take long for the location program to notify Flint that it knew where most of the Peyti clones were. At least, the ones that were lawyers. Lawyers had to bill for each waking hour, which meant they kept track of every single moment they worked. Most law firms used the same program. Once Flint got into that program, he could track a bunch of them, provided he had their names.

He had the names of four-hundred-and-eighty Peyti clones. The problem was, he still couldn't find the other twenty to thirty that he knew were on the Moon. And as DeRicci said, the takedown had to happen with all of the Peyti clones at once. If the security teams missed just one clone, then a dome might get destroyed—again.

No matter how many casualties there were, no matter how *few* casualties there were, another destroyed dome would demoralize the Moon's population. The very idea made Flint's heart sink.

He had no idea why anyone would target the Moon, and he knew DeRicci was right: that was a question for another day. On this day, he and DeRicci and everyone else had to prevent another devastating attack.

Popova had left the room to set up the complicated conference that DeRicci needed to have in just a few short minutes.

Flint had already sent word to some of the best techs in the building. They would meet him in DeRicci's office while she was having her conference. With luck, he and the others would find the remaining clones.

But what he was most worried about was that one or two or five of those clones had been smart enough to stay away from security cameras, and weren't lawyers or interns or law students.

He was afraid of clones who couldn't be tracked.

He also had one other worry, considering the names he had found in the Earth Alliance bar database. There were dozens of clones *not* on the Moon itself. Had they washed out? Given up?

Did they work for firms that didn't use the tracking program? Did they work off the grid?

Or were they planning another attack elsewhere?

DeRicci stood in the center of the room, surrounded by the creepy Peyti faces, working on a pad as if none of this bothered her. She managed to shut off everything.

Flint was having a tougher time. He didn't want to think about Talia, and yet he couldn't stop doing so. He was glad she was in school, but he wanted her here, where he could keep an eye on her.

He also wanted her brain. She would help him as no one else could.

Only he didn't want her to travel here. He felt that being out in the open right now would be worse than being in Aristotle Academy or the Security Building itself.

He really wanted to go get her, but he knew the best thing he could do was remain here and work, neutralize the threat so that she wouldn't even know she had been in any danger.

Only he couldn't do it all alone.

"Noelle," he said, "I need your attention for one minute."

She raised her head, her hand still clutching the pad. She frowned at him, and he wasn't sure how much of her brain was here, and how much of it was planning the takedown of all those Peyti clones.

"There are dozens of clones not on the Moon," he said.

"I know," she said. "We can't worry about that."

329

"We have to worry about it," Flint said. "We don't know what they're going to do."

"It's not an immediate threat, Miles. We—"

"I know," he said. "Which is why I propose we bring the Earth Alliance investigators in on this. We can have them take this information to the Alliance. Your Peyti friend couldn't do it, and you're busy with this. Let them do it."

DeRicci shook her head. "There's too much evidence that the Earth Alliance is involved. We can't trust them, Miles."

He was prepared for that argument. "It's not going to hurt. If we don't tell them anything, there might be attacks off-Moon. If the investigators don't inform anyone, the attacks will happen anyway. If they actually do their job, then we might be able to prevent those attacks as well."

"And if they warn the Peyti clones?" DeRicci asked. "The ones here?"

"It's on me," Flint said.

"You're willing to risk Talia's life for that?" DeRicci asked.

It was a low blow, but an effective one. DeRicci knew how to get to his heart with one quick question. Did he trust those two investigators enough to risk an attack on the Moon?

He had to think. His heart was pounding. He hadn't realized that until now.

"I trust Goudkins," he said after a moment.

"All right then," DeRicci said. "Bring—her? Him? I forget which one that is—"

"Her," Flint said.

"Bring her in, but don't let her tell the partner. Can we shut down her links?"

"I can," Flint said, "but that'll make contacting her people at the Alliance tougher."

"We have to minimize risk," DeRicci said, but her attention had already gone back to the pad.

She was right. Flint had to minimize risk. He could shut down the links for most anyone who might ruin the operation that DeRicci was trying to set up.

He sighed and sent for Goudkins. He hoped to hell she could get someone in the Alliance to listen to her.

Because if she didn't do it, if he couldn't find all the clones, if De-Ricci couldn't get law enforcement Moonwide to cooperate, this would be a very bad day.

Worse than Anniversary Day ever was.

And he didn't want to even try to imagine that.

57

THE SECONDARY CONFERENCE ROOM FELT CROWDED EVEN THOUGH Noelle DeRicci stood in it alone. Popova had coordinated every mayor, every acting mayor, all the members of the United Domes Council, and all the heads of law enforcement all over the Moon, and put them on visual, with their names underneath the images (thankfully). Some of the faces floated like the Peyti clone faces had, and DeRicci wanted to swat them away from her.

Instead, she stood awkwardly like a schoolgirl waiting for a date, her mouth dry and her hands shaking.

"First," DeRicci said loudly, trying to get their attention, "I need you all to be alone in your rooms. I need you to shut off all of your links except emergency links, and I need your word of honor that you have done so. I don't have time to check, but believe me, I will know if you failed, and I will know rather quickly."

She sounded ominous. She felt ominous, and all alone.

Popova worked in an alcove off the conference room that had its own secure link, so DeRicci could tell her if something went wrong. Normally a high-level tech would be inside the room, making sure everything worked smoothly, but the high-level techs that DeRicci had on staff were working with Flint, trying to find all of the Peyti clones on the Moon.

She was terrified they would miss one.

She was certain they would miss one.

She waited as various people turned away from their cameras or clearly waved a hand, instructing someone to leave the room. Her heart pounded.

As the faces turned back to her, she said, "I'm sorry to be so harsh, but we have a situation that makes Anniversary Day look like practice."

Nods, responses to the affirmative, and some folks who didn't move at all.

"Do any of you have lawyers in the room with you?" she asked. She initially was going to ask if they had any Peyti on staff, but she decided against it. Too obvious, too easy a warning.

She heard a few yeses.

She cursed silently. She had already told them to clear the room, and they'd left lawyers in there. She had been around government long enough to know that some government officials didn't think of lawyers as people—which was why she asked the question.

She had hoped no one had made that mistake. The fact that a group of them had made her mad.

"Get them out," she said. "I know they are supposed to be good at this confidentiality stuff, but what I'm about to ask you to do will automatically put them in an ethical quandary. Better that they leave the room. You don't want them to hear what I have to tell you. It'll be bad for the future of your administrations."

She had thought of that as her excuse. too, even though it wasn't strictly true. She wasn't sure she had the legal authority to do what she needed to do, but the government lawyers and the lawmakers would back-date everything if she was successful, and crucify her if she was not. It didn't matter if lawyers were in the room.

She just didn't want Peyti in the room.

"Okay," she said after a moment. "Are we alone?"

She got a lot of yeses, didn't see any noes, even if there were any, and decided to proceed.

"Okay," she said. "That situation I was talking about, it's going to happen today. We have to work together to stop it, and we *cannot* miss. If we miss, thousands, maybe millions, maybe tens of millions will die. Am I being clear?"

Faces going gray, closed eyes, a few moans.

"I'm going to give you a plan of action, I'm going to give you a timeline, and if any of you deviate from that timeline by as much as one second, we are all doomed, am I clear?"

"Are you going to tell us what this situation is?" Dominic Hanrahan asked. Of course, he'd be one of the first to slow everything down. He was so afraid of everything, so afraid of being blamed for everything, and such a victim.

She took a breath. She was still angry at him for his comments the day before. (Just the day before? It felt like weeks ago.)

"Yes," she said. "Then I'm going to tell you what we all are going to do. I'm going to give you a very short time frame in order to act because once this information gets out, and it *will* get out, we will lose. After this conference ends, I will send you coordinates of where the potential attackers were last seen. You will use a jammer in the area where those attackers are. You will shut off *all* links, including emergency links. You will shut off foreign links. You will shut down every communication system, *including* your own. Am I clear?"

"What the hell are you afraid of, DeRicci?" asked Dmitri Tsepen, the mayor of Glenn Station. She gave him a hard look. He didn't seem to be drunk today, which was a good thing, since she probably had him dismiss his very competent assistant.

"You'll understand in a few minutes," she said.

Her gaze met that of Diane Limón, the acting mayor of Armstrong. Beside her, in a different bubble, was Olympia Hobell, chief of the Armstrong police department, and DeRicci's old boss in the First Detective Unit, Andrea Gumiela. So just judging from Armstrong, Popova had doubled up on the security forces, making sure the people in charge knew what was going on, and the people who could actually do something knew as well.

"I cannot stress how important this is," DeRicci said. "I also need to emphasize now that some of your actions today might result in civilian casualties. That can't be helped. If you cannot deal with it, then you need to bring in someone who can *right now*. Is that clear?"

She expected to lose half the mayors right there. Her gaze met Hanrahan's. He had gone gray but he hadn't moved. Tsepen actually looked awake. Terrified, but awake and ready to act.

Olympia Hobell hadn't moved. Neither had Andrea Gumiela. They watched with a coldness that DeRicci recognized in herself.

They would deal with the collateral damage later. They would do what they needed to do.

DeRicci wished she personally knew everyone of these people she was talking to. She wished she knew if she could trust them.

Surprisingly, though, she knew many of them, and she knew they'd do what they could.

That was all she could ask.

"Okay," she said. "I'm going to give you the timeline first, and I want you to keep track of it. Back it up, do what you must, but do *not* lose it. You *must* follow it. Am I being clear?"

Everyone nodded. Or so it seemed. It was hard to tell with the damn floating heads.

"I am telling you the timeline first," DeRicci said, "because this situation is so big and so difficult that I expect it to stun you for a few minutes. You have to plan for that, and figure out a way to set aside your emotional reaction. If you do not, you might harm everyone in a domed community on the Moon."

"That's everyone," said a woman she didn't recognize. "We all live in domed communities."

"Yes," DeRicci said. "I know."

Her words hung for a moment.

She took a deep breath. "Pay attention, because we don't have a lot of time to implement this, and the longer it takes to get you all on board, the greater the chance we have of losing everything."

She steeled her shoulders. She had to communicate clearly as well. This was on her as much as it was on them.

"Okay," she said. "Here we go."

58

SIXTEEN PEOPLE, HALF OF WHOM FLINT DIDN'T KNOW, CROWDED into DeRicci's office. They hunched over pads while sitting on chairs, on the floor, or leaning up against the wall. They had split the Moon into eight sections, by population, and two people concentrated on each section.

Flint had glanced quickly at their personnel files. He put one of the best on each team, going down by population. The most populous places, the ones with the most lawyers, got the best teams.

All of this seemed haphazard to him. It made his stomach twist. He collated all of the information, ran scans over the entire Moon on his own, and had Murray from Space Traffic send information from the private security system in the Port. The system that wasn't supposed to exist, but that Flint, as a former member of the Space Traffic Patrol squad, knew all about.

He found half a dozen other clones all on his own. The ship records showed that another eight had left the Moon in the past week on ships bound back to Peyla. He sent that information to DeRicci's contact on Peyla, without asking DeRicci's permission.

Someone had to take care of this, and DeRicci was already overwhelmed.

He was overwhelmed, too. He had to coordinate all of this information. He hadn't had a chance to absorb it, verify it, or examine it as closely as he would have liked. If someone asked him directly where all the clones were, he couldn't say. He would have to refer to the information in front of him.

There was simply too much information to absorb, so he didn't try to absorb any of it. Instead, he gathered it, and put it in easily understandable packets for the leaders and law enforcement officials DeRicci was still talking to. As soon as she was done, he would have to send all of this information to them, whether it was complete or not.

He wasn't going to believe it was complete, either. He planned to keep working on finding more clones even after the information got sent. He really didn't want someone—anyone—to slip through on this. It could be devastating.

Goudkins agreed. She had taken a spot in the far end of the room. She was using the Security Office's equipment to contact the Earth Alliance. She didn't use her links at all, trusting DeRicci's system to get her through. DeRicci's system and Goudkins' identification.

Flint didn't know what Goudkins had told her partner and he didn't care. All he cared about was that she was sending information throughout the Earth Alliance about the clones. She was going outside of the investigative unit and to upper-echelon people, letting them know that the Moon had decided these clones were some kind of threat.

Goudkins had also decided that if she felt like she was getting a runaround, she would go directly to as many government leaders as she could before someone in the Alliance shut her down.

Flint trusted her more than he had earlier, but he would make sure the information got out once this day was over. He also warned her not to say that the Moon was taking action today or to say what the exact problem was.

They would save all of that until after the success or the failure of the Moon mission.

He glanced at the information pouring across the screen. They had most of the clones' locations down to the second. But most wasn't enough. Some had been seen a minute or two before, some five minutes before, and some thirty minutes before.

He was worried about them, but the ones he worried about the most were the ones that were off the grid, the ones that hadn't been seen for a day or two.

Just one of those clones on the loose, just one, could ruin everything they were working toward.

He tried not to think about it.

But it seemed he could think about nothing else.

59

THE CONFERENCE ROOM EMPTIED, FACES WINKING OUT IN GROUPS OF two, three, and five. DeRicci still stood, hands clasped. They weren't shaking any longer, but her stomach was so upset she wondered if she was going to be ill.

She made herself breathe. She couldn't do much else. She couldn't do *anything* else. It was all on them now.

And she hated that.

The last face vanished and she sank into a chair. It creaked slightly, as if no one had bothered it for a very long time.

She sent a message to Flint and Popova, *Release the whereabouts information.*

Then she put her hands over her face and closed her eyes. She felt absolutely helpless.

Perfection was not a human trait. Humans did not do things one-hundred percent. They usually missed by five to ten percent on everything they did, and usually that was acceptable.

Now she was trusting people whom she knew to be incompetent boobs, like Dmitri Tsepen, to not only rise above themselves but do so at one-hundred percent.

Maybe fear would make them do well. Because she hadn't doubted the fear she had seen on all of those faces.

Some, like Gumiela, had hidden it quickly, but it had been there.

Everyone knew what was at stake. In that, at least, DeRicci had done her job. Whether or not they completely understood the plan was another matter. But they understood the stakes.

DeRicci couldn't do anything now except monitor.

And give the order for the dome sectioning so that destruction— again—would be on her.

She had fifty minutes before she gave that order.

Fifty minutes in which she had to trust others to do work she wasn't even sure she could do.

Fifty minutes in which everything in her world could disappear— and very well might.

60

Mayor Dominic Hanrahan stood in the center of his office, his hands clenched into fists. He could barely breathe. That bitch DeRicci had been right. The news was paralyzing, and he had to take action.

For himself and for his city.

And because one of the last things DeRicci had said to him when she had visited here yesterday haunted him: *If you don't want to make the hard decisions for your city, we'll find someone who can. And we'll instate him as mayor of this city. I'm sure everyone in Tycho Crater will be relieved.*

Right now, he wanted someone else to be mayor. He *needed* someone else to be mayor. He didn't want this responsibility.

But he had gotten in trouble for freezing when the Top of the Dome collapsed six months ago. He couldn't freeze now.

He had to take action.

Even though all he could think about was his favorite lawyer, who happened to be Peyti, who for some reason hadn't come into work today. Or that Peyti lawyer who'd sat in this very room yesterday, talking about lawsuits against Tycho Crater for all the deaths that happened on Anniversary Day.

Lawsuits. Deaths. And he had only his memory of those lawyers to check against the database. At least for the moment, at least until

DeRicci's people sent him the information about where Peyti lawyers would be.

He wished he could call in his assistants, but he couldn't. He needed to talk directly to law enforcement here and he had to set it up. Fortunately, at least three of them had been involved in that conference call. If he were acting on his own, he would wait for them to contact him.

But he didn't have time to wait.

If he waited, Tycho Crater could be obliterated.

The information packet that DeRicci had promised hit his links accompanied by actual alarm bells. Like he needed alarm bells. Like he wasn't alarmed enough already.

He combed through the information, found five of the clones here in Tycho Crater, all of them with their locations known. As he examined them, his emergency links opened.

Law enforcement contacting him. Of course. They had only a few minutes to coordinate everything, too.

Five. Known. None of them his lawyer.

He hoped to hell DeRicci's people were good. He would tell his own officials to make sure they didn't find more clones on their own security feeds. He had no idea if they would.

But he didn't want to fail at this. If someone was going to fail, it couldn't be him.

He couldn't lose Tycho Crater—again.

61

TALIA HOVERED. SHE NEVER HOVERED. SHE WAS USUALLY outrageously decisive.

But seeing Kaleb inside that conference room, his head down, made her nervous. His father's face had grown red, and his gestures curt, almost violent. One of the men sitting next to him actually put a hand on Kaleb's father's arm, as if to calm him down.

Ms. Rutledge didn't seem upset. She had templed her fingers, and was tapping them together as she listened. She wasn't watching Kaleb's father.

She was watching Kaleb.

Talia stood a few meters away, mesmerized. She really needed to get back to class, but she didn't want to leave this. She wanted to know what was going to happen.

One of the security guards looked up and frowned. Then he glanced at his companion who seemed to be working really really hard not to show any surprise.

But something had happened.

Talia felt the beginnings of a headache, and heard an ache in her ears. She recognized this feeling. She'd had it once before, in her closet in Valhalla Basin, after those idiots who killed her mother—who would kill her mother at that point, but hadn't yet—shut off the links.

She was just imagining it. No one shut off all the links in Armstrong. It just wasn't safe. Armstrong was all about safety.

She tried to access the school links, and couldn't. Maybe the school system was down.

Then she decided to use her private link to contact Kaleb, see if he wanted her in there. The message she planned to send bounced back at her, something that had never happened on any links before. At least to her. At least here.

"C'mon, honey." A security guard put his arm around her waist and pulled her backward. "We need to move you."

He was already moving her. She elbowed him—hard— in the stomach. Nobody touched her without her permission. Nobody. Not after what happened with her mom all those years ago. Talia took care of herself and didn't let anyone force her to do anything.

The guard grunted, but didn't let go. He pulled her behind one of the plants.

She sent a help message to her dad—*Something's weird. Get here at once!*—through her emergency links, and that message just fizzled.

The emergency links were down, too.

She struggled. "Let me go."

"I can't, hon. We have to get you out of here. Let's get you to class, okay? Where are you supposed to be?"

His voice sounded calm, as if he weren't holding her in a death grip. Five Armstrong police officers came down the hall, pointing and nodding. They didn't seem to be using links either.

Had they come to arrest Kaleb's father?

She planted her feet, hard, and the security guard couldn't budge her. "What's going on?"

"It's none of your business, hon," he said. "Let's get you out of here."

"It is too my business!" she said loudly, even though she wasn't exactly sure why.

"Shut her up," one of the police officers hissed, "and take her somewhere else."

"I'm going to need help with that," the guard said.

"We can't spare anyone," the officer said. "Don't cause trouble, kid, or we'll have to restrain you."

"You can't do that. My dad works with Security Chief DeRicci. They'll—"

"This is on their orders," the officer hissed, his voice very soft. "Now shut up and get out of the way."

Something about his tone convinced her. She stopped struggling. The guard tried to pull her down the hall, but she kept her feet planted hard. He'd have to lift her to move her.

She wasn't going to yell any more, though.

"I can't check the specs," one of the other officers said to one of the guards. "Every room here have its own environmental system?"

"Of course," the guard said.

"Where do we get to it?" the officer asked.

"I'll show you," the guard said.

They took off at a run down the hall.

Talia stared at the conference room. No one in there seemed to notice what was going on in the hallway. Kaleb had raised his head, but his hand shielded his eyes.

He looked miserable.

She wanted to catch his attention, but she couldn't. The guard held her arms. She'd been in that conference room once. It was soundproof, so it didn't matter how much she yelled.

Still, she felt like Kaleb should know something weird was going on. If nothing else, it would stop the stupid talks about him leaving school. It would give her a chance to think about whether she wanted to help him or not.

Maybe she wouldn't have to do anything. Maybe the police were here for his dad. Her dad knew she was worried about that whole family. Maybe he had told Security Chief DeRicci. Maybe they found something. Maybe they could arrest him, and Kaleb would become the state's problem.

She wanted Kaleb to be the state's problem.

The police officers had moved into a weird line, like they needed to see each other to relay information.

Only one stood in the hallway now, and he looked really, really nervous.

He gave a small hand signal to his other officers. The guard put his hand over Talia's mouth. His fingers smelled of onions. She tried to move away, but his grip got tight.

The police officer opened the door to the conference room.

"I need to speak to the lawyers, please," he said. "Outside. Right now."

The lawyers looked at each other, clearly confused. But they didn't get up. No one did.

And Talia had a feeling that was a very, very bad thing.

62

DeRicci's office was a hub of activity. Techs she barely recognized scanned information from every part of the office, sitting everywhere, including the edge of some of the planter pots. Flint stood at her desk, tapping away, looking stressed. That Earth Alliance investigator, Goudkins, bowed over some kind of pad, recording information or making notes or doing something during this time of silence. DeRicci wasn't sure what, and at the moment, she didn't care.

Goudkins couldn't communicate with anyone. Hell, no one could communicate, and DeRicci hated that.

But she liked it, too. It meant that she didn't have to worry about this Earth Alliance investigator for another thirty minutes or so.

Popova was in the other conference room with the remaining Earth Alliance investigator, trying to get him to take the afternoon off so he wouldn't see what was going on. Eventually they would have to trust him, but DeRicci didn't want to think about that right now.

In fact, all she could think about were the screens someone had lowered in the center of the room. Just before she left for the conference, she set up the screens to show law enforcement offices all over the Moon. She had opaqued the screens so they wouldn't bother anyone else, but she wanted the screens working when she came back.

She looked at the blank screens. She hadn't thought about her one, simple, *important*, order. Keep the links down. They were down now, and she couldn't get information—at least not the information she wanted.

She wanted to know how well it was going. And she had no idea. Because all she could learn was negative right now. No one had reported an explosion, no one knew of a dome breach, no one heard of some Peyti going nuts on the street.

Or if they had heard, they couldn't report to her.

She used to hate her links. Now she hated the silence. She wanted everything back to normal, but she had no idea what normal was any more.

She threaded her fingers together, took a deep sigh, and waited.

She couldn't do anything else.

63

BARTHOLOMEW NYQUIST WASN'T MUCH OF AN ACTOR, BUT HE KNEW the importance of his role this afternoon. He had to remain calm and pretend like everything was normal, even though the links had gone down and he had to catch one of hundreds of mass murderers who had infiltrated the Moon.

He greeted Uzvaan, the Peyti lawyer who represented Ursula Palmette, Nyquist's old partner and the woman who had tried to bomb Armstrong on Anniversary Day. He had told Uzvaan that Palmette had information, that they were bringing her to the precinct to question her again, and that Uzvaan probably wanted to be present.

Since Uzvaan worked in a law office nearby, it hadn't taken him long to get here.

Most of the detectives in the First Detective Unit were gone, tracking down other Peyti clones. No one had said anything when the orders came through; they had all looked at each other with a resignation that he found familiar.

This was the new normal. They would constantly be under threat until they figured out who or what was behind the attacks. That they faced clones again didn't surprise Nyquist. He felt weirdly unsurprised by it, maybe because of the discussions he'd had with Flint.

What had surprised Nyquist was the fact that the clones were Peyti. Somehow he had gotten it in his head that these attacks were human-based.

"They're bringing her to Interrogation One," he said to Uzvaan.

Uzvaan clutched a small pad in his long fingers. He always carried one. He was slender, even for a Peyti, and fussy about everything. Nyquist had known him for years now, and always thought of him as a competent lawyer, but not a great one. He sometimes seemed like he wasn't paying attention, which Nyquist had always thought of as strange in a Peyti. Usually they had a fanatical attention to detail.

Uzvaan didn't move. He tilted his head. Nyquist tried not to look at his mask. If he hadn't been told about the difference, he might not even have noticed it. The mask looked a little thicker on the bottom. That was it.

"Are the links off here?" Uzvaan asked.

Nyquist had expected the question, but it still made his heart race to hear it. "Yeah. They went down a few minutes ago."

"This does not worry you?"

"Everything worries me," Nyquist said, "but we've had issues like this for weeks now. I think someone has been monkeying with our system."

Uzvaan did not visibly react to that. Instead, he turned and headed toward the interrogation rooms.

Nyquist wasn't sure what kind of reaction he wanted to see from Uzvaan, if any. He'd always found Uzvaan unreadable, even for a Peyti. And he used to think Uzvaan was nondescript, rather forgettable. He would have been hard-pressed to describe him at all. Privately, Nyquist used to think to himself that Uzvaan looked like every other Peyti, and then Nyquist would worry about that thought, thinking maybe it was bigoted.

Now he realized that Uzvaan did look like other Peyti that Nyquist had seen. He hoped that his colleagues were taking care of those Peyti. Because he had to take care of this one.

"I do not understand what she can tell you now that she has not already told you," Uzvaan said as he pulled open the door to the interrogation rooms.

"We've gotten some fascinating information concerning the zoodeh," Nyquist said truthfully. "I think some of our assumptions might be wrong. We can shorten her sentence if she can give us information of value."

Uzvaan grunted, as if in acknowledgement. He headed toward Interrogation One. He certainly knew his way around here.

Nyquist's heart was pounding.

"I do not know why you could not have talked with her in the prison," Uzvaan said.

"I would've thought she'd be happy to have a day on the outside," Nyquist said.

"Since when do you care about her happiness?" Uzvaan asked.

Nyquist smiled slightly to himself. That was the Uzvaan he knew.

"I don't," Nyquist said. "I have information here that I'm not taking near that prison."

"You are afraid it will be compromised?" Uzvaan asked.

"I'm sure of it."

They reached Interrogation One. The window was clear, showing no one in that white-on-white room.

"I'd find out where she is," Nyquist said, "but my links are still down. Why don't you just wait in there, while I check."

Uzvaan shook his head, and for a moment, Nyquist thought they might have a problem. "You do realize that each minute I sit in there wastes my time. She is not a paying client. I will bill this to the city itself."

"That's not my concern," Nyquist said. "But I'll do what I can to get her here faster."

Uzvaan went inside the room. He peered at the white table as if it were covered in filth.

Normal procedure meant that Nyquist left the door open. But there was nothing normal about this afternoon.

He slammed the door shut and locked it. Then he hit the control panel hidden in the wall and immediately changed the environment inside Interrogation One to Peyti Normal.

Uzvaan whirled. He grabbed his mask by the bottom and removed the bomb. Then he took off the mask itself.

Nyquist wasn't sure he had ever seen a maskless Peyti before. Uzvaan looked less intimidating, not more. Blue flooded his face, and for a moment, Nyquist wondered if the environmental mix was wrong.

Uzvaan threw the mask on the table and squeezed the bomb.

Nyquist shook. He reached for his own weapon, not sure what would happen.

But the bomb did not go off.

Uzvaan's skin continued to cycle through a variety of colors. Then he tossed the bomb across the room as if in fury.

Nyquist had never seen an angry Peyti before.

"You do not have the right to hold me here," Uzvaan said through the open intercom.

"Oh, yeah, I do," Nyquist said. "We just got a recording of that. You tried to bring down the entire station. And yes, I know what you were holding. You might want to think about your own defense, counselor. Because what's going to happen to you in Earth Alliance courts won't be very pretty."

Then he shut off the intercom, and moved away from the window so that Uzvaan couldn't see him.

Nyquist leaned against the wall and closed his eyes for a second. One down. Hundreds more to go.

He had no idea if the other takedowns were going well. He hated the silence on the links. But he now knew why that silence was mandatory.

He set up an automated message to go to DeRicci the moment the links returned:

I have one of the bastards in Interrogation Room One. He's neutralized.

Nyquist took a deep breath and opened his eyes. His instructions were to remain in case something went wrong with the environment, the interrogation room, or the bomb.

He hoped to hell this thing would get resolved soon, because he felt like a potential victim just standing here.

And he hated that feeling more than anything else.

64

FLINT DOUBLE- AND TRIPLE-CHECKED THE INFORMATION IN FRONT OF him. He couldn't get past the feeling that he had missed something. He used this time when the links were down to review everything he and the others had done.

His neck ached. So did his back. He hadn't moved for hours. His eyes burned because he sometimes forgot to blink.

He had also ordered the techs in the room to review their information. Goudkins had started reviewing information as well, because she couldn't communicate with the Alliance at the moment.

DeRicci paced, clearly too distracted to think about anything else. Flint thought that was all right, because she wasn't the best with information gathering.

He hadn't found any clones that his system had missed, so he couldn't quite figure out where this odd feeling came from. He had dispatched some security guards in this building to the first floor because one Peyti lawyer had arrived with a delegation from Moscow Dome, trying to extort some nonexistent money out of the United Domes of the Moon. That Peyti lawyer had been a clone.

The guards were supposed to move him to a different section of the building and then change the environment in that area. The fact that nothing had exploded yet probably meant the capture of the Peyti clone had been successful.

But Flint still couldn't figure out the cause of his unease. Clearly his eye had seen something that registered with his subconscious, but not with his conscious brain. His main concern was always Armstrong, so he decided to go through its files first.

And then he found it:

A Peyti lawyer—a Peyti clone of Uzvekmt—had entered the Aristotle Academy about the point when Flint had dropped off Talia. The lawyer worked for one of the most respected firms in Armstrong.

Flint had seen a crowd of people surrounding that kid who had started the melee the day before. Maybe that crowd hadn't been handlers for the father, like Flint had assumed, but lawyers.

Lawyers trying to protect something, or do something, or change something.

He wished the links were open, the networks were open, the information system was open. Because he needed to hack into the law firm right now and see if Kaleb Lamber's father was a client.

Hell, Flint needed to get in touch with Talia, right now. She had to get out of that building.

He tapped the computer screen, shutting down the program.

"I gotta go," he said to DeRicci.

She looked at him as if his words made no sense. "Go where?" she asked.

"One of the lawyers is at Aristotle Academy," Flint said. "With Talia."

Goudkins looked up, so did a few of the other techs.

"You can't go anywhere, Miles," DeRicci said. "It's not safe."

"It's not safe for her," he said.

"If something had exploded, the dome would have sectioned," DeRicci said. "It hasn't. She's all right. You have to trust that this will get taken care of. It's in your files, right?"

"That's how I found it," Flint said.

"Then someone is on it," DeRicci said. "You have to trust them."

356

"It's my daughter," he said, and pushed past a pile of techs. He had to get out of here. He had to make sure she was all right.

He reached the door when he heard DeRicci behind him.

"I'm going to section the dome right on schedule," she said. "Make sure you're nowhere near one of the dividers."

Permission to leave. As if he needed that.

"When, exactly?" he asked. He couldn't remember. It seemed like everything had left his mind when he discovered Talia was in danger.

"Six minutes from now."

He set one of his internal alarms. When he got in the car, he would make sure he avoided the divider.

But he also had to figure out if he could get to Aristotle Academy fast enough to be in the correct section with Talia.

He ran out the door and down the hall, avoiding guards, avoiding people who looked both panicked and busy and lost without their links. He pulled open the stairwell and took the stairs down three at a time.

It would be a push to get to the correct section of the dome before the dividers came down.

But he would do it, no matter what.

65

"WE'RE IN THE MIDDLE OF A MEETING," MS. RUTLEDGE SAID TO THE officer standing at the door of the conference room. She had used that powerful headmistress voice, the one that made Talia nervous.

The guard holding Talia shifted slightly. He was clearly nervous, too.

"I know, ma'am," the officer said in a respectful tone. "But this is important. I need to speak to the lawyers, please."

"It will wait," Ms. Rutledge said. "We'll be done in just a few minutes."

"No, ma'am, it will not, and I can't talk to them in front of you. If you would kindly leave the room, I can talk to them inside."

Ms. Rutledge sighed audibly and got up. One of the police officers hidden down the hallway was holding up his fingers, as if he were counting down. If he was marking time, they were running out.

Talia wanted to know what was going on. Something bad. Something these guys said Chief DeRicci wanted stopped. And the links were down. She wanted to squirm away, but she had the good sense not to. She would be interrupting something.

Ms. Rutledge got to the door. "Officer, please, tell me what it is, and I'll see if it's worth taking the time."

The officer doing the countdown only had four fingers remaining. The officer closest to the one at the door hissed, "Now or never," and the officer at the door grabbed Ms. Rutledge and threw her into the hallway.

Then he slammed the door shut.

"Now!" he yelled. "Now!"

Talia's heart pounded. Ms. Rutledge lost her footing and sprawled on the floor. Someone should have helped her, but no one did. The guard holding Talia tightened his grip, pushing up on her nose, blocking her air.

She elbowed him in the stomach again, and when that didn't work, she grabbed at his hand and pulled down, hoping he would get the message.

He did. He shifted his hand slightly, but he didn't relax his grip on her.

At the same time, Kaleb's dad and two of the lawyers stood up. Kaleb still sat at the table, looking stunned. One of the lawyers, the Peyti, tugged on his mask.

Talia had never seen a Peyti touch his mask, let alone tug on it.

It looked like he broke it.

The guard holding Talia cursed. He let her go and sprinted down the hallway toward the others.

She stumbled, her mouth bruised, then she staggered over to Ms. Rutledge.

"What's going on?" the headmistress asked.

"I don't know," Talia said. "Are you okay?"

She glanced over her shoulder as she asked it. The officer near the door still held it shut. Another officer and a guard flanked him.

"*Now!*" the officer screamed. "I'm not kidding! *Now!*"

Ms. Rutledge pushed herself up. "I'm fine."

She sounded as distracted as Talia. Ms. Rutledge leaned forward and then said, "What—?"

And stopped herself, hand over her mouth.

Talia looked at the room. The air was no longer clear. It was...orange? Yellow? She couldn't quite tell. But Kaleb was screaming, he was clearly screaming, even though she couldn't hear him.

Kaleb's dad was pounding on the windows, and two of the lawyers were pulling on the door, but they weren't getting it open. Their faces were turning red, their eyes were watering, and they were clearly yelling too.

Talia stood up. The officers had let go of the door. They were backing away.

"What are you doing?" she asked them.

They didn't answer her.

Kaleb collapsed, then one of the lawyers, followed by another. They twitched on the floor, partially obscured by that weird-colored air. Then Kaleb's dad dropped, and two more lawyers.

Talia was shaking. This was deliberate. They were deliberately killing the people in the room.

She took another step forward and no one stopped her.

Through the yellowish air, she saw one figure still sitting at the table. The Peyti. He had removed his mask.

She'd never seen a Peyti face outside of holoimages. He looked almost human. He didn't seem upset at all. He still held the part of his mask that he had broken. He held it up for everyone to see, and then brought his other hand over and grabbed it tightly.

The officers froze. The guards looked terrified.

And nothing happened.

Nothing at all.

The Peyti looked at the mask.

Talia looked at the floor, the people hunched down there. If the Peyti could breathe, then the atmosphere in there was toxic. She knew that much, even though she'd never been to Peyla.

"You killed them," she said, her voice shaking. "You killed everyone in that room."

"Yeah," one of the guards said and turned his back on the carnage. "We know."

66

DeRicci watched the clock she had put in front of her left eye. A timer, set to the exact moment when she would release the domes. Three more minutes.

She hoped to hell that Flint had paid attention to her warning; she hoped he was nowhere near the dome dividers.

She also knew she was worried about him so that she wouldn't think about all of the people who would get hurt when the domes sectioned. Sectioning them wasn't something she did lightly. Depending on where the dividers were, their rapid fall could cause injury and death.

She toyed with opening the links a full minute before the domes sectioned, but an order to explode the domes could go through the links as rapidly as an order to section the domes. She didn't dare risk it.

She had to trust her people to know when those domes would come down.

She would open the links ten seconds ahead and hoped they worked all over the Moon.

Popova had moved to her side. The techs had stopped working. They were looking at her.

Goudkins stood at her other side, as if supporting her. Maybe she was. The woman had worked hard this afternoon. Even Goudkins' partner had come into DeRicci's office. Apparently the guy finally figured out that something was up.

He was no threat, because he couldn't contact anyone.

One minute left. DeRicci counted down mentally along with the seconds clock. She wanted to anticipate, she wanted to be early, but she didn't dare.

She glanced at Popova. Popova was staring at the blank screens, her hands clasped tightly in front of her, as if she were holding herself together.

Fifteen seconds.

She could feel the techs' eyes on her.

Thirteen.

She had no idea seconds could last so long.

Eleven.

"Now," she said, and the links opened.

The screens sprang to life, images everywhere, things she didn't entirely understand. The floating faces returned, and so did some other images she couldn't look at right now.

She sent the order to everyone from the conference, every Moon government, everyone in charge of domes.

Section the domes, she sent. *Now.*

67

HE WASN'T GOING TO MAKE IT. FLINT HAD BEEN FIGHTING WITH HIS aircar from the moment he got in it. He'd taken off most of the fail-safes long ago, but he never thought to take off a maximum speed fail-safe. Yeah, he'd set the maximum speed fifty kilometers per hour higher than it was supposed to go, but that wasn't enough.

He never thought he'd have to go faster than that.

And he needed to now.

He was half a kilometer away from the Aristotle Academy. For some reason, he thought the dome section was a kilometer closer. When he got into the aircar and realized his mistake, he'd tried to punch the speed, and he wasn't able to.

So he was driving too fast and he was trying to reprogram his air-car and he was trying to stay out of the way of other vehicles because at this speed, the automatic pilot did not work, and he was only a few meters away from the dome divider when the links opened.

"This dome is going to section right in front of us and we're going to crash," he said out loud to his stupid aircar, hoping that at least an emergen-cy—a proven emergency—would break the vehicle's stranglehold on speed.

He was afraid the aircar would brake, but apparently, they were too close for that and going too fast, because the aircar shot forward. He lost control.

The automatic pilot was back, taking care of things at a speed so fast the buildings around him were blurs. The aircar ducked and swerved and slowed down.

And as it did, Flint looked behind him. The section had dropped. He hadn't felt it because he'd been in the air.

He couldn't see if anything—or anyone—had gotten caught in the sectioning. And he wasn't going to go back to help.

Not with a Peyti lawyer on the grounds of Aristotle Academy.

Not with the links back up.

He sent to Talia, *I'm coming. I'll be there in just a few minutes,* but she didn't respond. He didn't know if her links were back up yet or if she couldn't respond.

Half a kilometer wasn't much at this speed. But it still seemed like it would take too long.

He set his message to Talia on repeat, and hoped to hell he would hear from her any second now.

68

THE LINKS OPENED. BARTHOLOMEW NYQUIST DROPPED TO THE FLOOR outside Interrogation Room One and covered his head with his hands. He'd been through too many dome sectionings to ever experience one on his feet again.

The building shook, and he heard the sound of falling debris. Nothing fell around him. The entire building was solid and had been fortified since Anniversary Day—at least parts of it, anyway—but that didn't stop things from falling off desks or lights from coming out of ceilings.

He hoped the entire ceiling collapsed inside Interrogation Room One. He hoped it would fall on Uzvaan's head and kill the bastard slowly and painfully.

But he also hoped that the atmosphere wouldn't escape and Uzvaan's stupid bomb wouldn't go off.

The thought made Nyquist pop to his feet the moment the shaking stopped.

Uzvaan still sat on his chair, looking calmer than he had a right to. The mask had slipped to the ground, as had the bomb component. The air still looked yellowish, but Nyquist double-checked the reading to make sure nothing leaked from the room.

He didn't want any change in that atmosphere. He didn't want a bomb to go off in this building, even if the dome had sectioned.

He wanted this day to be over.

A cacophony started through his links and he welcomed it. Damage reports, updates, voices sounding stressed. He left the emergency links on, but isolated it to audio only, so that he'd hear any warning as it came in.

Instead, he went to the secure links that DeRicci had set up. Report after report of imprisoned Peyti clones. Trapped. Looking frustrated. Looking angry.

He sighed for just a moment and leaned against the wall. They'd averted the worst of it.

Now they'd have to figure out what to do with these bastards.

But they could do that. They had the clones trapped.

This wasn't Anniversary Day times a hundred. Times five hundred. This was bad, yes, but solvable.

And now they had prisoners. Prisoners who might know something. Prisoners who were logical and who might be amenable to making a deal to save their own skins.

He glared at Uzvaan and smiled slowly.

"Got you, you bastard," Nyquist said softly. "We got you all."

69

DeRicci had managed to stay on her feet during the dome sectioning. She didn't want to sit down, she didn't want to cover her head, she didn't want to hide.

Not from anything or anyone.

Several others in the room dropped when she gave the order. She didn't look at them.

Instead, she watched the screens, listened to the sounds that came through her links.

Once, just once, she glanced at her desk, and thought of Flint. The thought had built-in conflict: She wanted him here because she wanted his help, and she hoped he made it to Aristotle Academy without trouble.

Then she looked away. She instructed Popova to compile a casualties list in real time. DeRicci wanted to know how many were injured, how many dead, and how many of those injuries and deaths came from the domes sectioning, how many were collateral damage from stopping the Peyti clones, and how many were due to the clones themselves.

She could see, at a glance, that all of the domes had survived.

All of them.

She considered that a huge victory. One she would not celebrate, of course, because there had been casualties. But personally, privately, she pumped a tiny mental fist of joy that none of the domes disintegrated.

Somehow, her people had worked together. Somehow, even the idiots had risen above their petty politics and had managed to do something within a short space of time. Somehow, everyone managed to neutralize the threat before any of the bombs went off.

"Chief?" someone spoke behind her. She didn't like the tone. She turned.

A young man, one of the techs whose name got lost in the chaos of the day, had paled. He clutched a pad.

"There was an explosion about half an hour ago," he said.

Her heart sank. She hadn't seen it. Nor had any of the government officials contacted her.

"Where?"

"In one of the Growing Pits twenty kilometers from Armstrong," he said.

"And another one," said one of the middle-aged female techs, "in a mining company near Tycho Crater."

"And a third," said an older male tech, "in a resort not too far from Gagarin Dome."

DeRicci let out a breath, the feeling of jubilation gone. Somehow the links hadn't failed in those places, the domes hadn't sectioned—

What a minute. She blinked, her brain working again. "All three of those businesses, were they outside domes or inside domes?"

"Outside," the younger tech said.

"There were Peyti clones outside the domes?" asked another tech.

"Lawyers work everywhere," Goudkins said drily.

"When the links went down, they knew something was up," DeRicci said. "So the clones activated their bombs, and no one in the companies knew what was coming."

She had known that they would miss. Only this one was on her. She hadn't thought about all the businesses outside the domes. She didn't dare speak her next thought either, but she had been lucky: Considering how many businesses did operate outside a dome, the fact that only three had exploded was amazing.

"Send help to all of these sites," she said. "And get eyes on them. I want to know the extent of the damage."

"That Growing Pit company was obliterated," the first tech said.

"Some of the mines collapsed," the female tech said, "but that didn't mean deaths, just a loss of equipment."

"Only one building in the resort blew," the third tech said. "I have no idea how big that building was or how many casualties there were."

DeRicci let out a small breath. She had been through this before. She would not rest until she had answers.

Only now, she had five hundred suspects in custody, five hundred Peyti who knew something, even if it was only the name of the person or organization that ordered this massive attack.

This attack on the Moon.

This wasn't an attack against the Earth Alliance. This was an attack against the Moon, just like Anniversary Day had been. Someone wanted to obliterate Earth's moon.

And she would find out who. She wasn't going to ask for help from the Alliance, especially since it looked like they were involved in some way. She would learn from Flint.

She would use any resources she had, from the police forces all over the Moon to criminals like Luc Deshin to non-security personnel like Flint himself.

She would find whoever—or whatever—was behind all of this, and she would make them pay.

70

THE AIRCAR HAD BARELY STOPPED WHEN FLINT LEAPT OUT OF IT AND ran into Aristotle Academy. He had been shocked at the lack of security. Not that it was down—at least outside the Academy—but it had remained at normal levels.

He would have figured after a dome sectioning, someone would have implemented high security protocols.

He still couldn't reach anyone through his links. He suspected the problem was the network inside the Academy.

At least the building was still here. At least nothing had exploded.

And that was a good sign.

He ran inside, further shocked that no guards stood near the doors. He used a locator through his links to find Talia.

She wasn't far from Selah Rutledge's office.

He ran past students still sprawled on the floor, some injured, others taking care of them. The walls and ceilings of the building held, but plants had fallen over, tiles had fallen off the wall, and a couple of doors hung sideways.

The entire place smelled of fear. He wished he'd never learned to recognize that scent. He certainly didn't want to smell it in his daughter's school.

He ran to Rutledge's office, and slid to a stop when he reached the conference area.

Selah Rutledge sat on the ground, her face buried in her hands. Guards and police officers ringed a conference room.

Talia was pressed up against the window, the outside window—not inside the room, thank heavens, because the air was yellow. It had a Peyti environment, not a human one. Her fists were balled against it.

She looked devastated.

"Talia," he said.

She turned, but she didn't run to him like he thought she would. "They just killed ten people, Dad. They're all dead."

He took a step toward her. Over her shoulder, he could see one Peyti clone, long fingers tapping a tabletop, a discarded bomb not far from him. He watched Flint approach with something that might've been curiosity.

Or it might've been contempt.

Flint didn't know what to say to Talia. That he had helped devise this plan? That he had known people would die? That the ten dead people would have died anyway if that hideous bomber inside that room had succeeded?

"I know," Flint said, and it sounded lame.

"*Kaleb* is dead, Dad." Talia pounded a fist on the window.

Kaleb. It took a moment for the name to compute. The kid who had taunted her. The kid who had caused all that turmoil just the day before.

"He wanted me to go in there with him." Talia's voice was watery. "I was thinking about it. I would've been in there—"

Flint wrapped her in his arms. He didn't care what she wanted, he needed it. For a moment she struggled against him, and then she clung to him, her body shaking.

He looked over her shoulder. That Peyti clone inside that room, that *assassin*, was watching all of this. He looked pleased.

No matter what DeRicci said, Flint would deal with this one on his own. He would do whatever it took to make this assassin give up information, and then suffer for what he had done.

To Flint's daughter. Flint's beloved daughter.
Who just happened to be a clone herself.
This whole thing wasn't over yet.
But it would be.
He would see to it himself.

71

Iniko Zagrando stood up from his computer. He felt dizzy.

A quick search for information had given him too much. This thing was big, and it seemed to infect the entire Earth Alliance. He couldn't just report to a superior or try to bring down Jarvis.

He had to figure out who inside the Alliance was causing this. Or how many people. Or how many people and corporations. He needed to know how far up this thing went before he could do anything.

And although he was good, he wasn't that good. He didn't know how to track and trace things aside from a superficial look as part of an investigation. He had let other people do that back when he was a police officer. He hadn't had to do it much at all when he had been undercover.

The problem was, the entire Alliance was involved, the government itself. He couldn't just ask them for help, and he couldn't go through channels anywhere inside the Alliance.

And dammit, he couldn't walk away. He wasn't that kind of guy.

He rubbed a hand over his face.

He knew a lot of people who could help him get this information, but only one person he trusted. Only one person who understood how corrupt the system could be and how to work outside that system.

The problem was, that person was in the center of the Earth Alliance, on Earth's Moon.

He would have to contact Miles Flint.

Only Zagrando couldn't do it through links or secret communications. Nor could he do it by asking Flint to come to him. Flint wouldn't leave Alliance space. Not with a daughter to raise.

Zagrando had to go to Flint.

Instead of fleeing the Alliance, Zagrando had to go into the very heart of it.

The upside was that no one expected him to do so.

The downside was that he would be completely alone until he reached Flint.

Zagrando took a deep breath. This was one of those moments when a man, standing alone, would find out what he was made of.

He had been right: He wasn't the kind of man who ran away.

He went directly into the crisis.

He would stop these criminals from bringing down the Alliance.

The criminals would have some time to regroup. It would take Zagrando a while to get to the Moon, even in this ship.

But he would do it.

And he would stop them—if it was the last thing he would ever do.

The thrilling adventure continues with the third book
in the Anniversary Day Saga, *A Murder of Clones.*

A deadly conspiracy...

The Anniversary Day bombings on the Moon sent shockwaves throughout the Earth Alliance. No one knows who created the clones responsible and turned them into ruthless killers. No one knows where or when they'll strike next.

The bombings compel Earth Alliance Frontier Marshall Judita Gomez to launch an unauthorized investigation into a case from her past involving the murder of clones. An investigation that might cost Judita not only her career but the lives of her crew.

This third book of the Anniversary Day Saga sheds further light on the Anniversary Day events, and introduces several new key characters.

Turn the page for the first chapter of *A Murder of Clones.*

FIFTEEN YEARS AGO

1

THE STENCH MADE HER EYES WATER. MARSHAL JUDITA GOMEZ HAD A protect-strip over her mouth and nose, but the stench still got through. Something had died here. Something big, or many somethings big. The fact that the stench was so strong meant she would have to destroy her clothes. Nothing anyone had invented had been able to take the overpowering smell of corpses out of clothing.

At least nothing had done it to her satisfaction.

And perhaps nothing could have satisfied her. Every time she found a corpse, she felt the death viscerally. It became part of her. Perhaps it made sense, then, that it would seem to be part of her clothing as well.

She carefully moved several flat leaves, following the Eaufasse into the cluster of trees. She hadn't studied this culture at all, just responded to their call. So she touched what the Eaufasse touched and stepped where the Eaufasse stepped, which was hard, since the Eaufasse was the size of a thin twelve-year-old human child with extra-long legs and feet the size of fists.

Be extremely careful, she sent to her partners Kyle Washington and Shakir Rainger through their links. They'd been with the Earth Alliance Frontier Security Squad for years, but she wasn't sure they'd ever been in a situation like this before.

She wasn't sure *she* had ever been in a situation like this before.

The Eaufasse Emir had contacted the Earth Alliance about an enclave of humans hiding in the back country, near one of the Eaufasse's major cities. The Eaufasse was one of sixteen different sentient species on Epriccom, the habitable moon of an uninhabitable planet in a sector of space that the Earth Alliance dubbed the Frontier.

Ever since its formation, the Earth Alliance had given several sectors of space the Frontier designation. That meant most of the planets within the sector had applied for Earth Alliance membership—or were potential applicants for membership. Most sectors ended up becoming part of the Alliance, but every once in a while, the designation backfired, leaving the sector unapproved or with only a few Alliance planets, making it difficult for anyone from the Alliance to do business there.

And no matter what the Alliance said, what its propaganda dictated, the Alliance was always about business.

Gomez moved slowly. She loved her job, even at moments like this, moments when a single misplaced footstep could cause an interstellar incident. Her work was not the same from hour to hour, let alone day to day or week to week, and she saw parts of the known universe that most people never got to see.

She focused on the steps in the dirt before her, noting the strange plants that slid toward her feet. They seemed to move without wind or even being touched.

She'd been trained to watch for cues like that, things that might mean whatever she was looking at was sentient. She carefully avoided those plants, and she sent a message through the secured link to her deputies to do the same.

She didn't expect them to answer. One reason she had chosen Washington and Rainger for this mission was because they had the most experience of all her deputies in first-contact situations. Not that this was the first time humans had contact with the Eaufasse, but as far as she could tell, this was the first time that the Earth Alliance authorities—not diplomats—had in-person contact. And in-person contact was always different from contact through networks and links.

For one thing, it was infinitely more dangerous.

The Earth Alliance Frontier Security Squad had jurisdiction in any sector designated Frontier. But jurisdiction didn't mean they could override local laws. It simply meant that the FSS investigated, policed, and patrolled any Earth Alliance members who found their way to a Frontier planet.

And usually, the shadiest Earth Alliance members found their way to the outskirts of Earth Alliance territory, knowing that the FSS was underfunded and spread much too thin.

Gomez was deeply aware of that right now. She needed half a dozen deputies, not the two she always traveled with. The Emir believed that the human enclave was up to no good—at least that was how the translation program had filtered the Eaufasse's extremely complex language.

The relationship with the Eaufasse was so new that very few Eaufasse spoke Standard, and those who did didn't speak it very well.

One of those Standard-speaking Eaufasse was just outside the investigation area, listening in on a link hooked up to both Gomez and the Eaufasse tracker/police officer/military official who led the small group to the corpses.

The language barrier was still so complete that she wasn't sure what job the Eaufasse in front of her actually had.

Finally, the group reached a clearing. The ground dipped here in a bowl shape, and she knew without looking that the corpses were here. The nose never lied.

She held up a fist, so that her deputies stopped moving. They froze. They didn't dare do anything else. One wrong word, one wrong gesture, one wrong step, and the FSS officer could find herself on the wrong side of an alien judicial system.

There were exceptions for marshals. Exceptions were part of the agreements made with Frontier planets. But that didn't mean every single culture on those planets abided by the rules, nor did it mean that the Earth Alliance would always defend a marshal's behavior, particularly if some authority in the Alliance felt the marshal was out of line.

We would like to spread out along the rim of this small clearing, Gomez sent through the joint alien-marshal link. *Do we have your permission to do so? If not, where should we stand?*

The Eaufasse responded quickly. *Of course, permission.*

And she had no idea if that meant she had permission to stand wherever she wanted or if she had to wait while it translated her request to the Eaufasse leading her.

That Eaufasse turned its pointed head toward her. Its eyes, large and liquid, fixed on hers. Then it waved one of its extra-long limbs toward her, in what seemed like a very human gesture for *Continue.*

She knew better than to assume she knew what the Eaufasse meant by the gesture.

After a moment, it tilted its head away from her, and another message came through the link.

Of course. Permission. Stand you want. Okay.

She cursed silently. She hoped that meant it was okay to stand where she wanted. At least she had it on record.

She put down her fist, gestured for the others to join her, and moved near the Eaufasse. It hunched toward the bowl like a mangled question mark.

The two deputies fanned out beside her, moving as cautiously as she was.

The clearing had an open view to the sky. Epriccom's bright sun made the plants glow bluish green. Epriccom had the right oxygen mix for humans, which made it an enticing planet for development, but it was clearly an alien place.

So alien, in fact, that it took her a moment to recognize the bodies in the tangle of vines, leaves, and branches that passed for ground cover here.

The bodies were equidistant apart. They sprawled face down, heads turned toward her, arms outward, feet bent. They were so bloated she couldn't tell much about them—male, female, age. Nor could she quite comprehend what they were wearing; in most areas the bloating was so severe that they had burst through their clothes.

The identical positions, and the fact that they sprawled face down, however, led her to believe they had been killed. Whether or not they had been dumped here was another matter.

She suppressed a sigh. She also didn't know what kind of killings Eaufasse did, if any, and how they treated their dead.

May we approach the corpses? She sent through the links.

Of course. Permission. Stand you want. Okay.

"Okay," she muttered. Washington glanced at her, his mouth a thin line.

She started down the incline, leading the way. Washington and Rainger followed, doing their best to walk where she had. Branches clawed at her boots, and she had the impression that some of the stuff had scuttled away from her feet.

Her heart pounded. She hated this kind of thing. She always felt out of her depth in situations that involved killings in Frontier planets. She had no idea what the temperature ranges were, how the local flora and fauna interacted with rotting material, what kind of insects—if any— went after corpses, and on and on.

She could only guess at things, and she was terrified she would guess wrong. Not only did her future depend on the correct moves, but often so did the future relationship between the Earth Alliance and the Frontier planet.

When she was within a few meters of the bodies, she turned slightly toward the deputies.

Spread out, she sent through the private links. *Tell me if you can make any sense of this. Try to limit your guesses to the ones you're at least half certain of.*

Rainger gave her a grim smile. Washington nodded once. They picked their way around the other side, with Rainger continuing until he stopped above the corpses' heads. He crouched. So did Washington near one of the corpse's backs.

Gomez stood near the feet, gazing upward. As she'd been traveling here, she had downloaded all the information she could find on the Eaufasse. She'd stored a backup copy on a chip in her thumb. Not that there had been a lot of information, just the preliminary report, filled with the usual happy-shiny crap about what a great planet it was, how accommodating the locals were, and how happy they would be to cooperate with any Earth Alliance culture that wanted to set up a base here.

No initial cultural difficulties, not with the advance team, and no mention of crime at all. Now whether that meant that the Eaufasse didn't commit crimes against each other or whether it meant that the Eaufasse had a different conception of crime than the Alliance did was anyone's guess.

And search she did, but hadn't found anything on Eaufasse death rituals. So that meant the advance teams and the later observers weren't allowed to see what the Eaufasse did. But she had learned not to interpret that either. It might mean that they kept the rituals private like some cultures kept bathing private or it might mean that the teams simply hadn't been near a death so didn't get to see what the Eaufasse did in that circumstance.

Not that it mattered now. She couldn't find the answer she wanted. She had no idea if these corpses were arranged in an Eaufasse death position or one of the other fifteen species on this planet had been involved in any way or if she was looking at a human-on-human crime.

She sighed softly. She had hoped for a simple knife in the back of one of the deceased, with a note attached, explaining all the reasons for the crime—or at least something similar, something that was obvious and unambiguously human-on-human.

Something she could deal with.

"Rainger," she said out loud, knowing that the Eaufasse could hear her conversation and would do its best to translate it for the other Eaufasse. "Send for the collection team. Tell them you'll meet them here, and remind them of the delicacy of the recovery effort."

"Yes, sir," Rainger said. "Mind if I continue to examine the scene, sir?"

"Don't touch anything," she said. "In fact, make a secondary recording. Get up close. The more information we have the better."

He nodded.

"Washington," she said. "You're with me."

"Sir?" he said, looking startled.

"We came here to remove a human enclave," she said. "I think we should see what we're facing."

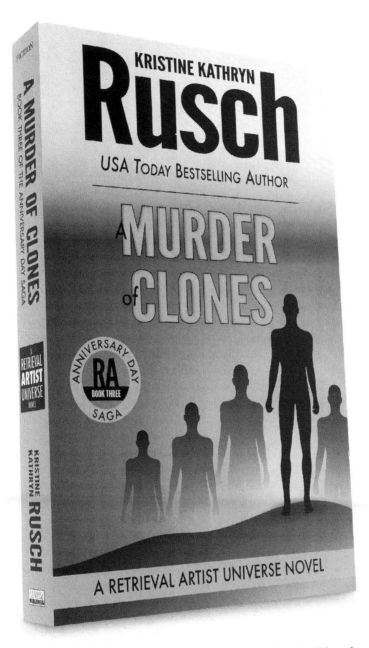

The thrilling adventure continues with the third book
in the Anniversary Day Saga, *A Murder of Clones*,
available now from your favorite bookseller.

ABOUT THE AUTHOR

USA Today bestselling author Kristine Kathryn Rusch writes in almost every genre. Generally, she uses her real name (Rusch) for most of her writing. Under that name, she publishes bestselling science fiction and fantasy, award-winning mysteries, acclaimed mainstream fiction, controversial nonfiction, and the occasional romance. Her novels have made bestseller lists around the world and her short fiction has appeared in eighteen best of the year collections. She has won more than twenty-five awards for her fiction, including the Hugo, *Le Prix Imaginales,* the *Asimov's* Readers Choice award, and the *Ellery Queen Mystery Magazine* Readers Choice Award.

To keep up with everything she does, go to kriswrites.com. To track her many pen names and series, see their individual websites (krisnelscott.com, kristinegrayson.com, krisdelake.com, retrievalartist.com, divingintothewreck. com, fictionriver.com). She lives and occasionally sleeps in Oregon.

Made in the USA
San Bernardino, CA
22 August 2018